Violent Ends

Also by Neil Broadfoot

No Man's Land
No Place to Die
The Point of No Return
No Quarter Given

Neil
Broadfoot
Violent
Ends

CONSTABLE

CONSTABLE

First published in Great Britain in 2022 by Constable

Copyright © Neil Broadfoot, 2022

1 3 5 7 9 10 8 6 4 2

The moral right of the author has been asserted.

A CIP catalogue record for this book
is available from the British Library.

ISBN: 978-1-47213-497-4

Typeset in Minion Pro by Initial Typesetting Services, Edinburgh
Printed and bound in Great Britain by Clays Ltd, Elcograf S.p.A.

Papers used by Constable are from well-managed forests and
other responsible sources.

Constable
An imprint of
Little, Brown Book Group
Carmelite House
50 Victoria Embankment
London EC4Y 0DZ

An Hachette UK Company
www.hachette.co.uk

www.littlebrown.co.uk

To the memory of my dad, John Broadfoot, who, in his last days, showed me what real courage is. Love you, Dad, always.

CHAPTER 1

He had been taught it was nothing more than the by-product of a chemical reaction, energy expressing itself in heat and flame. Over the years he had studied it, and the ways in which it could be controlled and suppressed. He had seen the devastation it could wreak on homes mapped out in the gutted, blackened skeletons of collapsed roofs and scorched walls, seen what it could do to bodies shrivelled into a foetal position by heat, faces pulled taut in rictus grins, hands palsied talons, the muscles and skin sloughing off the bones, like slow-cooked chicken, the bodies filling the room with a smell that was at once acrid and sickly sweet.

He had fought it in tenements and staircases, cars and forests, developed a grudging respect for it. But lying there, he suddenly knew the lie at the heart of all his years' facing fire. It was not merely the result of a kinetic reaction, fuelled by oxygen until it was starved of fuel or doused.

No. The truth was the fire was alive.

And it was laughing at him.

He could hear it even over the laboured hiss and spit of his respirator, a rumbling chuckle that accompanied the flames that danced and capered across the floors and up the walls surrounding him. He braced his arms again, pushed with all his strength against the beam that had fallen over his chest when the roof had collapsed on him. He closed his eyes, filled his mind with images of Caroline and his son as he pushed, bit back the scream that was clawing up his throat as he willed the beam to move. After a moment, he sagged back, arms shaking and spent, heard the fire's laughter grow harsher, crueller at his latest failure.

He tried again to reach for the radio on his chest, found he still could not slip his hand between the beam and his bulky overalls. Considered, in a moment of desperation, removing one of his gloves to try to squeeze through the gap. Knew he could not. The world around him was a roaring flame, hell made real. His hand would blister and burn the moment his naked skin touched the air.

And he would be damned if he was going to give the fire something else to laugh at.

He sagged back, forced himself to breathe slowly and regularly, just as he had been trained to. Used facts to hold back the rising terror that threatened to overtake his thoughts, like a tide overtaking a beach. He had entered this building as part of a three-man team. The control team outside knew he was here, had his tally to prove it. They would come for him. Find him. Save him.

After all, wasn't that what they were all here to do?

A splintering bang shook his world. The fire roared its approval and seemed to swell in the room. He swivelled his head desperately, trying to see through a visor quickly blackening with soot and the charred remains of whatever had been in the room before it had been transformed into a scene from Dante. Could feel the heat for the first time now, pressing on his protective jacket and trousers, probing for weaknesses, vulnerabilities. He felt a sudden, desperate thirst, ran his tongue over lips that were cracked and dry, any moisture vaporised by the fire.

'Please, God,' he whispered, the words thick and alien in his mouth. He had been told this was all a part of His great plan, a holy undertaking. He was one of the chosen, the anointed. It was his destiny to be in this building now. Why shouldn't God help him?

Another shuddering crack, this time closer, louder. He craned his head back, the world turning upside down. Barked a harsh laugh that sounded more like a scream as he saw boots stomp towards him. Felt a flash of shame at his earlier doubt. They had been right. He was the anointed, the chosen. God had not forsaken him. After all, this was a part of his plan.

He dropped his hands from the beam across his chest, reached back towards his saviour.

'Please,' he shouted, his throat burning as though the air from his respirator had become toxic. 'Trapped. Help me move this beam, we can get . . .'

The figure beside him crouched, features hidden behind a breathing mask and visor that danced with reflected flame. He felt a pressure on his helmet, realised his saviour was assessing for injuries, trying to stabilise his neck. Relief flooded through him again, and tears sprang into his eyes. A professional, acting just as they had been trained. He would be safe now.

'I'm okay,' he said. 'Spine is intact, can feel my extremities, even with this bastard weight on me. I just need you to . . .'

A sudden harsh jerk and the world became a thing of searing agony and blurred images as his helmet and mask were ripped off. He felt a momentary scalding as the heat of the room crawled over his now-exposed flesh. Tears streamed down his face as the smoke bit into his eyes, blinding him. He coughed and gagged, head thrashing from side to side as the bitter, acrid air that filled the room forced its way into him.

He felt a shape being drawn on his forehead, a momentary coolness that gave way to a terrible, final numbness. And in that moment, he knew. Knew he would never see his family again. Knew that he was not one of God's anointed after all. He had been chosen, yes, but not in the way he had thought. He was not a saviour doing God's work. He was a lamb led to the slaughter. A sacrifice to the flame.

Even as he felt his mind crumble and fracture under the crushing weight of this new certainty, he called out to God. Begged, pleaded. For his life. For his sister. For his child. Forced his eyes open, his frantic, begging sobs giving way to a hoarse, rasping scream as he saw something cold and bright flare across his vision, as hard and final as the voice that still spoke.

The respirator's rasp drowned the fire for an instant as the figure loomed over him, closer now, intimate, almost as if there were great secrets to share.

A scorching fire flashed across his throat. Then the numbness again as his vision dimmed, as though the fire was now burning the very light in the room. But even as the suffocating blackness took him, he heard it again, knew he was right.

The fire was a living thing. And it was laughing at him.

CHAPTER 2

Strong hands clamped around the back of Connor Fraser's neck, their touch as cold as the steel he could feel in their grasp. They forced his head down, bending him over. Instinctively, he brought his hands up to his face, blocking the knees directed at his chin and temple.

He heard a grunt of laughter as his opponent changed tactic in response to Connor's defence and started stabbing at his side with knee strikes. Connor rolled away from the kicks as much as he could, focused on his breathing. Closed his eyes, felt the blows pepper his ribs. Ignored the pain, searched for the rhythm.

There.

He dropped his guard, grabbed the knee aimed for his left side. Felt his opponent stagger back, pirouetted with the sudden shift in weight and swept his leg out, shin scything his attacker's legs from under him. A moment of weightlessness as the pressure on his neck eased as his opponent crashed to the floor. Connor twisted, pounced. Grabbed his attacker's shoulder and dragged him onto his back, then fell on him, his knees pinning him as he sat on his chest. Connor grunted, pulled back his fist, ready to strike, to destroy the face of the man who had dared attack him.

'Jesus, big lad, catch yerself on! You look like you're gonna fuckin' do me one!'

Connor blinked, lowered his fist slowly. Simon McCartney grinned up at him warily, as though he was laughing at a joke he knew he should find funny but somehow couldn't.

Connor rolled off his friend, bounced onto his feet, then stretched down, offering his hand.

Simon took it, hauled himself upright, the wariness in his smile now bleeding into his eyes.

'Thought you said this was going to be a bit of light sparring, nothing serious?' Simon said, as he peeled off his boxing mitts and threw them to the floor.

'Says the man who was trying to rearrange my teeth with his knee,' Connor replied.

Simon gave another smile, this time more genuine. 'Aye, fair play,' he said. 'Though you're getting better all the time, Connor. Not sure how much more I can teach you here.'

Connor shrugged off the compliment as he headed for his kit bag at the far end of the room. He had found the place three months ago: a slightly tired, utilitarian gym on an industrial estate on the western edge of Stirling. He had been looking for a place to train that was free from the ghosts and painful memories of the gym he had used on Craigs Roundabout. It was nothing more than it said it was: an industrial unit filled with weights and machines, a place to work, not spend two hours between sets as you updated Facebook or Instagram or TikTok with a livestream of how well your workout was going.

It was on one of his early-morning visits to the gym, a visit fuelled by a night of bad dreams and a vague, unformed dread about how Jen's rehabilitation was going, that Connor had met Dean Lawson, the gym's owner. About fifty, with a smile that was full of teeth and devoid of humour, Dean was essentially an extension of his gym – all business, no bullshit. He had been a prison officer for eighteen years, and decided a career change was in order after an inmate tried to give him some free cosmetic surgery with the end of a sharpened toothbrush.

Dean had always been interested in fitness ('In my line of work, I'd be a fool not to be, son'), so he had opened the gym. Simply called Lawson's, it had started off with Dean and a few of his friends. Over time, the clientele had grown, and soon Dean had leased the next-door unit and expanded. With the explosion of housing developments around Stirling as families were driven further from Glasgow and Edinburgh by rocketing property prices, he was soon inundated with a flood of young professionals who thought they should look like their favourite movie stars, retirees with too much time on their hands and bored stay-at-home parents who mistook a trip to the gym for an afternoon coffee and catch-up with their friends. The place had been so successful that Dean had partnered with a local martial-arts dojo and started offering classes in the expanded gym.

And then the pandemic struck. Overnight, Dean saw his business collapse. He kept the place going, first with his own money, then with government aid, until in desperation he started dragging pieces of equipment outside and offering workouts in the car park. Lawson's survived, barely, but the martial arts school didn't. Which meant a dojo with punchbags, mats and all the other equipment you could ask for was lying empty.

Until Connor found out about it. He made a deal with Dean to rent out the dojo, then persuaded Simon, who was staying with him on leave of absence from the Police Service of Northern Ireland, to train him in mixed martial arts, kickboxing and anything else he knew. Connor had always known how to handle himself, but with Jen slowly recovering, Duncan MacKenzie lurking in the shadows and the sex-abuse ring he and Simon had exposed months earlier no doubt baying for his blood, Connor wanted to be more than just competent in a fight.

He wanted to be lethal.

'So what's the plan now, then?'

'Huh?' Connor grunted, as Simon's words pulled him from his thoughts.

Simon smiled, shook his head. 'You know, for a smart guy, you're an idiot sometimes, Connor. I asked what you wanted to do now. We could go and get a—'

He was cut off by the shrill ring of a phone in Connor's kit bag. Connor gave him an apologetic shrug.

'Thought you were going to leave that bloody thing in the car,' Simon said.

'Sorry, force of habit,' Connor replied, the lie sounding hollow in his ears. They both knew that, with Jen at the spinal rehabilitation unit in Glasgow and his gran in a nursing home in Bannockburn, Connor was never going to be more than six feet away from his phone.

He peeled off his gloves, the Velcro rasping as if in competition with his ringtone, then fished his phone out of his bag. Frowned when he saw the name of the person calling, then hit answer.

'Robbie? Wasn't expecting to hear from you today, my day off.' He winced at the harshness of his words.

'S-sorry, boss,' Robbie Lindsay was one of Connor's employees at Sentinel Securities. 'It's just that, well, something's come up. And we thought you should know about it.'

'Oh?' Connor said, a wisp of unease cooling the sweat he could feel trickling down his back. 'And what would that be?'

'Well, there's two things, boss. We've had a payment made into the main business account. Only reference on it is your name and what looks like a four-digit code.'

'Could be anything,' Connor said. 'We've plenty of invoices outstanding, and it's not unusual for me to be referenced in them.'

'True,' Robbie replied, his tone telling Connor he had already thought of that and was waiting for his boss to catch up. 'But there's nothing outstanding to the tune of seventy thousand pounds.'

'What?' Connor said. 'You mean someone's just paid seventy grand into our business account? You checked with the bank? Must be a clerical error.'

'Yeah,' Robbie said slowly. 'That's the second thing, boss. The bank this transfer came from is in Delaware, United States. We've not had any dealings with US-based clients in the last three months.'

Connor heard a chirp at the other end of the line. Ignored it. 'Must be some kind of mistake,' he repeated, even as his gut whispered that it wasn't. 'Check again with the—'

'Oh, shit,' Robbie said, cutting Connor off.

'What? Robbie, what—'

'Just got an email, boss,' his tone indicating he was talking more to himself than Connor now, 'about the money we received. Email address is generic, could be from anywhere. But the header is, well, it's addressed to you, boss.'

'For me?' Connor said. He felt Simon drawing closer to him, as though he had sensed something was wrong.

'Yeah. The title of the email is "FAO Connor Fraser. Contract and commission. Use code to read."'

'"Use code to read" – What the hell does that mean?' Connor said, his mouth forming the words a second before his brain made the connection. 'The code in the bank reference. Must be that. Is the email password protected?'

'Yeah, boss, it is. Hold on.' Silence on the line, quickly filled with the chattering of keys as Robbie turned to his laptop.

'Go on, then, Robbie,' Connor said, impatience sharpening his tone. 'What does it say?'

'Boss,' Robbie said, his voice cold, sterile, almost clinical. Connor had heard the tone too many times before, usually when he had been taking statements from someone who had witnessed a horror that was beyond their comprehension.

'Robbie, what is it? What's—'

'Boss. Get to your gran. Now. Jen's in Glasgow, right? It'll take you longer to get there. We've got people in the area. I'll make sure she's covered. Just get to your gran, now.'

Connor felt panic stab into his guts, freeze his blood. The world took on a harsh, metallic hue as his eyes developed an almost supernatural focus. 'Robbie, you're not making any sense. What—'

'The email,' Robbie replied, his voice somehow colder now. 'It's got a contract attached to it. Along with pictures of Jen and your gran. Says one of them will die if you don't sign this contract. So get to your gran in Bannockburn. It's only ten minutes from you. I'll keep Jen safe, I promise. But get moving. Now.'

Connor ended the call, looked desperately around the room. Saw Simon staring at him, fear and determination painted into the set of his jaw and the way he was bouncing softly on the balls of his feet.

'Connor, what the hell is going on? What do you need?'

Connor opened his mouth. Closed it. Found he couldn't articulate the maelstrom of rage, terror and confusion that was screaming through his mind, like a tornado.

Instead, he took Robbie's advice. He got moving.

CHAPTER 3

The car seemed to give a sigh of relief as Connor pulled to a halt in the care home's car park and killed the engine.

Simon could sympathise.

After ending the call to Robbie, Connor had paused for a moment, as though digesting what he had been told. Then he got moving with that lithe grace that always unsettled Simon: watching a man of Connor's size move like a dancer was a little like watching a great white shark swim through the ocean.

He turned to Simon, tossing the phone to him as he did so.

'You read, I'll drive,' he said, as he strode towards the gym door.

Outside, the sky was a canvas of azure blue, marred only by the bone-white slash of a jet trail from a plane. Simon sprinted to Connor, got a hand on his shoulder and pulled his friend back.

'Connor, wait,' he said, forcing his voice to remain calm even as he saw the naked fury and, yes, hatred, spark in Connor's jade-green eyes.

'What the fuck?' he hissed. 'Simon, we've not got time for this. We need to get to—'

'Exactly,' Simon said, eyes not leaving Connor's. He was taller than him by about three inches, but what Connor lost in height to Simon, he made up for in bulk. Simon had seen how effectively Connor could use that bulk, had no desire to be on the wrong end of his wrath.

'Come on, man,' he said. 'Think about it. We get a call, you charge off straight for the car. No time, got to get there now. You hop in, start the engine then . . . what?'

'Even in peace time, you always check under the car,' Connor rumbled absently, repeating the mantra Simon had taught him years ago when they were police officers in Belfast.

'Exactly,' Simon said, and felt something ease in his chest as the fury in Connor's eyes slowly abated. 'Look, big man. This could be a hoax, it could be real. But we both know you've got few friends and a lot of enemies at the moment. What if this is their way of getting to you? Wind you up, get you running to a booby-trapped car. Sure, we saw it enough times in Belfast.'

Connor gave the slightest of nods, his jaw set tight, a muscle fluttering in his cheek, as though he was chewing on something vile. 'Okay,' he said softly. 'We check the car.'

Five minutes later, they were on the move, having checked under the wheel arches, the exhaust track, the engine block, anywhere a device might have been hidden. Simon was glad of the distraction of Connor's phone as they drove, the V8 of the Audi roaring like a wounded animal as Connor red-lined every gear.

The email Robbie had forwarded to Connor originated from an email address so generic it might as well have had 'delivered from a dark web server' watermarked on it. Attached to it were three items: a password-protected document labelled 'CONTRACT', and two jpegs, 'OLD BITCH' and 'YOUNG SLUT'.

Opening the images, Simon found pictures of Connor's grandmother, Ida, and his girlfriend, Jen MacKenzie. Pushing his revulsion and panic aside, he forced himself to examine the pictures as dispassionately as possible, see them as evidence, not intimidation.

They were professionally framed shots, the faces of both women clear and distinct. In the first, Ida Fraser was seen through the window of her care-home flat, grey cardigan draped around increasingly slender shoulders, her head crowned in a tight halo of permed grey curls, her left shoulder drooping slightly as she leant on her walking stick. In the second image, Jen was sitting in her wheelchair, a woman pushing her, long hair frozen in streamers as it was caught by the wind. She was, Simon realised, smiling in a way he had not seen in a long time. Carefree, happy, almost as if someone had not tried to kill her to settle an old score with her father.

He took a moment, considered. Two pictures. Both seemingly at long range. So a zoom lens, then. He thought back to his visits to Ida's care home, a grand old converted Victorian townhouse that sat nestled behind a thick copse of trees to protect it from the outside world. Easy enough to conceal yourself in those trees with a camera and wait for the perfect picture to present itself. The same held true for Jen. She was outside in the picture, her face bathed in early-afternoon sun, the same flawless sky above her that Connor and Simon had seen when they left the gym.

Simon flicked between the pictures, looking for a date stamp, anything to give him a clue as to when they were taken. There was nothing, apart from Jen's hair, which she had been growing out for a few months now. He felt a chill twist down his spine at the realisation: these images were relatively new, which meant the danger, whatever it was, was present and active, now.

He was startled from his thoughts by Connor shifting in his seat, the car rocking gently. He leant forward, eyes strobing across the front of the care home.

'All looks normal enough,' he muttered. 'But I've got to get inside, see her, make sure . . .'

Simon nodded, placed a hand on Connor's forearm. 'Connor, take a breath. We don't know what we're dealing with here. But the last thing your gran needs is you barging in there like the Terminator. Be calm. Go to Reception, see if anything feels out of place. Get to your gran. If something doesn't fit, call me.'

Connor looked at him, confusion flitting across his face. 'You're not coming in with me?'

'No,' Simon replied. 'Think about it. If I go in there with you and there's a problem, we're trapped, and whoever's running this shitshow has us locked down. You go in alone, I stay behind, gives us two possible lines of attack. Besides . . .' he paused, flicked at Connor's phone, then passed it back to him '. . . there's something I want to check out.'

Connor nodded, his impatience to reach his gran obviously

overwhelming his desire to get any more answers from Simon. They got out of the car and Simon watched as Connor approached the care home, looking for signs of another car door opening or someone emerging from the grounds to follow him.

Satisfied that his friend was not being followed, Simon pulled his phone out of his pocket, called up the picture he had forwarded from Connor's phone and slowly wandered around outside of the care home. To the left of the main house, connected to it by an umbilical-like glass corridor, was a smaller, more recent building. The architects had obviously tried to blend it in with the imposing sandstone-and-glass façade of the main house, but no amount of sympathetic cornicing or stone pillars could hide what the second building was: a block of flats.

Simon closed his eyes, recalled previous visits to Ida. She was on the second floor of the building, on the south elevation. Simon glanced in that direction, smiled slightly as he saw that that side of the house faced directly onto the towering pines and oaks that surrounded the facility.

He walked briskly to the trees, then stepped into them, glancing back occasionally to orient himself. He remembered Ida serving them tea late one afternoon, the light dancing off the ornate silver teapot she used. He closed his eyes again, tracing the setting of the sun across the sky, trying to match the angle of that afternoon. That, coupled with Ida's room number, gave him a fairly good idea of the room's position. About twenty metres into the copse, he found an old oak, its bark like soot-stained silver. It was similar to the dozens of other trees around it, except for one difference: a massive branch at the bottom of it, fingers of wood stretching back to the main bulk of the tree, as though silently pleading with the trunk to bring it home. Simon bent down, examined the end of the branch. Felt excitement and adrenalin quicken his pulse and sharpen his senses as he ran a finger over the smooth, cut end. It was still slightly tacky to the touch with sap.

He took a breath, held it. Strained his senses for the smallest hint that someone was there with him. But, no, he was alone: he could feel it. Whoever it had been had done their job, then left.

Simon didn't want to think about where they were going next.

He glanced up, saw another thick branch jutting out from the trunk, about eight feet up. Stood up and studied the tree, then jumped, grabbed a branch and hauled himself up. Felt no surprise when he saw fresh grazes in the bark: boots scrabbling up it. He kept climbing, found the branch he wanted, sat down. Looked up and saw another fresh cut mark on the tree, the same smooth saw marks where the branch that was now on the ground below had been cut from. Took out his phone, held it up. It wasn't conclusive, but the angle and the height seemed right. Whoever had taken the picture sent to Connor had come here, cut down the branch above him to clear his line of sight, then taken the shot.

Simon sat there for a moment, trying to get a feel for the photographer. Fit enough to climb a tree with a camera and a zoom lens on their back, smart enough to use an untraceable email address, prepared enough to come here with a blade or a saw to remove any obstacles that might get in their way.

But who would do this? And why? For a contract? It made no sense.

Simon climbed down, then looked around the trunk, searching for clues. He didn't think he would find any. The person who had done this was obviously . . .

He froze halfway around the tree trunk, on the opposite side to where he had found the cut branch. Glanced around again, suddenly convinced he had been wrong and someone had been there the whole time, watching him. But there was no one, just the rustle of the wind in the leaves, as though it was quietly mocking him.

Impaled on a branch in front of him was a single sheet of paper. Simon approached slowly, wishing he had something, anything, more than his fists and his feet as weapons.

It was a sheet of A4, thick and rich. Expensive. Scrawled on it in thick black letters was a simple message. Twelve words that told Simon he and Connor had just stepped into a world of trouble.

Sign the fucking contract. Or there will be holy hell to pay.

CHAPTER 4

He was the type of man who made an expensive watch look cheap. There was something in the way he constantly adjusted the cuff of his shirt and tailored suit jacket, pulling them up, then tucking them under the band of the watch, ensuring it was always on show, flashing 'I'm a pretentious twat' in Morse code as it caught the early-afternoon sun.

Not that being a twat had harmed Tom McGovern's business acumen. A joiner by trade, McGovern had served his apprenticeship on building sites across central Scotland. When he was twenty-five, he had bought a small piece of land just outside a town in Midlothian that had been long forgotten by the mining industry that had given birth to it. According to his autobiography, McGovern had sold his car, his flat, and scrounged loans from his parents, his friends and anyone else who would open their wallet for him. And there were rumours, some of which Donna Blake had unsuccessfully investigated, that some of those wallets had not been filled through legal means.

McGovern, along with friends he had made on building sites, built ten homes on that patch of land. He had sold them for a ridiculous profit, and used the money to set up McGovern Homes. Over the following twenty-five years, McGovern had grown from a small developer to one of the biggest house-building operations in Scotland. Lauded as a magnate of Scottish business, he had been recruited as an adviser to government on industry and economic growth, attracted the attention of TV producers, who created a fly-on-the-wall documentary series about his life and work, and even gone down on one knee to collect a knighthood in London.

All of which had led Donna Blake to this moment: she was standing on another piece of forgotten ground about ten miles outside Stirling, watching McGovern as his PR people swarmed around him like flies as he constantly fiddled with his watch and paced around the makeshift stage that had been erected for the day.

The story had been a routine one to begin with: McGovern Homes had bought a slice of land just outside Banknock, a village south of Stirling, on the road to Glasgow. It was to be the site of a 'development of twenty-five executive homes, offering both exceptional comfort in a rural location and easy transport links for commuting'.

Unfortunately for McGovern, Archie Baldwin had other ideas.

A retired history teacher, Archie had spent his retirement building up an encyclopaedic knowledge of Banknock and its surrounding area. So when he had heard about McGovern's plans, he had objected on the grounds that the development would change the water plain in the area, which would ultimately flood an almost-forgotten graveyard that, Archie claimed, dated back to the time of Robert the Bruce and William Wallace.

Then, just as the press and the media were raising their noses and sniffing an interesting David v. Goliath story, Archie stepped into a council planning meeting in Falkirk and delivered a headline that propelled the story from local interest to the national agenda.

Donna smiled as she remembered the cutting she had read from the local paper:

A meeting to consider McGovern Homes' application to build twenty-five homes near the village of Banknock was dramatically interrupted today, as on objector to the plans claimed the development would see 'the streets of Banknock flooded with the remains of the dead and haunted by the avenging spirit of William Wallace'.

The story had dragged on under the full glare of the press, with the planning application eventually referred back to Scottish ministers for the final ruling. They had agreed to a modified plan for eighteen homes, citing the boost for local business and the pressing need for new accommodation in a post-pandemic world.

Finally, after almost two years, and with Archie still muttering darkly to any reporter who would listen, work was about to begin on the Middletrees Rise Development. With the interest in the story, McGovern had decided to spin it, getting a minor TV star with tenuous links to the area to cut the first sod.

Donna looked around at the assembled throng of reporters. She recognised people from STV, the BBC and a few other channels, all there for the same reason she was for Sky – hoping Archie or someone else would turn up and cause a scene.

A few minutes later, an immaculately tailored woman with a smile that was all teeth and lipstick tapped on a microphone that was set on a lectern at the centre of the stage. 'Ah, ah, good afternoon,' she said, her voice as bright as the gleam from McGovern's watch. 'Thank you all for coming. As you know, we're here today to celebrate the start of work on the Middletrees Rise Development, and the jobs and homes it will bring to this community. There will be time for questions shortly, but first, Mr McGovern would like to say a few words.'

She shuffled to the side as McGovern lumbered towards the lectern. He was a large, broad-shouldered man, white-blond hair slicked back to reveal a forehead that wasn't so much wrinkled as ploughed. He engulfed the microphone in one massive hand, then cleared his throat with a noise that sounded as if someone was taking a chainsaw to a tree.

'Ah, good afternoon,' he said, in a deep west-coast lilt that seemed to push his voice up half an octave at the end of every sentence. 'It's good to see you all here today. It's been a long road getting Middletrees off the ground, and it wouldn't have been possible without the help of my incredible team of—'

'Lobbyists and well-connected friends?' a voice called from the crowd.

Donna turned to see a thin man with a wild mop of dark brown hair glaring at McGovern on the podium, a small smile crawling across his thin lips. She turned back as McGovern jostled his assistant aside and craned forward to peer into the crowd.

'I'm sorry,' he said, every word slow and deliberate. 'Who are you, and what are you insinuating?'

'Doug McGregor, PA News,' the wild-haired man shouted back. 'And I'm not insinuating anything, sir. I'm just asking a question. Everyone here knows this development had a . . . shall we say difficult time getting approved? You yourself said it wouldn't have been possible without a team. I'm just asking if that team included lobbyists and well-connected friends.'

'I don't believe a question of that sort should be dignified with an answer,' McGovern said. His tone was all threat now, the lilt flattened by anger, every word designed to bite. 'Let me guess. You're another of those green-leaning fake-newsers who believes every entrepreneur is a money-grabbing monster, out to make a buck no matter the cost.'

McGregor laughed, shook his head as though McGovern had just told a joke he'd heard a hundred times before. 'Nah, not at all, Mr McGovern. Got nothing against making a few quid myself, though I guess I'm in the wrong game for that.' A ripple of laughter from some of the other journalists, Donna included. 'What I do have a problem with, and what I do have questions about, are the five private dining events you hosted with this region's list MSP throughout the planning process, and the donations made to his election fund by a company with which you have a direct yet undeclared connection through your work.' He paused and theatrically checked a notepad he had produced from his back pocket. 'Ah, yes, the Stephen Foundation.'

McGovern grew very still as the assembled crowd fell silent, the only sound the burst of flashes and the snapping of cameras. Then, as if some invisible dam had broken, the questions began, a wall of sound that seemed to send McGovern staggering back.

Donna watched as he was bustled off the stage, then whirled towards McGregor, who was standing rocking back and forth gently on his heels and raking one hand through his hair.

She strode over to him. 'Nice work, genius,' she said. 'Now none of us will get anything from him other than a no-comment comment from his PR team later on. And what was that "PA" bullshit? I know all the reporters in the pool, and you're not one of them.'

McGregor stared down at her, dark eyes dancing over her face. Then he smiled, offered her his hand. Surprised by the move, Donna took it and shook.

'Doug McGregor,' he said, his voice clipped and exact in only the way an Edinburgh boy's can be. 'Bullshitter extraordinaire and sometime crime reporter. And you're Donna Blake from Sky TV, aren't you? Thought I recognised you. Sorry I messed this up for you and everyone here, but I . . . Well, let's just say I have my reasons.'

'And what the hell might those be?' Donna asked, frustration, confusion and curiosity robbing her words of any real anger.

McGregor looked at her for a moment, as though making a decision. 'Why don't we find a coffee shop and have a word?' he said. 'I can wait while you file your report. And, if you're still not convinced, you can give Susie Drummond a quick call. She can vouch that I'm not a nutcase.' The smile crawled back to his lips. 'Well, not too much of one anyway.'

Donna felt her mouth open. Closed it. Who was this guy? He had shown up from nowhere, thrown some fairly damning accusations at a leading businessman and a local MSP, then asked her to go for a coffee.

And, more importantly, how the hell did he know her friend, Detective Sergeant Susie Drummond?

CHAPTER 5

Connor paced around the car, the sound of gravel crunching under his feet seeming to echo the grinding, incessant buzz of his thoughts.

He had forced himself to be calm when he walked into the care home, checked in with the front desk about his gran. A young woman, whom Connor vaguely recognised, answered his questions warily, as though she could read the storm of confusion and terror in his clipped, precise words and balled fists.

Yes, his gran was fine. Better than fine, actually. She'd taken a walk in the gardens earlier, seemed to enjoy the flowerbeds. No, no one had visited her in the last few hours, or approached the desk and asked about her. Was she expecting someone?

Good question, Connor had thought.

He had made his way to his gran's flat, his guts lurching with a cocktail of relief and blind fury when she had opened the door and peered up at him, a smile creasing her face. She bustled him inside the flat, even as she launched into a stream of apologies about not having his favourite biscuits in as she hadn't known he was coming. He made up an excuse he now couldn't remember for his unannounced visit to her, then spent ten minutes on small-talk even as he checked the flat for signs of an intruder.

He found nothing, which only fuelled his rage. Someone was using his gran to get to him. But who?

And why?

He made his excuses after about twenty minutes, promising to return for a proper visit as soon as he could, then headed back outside, found Simon waiting for him, nothing good in his friend's blank gaze. Simon had told him about his discovery in the woodland surrounding the home, which had set Connor pacing around the car, trying to understand what was going on.

'Connor,' Simon called, after a minute of silence. Connor looked up, saw Simon holding his phone away from his ear. 'Just heard from Robbie. He's got people with Jen now, says she's fine. Seems she's been out with her physio for a walk, which means . . .'

'Which means the pictures were taken today,' Connor muttered even as he felt oily guilt curl in his stomach. He should have called Jen, made sure she was all right.

He forced the thought aside. Focused. 'But if they were taken today, does that—'

He was cut off by the chirp of his own mobile. He pulled it out of his pocket, wasn't surprised when he saw 'No Caller ID'. Gestured for Simon to come closer as he hit answer.

'Connor Fraser,' he said.

The voice that oozed out of the phone was smooth, cultured, almost tender. But there was something wrong with it, distorted, the vowels warped and consonants lifted. Autotune or something similar, Connor thought. A coward's way of masking his voice.

'Ah, Mr Fraser. Good. My apologies for waiting to call you, but I can imagine you've had a busy time since you got my email and my deposit.'

Connor clicked his phone onto speaker mode before he replied. 'Busy time?' he hissed, as he forced his jaw to unclench. 'You could say that. Who are you? What's this all about?'

A small, amused laugh down the line, the autotune twisting the sound in Connor's ear. 'You can call me a fan, I suppose, Mr Fraser. You see, I've read about you, and I'm very impressed by your work. So, I've decided to employ you. I am going to kill Father John Donnelly sometime in the next seven days. And you are going to stop me – or die trying. I'm not sure what the going rate is for a security consultant, but I trust the seventy thousand I've deposited with you will be enough for a week's work.'

Connor looked up at Simon, whose expression was unreadable. 'Listen, whoever you are, you just threatened two of the—'

'I can see that you've accessed the pictures I sent you, Mr Fraser, so you know I'm serious in my intentions,' the voice replied, cold cruelty clipping the vowels despite the distortion. 'I can also see you've not accessed the contract I sent you yet. Refuse my offer, and either your grandmother, or the delightful Ms MacKenzie or someone else you love will die. So, reply with your agreement to the terms within ten minutes or my next call will be a very lurid, very detailed account of a death you could have prevented. A death that I promise will shatter your heart. And, just to be fair, I'll give you an hour, starting now, to find Father Donnelly before the games begin. Good hunting, Mr Fraser, to both of us.'

Connor took a breath to reply, heard the click of the call ending before he could speak.

'Jesus,' Simon said, as Connor stared down at his phone. 'What the fuck is all that about?'

'No idea,' Connor said. 'But we've got a clock ticking now. Thoughts?'

Simon blew out a deep breath, dropped his head. Connor could almost hear the thoughts thundering through his friend's mind as he ran every possible scenario. Someone had profiled Connor closely enough to know about Jen and his gran. They also knew how to surveil both women without being detected, and were tech-savvy enough to use bank transfers from American shell accounts that did not list account ownerships. And, given the seventy thousand pounds they had just thrown away to get Connor's attention, they had deep pockets.

'Play for time,' Simon said after a moment. 'We don't have enough facts yet to know what the hell we're dealing with. Scan that fucking contract, then sign it, buy us some time.'

Connor nodded. He hated being so reactive, responding to events rather than dictating them, but he couldn't see much choice. He would make sure Jen and his gran were safe, then find whoever had threatened them. And end them.

'Agreed,' he said. 'But do me one favour?'

Simon's brow furrowed. 'Sure. But what . . .'

'You check out the contract. Not sure how legally binding it is under the circumstances, but it's important to whoever our mystery caller is so we play along. If there are no glaring fuck-ups in it, tell me and I'll do as he asks.'

'And what are you going to be doing in the meantime?' Simon asked.

Connor felt a smile slither onto his lips. It felt cold, alien. Cruel.

'What else?' he said. 'I'm going to look for Father John Donnelly.'

CHAPTER 6

He laid the phone down gently, as though it was a pet he had not quite tamed. Stared at it for a moment as he let the silence of the room seep into him, soothe him, as it had so many times before.

It was done. After all these years, after all the planning and the agonising and the soul searching, it was done. The first step had been taken. There was no going back now.

For any of them.

He glanced around the room, his eyes falling on the Bible that sat on the table in front of him, a bottle of whisky beside it. He considered both objects carefully – his life represented by two objects, one offering salvation, one promising only ruin. He reached for the Bible, stopped himself. What he had just done was a grievous sin, mortal even. Yet he could not find it within himself to regret his actions. From evil had come good. It was always the way.

'Bless me, Father, for I have sinned,' he muttered, as he reached for the whisky instead. 'And I intend to continue sinning for a long, long time.'

The whisky seared his throat as he swigged from the bottle, stirring up a memory of another time when the fire had seemed ready to consume him. A smoke-filled room, the world seen in snatches of soot-smeared orange and flaring white as the fire raged, the heat an almost physical weight as it licked at his skin, blistering it with acid-laced kisses that blackened his flesh and . . .

He closed his eyes, told himself the tears he felt were from the whisky. It had begun. He could mourn himself and his lost soul later.

Fraser had not been what he had expected. Studying him, he had formed the impression of a bruiser who intimidated with his size and thought with his fists. But speaking to him now, he had felt the presence of the man, the force of personality that lurked behind his words. There had been no fear in that voice. Confusion, yes, and an understandable frustration and tension, but fear? No. He had seen fear in all its forms, from the haunted eyes that swung open the front door to him, begging him silently not to end their world with a simple statement, or the desperate, wide-eyed animalistic terror of a person who was trapped and knew they were going to die.

Like the fire, fear was a living thing. But it found no comfort in Connor Fraser.

He lifted the whisky bottle in a silent toast, took another long swig, then held it in his mouth, feeling it blister and burn.

Yes, he had chosen well. Connor Fraser would be more than adequate for the task at hand, a fine implement of justice. When he had completed his unwitting mission, Connor Fraser would die. But before he did, he would know the fear and the fire.

And in that moment, they would be brothers.

CHAPTER 7

Finding Father Donnelly had been a lot easier than Connor had thought it was going to be. Not thanks to the power of the Almighty or the divine insight of an omniscient God, but with the help of the twenty-first century's equivalent.

Connor had turned to Google.

He started with what he knew. He'd been given an hour to find Donnelly. Given that whoever he was dealing with wanted Connor to protect him, he had to be somewhere close, somewhere Connor could get to in under an hour. So that meant Catholic churches in the Stirling and Bannockburn area, maybe stretching out as far as Falkirk.

Armed with this information, Connor had flicked onto the web app on his phone and started searching. He was surprised to find his initial request led him to a searchable website that listed not only Catholic churches across the UK but also the names of those working there. Despite himself, Connor laughed at that. After the scandals of the last few years, from child abuse to priests having affairs with married parishioners, he would have expected the Church to be playing the quiet game. But, no, there they were, online and advertising, no different from a plumber or any other tradesman, and open for business.

It made a certain sense. After all, wasn't the main man the son of a carpenter?

The listing was for a small church called St Ninian's in Lenton Barns, a tiny, forgotten village nestled in the farmlands south of Stirling. Connor flicked through the website, found a picture of Father John Donnelly. He was a nondescript man, probably in his late fifties, judging from the salt-and-pepper hair and forehead that was as lined as a topological map. Dark brown eyes peered out from behind lenses so thick they gave him a vaguely owlish appearance. His only remarkable feature was a scarlet blotch that ran from his bottom lip and across his chin, almost as if he had snuck a swig of the Communion wine and dribbled it. Scar or birthmark, Connor couldn't tell.

But the question remained, who was this man? And why did someone want to kill him?

Connor phoned the number listed on the website, wasn't surprised when it rang out and went to an answerphone message so abrupt and perfunctory that all it told him was that Donnelly was from the west coast and no fan of technology.

He decided not to leave a message. Lenton Barns was only a twenty-minute drive from his current location, and he had the feeling that a personal visit was in order.

'Well,' Simon said, as he walked towards him, waggling his phone. 'I've read this "contract". Load of shite, so whoever wrote it could be a high-court judge. Basically says you agree to protect this Donnelly character for the agreed fee of seventy grand. A "fair day's work for a fair day's pay". Nothing more, nothing less.'

'Guess I should sign it then, keep this lunatic happy until we know what we're dealing with.'

A sly smile played across Simon's lips. 'Too late, big man,' he said. 'I've already done it. Forged your signature, signed into your email account and sent it. This bugger's going to learn he's not the only one who can play sneaky.'

Connor returned his friend's smile, but he could see the anger and determination behind Simon's banter. They had first met when Connor was a probationary police officer with the Police Service of Northern Ireland. And while Connor's police career had been neither long nor glorious, thanks to a run-in with a small-time thug who called himself the Librarian, Simon had taught him everything he knew about policing and, more importantly, friendship. He worked from a simple code: come at me in the line of duty, fine. Fuck with me or mine as a way to get to me, then your bones will enjoy a long interment in some very, very cold ground.

He filled Simon in on what he had found out about Father Donnelly and they headed to the car, Simon assuring Connor that he'd arranged for Sentinel Securities staff to put his gran's care home under surveillance. Connor wondered what Gordon Argyll, an accountant who was one of his fellow directors at Sentinel, would think about company resources being used for personal gain, and found he didn't really care.

Until he knew what was going on, he would do whatever it took to keep his gran and Jen safe.

They drove to Lenton Barns in silence, each man alone with his thoughts. Again, Connor felt a snarl of unease at being a player in someone else's game, tried to calm himself with the thought that Jen and his gran were safe, and he would find his mysterious 'client' soon enough.

A thought occurred to him as he drove. Was this Duncan MacKenzie's doing? He had clashed with Jen's father the previous year, uncovered some nasty family secrets that meant Connor had been moved from Duncan's Christmas card list to his hit list. The only thing that had stayed his hand, so far, was Jen. Still recovering from being run over as part of a twisted message to Duncan, Connor had been there for her through surgery and rehabilitation. Duncan had seen this, deemed his desire for vengeance was less important than his daughter's happiness and recovery.

But had that changed? Duncan had shown he could and would use anyone to get what he wanted. Had he decided Jen was now recovered enough to be a pawn in his game, a game that would lead to him standing over Connor's bloodied corpse?

Connor pushed the thought away as he saw the road sign that indicated they were entering Lenton Barns. He slowed the car, felt the air grow thick as Simon snapped to attention in his seat. It was like being back on patrol in Belfast, both men on alert, ready for anything.

28

Connor found it strangely comforting.

The village was typical affluent rural central Scotland: a neat high street with narrow side streets leading off it, the buildings hewn from sandstone and granite that seemed to glisten in the afternoon sun. Well-manicured trees and bushes dotted the street, which contained a butcher, a hairdresser, a pub that looked like it had been set up in someone's front room, and a small post office, a freshly painted letterbox standing to attention on the kerb. They drove on, found the church just as the village was petering out and the countryside was starting to express its dominance once again.

It was as if the church had hunkered down at the border of the village and dug in: religion by attrition. The Catholic Church as a whole might have professed love and light, but in Lenton Barns, it looked like it was ready for war.

The walls that surrounded it were low, blunt, utilitarian, an aesthetic that was continued by the church itself, which looked as though it had been hewn from rocks that had grown sour and warped when they had been dragged from the earth. Sitting beside it was a small, squat house, all white windows and harling that clung to the walls like patches of acne. The presbytery, Connor assumed.

He pulled up at the closed wrought-iron gates at the entrance to the church.

'Jesus, cheery place,' Simon said, peering forward.

'Aye,' Connor agreed. There was something about the church, about the way the main stained-glass window that was set directly in the centre of the building like a jewel seemed to stare at you, that unsettled him.

'So, not exactly a warm welcome,' Simon said, nodding towards the closed gates. 'What do you want to do?'

'Take no chances,' Connor said, reversing the car and parallel parking next to the pavement. 'Split up. I'll take the front, you take the back, scout the location. See you at the front door of the church. Check the house if no one's there?'

'Take the back?' Simon asked, mock shock in his voice. 'So you want me, an officer of the law, to scale a wall and very probably sneak through a graveyard?'

'Yeah,' Connor said. 'Got a problem with that?'

'Naw.' Simon smiled. 'Not really. I'm already screwed anyway, as we should technically have reported the threat to this man's life, Jen and your gran to your pal Ford and his chums in Police Scotland. But if I get into trouble with the man upstairs for this, you're doing my bloody Hail Marys for me.'

'Deal,' Connor said, climbing out of the car. 'Though you're well past saving.'

CHAPTER 8

The coffee shop where Donna had agreed to meet Doug McGregor was on the high street in Banknock. Small and neat, it was crammed with tables draped in old-fashioned frilled cloths, while the beige and orange crockery looked like it had been shipped straight from 1976. The warm, rich smell of home baking filled Donna's nostrils, reminding her she had skipped breakfast to make McGovern's photo call.

She saw McGregor sitting at a table, engrossed in an iPad. He looked up and smiled at her, the light from the tablet accentuating the sharpness of his cheekbones and his nose. After filing her report with Sky, and promising the desk editor she would update the story as soon as she found out what the hell was going on, she had taken a minute to look into McGregor. A former crime reporter in Edinburgh, he had dropped off the map a couple of years ago, only to resurface two months back, working for a start-up investigative news website called the Crucible. Initially dismissed as a place old reporters went to fade away quietly after their mainstream career had gone from a front-page splash to a page-nineteen filler, the Crucible quickly built a reputation for a strong investigations team breaking stories that regularly dominated the news agenda. After breaking one such story herself, about a child sex-abuse ring that stretched across Scotland, Donna was no stranger to the type of attention such work could attract.

Which left her with more than a few questions about Doug McGregor.

'Hiya,' he said, standing and offering her a hand as she approached the table. She took it, surprised by how his almost skeletal hand engulfed hers. 'Get you anything? The coffee's great.'

Donna nodded, ignoring the rumbling in her stomach. Later. The last thing she was going to do was share a scone with the man who had just screwed up her morning.

Doug gestured to a waitress and ordered a coffee for Donna and a refill for himself. Then he settled into his seat again, folding away the iPad and dropping it into a scuffed satchel at his feet.

'So,' Donna said, after a pause just long enough to establish that McGregor had no intention of speaking first, 'you want to tell me what your amateur dramatics back at McGovern's press call were all about? Seems to me the Crucible is beyond cheap theatrics to noise up a property developer.'

Doug raised his mug to her in a small toast. 'So, you looked me up. Can't say I'm surprised. I looked you up as well.' He indicated the satchel at his feet. 'Impressive stuff, though I'm not sure I'll be asking you to pick my lottery numbers any time soon.'

Despite herself, Donna smiled. He was right. Over the last few years, she had made a name for herself reporting on some big stories, mostly since she had run into Connor Fraser. But while the stories had brought her success, they had also come at a price. One that had been paid in blood and loss and pain.

She shuddered, pushed down a sudden memory of her ex, Mark Sneddon. Murdered three years ago, she still saw him every day in the eyes and lips of their son, Andrew.

'So what were you up to this morning?' she asked. 'Can't see why McGovern would be of that much interest to you.'

Something like amusement flashed in Doug's dark eyes. He smiled, revealing small white teeth that were just a little too crooked. 'Ack, McGovern's an arsehole,' he said at last. 'I'm not interested in him, not really. Oh, I'm sure there are a few dodgy tax dealings and off-the-books contracts he's got tucked away, but it's not him I'm really after. I'm much more interested in his pals, Kerr Cunningham and Brian Clarke.'

Donna rocked back as she considered the names. 'Well, I know Cunningham,' she said, after a moment, 'polis turned politician, list

MSP for Central Scotland. But Clarke?'

'QC in Edinburgh,' Doug replied. She noticed he was balling his left hand into a fist and releasing it as he spoke. 'Pals with Cunningham and, of course, McGovern.'

Donna thanked the waitress who had just placed a coffee in front of her. 'So why tell me all this, and why confront McGovern like that?'

Doug fiddled with his mug before draining it and reaching for his refill.

'Okay, honesty time,' he said after a moment. 'I knew you'd be there this morning, Donna. I did what I did partly to unsettle McGovern and see what he'd do, and partly to make sure I had a chance to have coffee with you.'

Donna felt something between anger and fear roil in her guts, turning the smell of the coffee bitter and the warmth of the café cloying. 'What?' she said softly. 'You mean you stalked me. On a story? Why? And what . . .' She trailed off, unable to speak past the sudden urge to throw her coffee in McGregor's face and storm out of the café.

He held up his left hand in a placatory gesture, and Donna could see a thin, silvery trail of scars traced across the palm.

'I'm working on a story,' he said, his voice low now, serious. 'Could be big. National big. But the Crucible's resources only go so far, and I need your help. Like I said, I looked you up. I was impressed with what I found, especially on the child sex-abuse ring case you worked with Susie Drummond last year. So I thought we could help each other. You get the six p.m. headlines. I get the deep dive and the answers I'm looking for.'

Donna stared at McGregor. She should tell him to piss off and leave. Yet another part of her, the part that lived for the thrill of breaking a story or leading the news, wanted to stay. She had seen his cuttings, knew he had been a good reporter, not afraid to follow the big stories, even when they led to the door of a crooked politician or a Gulf War veteran hell-bent on revenge.

'Okay,' she said slowly. 'Promising nothing. But what have you got? And what do you need from me?'

Doug smiled, sipped his coffee. 'Let me tell you a story,' he said. 'But, first, a question. How well do you know a man called Connor Fraser?'

CHAPTER 9

Connor approached the church slowly, the thought that this was the second time that day he had heard gravel crunch under his feet randomly crossing his mind as he walked.

A closer look at the place did nothing to improve its appeal. The sandstone façade seemed to suck in the bright warmth of the day, turning the sunlight cold and somehow sterile. The main entrance was a huge arch, which was adorned with ornately sculpted angels and cherubs, their faces now blank and fading like an old memory after years of being exposed to the elements. The wooden double doors set into the arch were painted an almost lurid red that glistened jewel-like in the sun.

To Connor, it looked like a gaping maw.

He caught movement to his left, looked around to see Simon emerging from around the corner of the church. He moved quickly, his head darting in small bird-like motions as he took in his surroundings. Stooped low to stay below window height, he might as well have had 'I'm a copper' stamped on the back of his T-shirt.

'You find anything?' Connor asked, as Simon stopped beside him, bouncing on the balls of his feet as he did so.

'Nothing,' he said, head still swivelling, trying to take in everything at once. 'There's a door to a cellar or coal store round the back, but the lock and hinges are rusted to shit. Been a long time since anyone used that door. You?'

'Nothing,' Connor replied, eyes drifting between the church and the small, squat house that sat to their left. 'What do you think?' asked. 'Here or there?'

'Here,' Simon said, an empty smile curling his lips slightly. 'Whatever the hell is going on, the priest is the focus of it. Whoever is yanking our chain wants to make that point. So, if they've left any surprises for us, it'll be in the church, the main stage for all of this.'

Connor agreed with Simon's chain of thought. 'So what's the protocol for visiting a house of God?' he asked.

'Fucked if I know,' Simon replied bluntly. 'Knock on the door? See if one of us bursts into flames?'

Connor grunted a laugh, took a step forward. He reached for the black iron handle on the door, was about to try it, when a voice called, 'Can I help you, gentlemen?'

Connor and Simon spun round to see a man dressed in black walking towards them, following the path that led from the house to the church.

He was maybe five years older than in the picture Connor had seen online, his hair more salt than pepper now, the forehead encroaching further up his skull. He was both shorter and broader than Connor had imagined, with powerful shoulders and a solid, rotund build that was uncomfortably similar to that of a psychopath called Paulie King, with whom Connor had had a few runs in over the years.

'Father John Donnelly?' Connor stepped towards the approaching man and offered his hand.

'Yes, yes, I am,' Donnelly replied, in a sing-song tone that somehow elongated consonants, sharpened vowels and marked him out as having spent time in Ayrshire. 'But that doesn't answer my question. Who are you, gentlemen, and why do you feel the need to approach my church as if you're about to lay siege to it?'

Simon shuffled on his feet at Connor's side in a way that told him his friend was embarrassed to have been seen sneaking up on the place. Not that Connor believed he had moral objections to what he had done. No, Simon would be professionally embarrassed for being caught while on surveillance.

'I'm Connor Fraser,' Connor said, as Donnelly took his hand and pumped it with surprising strength. Connor thought he felt the rough edge of calluses in the grip. 'This is my friend, Simon McCartney. I wonder if we could have a moment of your time, Father. Perhaps inside?'

Donnelly's eyes slid from Connor to Simon, then back to Connor, the pupils magnified by his thick glasses. There was no recognition in those eyes, Connor thought, no fear either.

'I can give you a few minutes, yes,' he said. 'This way.'

He turned without waiting for a reply, and set off for the house. Connor and Simon exchanged a glance, then followed him.

Donnelly led them into the house, down a small hallway and into a surprisingly large, airy study. The walls were crammed with books, which seemed to bleed out of the inset bookcases, and, in the centre of a room, Connor noted a desk that looked as though it had been transported directly from the eighteenth century. Heavily lacquered and carved in a way that vaguely reminded him of the church's archway, it had been designed for purpose and status. Whoever owned this desk had paid for the privilege of sitting behind it. They were a person of wealth and influence, it said.

Question was, what type of influence did Donnelly have?

Opposite the desk, set into a bay window, there was an old leather couch. Donnelly didn't invite Connor or Simon to sit, instead standing beside his desk and turning to them, like a headmaster who had summoned two misbehaving students to his office.

'Right. Gentlemen, please tell me what I can do for you. And forgive me if I ask you to be brief, but I'm rather busy this afternoon.'

Connor glanced at Simon. Shrugged. Brief he wanted, fine. He started talking, telling Donnelly about the pictures of Jen and his gran, the seventy thousand pounds that had been deposited in Sentinel's account and the contract that demanded he do his best to keep Donnelly safe. As he spoke, Donnelly grew still, except for a finger that played across the scarlet scar that twisted from his lip down and underneath his jaw.

'Can you think of anyone who might want to hurt you, sir?' Simon asked gently, after Connor had finished speaking.

'What?' Donnelly said, his voice small and vague, as though he had just been jarred from a daydream. 'No, no, of course not. I mean, this is preposterous, isn't it? It must be some kind of sick joke.'

'Doubtful,' Connor said, some unformed idea rearing vaguely in his mind, more feeling than conscious rationalisation. 'The pictures are current, and the seventy thousand that has been deposited in my account is very real. Unless you know any priest-hating billionaires with a sick sense of humour, we have to take this seriously until we know what's going on. Have you been contacted by anyone threatening you in, say, the last week? Seen anyone suspicious hanging around here?'

'You mean apart from you and your friend?' Donnelly shot back, something that could almost be mistaken for humour in his eyes. 'No, nothing at all. This is a quiet village, Mr Fraser. Peaceful. It's one of the reasons I . . .' He trailed off, as though the daydream was calling to him again.

Connor felt frustration prickle across his scalp. Whatever was going on, this man was at the centre of it. He needed answers, not distraction and disbelief.

He turned away from the priest to Simon. He was leaning against the arm of the sofa, arms folded, face impassive. Connor knew the look well, had seen it in a thousand police interview rooms when they were sitting across from a suspect at a cheap, scarred table. Simon was assessing, rapidly. 'Ford,' he said, after a moment.

'What?' Connor asked.

Simon looked at him, focus returning to his eyes. 'I said it earlier on. We're fucked as we didn't report these threats as soon as they were made. So let's make it official now. Report this to Ford. Fudge the timeline a little to keep us in the clear. Make sure Father Donnelly here, Jen and your gran are safe. I dunno, maybe this isn't the first threat like this that's been made. Would make sense for the police to keep it quiet if there had been others like it. So we go official. See if Ford knows anything. If nothing else, it gives us another resource, maybe frees us up to dig a bit deeper. And it keeps Sentinel's nose clean with the authorities.'

Connor was forced to agree. But even as he reached into his pocket for his phone, he felt a thread of unease twist through his mind. DCI Malcolm Ford was a back-to-basics copper, a man who put results and the desire for justice before anything else. Connor knew part of his drive was a need to atone for past mistakes. They had worked well together on previous cases. But, still, the fact remained, every time Connor contacted Ford he was bringing him bad news. How much more could the man take? And what did it say about Connor that he felt relief at having Ford to turn to and share the burden with?

CHAPTER 10

While Connor stepped outside to call Ford, Simon waited in the presbytery with Father Donnelly. He had retreated to his desk and was sitting behind it, hands splaying, digging beneath the various papers that were strewn across it. He seemed to relax slightly as he touched the desktop, as though it was anchoring him, giving him comfort. Simon noticed a large, leather-bound Bible sitting on the corner, complete with the ornate gold-leaf lettering that he knew so well from his own childhood. Wondered what it said about the priest that he reached for his desk rather than the Bible. Next to it sat a laptop, a Mac from what Simon could see, half submerged by papers, flotsam caught in the incoming tide of documents Donnelly had collected through his work.

'I'm sorry about all this,' Simon said. 'I know it must be a shock. But, trust me, my friend and I aren't going to let anything happen to you. We'll find out what's going on.'

Donnelly looked up at him, eyes flashing quicksilver as his glasses caught the sun streaming through the bay windows. He gave a small, almost indulgent smile.

'Don't worry, Mr, ah, McCartney, wasn't it? I have all the protection I need,' he said, gesturing to the Bible.

Coming from Belfast, Simon knew the power of such faith. But he had also seen its ability to distort and corrupt, to fill the minds of young men and women with a fervent, feverish belief that drove them to pick up petrol bombs and pistols to defend their interpretation of the Bible above others'. To Simon, faith was just another alibi – a way to absolve the bigots, racists and murderers of their guilt. All they were doing was following the holy word, wasn't it?

'Aye, well, if you don't mind, I'll stick to more practical defences,' he said. 'Are you sure you can't think of any reason, any reason at all, why someone would want you dead? And why they would want to drag my friend into it?'

Donnelly sighed, looked up at the ceiling, then back at Simon. 'No, I cannot. As I said, Mr McCartney, Lenton Barns is a quiet, peaceful village. A place of community. I've been here for ten years now, and I can assure you that, other than some clashes with the Community Council over Midnight Mass and the village's festive decorations, I've no enemies here whatsoever.'

'What about elsewhere?' Simon asked.

'What do you mean?' Donnelly said, wariness cooling his voice.

'You said you've been here for about a decade, right? But, and forgive me, I'm not great at Scottish accents, it sounds like you're from the west coast. Glasgow maybe? Somewhere like that? So what did you do before you got here? And could any of that previous life have made you enemies, someone who bears a grudge?'

Donnelly opened his mouth, closed it. When he raised a finger to his chin to trace the line of his scar, Simon noticed his hand wasn't quite steady.

'Before I came here,' he said slowly, 'I did God's work, Mr McCartney. I ministered to heroes, men and women who put their lives on the line every day for people who were strangers to them. I was proud of the work I did then, and I'm proud of it now. So, no, I cannot think of anyone from that time who would consider me their enemy.'

Simon held Donnelly's defiant gaze. 'Fair enough,' he said. 'Only one line of thought. But there's someone out there, someone—'

He was cut off by Connor's return. He glanced at Donnelly, then looked at Simon, who shook his head slightly. *Nothing of interest yet,* the gesture said.

'How'd the big man take it?' Simon asked.

'About as well as you'd expect,' Connor replied, his tone not without humour. 'Tried out a few swear words on me, made a passing reference to my bloodline on my mother's side. But he's going to head out here,' he turned, 'to take a statement from you, Father, if that's okay?'

'Of course,' Donnelly said. 'The faster we get this mess sorted out, the better.'

'What about us?' Simon asked, already suspecting he knew the answer.

'Stay put until Ford arrives,' Connor said.

Simon nodded. Standard police procedure. Try to contain the locus, keep everyone together until you could establish what the hell was going on. He'd have done the same in Ford's position. 'Fair enough,' he said. 'But that doesn't stop us doing a little work while we're here, does it?'

Connor smiled. 'Already on it,' he said, waggling his phone. 'Robbie's preparing, ah,' his eyes slid towards Donnelly, 'a briefing. And I've put certain, ah, additional measures in place to make sure Jen and Gran are safe.'

Simon leant forward, about to ask Connor exactly what he meant, when Connor's phone chimed with an email alert. He looked down at it, his face setting as hard as the stone of the building they were standing in.

'What?' Simon said.

Connor said nothing, just passed him the phone. He looked down, read the message. Felt a sudden urge to get away from the bay window he was standing in front of.

Hour's up, Mr Fraser. The fun begins now. Hope you're able to earn your money, for Donnelly's sake. And your own.

CHAPTER 11

DS Susie Drummond looked down at her mobile phone as it flashed in her hand, and sighed internally. Ever since she had seen the morning news and had a cursory scan of her Twitter feed, she had known this call was coming.

So much for a morning off. It didn't bode well for the rest of the day.

She considered ignoring the call, decided it was futile. The caller was not known for their ability to let something go.

'Donna,' she said, as she answered the call. 'Can't imagine why you're calling me. Fun morning?'

'Oh, yeah,' Donna said, her voice so heavy with sarcasm Susie almost felt the phone take on extra weight in her hand. 'Met an old pal of yours, Doug McGregor. Interesting guy.'

Susie closed her eyes, sighed. She had seen the footage from the press conference, and McGovern's subsequent denial of impropriety on any and every media platform that would listen.

One thing about Doug McGregor, she thought, the man knew how to make a splash when he wanted to.

'Yeah,' she murmured into the phone. 'I suppose he is at that. What's up?'

'How well do you know this guy?' Donna asked, her voice taking on a clipped, professional tone that told Susie she was no longer talking to her friend. Now she was talking to a reporter. The thought wasn't exactly comforting.

'Well enough,' she replied. 'We met a few years ago when I first transferred to Edinburgh from the Borders. He's a good reporter for the most part. Can take a few risks, but knows right from wrong, a shite story from a real one.' She smiled, remembering her first meeting with Doug, and him using the same words.

'So he's credible?' Donna asked. 'You trust him?'

Good question, Susie thought. 'For the most part, yes. He's been away, though, dealing with personal stuff. I haven't really spoken to him for a while. Why? What's this about, Donna? What's he up to now?'

A pause on the phone, the background noise washing down the line telling Susie that Donna was on hands-free in a car.

'You got plans this afternoon?' Donna asked.

Susie shut her eyes again. Her first day off after a ten-day duty shift, which had seen her looking into one domestic-abuse case, an aggravated sexual assault on the Grassmarket and an attempted murder in Leith. All she wanted to do was have a lazy day, go for a run, then maybe to the bookshop on Princes Street to lose herself in the historical fiction section for a while.

Trust Doug McGregor to screw up her plans.

'Nothing much,' she said, hearing the tone of resignation in her voice, not caring. 'What are you thinking?'

'Coffee, maybe something to eat. I'm heading for Edinburgh now. Can meet you in an hour or so?'

'Okay,' Susie said slowly. 'But again, why? What's Doug done now?'

'He told me a story,' Donna replied. 'A story concerning a mutual friend of ours, Connor Fraser. But before I go any further with this, I want to know about Doug McGregor, if he's on the level.'

Susie took a breath, held it. On the level enough to fake a news story when Doug thought he was a murderer? Yes. On the level enough to bury a sordid gossip piece about Susie's one-night stand with a married superior officer? Yes. On the level enough to turn to the bottle when he was badly beaten by a murderer, the injuries inflicted both physical and mental? Oh, yes. But he was still Doug.

Her phone chirped in her ear, stirring her from her thoughts.

'Look, Donna, I've got another call coming in. Text me where and when you want to meet, okay, and I'll see you there.'

She ended the call before Donna could agree, the surge of relief she felt souring quickly as she read the ID of the new caller.

'John,' she said, the same resignation she had just heard when talking to Donna echoing in her voice as the last vestiges of her hopes for her day off withered and died. 'What can I do to help you on my day off?'

DS John Troughton coughed down the line, telling Susie her barbed comment had hit a tender spot. No surprise, really. The man was a walking soft target.

'Ah, sorry, Susie,' he said. 'Boss just had a call, thought you'd want to know about it.'

'Oh, and why would that be?' Susie asked. Whatever crap DCI Malcolm Ford was having to deal with, it wasn't her problem – at least, not until she got back on shift.

'Connor Fraser's been on the phone,' Troughton replied, in an and-you-know-what-that-means tone. 'Told the boss one hell of a story about death threats, five-figure sums and a village priest. Given our previous dealings with Fraser, thought you'd want to know.'

'Go on,' Susie said, even as she felt her mind begin to race.

She listened as Troughton told her what he knew about the email to Connor, the pictures, the threat to Father John Donnelly. And as she listened, two questions formed in her mind, almost drowning Troughton out.

What exactly had Connor got himself into? And what role in it did Doug McGregor have to play?

CHAPTER 12

At Simon's insistence, they had closed the heavy draped curtains of the bay window in Father Donnelly's study, leaving the room in a thick, oppressive gloom.

Somehow, Connor thought, it suited DCI Malcolm Ford perfectly.

He had arrived about twenty minutes after Connor had called, in an unmarked car driven by a younger man Connor recognised as his detective sergeant, Troughton. Unlike Connor, Troughton had no compunction about opening the church's gates and driving straight up the gravel driveway.

Connor offered Ford his hand when he opened the door to the policeman, received a handshake as cold and hard as the man's gaze.

'Troughton's going to have a look around,' he said, as Connor led him to the study, 'which gives us time to have a little chat about the latest pile of shit you've landed me in.'

Connor felt an answer burn his throat, swallowed it. True, he had brought Ford his share of trouble, but he had also brought him a case that had revived his career and offered the man a form of redemption. The child sex-abuse ring Connor had exposed had led Ford to make some very high-profile, very public arrests that had eased the invisible burden that seemed to hunch the man's shoulders and darken his brow with a permanent scowl. He looked more energised and, yes, alive, than Connor had seen him in a long time. And the reason was simple – Ford was a man who lived for crises and impossible tasks.

At least, that was what Connor told himself.

Introductions were made, and Connor recapped what had happened since Robbie's first phone call, the emailed contract and the photographs. Hoped Ford didn't look too closely at the timeline, Simon's warning echoing in his ears as he spoke.

Ford took it all in as he stood in the centre of the room, the shadows around him seeming to grow darker as he listened.

'And you say there have been no threats to you, sir?' he asked Donnelly. 'Nothing out of the ordinary?'

'Hmm?' Donnelly said, as though he had been roused from a doze. Connor wondered if the man was in shock, his apathy a way of dealing with the fact that someone had threatened his life and made a twisted game of it.

'No, no,' he said, as he adjusted his glasses. 'As I said to these two gentlemen, I have no reason to believe I warrant this level of attention.'

Ford grunted, his tone telling Connor he was thinking of the pub. 'So, Fraser, other than some pictures and this so-called "contract", what have you got? What makes you think this is a credible threat, not just an elaborate hoax? After all—'

He was cut off by a high buzzing sound that seemed to make the room vibrate. Connor glanced at Simon, who was already moving to the side of the window, drawing the curtains cautiously aside for a peek. 'What the hell?' Connor heard him mutter.

'Simon? What? Is there—'

'Guv!' Troughton's voice from outside. High and urgent. 'You should get out here, see this.'

Ford shot Connor a look. He turned to Donnelly as the policeman moved past him, heading for the door.

'Father, you stay here. My friend will be with you, make sure you're safe.'

Donnelly half rose from his chair, fell back into it. 'What is going on?' he said, his voice rising to be heard over the buzzing that was filling the room.

'I'll be back soon,' Connor said, sprinting after Ford.

He almost ran into the policeman on the doorstep. He looked up, following Ford's gaze into the cloudless sky.

'What the . . .'

On the horizon, about fifty feet in the air, were what looked like four toasters with rotors attached to each corner. They buzzed like angry bees as they swayed and lurched through the air, like a man leaving the pub and heading for the taxi rank after one too many.

'Drones, sir,' Troughton shouted. 'Definitely heading this way.'

Connor shielded his eyes, squinted. Troughton was right: their flight path, though erratic, was definitely heading for them.

'Could be anything,' Ford said. 'Those bloody things are all the rage now, could just be kids or—'

Before he could finish the sentence, one of the drones suddenly sped up, as though it had seen someone it recognised across a crowded room and wanted to say hello. It dipped violently, its rotors buzzing frantically, and darted towards the church.

Connor was moving before he was aware of it. He cried out, warning Troughton, bent low and sprang, grabbing Ford around the waist and bowling him off the front step of the house. The policeman's sudden cry was drowned in the roar of an explosion from behind Connor. It sounded as though the world was screaming, the force from the blast like a massive hand, swatting him aside as though he were a fly.

He rolled, forcing Ford down, trying to shield the policeman with his own body. Darted his head up to check on Troughton, then looked back at the church.

It looked as if it was bleeding fire. A black, charred crater had bloomed on the sandstone façade where the drone had crashed into it, whatever accelerant it was carrying dripping from the wreckage that was wedged into the stone, like the blade of a broken dagger.

Connor leapt to his feet, got Ford by the scruff of the neck and threw him towards the side of the house.

'Go!' he yelled, his voice muffled and alien, due to the scream of the drones and the after-effects of the explosion. 'Get round to the back of the house. For fuck's sake, get going!'

Another drone dived forward, this time heading for the church. Another explosion, almost knocking Connor off his feet, then musical tinkling as the stained-glass window shattered and rained down onto the ground.

Connor looked about desperately for something, anything he could use as a weapon. Saw a rock about two feet in front of him, part of the border between the gravel path and the lawn that surrounded the church. He surged forward, bent low and scooped it up, kept moving, adding his momentum to his throw as he said a silent prayer.

The rock bounced off the third drone, which listed to the side, like a pheasant winged by a bad shot. It fell from the sky, exploding ten feet from Connor, sending up a shower of grass and mud as it tore a chunk out of the lawn. Connor spun, saw Troughton and Ford disappear around the back of the church, just as the last drone made its kamikaze run. Felt his blood freeze as the drone seemed to bear down on him, then corrected itself, changing course for the church and its bright red double doors.

Connor dropped to the ground, hands covering his head. The explosion seemed to engulf him, scald him, as though a wave of boiling water had washed over his body. He felt shards of wood and stone pepper his back, cried out when something heavy slashed into his shoulder. He rolled over and kicked away, looking at the ruin the front of the church had become.

The explosion had obliterated the double doors, making the entrance look even more like a dark, gaping maw. Fire capered among the carvings on the archway, the stone blackening, the cherubs and angels' faces darkening, as though in fury at this outrage.

The silence that rushed into Connor's ears was overwhelming. He forced himself to breathe, swallowed the bile he felt rise in his throat. Sat up slowly, cold agony scalding his shoulder when he felt the shard of wood now embedded in it.

'Connor! Connor!' Simon's cries seemed to be coming from very far away. Connor turned, saw Simon sprinting towards him, head still swivelling as he moved, taking everything in, looking for fresh dangers.

'Christ, man, you okay?' Simon said, as he dropped to his knees beside Connor.

Despite himself, Connor smiled. 'Oh, aye, I'm fine,' he said, wincing again as he closed his hand around the shard in his shoulder. He knew he should leave it in, wait for medical help. Didn't care.

He tightened his grip, pulled. Felt his stomach lurch as the world filled with dark stars and agony exploded in his back. Held up the blood-smeared wood for Simon to see, his hand shaking badly.

'Think Ford will take this as evidence of a credible threat?' he said, slumping back to the ground.

CHAPTER 13

It didn't take long for the attack on the church to make its way online. A group of kids, attracted by the commotion, had made their way there and, phones in hand, gleefully filmed the devastation.

Not one of them thought to call the police.

News agencies quickly picked up on the story. Donna saw the snap on the PA news wire service just as she was getting ready to head to her meeting with Susie. 'Arson attack on church in county of Stirling'. She grabbed her phone, found one of the videos posted by the kids, a jerky long shot of the church, smoke billowing from the church into a flawless sky, the kids' excited whoops the soundtrack. The camera then panned down and did a stuttering zoom out, giving a wider shot of the church.

Donna felt something cold wrap itself around her throat and freeze her breath. She hastily scrolled back the video. Paused it and zoomed in, praying she was wrong.

She wasn't. Sitting in front of the church, low and sleek, like a predator about to pounce, was a car she knew very well. An Audi coupé, V8 engine.

Owned by Connor Fraser.

She flicked off the video, clicked on her phone contacts. Found the number for her cameraman Keith, told him to grab a van and head for Lenton Barns. Hung up before he could object, then dialled her editor at Sky, Fiona Young. Told her what was happening, that the story was hers. Satisfied, she grabbed her keys and headed for her car.

Susie would have to wait.

She made the drive to Lenton Barns on autopilot, her mind racing. What had Connor got involved in now? She couldn't see how it was related to the story Doug McGregor had told her, but could it be? And if it was, might that mean McGregor was right in his theory?

By the time she arrived at Lenton Barns, the emergency services had been called and descended on the church. It was cordoned off with police tape, two officers standing sentry at the gates, waving curious locals away. Peering up the long driveway of the church as she went slowly past, Donna could see a fire engine and an ambulance. She turned back to the road, cursed under her breath as she saw broadcasting vans from both STV and the BBC had already arrived. Looked around for Keith's Sky-branded van, saw it up the street.

She found a space close to it and parked, looked in her rear-view mirror at the scrum in front of the church. No point in just joining it: every other reporter on the scene would have the same shot. So what was the best way to—

She was startled from her thoughts by a soft tapping on the passenger-side window of the car. She turned, felt a prickle of irritation to see Doug McGregor leaning down, smiling at her as he waved.

'Hiya,' he said, as she got out of the car. 'Fancy seeing you here. Take it you spotted the story online as well?'

'Well, yeah,' she said, casting a glance back at the Sky van, hoping Keith had seen her.

Doug seemed to read her thoughts. 'If you're looking for your pal, he's in the fields round the back, getting some different angles on shots for you. I had a wee look myself, sent some shots and footage to the Crucible, but they'll look better on a TV screen than online, so I thought there was no harm in sharing.'

'Hold on,' Donna said. 'You've filed already?'

McGregor gave a smile that could almost have been mistaken for apologetic, if it weren't for the hard glint in his eyes. 'Well, yeah,' he said. 'Got here pretty sharpish when I saw the story, called a few contacts, got some initial statements. Wrote it up for the Crucible, sent it

51

over with some images. Already heard back from Andy on the desk – seems some of the agencies want to use our copy for now.'

'How the hell did you get here so fast?' Donna asked. She hated being scooped on any story. But to be scooped on her own patch by a newcomer who was hinting at having possibly the biggest story in a decade? No. No way.

'Like I said,' Doug replied, 'contacts. Besides, I have the feeling we're both here to see the same man, so it made sense for me to get here as soon as I could.'

'I need to find my cameraman,' Donna said, as she tried to compose herself.

'Take your time,' Doug replied. 'Police comms team have scheduled a briefing in ...' he glanced down at his watch '... twenty minutes' time at the Mercat Cross in the village square. Seems it's a joint presser, police and fire service. So, your cameraman can get his establishing shots and you've time to get ready to go live if needed.'

Donna was about to say something when she heard the honk of a horn. A red Ford Fiesta slid by, Susie Drummond at the wheel. She raised a hand to Donna, pointed down the road.

Donna turned back to Doug, whose face was now set, almost pale. 'Take it you know who that was?' she said.

'Aye,' Doug said, shifting his stance slightly. 'Susie Drummond. You'd best go and say hello.'

***

Connor thanked the paramedic who had patched up his shoulder, glad to be free of the ambulance and the overpoweringly antiseptic stench that hurt him in ways that a piece of wood lodged in his shoulder never could. He stepped out of the ambulance and took deep, cleansing breaths, as though filling his lungs could banish the memories of Jen lying in a hospital bed, her face a stain of bruises, naked anguish in her eyes as she whispered seven words, words he still had trouble believing today. *I was pregnant. But I lost it.*

He felt the familiar heat behind his eyes, shook his head angrily. Saw Ford standing at the ruined door to the church, conferring with a firefighter, who was pointing at the various scorch marks where the drones had exploded.

'Anything interesting?' Connor asked, as he approached the men.

They turned as one, giving Connor the kind of suspicious look those in the emergency services gave civilians. *You're not one of us*, it said.

Ford's eyes roamed over Connor. 'You okay?' he asked, his voice gruff, business-like.

Connor shrugged, rotated his shoulder. 'Could be worse,' he said, as pain crawled from his shoulder to his spine. 'Just got a bit of that bloody door wedged in my shoulder when it exploded. Be okay in a couple of days. How about you? Sorry I was a bit rough with you.'

Ford waved away the apology. 'You saved me, Fraser. I won't forget that.' He paused, a smile creasing his lips. It looked foreign to Connor, vaguely unhealthy, as if the policeman was laughing at a joke at Connor's expense. 'Nor will I forget that you dragged me into this shit-show in the first place,' he added. 'A shit-show that has attracted the attention of the chief constable and,' he jutted his jaw to the firefighter standing beside him, 'Gary's boss.'

The firefighter extended a hand to Connor. He was short, compact, with a hard, set face softened by intent blue eyes that seemed to shine with intelligence and humour. His handshake was like a warm, callused vice.

'Gary Strachan, head of service delivery for Central Scotland. You must be Connor Fraser. Malcolm's told me a lot about you.'

'Not sure if that's good news for me or not,' Connor said with a smile, his eyes drifting towards the ruin of the door, which was still giving off wisps of acrid smoke, like a stubbed cigarette that refused to die.

'So,' he asked, 'what have we got?'

Strachan glanced at Ford, who shrugged, then nodded. It was in that moment Connor saw how tired the man was, and the toll the events of the day had taken on him. What was it Ford had said? *You dragged me into this shit-show.* Connor felt a sudden stab of guilt.

'Well,' Strachan said, 'you know almost as much as we do. We've only started our survey of the property, but it looks like you were targeted with modified drones. We found the remnants of a plastic vial in the wreckage of one of the drones. It had been filled with an accelerant, probably petrol. Looks like it had a little Vaseline added to it to give it an extra kick.' He indicated the scorch mark further up the wall and the star-like pattern that radiated from the point of impact. 'That's consistent with the blast patterns on the wall. The drone acted as the ignition device for the accelerant, and it burnt on contact with the stone and the door, also amplifying the explosion.'

'Napalm,' Connor said, more to himself than anyone else. It was a tactic he remembered from Belfast, where gangs had added Vaseline or coconut oil to petrol bombs, then hurled them at the police or anyone else who got in their way. The Vaseline and coconut oil acted as binding agents, making the ignited liquid stick to whatever it hit. Cars. Buildings. People.

'Yes, I suppose so,' Strachan said. 'Crude, maybe, but ultimately effective.'

'Anything more than that, Gary?' Ford asked.

'Not yet,' Strachan replied. 'Like I said, we've got some wreckage, hopefully enough that we can trace the type of drone we're dealing with. See if it's exotic or domestic.'

'Exotic,' Connor said, his mind filling with the machines' angry buzz as they swooped from the sky. 'They'd have to be to carry the accelerant. It's why they were so bloody noisy when they were coming in – I'll bet the rotors and engines had been modified to carry the payload.'

Strachan gave Connor an appraising look. 'Makes sense,' he said. 'But identifying the type of drone will also help with establishing a radius for where whoever is after you and the priest launched their attack. The controls on these things have a specific range. When we know that, Malcolm and his men can start a search. I'm sure whoever did this is too cautious to stick around, but it might give you some-where to start looking.'

'Thanks, Gary,' Ford mumbled, his eyes roaming across the ruined face of the church.

'No problem, Malcolm,' the firefighter said. 'You tell Mary I said hello, will you?'

Ford gave a smile crafted by sadness and years of regret. 'Will do, Gary. You take care. I'll see you at this bloody press call we're doing.'

He moved off without waiting for a reply, heading back towards the presbytery, gesturing for Connor to follow him.

'So, the chief constable,' Connor said. 'You want Simon and me to make ourselves scarce?'

'Christ, no,' Ford barked. 'I'm going to get shite for this, and you're going to take your dose with me. Besides, you know what Guthrie's like. He'll just hunt you down and see if he can blame you for all of this anyway.'

Connor nodded. Peter Guthrie had been made the chief of Police Scotland after the previous holder of the post had attracted one too many unforgiving headlines, thanks to a habit of taking the law into his own hands and dispensing summary justice on those he deemed worthy of it. Guthrie had been installed by the government as a safe pair of hands, more bureaucrat than bobby, a man who could be trusted to make the police look competent and caring. But he also had a politician's instincts – and the first was self-preservation, no matter whom he had to sacrifice to save his own skin.

'How's Donnelly?' Connor asked, deciding to change the subject.

'About how you'd expect,' Ford replied. 'Shocked, outraged. We've got him in the house now, but he's refusing protection, says this is a house of God, and he won't be cowed into hiding behind the police.'

Connor looked up at Ford, a sudden thought scuttling across his mind. He grasped for it. Something about hiding behind the police. And Guthrie. Something . . .

He was startled from his thoughts by Simon calling his name. He turned, saw him approaching quickly, phone held aloft. He shot a wary glance at Ford, then shrugged, handed the phone to Connor.

'What?' Connor asked.

'Friend of yours who wants to talk to you, big man,' Simon said, his face impassive. 'Says she's got someone you just have to meet. Someone with a hell of a story to tell.'

CHAPTER 14

Standing just off to the side of the Mercat Cross on the village green in the centre of Lenton Barns, Connor watched as the various media outlets and reporters jostled for position at the base of the sandstone spire that reached into the sky. It was typical of Mercat Crosses that could be found in towns and villages across Scotland: a large, sandstone column mounted on a stone plinth, the top adorned with a carved unicorn rearing into the sky, seeming to give off a faint golden glow as it basked in the afternoon sun. Centuries ago, Mercat Crosses had been erected to symbolise the right of the town or village to hold a market or fair. Connor smiled at the irony of that: the market had returned to town, but this time, instead of goods or cattle the product being sold was information.

Or, more accurately, propaganda.

On the steps leading up the cross, two men stood, both in full uniform. The figure on the left Connor recognised as Chief Constable Peter Guthrie, the man in charge of Police Scotland. He stood with his back ramrod straight, almost like a condemned man standing in front of a firing squad. He squinted out at the day from beneath the peak of his hat, the ornate silver embroidery catching the light and reflecting it back on the waiting press. There was something in the way he wore his uniform that accentuated how out of his depth he was, a bureaucrat who had been dragged through a fancy-dress store, told to dress up as a policeman and face the press.

The impression was only intensified by the man who stood opposite him. While Guthrie looked uncomfortable and ill at ease, his counterpart looked as though he had been born in his uniform and it had grown with him to accommodate his massive frame. He was tall where Guthrie was short, lean and powerfully built where Guthrie was pot-bellied and slope-shouldered. Unlike Guthrie, he wore no hat, and his close-cropped hair seemed to soak in the light that Guthrie's hat reflected. Connor had looked him up on his phone, found that Arthur MacAlister had a CV almost as intimidating as his appearance. He had enrolled as a firefighter after leaving school at eighteen, worked his way through the ranks in what had been the old Strathclyde Fire and Rescue Service on the west coast. When Strathclyde had been merged with Scotland's seven other fire and rescue services to create the Scottish Fire and Rescue Service, MacAlister had been made an assistant chief officer. He had campaigned vigorously against cuts to the fire service, both during the amalgamation and after, and had finally been named as chief officer a year before.

Connor looked across the press scrum, saw Donna standing near the front, her cameraman to her left. Beside her stood a thin, almost angular man, whose hair was nearly as rumpled and unkempt as the battered old suit jacket and jeans he wore.

Doug McGregor. When Simon had handed him the phone outside the presbytery, Donna had been on the other end, telling him that he had to meet McGregor: he had approached her with a story earlier in the day that was connected to Connor.

'That can't be a coincidence with everything that's going on, can it?' she said, her voice tight, serious.

'Not sure, but it's worth looking into. I'll see you after the press conference. You can introduce me to this guy then.'

He had followed Ford down to the press conference, keeping a discreet distance. Simon had agreed to stay at the presbytery with Father Donnelly, despite the uniformed officers Ford had left there as a guard. Simon's professional pride again. Someone had taken a shot at a person in his care. He was damned if he was going to let them take a second.

'Ladies and gentlemen,' MacAlister called, his voice a low, deep rumble, like the first warnings of a storm on the horizon. 'Thank you all for coming. Chief Constable Guthrie and I appreciate your help in spreading the vital public-safety messaging that today's regrettable incident has made so necessary.'

'Incident?' Connor saw McGregor leaning forward, his phone held aloft. 'I understand from sources that a firebomb attack took place at St Ninian's Church earlier today. Can you confirm if this is the case and, if so, are you looking at a religious motivation for the attack?'

MacAlister gave a smile that was somehow placatory and predatory at the same time. 'And you are?' he asked, his voice cool, calm.

'Doug McGregor, the Crucible,' Doug called back.

'Well, Mr McGregor,' MacAlister said, 'I can't speak about investigations - that's for the chief constable - but I can correct you on one matter, which is the reason we're here. This was not an "attack". Drones that were being flown by person or persons unknown crashed accidentally into the church at just after one p.m., causing significant damage to that historic building and the presbytery nearby. The chief constable and I wanted to visit personally to underline the dangers of these unlicensed drones, and repeat our call that members of the public refrain from flying them in built-up or rural areas, where there is an increased risk of injuries to people and damage to buildings and property.'

Connor caught the pointed glance Donna cast him, gave a short, sharp nod. He had been expecting this. The last thing the police wanted was a public panicked that drones were now being used as weapons and could swoop from the sky to strike at any time. No, better to get a lie out, try to control the narrative. Thanks to the footage that was already online, the story was out there, so why not write it off as an accident, tie it up with a nice PR-friendly bow? Nothing to see here, folks. Just a couple of career bosses trying to make a point and score some headlines. The line had already been deployed on social media by the police and the fire service. Their chiefs were in front of the cameras as icing on the cake.

Connor pulled out his phone, read the last message he had received: *The fun begins now. Hope you're able to earn your money, for Donnelly's sake. And your own.*

Let the authorities peddle their lie, he thought. Whoever was doing this had made it personal the moment he had targeted Jen and his gran. So Connor would find him and, far from the cameras that were arrayed before him now, he would have a very long, very pointed discussion with whoever had thought this twisted game was a good idea.

His phone buzzed in his hand. A text message from Robbie at Sentinel: *Background information you requested, boss. Sorry it took a while. The father obviously isn't the kind to like attention. I've put it on your drive. Let me know if you need anything else. Everything is in place for the assets. They're safe, I promise.*

Connor laughed at that. Since being recruited from Police Scotland's call-handling centre, Robbie Lindsay had become a valuable member of the Sentinel team. A savvy investigator with a talent for finding the facts many people wanted buried, he was growing in confidence as a field agent as well, and had performed well, protecting a controversial judge who had received death threats a couple of months ago. But the inexperience could still show through, like a flick of grey in dyed hair. It was why he thought it was a good idea to call Ida Fraser and Jen, the two women in the world who meant the most to Connor, 'assets'.

He flicked over to a web app on his phone, logged onto Sentinel's secure server and found his personal drive. Saw the file Robbie had placed there, simply marked 'Donnelly, J., Fthr. Background'.

He clicked on it, scanned it. Felt his mouth grow dry. Took a moment, then looked back up at the press conference, and the journalists clamouring to ask Guthrie and MacAlister questions.

He couldn't tear his eyes from MacAlister. Fought back the urge to shout his own question, the one Robbie's background file had just thrown up.

What had Donnelly said to Simon? *I did God's work, Mr McCartney. I ministered to heroes, men and women who put their lives on the line every day for people who were strangers to them.*

Connor looked back at his phone, and the file Robbie had sent. Donnelly's statement made sense now. It also explained why MacAlister had decided to attend this incident personally. What didn't make sense was the picture Robbie had appended to the file. It showed Donnelly standing in front a group of firefighters, their heads bowed, helmets held under arms. It was a cutting from a newspaper, with the caption 'PAYING RESPECTS: Father John Donnelly, chaplain to Strathclyde Fire and Rescue, leads firefighters in prayer on the third anniversary of the Harbour Street fire disaster.'

Connor glanced up at MacAlister, then back to his phone. No doubt about it. His hair was thicker and darker, but he was definitely the man who was standing in front of Donnelly in the picture. So he knew the priest.

The question was, how well? And did that relationship have anything to do with what was happening now?

CHAPTER 15

Donna was just finishing a to-camera report on the press conference when Connor approached her, the assembled reporters parting before him, like paper splitting as a blade ran through it. He saw the tousled man standing close to her, fiddling with his phone, his cheek twitching as he did so. Connor noticed that he was juggling the phone between his hands, squeezing his left and rotating it every time it was free.

'Donna,' he said, his voice sharper than he had intended. After reading Robbie's file on Donnelly, he wanted to get back to the presbytery, ask the priest a few questions. But Donna had said McGregor had potentially important information. And, given everything that was going on, the last thing Connor needed was to be sloppy.

She looked up at him, her smile quickly fading to concern as her eyes roved across the scratches peppering his face and neck. Luckily, he'd had a spare T-shirt in the car to replace the one shredded by the exploding door, but Connor could only imagine what he looked like.

'You okay?' she asked. 'I get the feeling more happened up at the church than Guthrie or MacAlister is admitting to.'

Connor shrugged, felt pain dig into his shoulder, became aware of the stranger who was approaching them. 'Ack,' he said, 'just another day at the office. Can we make this quick? I really need to get back to Simon.'

'That Simon McCartney by any chance?' the man approaching them asked. 'Your old partner from your Belfast days?'

'Yes,' Connor said, drawing the word out. 'And I take it you're Doug McGregor, formally of the *Capital Tribune* in Edinburgh, now working on the Crucible website. Tell me, how's the hand, Mr McGregor? I understand it got pretty badly banged up a few years ago.'

Doug gave a smile that would have made a Tory politician proud – maximum leering, no sincerity. 'Touché,' he said as he flexed his left hand. 'I see you've done your research as well, Mr Fraser.'

It hadn't been hard. Connor had tracked down the stories from a couple of years ago, how Doug had watched his editor being murdered in front of him, hunted down a Gulf War veteran with an axe to grind and a wife who was even more deranged than he was. He had been hurt along the way, badly. And while the extent of his injuries had never been made public, Connor had enough contacts in Edinburgh's physiotherapy clinics and hospitals to know Doug's left hand had been badly broken and he'd suffered nerve damage as a result. The thought brought Jen to mind, and he felt another flash of guilt at not having phoned her yet.

'So,' he said, keen to get the conversation moving, 'Donna tells me you have something you'd like to talk to me about. Not sure how much I'll be able to help, and my time really is short.'

'Yeah, you said,' Doug replied, his voice hardening. 'I could ask why a private security consultant like you was on the scene when the church was attacked, and why you look like you've just been in a mud fight with a bear, but I'll keep that for later. For now, I wonder if you can tell me what you remember about a man called Gareth Hogan and a company called Paradigm Energy.'

Connor frowned as he dredged his memory. It took a moment, and then the image of a gaunt, skeletal man with hair so slick it glinted like sealskin in the light came to mind.

'Yeah, I remember Hogan. I ran security for him a couple of years ago, back when his company was proposing fracking in old mining areas around Scotland. He got a few death threats, so we, Sentinel that is, were called in. Nothing came of it. Why?'

'A few death threats?' Doug said, a warmer smile playing on his lips. 'He had his car daubed with acid, doughnuts filled with oil delivered to his offices and a petrol-refining site in the Borders targeted by arsonists. That's a little more than "a few death threats", wouldn't you say?

McGregor was right, of course. Fracking was a controversial subject, a red flag to conservationists and environmentalists alike. The process of drilling into the earth, then pumping water into the hole to release gas inside rocks had been deemed unsafe by the Scottish Government and effectively banned in 2019, but not before Hogan and Paradigm had lobbied fairly heavily for licences to be granted and Scotland to 'take advantage of this new energy boom'.

'Okay, fair enough. But you're not saying a firebombing a few years ago is somehow linked to what happened today, are you?' Connor asked.

'I didn't say firebombing, I said arson,' Doug replied, before waving his hand in the air, as though a bee was bothering him. 'But, again, I'll get to that later. Mr Fraser, Connor, I think there was a lot more going on with Mr Hogan than many people thought. And I think you can help me prove it.'

Connor kept his face impassive, wary now. McGregor catching his comment about the firebombing showed he was as sharp as his biography suggested. He would have to be careful. 'How?' he said, his voice that of a man asking for his last card at a Vegas poker table.

'You ran close security on Hogan, right? Which means bodyguarding. So you'd know where he went and, more importantly, who he met?' There was an eager, hopeful tone in McGregor's voice now. It reminded Connor of Donna when she was on a story.

'Yes,' he said. 'But I'm not sure I can help you. Those records are confidential, they're—'

'Yes, yes, I know that,' Doug said, impatience sharpening his voice now. 'I'm not asking you to betray any confidences. But if I gave you a list of names and places, could you check them for me, confirm what I already know?'

'And what, exactly, is that?' Connor asked, not entirely convinced he wanted to hear the answer.

Doug took a deep breath, glanced at Donna. She held his eyes for just a moment, then turned back to Connor and nodded slightly.

McGregor took a breath, blew it out. 'I think Hogan was working with a man called Kerr Cunningham to push fracking as a way to destabilise the Scottish Government, put them on a collision course with Westminster. I believe both Hogan and Cunningham were paid to do this, and given access to both the Scotland Office and the resources of GCHQ to do so. I also believe the "attacks" on Mr Hogan were false flags, designed to be used against groups and political parties who oppose the Westminster Government and support the devolution settlement. Ultimately, Mr Fraser, I think you were pro-tecting a man who was the head of a conspiracy against the Scottish Government.'

Connor felt a sudden tickle of laughter scurry up his throat. Swallowed it. He looked from McGregor to Donna, both of whom were looking back at him with cold, professional eyes. Was it really that unbelievable? In an age when disinformation campaigns, cyber attacks by foreign nations and political assassinations were no longer confined to the big screen but reported as fact every night on the news, was it really unthinkable? Successive UK governments had weaponised oil, gas and the energy debate against Scottish independ-ence for decades, so why not go one step further and act in the way McGregor suggested?

Connor let out a breath. 'I'm sorry, I can't get into this with you now,' he said. 'I've got to get back to—'

'Simon,' Doug cut him off. 'You said. I understand, Mr Fraser, I really do. If my girlfriend and gran had been threatened and I'd been firebombed by drones, I'd be anxious to get back as well. But, please, this is important.'

Connor felt his mouth fall open. It was an expression he could see mirrored on Donna's face. 'How the hell did you . . .?'

'Contacts,' Doug said simply. 'You have your ways of digging into things, Mr Fraser. I have mine. I understand your urgency and, please, believe me, I'm very interested in your story, so I'll help you with that in any way I can. Just tell me you'll think about what I've told you. I can show you my research. All I - sorry, all *we* - need,' a nod to Donna, 'is for you to verify what I've found with times, dates and locations. And, don't worry, your name will never see print, I promise.'

'"We"?' Connor said, directing the word at Donna. 'You're working with him on this?'

'Yeah,' she said, her gaze steady, tone defiant. 'I have to, Connor. If he's right it's a massive story. So if you can help—'

She was cut off by a man calling Connor's name. He turned, saw Ford gesturing for him, flanked by Susie, who seemed to grow stiff and tense as she saw who Connor was talking to.

'Fraser, need a word with you. Now,' Ford shouted.

'On my way,' Connor replied. He turned to McGregor and Donna.

'I have to go,' he said. 'But if you know anything about what is going on here, and why I'm being targeted, I need to know.' The words came out as more of a threat than he had intended. He closed his eyes, took a breath. 'Sorry. Been a long day. Donna, call me later. We'll meet up and discuss all this. I'll see what I can do.'

'Thank you,' McGregor said. 'That's all I can ask. Looks like your polis friend isn't too happy. Good luck with that. Just do me one favour, will you?'

Connor made no effort to keep the surprise out of his voice. 'Oh, what's that?'

The smile returned to McGregor's face. 'Tell Susie I'll buy her a drink when I see her. Least I can do.'

CHAPTER 16

After leaving Donna with her cameraman, a doughy-faced man called Keith, who had the complexion of a thirteen-year-old with a sugar addiction and the boundless enthusiasm to match, Doug made his way back to his car, which he'd parked outside the local pub. It was a small, detached building, almost identical to the houses that lined the main street of the village. The only thing that marked it out as a commercial property rather than a private one was the sign over the door proclaiming it was 'The Cross Keys, home of real ale and good food' and the billboard at the door advising that the pub was dog-friendly.

Doug stopped beside his car, looked at the door of the pub for a long moment. Susie would get his crack about buying a drink for the joke it was, but standing there, the pub only a few feet away, it didn't seem so funny any more.

It had started about eighteen months ago. After one particularly bad story, which had dragged up more of Susie's past than she was comfortable with, he had started reaching for the bottle more often. He had told himself it was understandable: the long hours, the stress, the pain in his still-healing hand, the break-up with his girlfriend, Rebecca, who had moved from Edinburgh to Newcastle just after telling him she was pregnant and didn't want him in her life until he got his act together.

The trouble was, Doug knew he was selling himself a lie. The truth was much simpler: he was drinking because he was scared. He had been badly beaten by a woman he had identified as having manipulated her war-veteran husband into committing an act of vengeance. She had stamped on his hand, breaking the bones and damaging the nerves, leaving him in permanent pain. He had undergone surgery and rehabilitation, but the real damage, the damage that had sent Doug scuttling for the bottle, had never healed.

For the first time in his career, he had come face to face with the very real possibility that he was going to die, and the reality of that had opened up a chasm of terror inside him that could not be filled with surgery or rehabilitation or even his work.

It was only the intervention of his friend Hal Damon that had saved him. He had met Hal, who was a PR consultant in London, years earlier, when he had been brought in to try to rehabilitate the reputation of a Tory MSP Doug had had in his sights. Over the years, a close friendship had developed between them, despite Hal's constant, good-natured joking badgering of Doug to give up journalism and write copy for him in London.

It had been a Thursday night, the rain spattering on the windows of Doug's flat in Musselburgh. It was funny, he thought, that the rain was one of the few facts about the night he remembered. It was just after Rebecca had told him she was pregnant, and moving away. He didn't remember emptying the bottle of whisky, then dropping it off the coffee-table, could recall only snatches of a tear-filled conversation with Hal on the phone as he played with a shard of glass from the broken bottle, fascinated by the way it caught the light. He did remember waking half on his couch the next morning, his head as broken as the bottle that lay strewn across the floor.

The moment of clarity had come when he caught himself in the kitchen. He had headed there for a glass of water and the brush and dustpan to sweep up the whisky bottle. Except he hadn't grabbed either item – he'd grabbed another bottle of whisky. Cracking the seal on the bottle was like cracking some seal inside himself. He set the bottle down, headed through to the living room and found his phone, which was jammed with missed calls and worried messages from Hal. He sat on the couch, hit redial and told his friend as calmly as he could that he needed help.

Doug spent the next three months in London, camped out in the spare room of Hal's house. Hal and his husband, Colin, looked after him, spoke to him through the long nights, assured him everything would be okay. Not once did they mention the word 'alcoholic', but it seemed to scream at Doug every time he glanced in a mirror or was left alone for more than a minute.

After the first month, he had felt the need to get back to some type of work, so he finally took up Hal's offer of writing copy for his PR firm. And that was how he had found Gareth Hogan. Hal had been commissioned to develop a marketing campaign for one of Paradigm Energy's spin-off companies, so he had asked Doug to help. Doug, vaguely remembering the story of the death threats made against Hogan during his foray into Scottish fracking, did a little background digging – and ended up falling down a rabbit hole. At first, he thought it was his imagination, a way to distract himself from the constant desire for just one drink, but the deeper he dug, the more connections he found between Hogan and Kerr Cunningham, the list MSP for Central Scotland, who just happened to be a former army colleague of the private secretary to the secretary of state for Scotland.

Doug had investigated as thoroughly as he could but, as he had told Donna, the resources of the Crucible were limited. Which was why he had sought her out. If he could get Fraser to tell him what he knew about Cunningham and Hogan's movements, he could prove he was right. Donna could broadcast the story ten minutes after it appeared on the Crucible website. Doug closed his eyes, imagined Rebecca seeing it, their daughter cradled in her arms. Would that be enough to convince her he had changed, that he was ready to be a partner and a father?

Maybe.

He sighed, turned away from the pub, got into the car. He could daydream later. And if he was going to make those dreams a reality, he needed Connor Fraser's help. And the best way he could get that was by helping Fraser with his current problem. It hadn't taken much to find out about the threats to Fraser's girlfriend and grandmother: when Doug had realised he would need his help, he had dug into Connor Fraser's past and present. Hacking his phone wasn't quite as easy as hacking a celebrity's voicemail, but it wasn't a million miles from it. And while Doug was uneasy at employing the tactics of the tabloids, he comforted himself with the knowledge that he would never publish what he found.

Well, probably not.

He reached into the back seat, hauled his bag into the front, dug out his laptop and fired it up. He checked on the Crucible site to make sure the story was running as he had filed it, then flicked over to a search window on the internet. Found what he needed, then started the car.

Fraser would have to head back to Stirling at some point. And when he did, Doug would be ready.

CHAPTER 17

Ford filled Connor in on the short walk back to the presbytery: Chief Constable Guthrie had been called to Edinburgh to brief the First Minister on what had happened at the church, leaving Ford in charge of the investigation on the ground.

'Apparently the FM is shitting a brick that this could be religiously motivated terrorism,' Ford said, eyes locked ahead as the church came into view. 'So Guthrie's had to go and calm her down. That's what that line of crap was about at the presser – public reassurance.'

Connor nodded. It made sense. In Scotland, as in Northern Ireland, religion and sectarianism were barely healed wounds on the collective psyche. After centuries of fighting and dying over the best way to honour an omnipotent being that was powerful enough to create the universe but petty enough to worry about where you went to pray on a Sunday morning, the scab over the wound was still fragile, and could be made to bleed without much picking.

But, thanks to Robbie, he knew it wasn't terrorism – at least in the traditional sense. No, the targeting of Father Donnelly and Connor's loved ones was personal.

'So what about Simon and me?' Connor asked. If anti-terror officers got involved in the investigation, it would make Connor's life, and his own enquiries, infinitely more complicated. And he didn't have time for complications.

Ford stopped, turned to Connor for the first time.

'Drummond,' he said, eyes not leaving Connor's face, 'go on ahead, will you? Make sure Troughton has Father Donnelly and Mr McCartney's statements sorted out. We'll be there in a moment.'

'Yes, ah, yes, sir,' Susie said. Connor could see wariness in her face as she spoke – the same wariness she had shown when she had seen him talking to the reporter, McGregor. What, he wondered, was the story there?

Something to look into later.

Ford waited a moment, turned briefly to watch Susie walk off towards the church. Then he turned back to Connor, his eyes as cold and dark as the scars that were still smouldering on the church walls.

'We both know this isn't anyone looking to wage a holy war on the Catholic Church,' he said. 'Whatever is going on, it's targeted at you and this Father Donnelly. I've tried to keep as much of what you told me away from the chief at the moment, give us both some time to figure out what the hell is going on. I know you've got a few people out for your blood at the moment, Fraser. The question is, is one of them capable of this or is this targeted solely at Father Donnelly?'

Connor was stopped from replying by a sudden image of Duncan MacKenzie, Jen's father. He had been lying on a floor the last time Connor had seen him, spitting blood-flecked vows of revenge and painful death as Connor stood over him. Could this have been MacKenzie's doing? Was he finally moving against Connor as he had promised? But, then, why drag the priest into it? And what about that file Robbie had produced?

Connor shook his head. 'I don't know, but I might have a place to start searching. Look, sir, I've got some information that might help. I'll hand all of it over to you, but if you're so concerned about getting to the bottom of this quickly, will you let me talk to Donnelly, try to figure out what's going on?'

Anger flared in Ford's eyes, replaced by a weary acceptance. Over the last few years, Connor had come to know him as a pragmatic policeman who put getting results above sticking to procedure. He also knew that Ford had more than a few skeletons in his cupboard, skeletons that he was happy to rattle when he had to put the chief constable in his place. But, at heart, he was still a policeman and, although he had once served, Connor was now a civilian. And letting civilians in on police matters never sat well with any copper.

'Aye, okay,' he said at last. 'But this has to be made official at some point, Fraser. Whatever Donnelly says, we'll have to follow it up.'

Connor almost asked which *we* Ford was referring to. Swallowed the question. The look in the policeman's eyes told him Ford knew all too well that Connor was going to be part of this investigation, with or without his approval.

***

They assembled in the study into which Donnelly had first shown Connor and Simon. The curtains had been reopened, the general consensus being that, with so many police officers camped outside, Donnelly was probably fairly safe.

For the moment.

The priest had barricaded himself behind his desk, made a show of shuffling papers around it. His shoulders were stiff, his movements jerky and erratic, as though the presence of Ford, Connor and Simon in the room was somehow offensive to him.

'I really do have a lot of work to be getting on with,' he muttered as he looked up, his eyes roving from Connor to Ford. 'And I plan to do it. I will not see God's work interrupted by this madness.'

Connor considered Donnelly's words. Ford had sent Troughton and Drummond to arrange a protective detail for the priest, a move he had objected to as 'getting in the way'. Connor wondered what he thought a couple of police officers on the premises would get in the way of.

'Okay, Father, won't keep you long,' Connor said, after getting a nod of approval from Ford. 'I just have a couple of questions to ask, try to clear things up a bit.'

'If you must, but I've already given my statement,' Donnelly replied, confusion dulling the edge of impatience in his voice.

'Great, thanks,' Connor said. 'But first, tell me, was it good to see your old pal Chief MacAlister again? It's been what? Ten years or so?'

Donnelly bucked in his seat as though it had suddenly been electrified. He looked up at Connor, glasses catching the late-afternoon sun, reflections stabbing at Connor as if in accusation.

72

'Wh-what do you mean?' he said.

'I mean,' Connor said, taking a step towards Donnelly's desk, 'we found a picture of you leading the service of remembrance for those who died at Harbour Street back in 2011. So tell me, Father Donnelly, why does a chaplain "doing God's work" for the fire service suddenly quit and retire to a quiet church in the countryside?'

Donnelly's head darted to Ford then Simon, as though pleading for help.

'That's ...' he cleared his throat '... that's personal, Mr Fraser. Now if you don't mind ...'

'Mind?' Connor said, the sudden snarl of anger he felt turning his voice into a cold, hard growl. 'Sorry, Father, but I mind very much. See, whatever the hell is going on has put people I love in danger. So I'm sorry if this is inconvenient to you, but I really do mind, and I really do need you to tell me what happened. Now.'

Connor realised he had clenched his fists as he spoke. Took a breath, let it out and forced his fists to unclench.

The Fraser temper, son, he heard his father whisper in his mind. *Watch for it.*

Donnelly looked up at Connor, his face slack and waxy, the scar tracing down from his lip a slash of colour on flesh that was now a washed-out grey. He took off his glasses to reveal eyes that seemed too small for his face, eyes that were filled with a lifetime of regret and pain. As though trying to grind out that anguish, he pushed the heels of his palms into his eyes and rubbed. After a moment, he dropped his hands to the desk.

'You're right, of course,' he said. His voice was the sound of a breeze whispering through a graveyard. 'It was – what – eleven years ago. August the eleventh, 2011. A fire broke out in an old warehouse on Harbour Street in south Glasgow. It was filled with flammable materials and the whole thing went up like a Roman candle. Fire crews from around the city were sent in to tackle it. I was at Spaven Street station when the call came in, can't remember what for. I'd been a chaplain for the fire service for about six years by that point. Anyway, I persuaded the then station commander, Chief MacAlister now, to let me go along to offer support for the men tackling the fire. My God, but I wish ...'

Connor looked down at the priest, who had retreated into his memories. He didn't blame him. The report Robbie had prepared contained cuttings of the coverage of the Harbour Street fire. It looked like a scene from hell. An eight-storey building, its blackened skeleton etched against the crimson inferno that was engulfing it. At its height, more than a hundred firefighters had been on the scene, trying to contain the blaze before it spread to other buildings. It had taken them all night and into the next day, but they had succeeded. Three firefighters and four civilians had died in the fire, and Connor knew Donnelly had been instrumental in establishing the memorial for all those who had died, the memorial he had been pictured at with MacAlister.

'Okay, I get that it was traumatic,' Connor said, forcing himself to soften his voice as he spoke. 'But why move away? And could that have anything to do with what's happening now?'

Donnelly picked up his glasses, adjusted them on his face. Then he stared over Connor's shoulder, as though the words he was about to speak were written there.

'Have you ever looked into the face of the Devil, Mr Fraser?' he asked after a moment. 'I have. I saw it that night in those flames as they danced and capered around that building. They roared, Mr Fraser, as though the Devil himself was laughing at those brave men and women who dared to fight his fire. Of the seven men who died that night, four were of the faith, Mr Fraser, and I gave the last rites to two at the scene. I did my best to honour them with the memorial, yes, but to see the grief of their comrades day after day, well . . .' he took a deep breath '. . . it's enough to test any man's faith. You see, I'm a coward. Rather than stay and fight the good fight, I ran. Came here to get away from the memories of that night and the men who died. I came here looking for peace, Mr Fraser. I ran away. But I cannot see how that would lead to the insanity of today or the threats to your loved ones.'

Connor looked down at the priest. What he was saying made sense. Hell, he had done more or less the same thing when he had quit the police force in Belfast and come home. Rather than face his failure, he had started again.

74

But what price had Donnelly paid for his fresh start? And was someone trying to kill him for it?

Connor was about to ask another question when his phone beeped in his pocket. He started, cursed himself for not switching it to silent before he had come to talk to Donnelly.

'Sorry,' he mumbled, noticing the sharp glance he got from Ford, and Simon's slight shake of his head. He grabbed the phone from his pocket, felt the room grow cold as he opened it and read the message he had just received.

'Connor, what?' Simon said as he started forward.

Connor said nothing, just held up the phone to his friend. He saw the shock register on his face, then turned to Ford.

'What the hell is going on?' the policeman asked.

'See for yourself,' Connor said, as he handed him the phone, let him read the message that had just seared itself onto his memory.

Hope you enjoyed today. I did. Good to see so many old faces from the boys in blue came to show their support. Just for a bit of fun, I'll kill one of them as well. The napalm worked so well on the church, I'll use that. It'll be like an old family BBQ. But don't worry, I'll make sure you don't miss a moment.

'Jesus,' Ford whispered. 'Is he threatening . . .'

Connor nodded, even as he felt understanding rush through his mind like a shot of caffeine. *Good to see so many old faces from the boys in blue.* It had bothered him earlier. Why hadn't whoever was behind this insisted he didn't call the police? Answer: because they wanted the police involved, wanted to see who would respond and investigate.

Wanted to widen their pool of potential targets.

'Get in touch with everyone who was caught on camera or responded to this incident,' Connor said, his mind racing to Jen and his gran. 'Make sure they take every precaution. Do it now, before this psycho makes good on his threat.'

CHAPTER 18

They approached the flat warily, checking for signs it was being watched. But Park Terrace was as it always was when Simon and Connor drove up it: quiet, respectable, the sandstone façades of the houses betraying no secrets, the only sounds the rustling of the wind in the tall oak and birch trees that lined the street.

His flat was in the basement of a grand old Victorian townhouse, with only one way in. He continued up the gravel driveway that led behind the main house to the small, enclosed forecourt in front of the stairs that led down to the flat. Got out of the car, studying the gravel he had insisted on laying there. It served two purposes: to warn Connor if someone was approaching the flat, and tell him the story of any vehicles or people who had visited in his absence. But the gravel was unblemished, like sand on the beach after high tide.

If someone had been there, they had done a hell of a job of covering their tracks.

He checked the front door as Simon kept watch at the top of the stairs, found nothing that troubled him. Nodded to Simon, who came down quickly, following Connor into the flat. They moved quietly, leaving the lights off, splitting up in the hallway to sweep the rooms.

'Clear,' Simon called from the bathroom, after a moment.

Connor looked around the open-plan dining-living room. Nothing out of place from what he could see, everything as he and Simon had left it what now felt like a lifetime ago.

'Clear,' he called back, as he headed for the floor-to-ceiling patio doors that led out to the garden at the back of the flat. It was an enclosed, sunken space, the previous owners giving it a Japanese walled-garden theme and making a feature of the exposed chunk of limestone that served as the foundation to the street above. Unlikely anyone would be able to climb down into the garden, but Connor was taking no chances. He checked the doors for signs of tampering, found none. Unlocked one door, swung it open, the smell of freshly cut grass and flowers wafting towards him.

He looked across the garden. Saw cold, predatory eyes watching him.

'You,' he said. 'I should have known you'd be here. Waiting.'

'What's that?' Simon called from behind him.

'Nothing,' Connor said, with a grunting laugh. 'Just talking to your girlfriend. Looks like she's been waiting for you.'

Simon bustled past Connor, dropped to his knees, reached out a hand for the tortoiseshell cat that was sitting in the middle of the garden, as serene as a Buddha, its tail flicking languidly from side to side.

'Ah, Tom,' he called. 'Come on away in, lass. I'll get you something to eat.'

Connor smiled, stepped back into the flat. Tom had started visiting the garden about a year before, staking the place out, like a robber would approach a property they were looking to visit. Connor, not knowing much about cats, had christened it Tom and, at Jen's insistence, had started to feed it the odd can of tuna with a bowl of water. Connor had no idea if it was a stray or a local cat looking for an extra meal – it never let him get close enough to see if there was a tag on the collar it wore. That all changed with the arrival from Belfast of Simon. He had bonded instantly with the cat, which he had taken under his wing. He found that Tom was a female, and would happily approach him and enter the house if he was around. The affection the cat had for Simon had led Connor to call her Simon's girlfriend.

He watched as the cat trotted into the flat beside Simon, glancing up at him as it moved.

'I'll get you something to eat now,' Simon reassured her.

Connor grunted. 'I'll leave you two alone,' he said. 'I'm going to phone Jen.'

'Tell her I said hi,' Simon said.

Connor raised his hand in acknowledgement, headed for his bedroom. Sat down heavily on his bed, felt the weight of the day seem to press him into the mattress.

After the texted warning that a police officer would be attacked, Ford had moved with almost manic intensity to secure his officers. A protective detail was assigned to the chief constable, with every other officer being put on high alert of a possible imminent threat to them and their colleagues. Connor had arranged with his gran's care home that he be contacted before anyone was allowed to visit her, and he had stationed a two-man team of security guards from Sentinel nearby to watch the place. He had toyed briefly with the idea of moving Ida to a secure location, but had finally rejected the idea. She was increasingly frail, and the dementia that was robbing her of her present was getting progressively worse. To move her to a strange location, without her mementoes and other possessions, would be too much of a wrench for her. So he secured her care home the best he could, and hoped it would be enough.

All of which left Jen.

He had managed to text her once before leaving Ford. He had kept it light and non-specific, just a general query as to how she was getting on. Got a *Good! Call me when you can xx* in response. After being run down outside the gym she had worked at the year before, Jen had undergone a series of operations and was currently staying at a private residential clinic in Glasgow as she underwent rehab and physiotherapy. The fees were extortionate, as the facility was basically a five-star spa that employed specialists from the national spinal injuries unit that was also in the city. Not that cost was an issue: if Duncan MacKenzie, Jen's father, hadn't been footing the bill, Connor would have found a way.

He dug his phone out of his pocket. He had eventually persuaded Ford to let him keep it, the policeman wanting to confiscate it and get his technical experts to run a digital forensic analysis. Connor had argued that he needed the phone so whoever had targeted Father

Donnelly could get in touch with him whenever they wanted to, keeping the lines of communication open. Ford had agreed, reluctantly, but only after Connor had promised to share with him anything relevant he received.

He scrolled to Jen's contact number, hit dial. Wasn't surprised when she answered on the second ring.

'Connor Fraser,' she said, her voice as light and breezy as the evening sky. 'I never took you for an old romantic. Thank you, the flowers are lovely.'

'No problem,' Connor said slowly, dread rising in his gut. He hadn't sent flowers to her, so who had? The same person who had taken pictures of her? 'Just glad you like them.'

'I do!' she said. 'But won't you get into trouble using people from Sentinel to deliver them for you?'

Connor let out a small sigh of relief. What was it Robbie had said? *I'll get people to Jen. You get to your gran.* He must have sent someone to Jen, using the delivery of flowers from Connor as a decoy. Smart move. The boy was learning.

'Ack, privileges of being a partner in the firm,' Connor said, pulling himself from his thoughts. 'I can use staff as I see fit. And this was a critical assignment.'

Jen laughed. 'Flatterer. Anyway, how are you doing? I saw that story about the church getting hit by drones on the news. That was your car parked outside, wasn't it? You okay? What were you doing there?'

Connor closed his eyes, Jen's barrage of questions seeming to reawaken the pain in his wounded shoulder. 'Yeah, I'm okay,' he said. 'And, yes, I was there. A favour to DCI Ford, nothing big.'

He hated lying to her, wondered what it said about him that it came so naturally to him.

'Ah,' Jen said, her tone telling him she didn't quite believe him but wasn't going to push it. 'Well, hopefully Simon's keeping you out of trouble. When are you two going to come over and visit anyway? A girl could get bored here on her own.'

Connor swallowed. There it was. The question he had been dreading. After he had received the threat to Jen and his gran, Connor's first instinct had been to get his gran safe and then go to Jen. But if he visited her, would he be taking potential danger with him? The last thing he wanted was for Jen to get caught in the crossfire if whoever was threatening her decided to kill two birds with one stone and take a shot at Connor while they were together.

'Soon as we can,' he said as he rubbed his eyes hard enough to send dull sparks shooting across his vision. 'Just got an assignment to finish off here, and then I'm all yours.'

They spoke for another twenty minutes, keeping the conversation light, the unspoken truth underlined by every flirtatious comment or splutter of laughter that went on just a moment too long. Jen hadn't just lost her mobility when she had been run over, she had lost the child she was carrying too. They had spoken about it only once, when Jen had just regained consciousness and told Connor she had been pregnant. It had at once brought them closer together and driven them apart: they were bound together by a shared agony so great that acknowledging it would reopen a wound that would never heal.

He ended the conversation with a promise to call her in the morning, then lay back on the bed. Not telling her what was going on was for the best, wasn't it? The clinic was a secure facility, with excellent on-site security, and Robbie had made sure Sentinel staff were on hand as well. But, still, didn't Jen deserve to know the truth? Didn't he owe her that? Or would knowing that her life was again at risk, through no fault of her own, that she was once more being used as a pawn to get to the men who loved her, be too much for her to take, undo the progress she had already made in her recovery?

With a growl of frustration, Connor forced himself off the bed and made his way back to the living room. He found Simon sitting on the couch, Tom contentedly snuggled in beside him as he bent forward to the laptop open on the coffee-table in front of him.

'Jen okay?' he asked absently, eyes not leaving the laptop.

'Yeah, fine. Robbie was very discreet – she had no idea we were checking up on her. She saw the car at the church on TV, though.'

Simon turned to face him, studied him for a moment. Then, seemingly satisfied, he turned the laptop to Connor. 'Been doing a little more digging into the good father,' he said. 'Seems like he's just as he says he is

– got tired of preaching to firefighters after Harbour Street, then moved out to Lenton Barns. Few things in the local press about him becoming a community custodian, challenging local politicians on issues from gay rights to refugees fleeing Ukraine. Nothing that explains any of this . . .' he paused, perhaps to find the right word '. . . madness.'

Connor slumped into the couch opposite him. 'None of this makes any sense,' he said. 'Why target Donnelly in the first place? And if you do want to kill the man, why pay me seventy grand to try to stop you? Is whoever's behind this after me as well? Using this as a way to control my movements, get me where they want me? Would make sense, but why go to all this trouble?'

Simon gave Connor a you-know-better look. 'Come on, big lad,' he said. 'We both know you're not Mr Popularity just now. Thanks to you taking that child sex-abuse ring down, a few former police officers, lawyers and politicians would happily have a whip-round to put your head on a spike. And, let's not forget, you're hardly on Duncan MacKenzie's Christmas-card list, either.'

Connor grunted, sat forward, resting his elbows on his knees. Simon was right: he didn't have far to look for an enemy. But why the theatrics? What tied him to Father Donnelly? And why pay him seventy grand? Something about the number nagged at him, like a scrap of food stuck between his teeth. Something that . . .

He sighed, forced himself to sit up straight.

'What?' Simon said warily, obviously catching the thought that had just occurred to Connor in his expression.

'The enemy of my enemy is my friend,' Connor said. It was one of his grandfather's favourite phrases, often used when he was training Connor in his homemade gym behind the garage he ran in Newtownards, Northern Ireland. 'The pain you feel lifting weights is the enemy, Connor,' he would say, brimming glass of whiskey in one hand, a small dumbbell in the other. 'Embrace the enemy. Make it your ally. The enemy of my enemy is my friend.'

Connor grabbed his phone, paused. Then dialled. If he was being honest with himself, he had known this was a call he was going to have to make the moment he had seen those photos of Jen and his gran.

'What the bloody hell do you want?' a voice said as the call was answered.

Despite himself, Connor smiled. 'Paulie,' he said, watching as Simon lowered his head into his hands and shook it. 'Charming as ever. You got time to talk? I need a favour. And before you say it, yes, it affects Jen.'

'You should have bloody said that to start,' Paulie King rumbled down the phone. 'You know where I am. Come see me.'

The line went dead before Connor could reply.

CHAPTER 19

Murder is its own special form of alchemy.

He had realised this years ago when he had taken his first life. No, that wasn't quite true: when he had been God's instrument to take a life. Neither the sin nor the glory was his: he was but an instrument, a tool to be used for a greater purpose.

But, in doing God's work, he had been granted divine wisdom. And in that wisdom, he had discerned the truth of death: that it was transformation, from one state to another. Life to death. Man to symbol. Injustice to rallying call.

Alchemy.

He worked slowly, carefully, deliberately, ensuring the fire could not spring to life and turn on him. And as he worked, he reflected.

It had been a satisfying day. True, the attack on the church had not inflicted as much damage as he had hoped but, still, the wounds were clear to see in the mottled scorching that now traced across the stone, like smoke, and in the gaping chasm where the front door had once been.

He smiled at the memory of Fraser diving onto the policeman and dragging him clear of the blast. Felt something he could almost mistake for regret as he remembered the splinters from the exploding door stab at Fraser, one of them burying itself in his shoulder. He had worried for a moment that the injury would be serious, that Fraser would be taken from him too soon.

He chided himself for his lack of faith. He was but a servant. This was God's plan. And Fraser was part of that plan, whether he liked it or not.

His work completed, he leant back from the workbench, surveyed the fruit of his labours. Not as elegant or as refined as the drones, the originality of which he couldn't help but admire, but more than adequate for the next task.

And just as deadly.

He smiled, felt a shiver of pleasure as he thought of what lay ahead. Of releasing the fire, allowing it to feast, not on a church or a warehouse this time, but on flesh and blood and bone. He could almost smell the sweet, charcoal-bitter scent of burning flesh as he packed his bag, carefully checking his camera as he did so.

This was God's work. Alchemy. The transformation of a person into a symbol, a message. But he needed to get that message out there, make sure it was understood. A picture would suffice. Just one. It would tell Fraser everything he needed to know.

And it would tell him how he would die.

CHAPTER 20

Paulie King lived on a converted farm steading on the outskirts of Stirling, not far from Banknock, where Doug McGregor had derailed Tom McGovern's press event that morning. Connor thought about the man as he drove. With everything else that had happened, McGregor's request to see Sentinel's security logs and reports on Gareth Hogan's movements had slipped off Connor's radar. But if his allegations were true, and Hogan really had been working against the Scottish Government, wasn't that something Connor had a duty to help bring to light?

Or was it just a way to earn even more powerful enemies?

He sighed, made a mental note to talk to Robbie about McGregor's request, then pulled off the main road onto the short, rutted farm track that led to Paulie's house.

The bungalow squatted in the centre of a fenced-off paddock, windows aflame as they reflected the last of the evening sun, the sky a smear of rich, deep amber shot through with flashes of pink and gold, as if an artist had tried to express the word 'warmth' in visual form.

Connor pulled up his car beside Paulie's, a sleek black Mercedes saloon that glittered in the light. Paulie's pride and joy, it was immaculately maintained, like the house. Getting out of his own car, Connor glanced at the wheels, which were splashed with mud from the farm track. By comparison, Paulie's wheels gleamed as though they had never touched road. Yet Connor could see tyre tracks leading up to the car, so it had been moved. He wondered if Paulie cleaned the car every time he came home. It wouldn't surprise him. In Paulie's line of work, leaving a mess behind could prove fatal.

He heard a door chain rattle clear, turned to see Paulie emerge from the house. He was a small, squat man who wore his pendulous gut and weight like armour. A year before, he had broken Connor's nose during a fight. Payback, Connor mused, for him breaking Paulie's fingers on their first encounter.

'Fucking criminal the state you let that car get into,' Paulie barked as he gestured to Connor's car, amber liquid sloshing from the glass he was holding. Connor smiled despite himself, and approached Paulie warily. Over the last year they had forged an uneasy truce, partly through their shared concern for Jen, partly from their work together in exposing a paedophile ring. But despite this, and Paulie's choice to live a quieter life, distancing himself from Duncan MacKenzie and his work at MacKenzie Haulage, he remained a dangerous man to know.

'You should start up a valeting business,' Connor replied.

'Fuck off,' Paulie said. 'Not enough money in the world to make me clean up your shit. Speaking of which, you said something about Jen. What shite have you got her into this time?'

Connor felt a reply crawl up his throat, swallowed it. Paulie had watched Jen grow up, had been close to her father, Duncan, and her now-deceased mother, Hannah. He acted like a concerned uncle, overprotective of Jen, the psychopath redeeming himself with one true human relationship. Connor knew that his fondness for Jen made Paulie wary of him.

The problem was, he agreed with Paulie. Since he had met Jen at the gym she worked at in Stirling, she had almost died once, lost a child, and was now facing a long and painful rehabilitation. Connor felt a stab of guilt as he thought about it. Maybe Jen would be better off without him after all.

'Can we go inside and talk?' he asked.

Paulie seemed to consider this. Then he took a swig of his drink, turned and headed back into the house. 'Aye, 'mon, then.'

He led Connor down a long corridor to the living room, a large, open-plan space that was tastefully decorated and dominated by a huge log burner set in a stone fireplace. The room's restrained elegance was a stark contrast to its owner, who was dressed in a suit that looked as if it had just been rescued from the bottom of a laundry basket, unballed and thrown on.

'You want a drink?' Paulie asked, as he moved to a chest of drawers and the array of whiskies that sat on it.

'No, thanks,' Connor said, old pain flashing in his nose as he recalled the last time Paulie had offered him a drink. 'Won't be long, just need to ask you something.'

'Go on then,' Paulie said, suspicion flattening his tone. 'What have you got yourself into now, and how is Jen messed up in all of it?'

Connor told Paulie everything that had happened that day, from the pictures of Jen and his gran to the attack on the church and the warning that a police officer was in danger. Paulie listened silently, his eyes growing dark and as hard as the stone fireplace. Connor noticed his grip flexing on the whisky glass he held, wondered what effort of will it was taking for Paulie not to crush it in his hand.

'So,' he said, as he finished his story, 'that's it. I've made sure Jen is safe, but does this sound like something Duncan would try, using her as a decoy to draw me out? Or have you heard of anyone asking about me or this Father Donnelly?'

Paulie took a sip of his whisky, rolled it around his mouth, as though trying to rid himself of a bad taste, and swallowed.

'It's no' Duncan's style,' he said. 'He fuckin' hates you, make no mistake, but all this pissing around with the money and the priest isn't him. He comes for you, it'll be straight on. I've not heard of anyone asking about you, but I'll look into it. You sure Jen is safe?'

'Safe as I can make her,' Connor said, hating the defensiveness in his voice. 'The clinic is secure, keycard entry only, and I've got my people keeping an eye on both the hospital and Jen. If I take it any further, I'll have to tell her what's going on and—'

'Bad idea,' Paulie said, cutting him off. 'And your grandmother? She's safe as well?'

'Eh, yeah, yeah,' Connor said, surprised. The last thing he had expected was Paulie showing concern for another human being other than Jen – especially one who was important to Connor.

'Good,' Paulie rumbled, his eyes falling to his glass. 'Family shouldn't be targeted like that. But it tells us two things.'

'Oh?' Connor said. 'What's that?'

Paulie finished his whisky in a slug, then smiled. It was a cold, empty twisting of his lips, the face of a man desperately trying to mimic an emotion he had never experienced. The look made Connor suddenly nervous.

'It tells us that whoever is after you or Father Donnelly is a coward,' Paulie said. 'And it tells us that, whoever it is, they're a fucking dead man for trying to drag Jen into this. I'll find whoever this is, Fraser, trust me. I just need one thing from you in return.'

Connor let the silence in the room ask the question to which he already knew the answer.

'Aye,' Paulie said, as he refilled his glass. 'You just stay out of my way.'

CHAPTER 21

The moment was perfect.

The sky was the colour of fire as the sun sank to the horizon, the day burning away as it yielded to the night. The air was warm and clear, the smell of the pine trees nearby heady in his nostrils. He could hear animals and birds shift in the woods around him, feel the life that teemed around the forestry trail, almost as if he was part of it.

It was perfect.

Until the sobbing started.

He closed his eyes, centred himself. Fought down the sudden thrill of adrenalin that electrified his blood and sharpened his senses. The fire would soon be free, but he could not, would not rush this moment. There was too much at stake, too much to do.

He turned away from the forest, focused on the car that sat about ten feet away from him. A standard black taxi, its only crime its conformity. It was identical to the half-dozen like it that had been at the taxi rank at Stirling railway station, waiting for him. He had chosen this cab at random, knowing he was being guided by a power greater than him. Whether that power was God or the fire, he did not know – and at that moment, he did not care.

The sobbing intensified and the cab began to rock from side to side as the driver struggled against his bonds and screamed his terror into the gag stuffed in his mouth. A trickle of blood ran through his silver hair, like a route map to where he had been smashed on the head and knocked out.

He walked to the cab slowly, unslinging his bag from his shoulder. Felt his fingers tremble as they closed on the first bottle he had so carefully filled. He lifted it up, let it revel in the dying light of the day, its glinting only hinting at the majesty and glory he was about to bring to life. The driver's muffled screams intensified, and he lifted the camera that was slung around his neck and took a picture of him. He had planned to take only one, but this felt like a special moment, one that deserved to be documented.

He walked around the cab slowly, opening the bottle and trailing the liquid around it in a circle. When he came to the front he stopped, locked eyes with the driver. He had seen the look in the man's eyes before – the feral, impotent, wide-eyed terror when a person caught sight of their own death and understood that there was no way to escape it. The driver whipped his head from side to side manically, the cab still rocking, as he cried and screamed and gagged.

He smiled, pulled the second bottle from his bag and emptied it over the bonnet. Then he walked to the driver's side, pulled the last bottle from his bag, and tipped it into the open window, soaking the man. The liquid burnt away the foul stench of shit and piss, which told him the driver had voided himself in terror.

He stepped back, reached into his bag for two items. One he placed in front of the cab, three feet in front of the circle of liquid. The second he placed on the roof, adjusting it to make sure the angle was just right. He stepped back, framed the shot.

Perfection.

The driver's screams became inhuman howls as he took the first flare from his bag, broke it open. It fizzed and sparked to life. He lobbed the flare at the ring of liquid around the cab, felt an electric thrill arc through his spine and into his groin as the fire sprang to life and raced around the car, like a predator released from its cage and finally free to hunt. Bit back a laugh as the second flare bounced off the bonnet and orange flames exploded across the car, the fire digging in and taking root as the napalm stuck to the metalwork.

He stepped back, surveyed his work. The fire capered and cackled around the car, roaring its defiance at the driver. He smiled, lifted his camera, forced his hands to stop shaking and took the shot he needed. Studied it, took one more.

Perfection.

He begrudged the moments it took him to transfer the photo from the camera to his email and send it to Fraser. Precious moments when he had to look away from the fire and concentrate on his work. But it was, after all, the Lord's work, and what right did he have to argue against that?

Smoke was billowing from the cab now, the driver completely obscured. But he could smell him: the sickly sweet odour of burning flesh filled the dimming day.

Reluctantly, he turned away, tracing the path to the motorbike he had left hidden in the undergrowth days before when he had planned all of this. He wanted nothing more than to stay, watch the fire cavort over the cab, devouring it. But no. He had work to do. And, after all, there was no rest for the wicked.

He kicked down on the bike, revved the throttle. Took one moment to inhale the acrid smoke that burnt his nostrils, then drove away, not looking back.

A few moments later, he heard the explosion as the fire reached the cab's petrol tank. Unable to help himself, he laughed, the sudden tears that filled his eyes nothing to do with the wind that tore at his face as he drove. What, he wondered, would happen when the message was received? Would it be understood? Surely it must be. He thought of the cab driver's eyes, and the overwhelming, sanity-stripping terror in them.

What had the taxi driver seen in those last moments, when his mind was stripped from him and all that was left was the face of God and the certainty of his own death?

Connor Fraser would know soon enough. He would ask him before he died.

CHAPTER 22

'Jesus,' Strachan said, leaning back in his chair and looking up at the ceiling. 'There's a name I've not heard in a long time.'

They were in Ford's office at Randolphfield police station, where they had retreated after Connor had received the threat to anyone in uniform. Ford's shift had technically ended hours before, but he had been at the job for too long to tell himself the lie that he could just punch out, go home and forget about it until the next day. No, the truth was that the job lived with you; every case, every atrocity, every threat. Going home would only make it worse: he would fidget, be unable to settle, fall into sullen silences. Again, he wondered why Mary hadn't just upped and left him years ago.

Thanked God that she hadn't.

'Aye,' Ford said, offering Strachan what passed for a cup of coffee in a police station. Strachan took it, nodded his thanks. Ford wondered if he'd remain as grateful when he tasted the stuff. He should have been heading home himself, but when he had heard of the threat to police officers, he had insisted on staying to help out if he could. Ford knew his friend was offering support that was more moral than logistical, but it didn't matter. He was grateful for the company – and the chance to ask a few questions.

'So, Gary, what can you tell me about John Donnelly? You've heard of him, anything I should know?'

Strachan sipped his coffee, grimaced. Ford thought briefly about the half-bottle of malt he kept in his locked desk drawer, dismissed the idea. The last thing he needed was to be responsible for Gary Strachan going on a bender. He knew Strachan had his demons mostly under control but, still, he wasn't going to be the one to tempt them out to play with a snifter of whisky in his coffee.

'Not sure,' Strachan said, his eyes drifting back up to the ceiling. 'I mean, I never really met him, only heard about what he did after the Harbour Street fire.'

'Go on,' Ford said.

'Well, you know about the fire,' Strachan said, his voice growing low and cold as he spoke, the memory staining his voice. 'Absolute bastard of a job. Seven dead in total, three of our boys. Donnelly was at the scene, ministering to the lads who were called out. Performed the last rites on one, as I remember, poor bastard.'

Ford was about to ask if he was talking about the priest or the man who had died, ignored the thought. 'Okay,' he said. 'No doubt a tough job to be called to, but why would he quit and then move to a wee village in the country and keep preaching? Were there any rumours about him, any whiff of impropriety?'

Strachan swivelled his gaze from the ceiling, his eyes falling on Ford as an unspoken conversation passed between them. With all the scandals over priests, child abuse and the Catholic Church's preferred method of dealing with those scandals – moving the priests involved to quieter, more secluded parishes – it was a logical, if unpleasant, assumption to make.

'No, nothing. And if you know what's good for you, Malcolm, you won't go asking that question in too many fire stations around Scotland.'

'But why?' Ford asked, frustration edging his voice. 'What the hell did Donnelly actually do?'

'Depends on who you ask,' Strachan said, the hardness bleeding out of his voice as he spoke. 'The way some tell it, he practically saved the fire service in Scotland.'

'What?' Ford said, the thought of the whisky bottle rising in his mind again.

Strachan held up a callused hand. 'You've got to understand,

Malcolm, that Harbour Street happened in 2011. And, as you'll recall, that was roughly the time that the Scottish Government started to moot the idea of amalgamating our fire and police forces from regional to national bodies.'

'Hmm,' Ford grunted. He remembered it all too well. The plan had been to take the eight fire services that operated across Scotland and merge them into one national service. The strategy was replicated with the police, their eight regional forces being merged to create Police Scotland. The policy, and its delivery, had been controversial, with police officers being assigned to duties hundreds of miles from their normal base of operations, and problems with call-handling at a national level. There had, inevitably, been cutbacks as well, with older officers and administrative staff offered redundancy packages too good to ignore. The problem was that that left more work and less resource for everyone else.

'Okay,' Ford said. 'But how does Donnelly figure into all this?'

'At the time of Harbour Street, there was a lot of talk about how the national service would be run. If stations could be closed, what the shape of the map would look like. It was, basically, a turf war. Way it's told around fire stations, the priest used the deaths at Harbour Street to lobby everyone he could to keep fire stations open and firefighters on the ground. He and the chief made their case at every possible committee hearing, and Father Donnelly bent the ear of every priest he knew to preach the word that congregations should talk to their local MPs and MSPs about what was happening. It was rumoured that he took it as far as a private audience with the First Minister at the time, though who knows? What I do know is that Donnelly was seen as the patron saint of firefighters, the man who turned Harbour Street into a weapon to fight off the cuts that would have seen firefighters taken off the run.'

Ford sighed, thought it through, remembered what Donnelly had told Connor Fraser when they met in Lenton Barns.

I'm a coward. Rather than stay and fight the good fight, I ran. Came here to get away from the memories of that night and the men who died. I came here looking for peace, Mr Fraser. I ran away.

It didn't make sense. The man Strachan had just described didn't sound like a coward in any way that he recognised. He had taken a tragedy and used it to fight for what he believed in. So what was he running from?

'I don't get it,' Ford said, more to himself than to Strachan. 'We're missing something, Gary, we must be. I can understand him trying to forget that night, but why would he—' He was interrupted by the pinging of his phone. He grabbed it from his desk, felt tension clamp around his neck as he read the caller. 'Fraser?' he said. 'What—'

'I got another message,' Fraser said, his voice flat, clipped, as though he was giving an official report. 'Just came through. I'm sending it on to you now. Have a look.'

Ford pulled the phone from his ear, flipped into his email. Saw a message from Fraser, opened it to find a jpeg. Tasted bile in his throat as he opened the image, felt the world swim around him. He blinked, tried to swallow. Was dimly aware that Strachan was moving, pawing at his own phone.

'Jesus,' he whispered. 'Oh, Jesus.'

'No way to know where it was taken, or who the poor bastard is,' Connor said. 'I've checked the image, no distinguishing features other than it's a country lane. Must be somewhere remote to do . . . well, to do that undisturbed.'

'Get here now. I'm at Randolphfield,' Ford said. Then he abruptly hung up, suddenly desperate to get the phone, and the obscenity on it, as far away from him as possible.

'Malcolm?' Strachan asked, eyes darting from Ford to the phone in his hand and his own handset. There was something unreadable in the other man's eyes, almost as if he was about to ask a question he knew the answer to but wished he didn't.

'Here,' Ford said, handing Strachan his phone. The policeman suddenly looked bone weary, as if what he had seen had leached from him whatever vitality he had left.

Strachan looked down at the phone, jaw setting as his face tightened and seemed to draw in on itself. Ford simply nodded, the memory of the photograph Strachan was now studying seared into him.

The picture showed a standard black taxi, parked on a farm track that looked to be made of scree. The cab was encircled by a ring of flame that seemed frozen mid-leap in the image, as though the flames were trying to merge with the fireball that was roiling like a super-nova on the cab's bonnet. In the driver's seat, a man sat, his head flung back, cords standing out on his neck as he gave a silent scream: a snapshot of pure, terrified horror frozen for all time in one grue-some tableau.

In front of the cab, roughly a foot away from the ring of fire, was a simple sign. About three feet wide and two feet high, it had been buried in the ground like a signpost to a market or a village fair. Scrawled on it in what Ford prayed was red ink was a simple message:

This blood is on Donnelly's hands, Mr Fraser.
How bloody are you willing to get?

But there was worse, another detail that Ford knew Strachan had seen as soon as he gave a snarl that was somewhere between revulsion and fury.

'Jesus,' he whispered, looking up at Ford. 'Is that . . .'

Ford stepped forward, forced himself to look at the image. There was no mistake. Sitting on the roof of the cab, perched at an obscenely jaunty angle, was an old-fashioned conical police officer's helmet.

'Boys in blue,' Ford muttered. 'The bastard didn't have the balls to grab a real copper, so he went out and made himself one.'

'Come on,' Strachan said after a moment.

'What?' Ford said, the word little more than a confused cough.

'I got a message from Control when you were on the phone. Dog-walker outside Banknock reported a car ablaze on the Fordell Dyke trail. Don't know about you, Malcolm, but that doesn't sound like a curious little coincidence, does it?'

CHAPTER 23

The hotel sat at the top of Stirling, just down from the castle, which dominated Castle Hill and loomed over the city. A former school converted years ago, the hotel played up to its Scottish roots with tartan rugs, deep leather sofas, heavy pine furniture and large, candle-themed lamps that hung from the vaulted ceilings. A few guests milled around the bar, some in masks, some not, and Doug marvelled, again, at how the pandemic had changed the way people lived, the changes they were willing to accept, the ones they could not.

He knew the feeling all too well.

After his meeting with Fraser and Donna, he had decided to find a hotel in Stirling and book in for a few days. He could work from anywhere as long as he had his laptop and a phone signal, and it made more sense than the hour's drive back to an empty flat in Musselburgh. A flat where too many memories and regrets waited for him, ready to be unleashed the moment he cracked the seal on the bottle of whisky he kept under the kitchen sink.

'Well, well, Doug McGregor, fancy meeting you here,' a cheerful voice said, dragging Doug from his thoughts.

Doug looked up, smiled. 'Dave,' he said, moving around from the table he was sitting at and offering the newcomer his hand. 'Thanks for coming. How you doing?'

'Aye, well, well. Busy, but can't grumble, you know?' Dave said, as he shrugged off his coat and turned to the bar. 'Get you a drink?'

Doug held up a hand, gestured to the Coke that was sitting beside his laptop on the table. 'I'm good, thanks, but, here, let me get you one. Least I can do for you agreeing to see me. Pint?'

'Aye,' Dave replied, taking a seat. 'Please.'

Doug nodded, headed for the bar. He had met Dave Philp a few years ago, while working on a story about building standards and safety protocols after a storm had ripped through Edinburgh, toppling scaffolding and seriously injuring three workmen on a building site in the centre of the city. An expert in construction management, Dave was a rarity in Doug's field: an expert with a passion for his subject and the ability to translate the technical into the quotable. And it was that technical knowledge, and Dave's side passion for digital technologies, that Doug hoped would be useful. So he had called Dave after he had booked the hotel, asked him to meet up. Dave, who lived only a few miles away, happily agreed.

He ordered Dave's pint, then carried it back to the table, careful to use his right hand. The injuries to his left were healing, but still the pain lingered, and carrying a pint glass with his elbow at a right angle was just asking for trouble.

He put the pint in front of Dave, then settled into his seat.

'Cheers,' Dave said, holding the glass slightly towards Doug before taking a long drink. He sighed, then put it down and leant forward. 'So,' he said, as he rested his elbows on his knees. 'Why the call? What you working on now?'

Doug sipped his Coke, then turned his laptop to Dave. 'This,' he said, gesturing to a picture he had taken at the church earlier that day. 'Need your help with some tech questions.'

Dave gave a quiet whistle as he studied the photograph. Doug had managed to snap it on a zoom lens. It showed the church in the background, smoke wisping up from the ruined door that had been destroyed by one of the drones. But it was the foreground Doug was interested in. In front of the church was what had been a well-manicured lawn before a huge crater had been dug into it by a downed drone, a chunk of which had bounced free of the crater and lay on the border of the picture.

'I know you've used drones in site surveys and the like,' Doug said, thinking back to his research into Dave's recent work history. 'I was wondering what you could tell me about this one.'

Dave looked up from the laptop, the usual good humour in his eyes replaced by something sharper and more calculating. 'This from that accident at the church in Lenton Barns?' he asked, eyes drifting back to the screen.

'Yeah,' Doug said. 'I've blown up the image as much as I can, but I need to know more about drones. How they're controlled, how far away the controller would have to be, that sort of thing. Was hoping you could help me out.'

'Sounds like something more for the police,' Dave said, and had another swig of his pint.

'Aye, but I'm working on a deeper piece,' Doug said, comfortable with the white lie. 'And this would really help me out. So anything you can tell me, Dave . . .'

'May I?' Dave said, gesturing to the laptop.

'Be my guest,' Doug said, sliding the machine towards him.

Dave leant forward again, fingers flying across the keyboard with practised ease. He grunted to himself a few times as he worked, light from the laptop playing across his face. Then, after a minute, he sat back with a smile on his face. 'Maverick Reliant 4,' he said.

'What?'

'Here,' Dave said, turning the laptop back to Doug and leaning around it to point at the screen. 'See this part of the fuselage and that rotor?' Doug nodded as Dave pointed to the picture he had taken, what looked like a miniature helicopter rotor sticking out of the ground. 'Well,' Dave continued, 'that engine assembly is only used on the Maverick Reliant. It's an industrial drone, used in the construction industry and the like. Pricey piece of kit, costs around eight and a half grand for a top-of-the-line model. Doesn't sound much like the kids the firefighter on the TV said were messing around with this stuff.'

Doug nodded, thinking of the seventy thousand pounds that had been deposited in Connor Fraser's account by whoever was trying to pull his strings. Money didn't seem to be much of an issue. He felt something then, an undefined itch in the back of his mind as a random thought flared briefly to light then died, like a cheap match.

'Right,' he said. 'But what about controlling these things? How close would whoever was flying it have to be to operate it?'

Dave sucked on his teeth, raked his hand through thick greying hair. 'About seven kilometres,' he said, his voice distracted, as though he was already thinking ahead to the next problem. 'They're operated through radio or Wi-Fi – you can get phone apps and run them straight off your phone. We use proper handsets, though, and the better your Wi-Fi or stronger the radio antenna you're using, the less chance you've got of an outage that would make you lose track of your drone.'

'Right,' Doug said, his mind racing as Dave leant towards the laptop again. If he could track the location of the signal, or at least get a working range of how far the pilot had been, it might help him identify whoever had decided to bomb the church.

'Here,' Dave said, as he turned the laptop back to Doug. 'You might find this useful.'

Doug smiled as he looked at the screen. Dave had pulled up a map and overlaid a circle with the relative distance of seven kilometres radiating out from Lenton Barns on it.

'That's your search grid,' he said.

'Hmm,' Doug mused, as he studied the map. It was mostly open fields and farmland, a few small hamlets that were little more than a street around which a few houses clustered. Not many places to get a good Wi-Fi signal, or even reliable phone coverage.

He leant forward, clicked the map to show places of interest and public utilities. Frowned at it.

Dave leant forward, pointed to the map and the adjustment Doug had made. 'That's interesting,' he said.

'What?' Doug asked.

Dave tapped the screen, just on the icon that denoted Banknock community fire station.

'You know how I said those types of drones are used by the construction industry?' he said. 'Well, they're fitted with thermal cameras and used by the fire service as well. Easier to survey building fires and the like by remote control.'

Doug nodded, felt that itch return to the back of his mind. He was about to ask Dave another question when his phone rang. He gave Dave an apologetic smile, grabbed it.

'Don,' he said, to the Crucible's news editor. 'What's up?'

'You still in Stirling?' Don Amos asked, his clipped Dundonian accent reshaping the question into an accusation.

'Yeah. I told you I'd be here for a few days. What do you need?'

'Concerned member of the public just sent us in one hell of a picture. A cab on fire outside Banknock, where you were this morning. I'm going to send you the details now. Can you get out there, talk to him, see what we've got? Looks like it might be a lot more than just kids fucking about.'

'Yeah,' Doug said, glancing back at the laptop, and the tag for Banknock fire station. 'That sounds like just my type of story.'

CHAPTER 24

Connor arranged to meet Ford and Strachan at the site of the burnt-out cab, having been diverted there from Randolphfield by a call from a breathless DS Troughton. By the time he arrived, both police and fire service were at the scene and the entrance to the farm track where the taxi had been found had been cordoned off with garish yellow and black police tape; two officers standing guard at either side. In the distance, down the track, Connor could see the glow of spotlights and hear the soft, grinding splutter of the generator that powered them.

He parked his car, called Ford to tell him he had arrived.

'I'll send Troughton to get you at the perimeter,' Ford said, his voice as foreboding as the night that was drawing in around them. Then he hung up.

Connor waited for a moment, saw Troughton appear from the shadows of the farm track, like a theatre actor running from the wings to take to the stage. He got out of the car, felt panic whisper in the back of his mind like static, clouding his thoughts. The picture he had been sent of a man burning alive in a cab was bad enough: the last thing he needed was to see it in the flesh.

'Fraser,' Troughton said, his tone telling Connor he was trying to impersonate his boss and failing badly. 'DCI Ford is waiting for you. Please come with me.'

Connor ducked under the cordon, ignored the suspicious glance one of the uniformed officers gave him. Troughton led him up the track, the trees on either side seeming to thicken and crowd in on him, like the acrid tang of smoke and the horrible sickly-sweet odour that seemed to intensify with every step he took.

A minute later, he turned a corner on the path, a dull ache stabbing into his eyes as the harsh spotlights from a fire engine lighting tower beat back the night and illuminated the whole scene in horrific, stark detail.

The burnt-out cab sat in the middle of the scene, illuminated like a precious jewel on display. To its left, a fire crew milled around their engine, packing up after they had done what they could to quell a fire that had already done its worse. Parked opposite the engine, bracketing the remains of the cab, like oversized bookends, was a police forensics van. Connor could see a second cordon had been set up around the cab, the white paper suits of the SOCOs glowing, ethereal, as they buzzed around the remains of the vehicle, searching for any evidence they could find.

Connor studied the cab, his stomach giving a sickening lurch as he saw the blackened, smoking lump that was propped up in what had been the front seat. The skin had been stretched tight by the heat of the flames, pulling the face into a rictus leer made worse by the glint of hellishly pale teeth against the ashen flesh. The head, if you could still call it that, was thrown back, as if silently howling its agony to the stars overhead. Connor thought briefly of the image he had been sent – the man in the driver's seat had still been recognisably human then. How much longer after the photograph had been taken had he lived? How much agony had he endured, trapped with the flames licking hungrily at his body and sanity?

'Fraser.' Connor turned, startled from his thoughts, to see Ford approaching him, the firefighter he had seen at Lenton Barns earlier that day at his side. A towering figure, with sharp, hawkish eyes and a body that hadn't so much been built in a gym but grown there, hung back slightly. He looked like a bodyguard who had been given a firefighter's uniform and told to go undercover.

'Sir,' Connor said, willing his eyes to stay on Ford and not drift back to the horrors contained within the cab.

'You have any idea what this is about?' Ford asked, his voice cold and impatient. 'Seems clear you're at the centre of it, you and that priest.'

'No, sir,' Connor said, frustration mixing with the revulsion in his gut, curdling into something spiteful. 'The moment I got the picture, I forwarded it to you. Couldn't see a way of identifying the locus, couldn't think of a way to help this poor bastard, whoever he was.'

Ford nodded. 'We're pulling the VIN number from the chassis to see who the cab's registered to. That'll hopefully give us an ID. In the meantime, we need to figure out what the hell is going on here. What links you to Father Donnelly? Why are you being targeted?'

Connor thought briefly of Paulie, and his vow to get answers. 'I'm working on it now, sir. As I said, I can't think of any immediate connection, but there must be something. Whatever else is going on, I think this means Father Donnelly and I are of equal interest to whoever the hell is doing all of this.'

'Agreed,' Ford said, seeming then to lose himself in his own thoughts for a moment. The focus snapped back into his eyes, like quick-moving clouds skittering over a full moon and clearing. 'We're going to up security around Donnelly, and I think we should do the same for you until we know what the hell is going on.'

Connor had expected this. But there was no way he could let himself be hampered by a police officer watching his every move.

'Thank you, sir, but no,' he said, watching as anger rose in Ford's eyes. 'Think about it. Whoever is doing this is watching me. If he sees a uniform or a plain-clothes officer with me, he'll stay on the sidelines. If I'm on my own, he might get careless, try something. I'll be fine, sir. I've got Simon looking out for me, and I'm not exactly defenceless on my own.'

Ford grunted. 'Speaking of your friend, where is he?'

Connor had to bite back a smile as he saw the suspicion in Ford's eyes. Connor could have told him that Simon had headed to Lenton Barns to check on the priest, thought better of it. Ford was barely tolerating his involvement in a police operation as it was and the last thing he needed was to be told that an off-duty PSNI officer was double-checking the security arrangements he was making for Father Donnelly.

'Running errands,' Connor said. 'But he'll be around when I need him, sir.'

Ford grunted again as he glared at Connor with an expression caught between acceptance and fury.

'Did you find anything useful here?' Connor asked, keen to distract Ford from his ire.

'Nothing yet,' Ford spat. 'Though we've confirmed that the substance used in this fire is the same as that used in those bloody drones at the church.'

'Petroleum laced with Vaseline,' the firefighter, Strachan, said. 'Effectively budget napalm.' He turned his head back towards the smouldering cab. 'Whoever did this is a very sick individual.'

Connor was about to reply when Troughton appeared again, glancing nervously at Ford, as though he had news he knew his boss wouldn't like.

'Sir,' he said quickly. 'Sorry, sir, but just had a call from the boys at the perimeter. They say the press are here, Sky News. They're asking for you personally. And Mr Fraser.'

Ford gave Connor an accusatory look. Connor shrugged, then remembered his car was parked just beyond the police cordon. A car one reporter in particular knew well. 'Donna,' he said, watching Ford's jaw set. 'Donna Blake.'

Ford took a deep breath, closed his eyes. 'Perfect,' he said. 'Just bloody perfect.'

CHAPTER 25

Donna was waiting for them at the cordon, smiling at the uniformed officers whose eyes were darting between her, her cameraman Keith and a third figure Connor recognised as Doug McGregor.

'DCI Ford,' Donna called. Ford raised his hand and winced at the sudden glare of the light from Keith's camera as it swivelled on to him. 'Thanks for coming to see me. I understand there was a serious fire here this evening. Care to comment?'

Ford grunted, flashed small, predatory teeth. His posture told Connor he was holding back from what he really wanted to say.

'I'm afraid I can't comment on an ongoing situation, Ms Blake,' he said, his voice as clipped and strained as that of a politician making an apology. 'If you have any queries, please contact the Police Scotland press and communications team. I believe you have their details.'

Donna's smile intensified. 'I do, DCI Ford, I do. But since we're both here, would you care to comment on the fact that this is the second incident in the space of twelve hours that you've attended with members of the fire service? The first, at Lenton Barns, was dismissed as an act of irresponsible vandalism. Are you telling me that this is the same?'

Connor saw the flash of mischief in Donna's eyes as she spoke, felt concern bubble up in his gut. She was a damn good reporter, but when she got on the trail of something big and potentially exclusive, she could be reckless. Connor had seen the body count to prove that.

'As I said,' Ford replied, after a moment's pause, 'I cannot comment on an ongoing situation. If and when we're ready to issue a statement, I'll make sure you receive a copy, unless you'd prefer we take you off the mailing list.'

Ford let his voice trail off, the threat clear: fuck with me, I'll freeze you out. Connor watched as Donna's jaw set, eyes flicking between him and Ford as she decided how far to push it.

'Mr Fraser,' she said, decision made. 'Any comment to make? After all, you've been at both scenes today. Is Sentinel Securities consulting with the police in this matter? Perhaps that's why you were sent—'

'Sorry, Doug McGregor, the Crucible,' Doug said suddenly, cutting Donna off. 'DCI Ford, forgive me, but I'm not sure I've got the details of the press team you referred to. Could I have them, please?'

Ford smiled, whether at the easy out McGregor had given him or the waves of fury radiating off Donna, Connor couldn't tell. 'Well, of course,' he said. 'I'll make sure one of my officers gets that to you as soon as possible. Now, if you'll excuse me . . .'

Ford turned to leave. Connor saw his chance, stepped in front of him, careful to make sure they were both still on camera. 'I'll duck out here, sir,' he said. 'Nothing else I can add at this point. Of course I'll report to Randolphfield to give you my formal statement, and contact you immediately if whoever is behind this contacts me again.'

'Now, wait a minute,' Ford said, good humour evaporating as his voice hardened. 'You can't just—'

Connor jutted his jaw over Ford's shoulder to Donna and Doug. 'I think I can, sir,' he said. 'Unless you want to discuss grounds for arrest and custody in a very public forum.'

Ford's eyes darkened, the predatory smile he had given Donna a few moments ago resurfacing. It was not a pleasant sight. 'Fine,' he said slowly. 'But keep in touch.'

Connor nodded, moved off. Felt his phone buzz in his pocket as he walked towards his car. A message from McGregor.

Got something. Meet us at the Stirling Highland in town. Important.

Us? Connor thought, glancing up at McGregor, who was making a show of studying his phone and keeping out of Donna's line of sight. *Interesting.*

Donna waited until Ford had disappeared beyond the police cordon before she grabbed Doug by the arm and dragged him towards her car. She glanced about, then whirled him round, hard, causing dull sparks of pain to crawl up his left arm, from his palm to his elbow.

'What the fuck was that?' she hissed. 'We had him. Connor's on the scene. We've got the picture. And you pull that give-me-your-press-contacts bullshit? I thought we were working together on this, but it looks like you're only working to sabotage me.'

Doug took a breath, forced his breathing to slow as he tried to flex away the growing pain in his arm. 'We *are* working this together,' he said. 'Isn't the fact that I called you the moment I got the tip on this proof of that? I could have scooped you, but I didn't. I want your help, Donna. I mean that.'

'Then what the hell was that all about?' she asked, angry blotches of colour crawling up her neck as she spoke.

'Think about it,' Doug said. 'What have you got here tonight that you can use? A copper on camera giving you a no-comment comment, some establishing shots of a police cordon and a member of the public helping police with their enquiries. I'm no broadcast journalist, but that doesn't sound like much of a package to me.'

'But what about the picture?' Donna asked, her tone telling Doug that she could see where he was going.

'Useless,' he replied. 'I took a look at it. Your newsdesk would never run it, just like mine won't. Too graphic. So we tell Ford what we've got and he gets his media team to tie us up in non-publication threats and writs while the story goes cold. No, better to keep the picture back, use it when we're ready.'

'Okay,' Donna said, her posture telling Doug she agreed with him, her tone telling him she didn't like it. 'So, what now? This all seems to revolve around Connor somehow. Has he said anything about helping you out with the Sentinel logs on Gareth Hogan?'

Doug smiled. 'I'm hoping he's about to,' he said. 'Look, it's been a long day, how do you fancy a drink back at my hotel? Who knows? We might even bump into a familiar face while we're at it.'

CHAPTER 26

They met in the hotel bar, which was now filled with a scattering of guests looking for a drink after a day of sightseeing around Stirling.

'Ack,' Doug said. 'Too busy. Let's get drinks, go to my room. Quieter there.'

They ordered a round, whisky for Connor, a Diet Coke for Doug and a red wine for Donna, then Doug led Connor and Donna down a narrow, dim corridor. He stopped at the end, dug a keycard out of his pocket and led them into a large corner room that had windows in two walls: one looked out to the Wallace Monument and the Campsie Hills beyond, the other down Castle Hill to the centre of Stirling.

'Take a seat,' Doug said, gesturing to a small table bracketed by two oversized armchairs that sat below the window looking out to the hills. Connor nodded, manoeuvring himself along the narrow space between the double bed and the dressing-table that took up the far wall of the room. As he passed the dressing-table, he noted the objects there: a battered, scarred squash ball, an unopened half-bottle of whisky, two glasses neatly set beside it, along with a slightly battered picture of a little girl, maybe about a year old. Connor couldn't be sure but, judging from the hair and high cheekbones, she was related to McGregor.

'Thanks for coming, Connor,' Doug said, as he grabbed the squash ball in his left hand and started to squeeze it. 'Imagine you've had a hell of a day.'

Connor took a sip of his drink, exchanged a glance with Donna, who was sitting opposite him. As usual, she was camera ready, her make-up and hair perfect, the dark trouser suit she wore looking as though she had slipped it on twenty minutes before he arrived. But there was tiredness in her eyes, and gauntness to her features, which troubled Connor in a way he didn't fully understand.

'You said you had something for me,' he said, pushing the thought aside. 'What is it?'

Doug propped himself against the dressing-table, eyes darting to Connor's whisky briefly before settling on Donna. 'Before I start, I want to stress this is all off the record, for the moment. I'm still hopeful you'll agree to let us see the Sentinel files on Gareth Hogan. I think the way we're dealing with what I've found out is proof that we can be responsible with sensitive information, not just hacks looking for a splash.'

'I already know Donna isn't that,' Connor said. 'As for Hogan, we'll get to him later. For now, tell me what you've found.'

Doug smiled, the gesture making him appear younger, the keen reporter he had been years ago, perhaps. He briefly outlined his conversation with Dave Philp, the revelation that the drones used in the church attack were also used by the fire service and that Banknock fire station was one of the few places in the vicinity of Lenton Barns that the drones could have been controlled from.

Connor sat back in his seat, considered. Everything pointed back to the fire service; from Donnelly's involvement with them, the disaster at Harbour Street and now this. But what did it mean? And, again, why had he been dragged into it? A thought crossed his mind, and he made a mental note to follow it up as soon as the meeting was over.

'So, what's your next step?' Connor asked.

Doug opened his mouth to speak, but Donna got there first. 'Depends,' she said. 'First, we need to verify that Banknock fire station was involved in this somehow. That means we need the station logs for the time around when the drones attacked. Next step would be to find a way to check the fire service's equipment logs, see if these drones were theirs or just the same model as they use. Obviously, there's a bigger story here than Ford or his fire pals want us to know about, so we'll keep digging. But there's also Doug's story to consider . . .' She let her voice trail off, the question hanging unasked in the air.

Connor set his jaw, felt suddenly like a parent being looked at by expectant children who had just asked to be taken to the ice-cream parlour for a treat. He sighed, let his shoulders sag. Felt irritation itch in his mind even as the urge to move sank its fangs into his muscles. Too many things to think of at once, too many angles to cover. What he needed was a workout, a way to re-centre himself, focus his thoughts.

Focus . . .

'All right,' he said. 'Donna, you know Robbie Lindsay at Sentinel, yeah? He'll call you tomorrow afternoon. Tell him what you and Doug are looking for, specifically, and he'll help you out. I can't let you see the full files for obvious reasons, but I'll do what I can, okay?'

Donna exchanged a look with Doug. 'Okay,' she said. 'But why wait until tomorrow afternoon? Why not just get him to buzz me in the morning, keep things moving?'

Connor smiled, his earlier thoughts coalescing into a plan. 'Because,' he said, 'I'm going to have Robbie looking into something for me tomorrow morning. And, besides, you two are going to be busy doing me a favour.'

CHAPTER 27

Morning came too quickly, the bright sunshine and clear skies seeming to mock Connor, taunt him for his broken night's sleep that was crammed with too many thoughts and aches from the day before. He gave up on sleeping at six, tossed aside his quilt and padded through to the living room of the flat. Wasn't surprised to see Simon already set up on the couch, coffee in hand, Tom at his side as he pecked away at his laptop.

'Mornin',' Simon said cheerily as he looked up from the screen, his eyes as clear as the morning sky. 'I've checked in with the teams looking out for your gran and Jen. Both reported nothing unusual happened overnight, though the personal touch and contacting them won't hurt. There's coffee in the pot, though it looks like you could do with something stronger.'

Connor grunted, shrugged. His body was a mass of pain that seemed to radiate from his injured shoulder. He remembered an old saying his grandfather favoured. 'Not the years, Simon, it's the mileage,' he said.

Simon smiled. 'Aye, and the way you bloody drive, it's a miracle you've not had a write-off yet.' He paused, his face growing serious, his tone softer. 'Get some coffee, big lad. You could use it.'

Connor headed for the kitchen and the strong, rich aroma he could smell. It had been the same when he and Simon were partners in the police in Belfast: a live case seemed to invigorate Simon, sharpen his senses, make small matters like sleep and food mere distractions from the hunt. Connor, meanwhile, paid the price of the over-thinker as he became consumed with solving the problem at hand.

He poured himself a cup of coffee, savoured the first sip. Simon had been staying with him for a few months now, taking extended leave from the PSNI to help him in the aftermath of Jen's injury. And in that time he had somehow tracked down the best coffee in Stirling, maybe even in Scotland. A feat Connor had not equalled. But that was typical Simon, wasn't it? He got along with people in a way Connor could not, managed to fit into wherever he was with ease and find what he needed. It was a skill Connor admired and envied.

'So,' Simon said as he folded the laptop shut, 'what's the plan for today? Been looking around the tourist guides? Got to say, there are more than a few tasty-looking churches and historical monuments we could rain fire down on if you're in the mood.'

Connor grunted a laugh. 'No, thanks. Once was quite enough,' he said. 'No, today I thought we'd get a little closer to the fucker who's doing all of this.'

Simon's eyes narrowed as he leant forward. 'Liking the sound of this,' he said. 'Tell me.'

Connor sighed, the thoughts that had kept him awake most of the night crowding into his mind. He closed his eyes, forced himself to take one idea at a time.

'Whatever's going on, the priest and I seem to be the focus of it. Given what Donna and that reporter McGregor told me about the drones and Banknock fire station last night, it seems the fire service are tied up in it as well. So, the best thing we can do is dig. I've already got Paulie looking into whether Duncan MacKenzie or one of his cronies is involved, or whether someone else has been asking about me. So that leaves Father Donnelly and the fire service.'

Simon took a sip from his coffee. Connor could see the concern in his eyes at the mention of Paulie, knew Simon was pragmatic enough to know Paulie could go places and ask questions they couldn't. For now, he was a necessary evil, one that hopefully wouldn't turn on them, like Lucifer in the Garden of Eden.

'Okay, makes sense,' Simon said. 'So how are we going to do that?'

'I called Robbie last night,' Connor said. 'He's going to do a deep dive on Donnelly, see if there are any connections between him and me that might give us a clue. And while he's doing that, Donna and McGregor are going to be looking into the other side of this.'

'That fire at Harbour Street,' Simon said.

Connor raised his mug to him. 'Exactly. Whatever the hell happened there, it was enough to force Donnelly to move away from Glasgow. And I get the feeling there's something he's not telling us about that night. Might be wrong, but Donna and McGregor are going to pull all the cuttings and news reports from the time, see if they can find anything.'

'And, in return, you'll give them the files they wanted on that energy company you did some work for.'

'Paradigm,' Connor confirmed. 'I've told Robbie to talk to them. He can look into our files to make sure no confidentiality clauses are broken. Last thing I need is a fucking lawyer breathing down my neck on top of all of this.'

'Fair enough,' Simon said, one hand falling to Tom's head and scruffling her ears. 'So what does that leave us to do? Seems like a beautiful day out so we should make the most of it. Maybe go and see Jen.'

Connor winced. It had been playing on his mind – the desire to get into the car and go to see her, confirm she was all right with his own eyes. But he fought the urge with two simple realisations: she would read trouble in his face the moment he saw her, and he needed, no, *wanted*, to find whoever had threatened her and have a very long, personal chat with them about the cost of that threat.

'No,' he said. 'Not now. Not when there's work to be done and whoever is pulling our strings is out there. But, you're right, it looks like it's going to be a beautiful day, so we should take a drive.'

'I'm in your hands, big lad,' Simon said. 'Where are we going?'

'The Kingdom,' Connor said. 'I think, Simon, it's about time I showed you the Kingdom.'

CHAPTER 28

They took the M9 east, past the towering horse heads of the Kelpies monument that reared up into the flawless sky and the industrial scar of gunmetal grey petrol refineries at Grangemouth. Kincardine Bridge took them across the Forth into Fife, a name that had echoed from the region's past as a Pictish kingdom known as Fib. The royal connections were strengthened by Dunfermline's claim to be one of the ancient capitals of Scotland, and the current resting place of Robert the Bruce.

They were heading for Kirkcaldy, one of Fife's larger towns, where Gary Strachan was based. As the lead firefighter for Central Scotland, Strachan could have based himself at any station from Edinburgh to Loch Lomond, yet he had chosen to return to the fire station where he had started his career. Thanks to some digging by Robbie Lindsay, Connor had seen Strachan's biography, knew he was a career fire-fighter who had joined the service at nineteen and worked his way steadily up the ranks. But no matter how far his career had taken him, he had always chosen to stay close to home and the place where he had been brought up.

Connor understood the impulse, wished he had the kind of life that let him follow it.

They pulled up in front of Kirkcaldy fire station, a blunt, grey-harled box of a building that looked as if it had been ripped straight from the eighties and had a glass-fronted entrance grafted on to it as a half-hearted attempt at modernisation.

'I've said it before and I'll say it again,' Simon said, as he climbed out of Connor's Audi and slung his bag over his shoulder. 'You do bring me to the nicest places.'

Connor smiled, took another look at the fire station. 'Ah, but think of all the interesting people I introduce you to.'

Simon glanced across the roof of the car at him, his gaze growing serious. 'You sure we're going to get a warm welcome here?' he asked. 'After all, firefighters and coppers don't always mix.'

Connor smiled. They'd both seen it on the job in Belfast, the natural competitiveness between two very different bodies charged with keeping the public safe, each thinking they were better than the other.

'Ack, it'll be fine. I'm not a copper any more and you're on a sabbatical. Besides, I spoke to Ford before we left, and he's spoken to Strachan, told him we're coming. With the shit his boss was spouting at the press conference yesterday, it's in his interests to help us get to the bottom of all this as quickly, and quietly, as possible.'

'Oh, so you think involving Donna and that McGregor character is playing this quietly?' Simon asked, the humour returning to his gaze. 'Might have escaped your attention, big lad, but Donna's not exactly camera-shy, and McGregor seems every bit as headline hungry as she is.'

'I'll deal with that when it happens,' Connor said, a sudden memory of the candid pictures of Jen and his gran flitting across his mind. 'First, we need to find the bastard doing this. And if that means working with Donna and McGregor, so be it.'

Simon held up his hands. 'Fair play,' he said. 'Now, shall we go and see the nice firefighter, see if he can help us?'

They gave their names at the reception desk, which was manned by a short, rotund blonde woman with tired eyes and a demeanour that hinted she had been dragged from the eighties along with the rest of the building.

'Ah, yes, ACO Strachan is expecting you. Please, take a seat. Someone from his office will be down to collect you shortly,' she said, her tone as tired as her eyes.

They had barely had time to take a seat on the cheap plastic chairs that sat opposite the reception desk when a fridge dressed in a firefighter's uniform lumbered into the reception area from behind a secure door at the end of a small hallway. Connor recognised him from the site of the cab fire the previous night, and the daylight did little to dampen his impression. He was, Connor thought, the biggest man he had ever seen, almost as wide as he was tall, his uniform straining to hold in his massive physique. Small green-grey eyes swept the room from underneath the shelf-like overhang of his forehead, the size of which was accentuated by the harsh bristle-cut of his dark hair.

'Mr Fraser, Mr McCartney?' he said, his voice a soft, almost lilting whisper that didn't seem to belong to the body it came from. 'I'm Group Manager John Ogilvy. Please follow me. ACO Strachan is waiting for you.'

Ogilvy led them through the security door, along a corridor that seemed almost too narrow for his massive shoulders. Connor exchanged a glance and a smile with Simon, who mouthed, 'Hulk smash,' silently and bashed his fists together as they walked. At the end of the corridor, Ogilvy opened a door to a large conference room, an imposing heavy oak table in the centre, the far wall dominated by a video screen showing the Scottish Fire and Rescue logo. Strachan was seated at the head of the table. He didn't get up when Connor and Simon entered the room.

'Sir, Mr Fraser and Mr McCartney,' Ogilvy said, as he rose to his full height and threw back his shoulders, as though standing to attention on a parade ground. Connor had heard that the rank structure in the fire service was more militaristic than its equivalent in the police force, but hadn't known they took it quite so literally.

'Thank you, John, that will be all,' Strachan said.

'Sir,' Ogilvy replied, looking as though he had barely resisted the urge to offer a small salute and click his heels as he retreated from the room.

Strachan watched him go, then waited a moment, letting the silence in the room linger. 'Please, gentlemen,' he said at last, gesturing to the seats at either side of the table in front of him, 'take a seat. Can I offer you anything? Coffee? Tea?'

'No, thank you,' Connor said, taking the seat to Strachan's left as Simon slid into the chair opposite.

'So,' Strachan said, 'DCI Ford called me earlier, said you might have some information on what happened at Lenton Barns yesterday. I must say, it's not like him to involve civilians in his investigations, so this must be important.'

Connor let Strachan's implied dig with 'civilians' slide. 'First, thanks for seeing us,' he said, keeping his gaze on Strachan's. 'And, yes, you're right, we think we might have something on what happened yesterday, and we think there might be a link to the fire service somewhere.'

Strachan stiffened in his seat, weariness darkening his gaze. 'Go on,' he said slowly.

Connor nodded to Simon, who laid his bag on the table and retrieved his laptop. 'What do you know about the Maverick Reliant 4 drone?' he asked, as Simon tapped away at his keyboard.

Strachan leant forward. 'Standard model. We use it in search-and-rescue operations, and to reconnoitre potentially dangerous areas on the job. Usually fitted with thermal-imaging cameras. Why? Hold on, you don't . . .'

'Yes, sir,' Connor said. 'You'll be able to confirm it with police when they finish their forensic examinations, but we strongly believe that the drones employed in yesterday's attack were the same as those used by the fire service.'

'They're commonly used commercial drones,' Strachan said, a defensive tone giving his voice a hard edge. 'It doesn't mean—'

'No, sir, it doesn't,' Connor said, keeping his voice conciliatory. 'But it kind of blows the line you and the police are putting out there that the attack yesterday was an accident that probably involved some kids, doesn't it? Can't see many teenagers being able to stretch to the six or seven grand apiece these drones cost. And then there's this . . .' Connor gestured to Simon, who turned the laptop he was working on towards Strachan. He watched the firefighter's face grow pale and serious, as Simon explained to him what Doug McGregor had discovered about the working range of the drones and that the Banknock community fire station was the only place in range with

118

a radio tower and Wi-Fi transmitter capable of sending signals to the drones.

When Simon had finished, Strachan sat silent, as though digesting the news that a loved one had just died. When he spoke, his voice was a whisper almost as gentle and foreign as that of the giant who had led them into the room.

'Are you alleging that this attack was orchestrated from a fire station? And that the press are following this as a line for a story?'

Connor felt a guilty pang of pleasure. He had been counting on this – Strachan's natural fear of bad headlines could be useful, especially if he thought Connor had the journalists in question in his pocket. 'Don't worry,' he said. 'We're working with the journalists involved, and they've promised to keep this out of the public domain for the moment. But we need your help, sir. We need to find out who's doing this. If you could get Banknock to run an inventory check on their drones, see if there's anything missing? And I'm guessing there would be broadcast logs for the radio tower and Wi-Fi routers. Could you check them as well, see if anything unusual happened at the time of the attack?'

Strachan put his hands on the table, pushed himself back. He gave Connor a cool, impassive stare, then nodded, as though he had reached a conclusion. 'Ford was right about you,' he said.

'Sorry, sir?' Connor asked, not sure he wanted to hear the answer.

'He said you were ballsy. Determined, talented, but ballsy. Barging into a police investigation, pulling favours, asking me to investigate my own officers. Christ, I almost wish it was me you'd taken a swing at at Alloa House.'

Connor flinched back as though Strachan had reached across the table and slapped him. 'Alloa House?' he said, his mind racing back to another case, another fire.

'Yes. You remember, don't you, Fraser?' Strachan said, his voice as cold as his eyes. 'It was a couple of years ago. You were providing security for someone there, and a fire got out of hand. My men intervened to put the fire out, and you grabbed one of them by the throat. I wish it had been me. It wouldn't have gone so easily for you.'

Connor felt anger prickle across the back of his neck as his shoulders bunched at Strachan's implied threat. Sensed rather than saw Simon shift uneasily in his seat.

'I can only apologise, sir,' he said, his voice flat and emotionless. 'It was a fraught situation, and the officer I grabbed caught me unawares. In the heat of the moment, I thought I was being attacked. Now, that aside, will you help us with this, or would you prefer to give your answers to the press?'

A cold smile twisted across Strachan's face. It was a smile that told Connor he would remember this encounter – and one day he would seek revenge for it. 'I'll help you, if only to prove this has nothing to do with the fire service,' he said. 'In the meantime, Mr Fraser, I suggest you get back to Stirling, and stay out of my way until I get in touch.'

CHAPTER 29

Donna sat in the small room she had converted into a study at the rear of the flat, listening to the sound of Andrew's laughter as he played with his grandparents in the living room. When she had asked her mum to watch him for a couple of hours as she worked, she had been forced to do the well-worn dance with her: first, the recriminations over the demands of her job and all the times it took her away from her son, then the remonstrations that 'Neither your father nor I are getting any younger, and Andrew is a handful now that's he's older.' And, finally, Donna's personal favourite; the sucking of teeth, the grudging accept-ance, her mother's struggle to keep her delight at seeing her grandson out of her eyes. Andrew was due to start school in a couple of months' time and, as guilty as it made her feel, Donna found she couldn't wait.

She had her laptop open, and was logged into the databases of Sky and the *Western Chronicle*, the Glasgow-based paper she'd worked at before she'd fallen pregnant with Andrew. She wasn't meant to have the log-in, but had pulled in a few favours and made promises of shar-ing stories in the future to get it. And, as she had found, she needed it. Sky had only really increased its presence in Scotland over the last couple of years, mostly thanks to the stories Donna had managed to break, which meant that their library of stories based north of the Border before that time was somewhat threadbare.

Luckily enough, the old morgues at the *Western Chronicle* were anything but.

After speaking to Doug and Connor, and reluctantly agreeing to Connor's plan, they had decided that she would take the *Westie*'s coverage while Doug would focus on what his old paper, the Edinburgh-based *Capital Tribune*, had run on the Harbour Street fire. She knew that Connor had already had his man at Sentinel, Robbie Lindsay, skim the newspaper headlines at the time and had the bones of the story. The hope was that he had missed something, some nuance in the reporting or the details that Doug or Donna would spot.

At first glance, the fire seemed as straightforward as it was reported. Just after 3 p.m. on 9 August 2011, firefighters at the Spaven Street station in the south side of Glasgow had been alerted to a fire at the old Mason Brothers warehouses on the Harbour Street industrial estate. As it was the closest station, both fire engines had been dispatched, along with the station commander at the time, now Chief Fire Officer Arthur MacAlister. When the firefighters arrived, they found that the eight-storey building was engulfed in flame, the fire having started on the fourth floor and quickly devoured the industrial cleaning chemicals that were being stored in the warehouse. It wasn't long before the fire hit the headlines, partly because the thick, black smoke belching from the warehouse was caught by the summer winds and whipped towards the M8, the main motorway that cuts through the heart of Glasgow and encircles the city, like a diseased artery. Roads were closed and nearby homes evacuated, with other firefighters from several stations around Glasgow called in. And still the blaze raged on, angry and defiant, burning through the day and scorching itself into the memories of everyone who saw it.

'"It looked like a scene straight from Hell,"' Donna read in a quote from an eyewitness in one of the stories the *Westie* had run. 'The whole building was engulfed. Those firefighters tried their best, but who the hell thought it would be a good idea to store chemicals like that in an old warehouse?'

At some point, the alarm was raised that a night-watchman and a two-man security team who patrolled the industrial estate were unaccounted for. This left MacAlister with no choice but to send in firefighters to check the building for casualties.

And that was when it had all gone wrong.

The statement issued by the fire service after the event was typically terse and clipped, but Donna had seen enough death notices to read between the lines.

> While attending a well-established blaze at a premises in Harbour Street, firefighters entered the building to engage in life-saving search-and-rescue operations. During this operation, several sections of the building's substructure collapsed, and three firefighters, along with four members of the public were seriously injured. One firefighter died in the building, while the four members of the public, who were heroically led to safety by our firefighters, and two crew members from Harbour Street subsequently succumbed to their injuries. We will not be releasing the names of the deceased until their families have been informed.

Donna flicked forward to another story, two days after the fire. 'DEATH BLAZE FIREFIGHTERS NAMED,' the headline shouted in bold capitals, with the story running below.

> Three firefighters who died in the blaze which engulfed a warehouse on Harbour Street were last night named by Strathclyde Fire and Rescue. Firefighters George Logan and Derek MacRae died from injuries sustained while searching the Harbour Street warehouse, while crew manager Michael Lawson was trapped in the blaze and perished at the scene.
>
> The news comes a day after it was confirmed that three members of staff from the Harbour Street estate, Paul Fairlie, Richard Lamont and Evelyn Geddes, were killed in the fire, which brought central Glasgow to a standstill. The identity of a fourth victim has yet to be established.

Donna skimmed the rest of the article, which was mostly biographical details of those who had died, followed by glowing testimonials from their commanding officer, MacAlister, and Father Donnelly. She forced herself to slow down as she read his words.

> These brave firefighters were doing the Lord's work and made the ultimate sacrifice for their fellow man. We can only honour their sacrifice by holding them in our thoughts and our prayers, and I will commit myself to ensuring these deaths are not in vain. The fire service is a family, and today that family is united in grief. But through that grief, there will be a healing. And a resurrection.

Donna rocked back in her chair, bit her lip. Growing up, her parents had been at best lukewarm to religion, and attendance at church was a rare event, mostly triggered by marriages or funerals. She guessed Donnelly's words were standard for a man who had devoted himself to the service of God, but there was a tone in the language that bothered her, something that . . .

She flicked back to one of the reports from the night of the fire, and one of the most iconic images of the night. It was obvious the shot had been taken from a telephoto lens, by a photographer who was being kept away from the fire by a police cordon. It was a landscape shot, two ambulances in the forefront, the warehouse standing behind them, like a huge, burning effigy, billowing smoke and capering flames forever frozen in the flare of a flash.

In front of the ambulances paramedics crowded around two stretchers. On the stretcher to the right, Donna could see a pair of heavy boots dangling off the end, the cuffs of the legs rimmed with the distinctive fluorescent piping of a firefighter's uniform. Stooped over the body, obscuring any view of the wounded man, Father Donnelly had his back to the camera, his head turned to one of the paramedics, showing his profile. He was wearing overalls similar to those of the firefighters around him, the shoulders smeared with smoke and falling ash from the blaze. 'TENDING THE SICK', the caption below the photograph read. 'Father John Donnelly ministers to a wounded firefighter as he is treated for his injuries at the Harbour Street blaze in Glasgow.'

Donna studied the image for a second. Like Donnelly's statement, something about it disturbed her, like the sound of an off-key piano or an old-fashioned record played at the wrong speed. Something about the pose, something . . .

The fire service is a family.

She shook her head, scrolled on through the rest of the stories. Had just felt the first snarls of a headache that was part concentration and part frustration that she was wasting her time when she hit another story that made her jump up and lean forward in her chair. She had almost missed it, would have if she hadn't kept her search dates so open.

It was a small story at the bottom of an inside page of the *Westie*, what would have been called an 'anchor' back in the day.

'FUNERAL HELD FOR FINAL HARBOUR ST VICTIM', the headline read.

Donna read through the article, felt her heart begin to hammer in her chest as the sour thrill of adrenalin coated the back of her throat. She stopped, reread the article, then skimmed back to the article with Donnelly's quote.

Through that grief, there will be a healing. And a resurrection.

She leant back in her chair, staring at the screen. She had started this looking for answers, had found nothing but more questions.

But at least, she thought, they were the right questions. And she knew exactly who she needed to put them to.

CHAPTER 30

Paulie had always hated his hands. Or, more specifically, his fingers. They were blunt, dull things, twisted and scarred by a lifetime of manual labour and fights in which boxing gloves were never used and rules were rarely applied. But that wasn't what bothered him. Paulie had little concern for his physical appearance. He was what he was, would never be one of those wankers, like Fraser, who spent hours in the gym trying to sculpt the body beautiful, or agonising about his haircut or his skin routine.

No, the reason he hated his hands was that in shape, size and, yes, their ability to inflict pain they reminded Paulie of his dad. Paul King Senior had been a cruel, abusive husband and a worse father, all too eager to vent his drunken fury at the disappointments and failings of his life on Paulie or his mum. Over the years, the beatings Paulie had endured had blurred together into one miserable kaleidoscope that coalesced on one image: his father's hands, either balled into fists or wrapped around his mother's throat.

Paulie had put a stop to the beatings when he was seventeen with a baseball bat to his father's jaw and a vow that, if he ever touched him or his mother again, Paulie would kill him. His father must have seen the intent in his son's eyes because he never again raised a hand to either of them before he died of a heart attack four years later. But his legacy lived on in the shape of his son's hands and the capacity for violence he had beaten into him.

Paulie shook himself from his thoughts, focused on the present. Took his hands from under the tap, then turned it off, the sound of hitching, whimpering breaths rushing in to fill the sudden silence. He grabbed a handful of paper towels from the dispenser by the sink, dried his hands as he hunkered down beside the snivelling man propped up against the corner of the toilet, legs splayed out, his chest a bib of blood that gushed from his nose and mouth, the same blood Paulie was now rubbing off his hands.

'Now, Danny, let's try that again, shall we?' Paulie asked. 'Try not to be a daft cunt this time, eh?'

Danny nodded, like a puppy desperate to please its master, his eyes huge, tear-streaked orbs in his face. They were in the toilets of Leggatt's, a small, out-of-the-way bar a five-minute walk from Stirling railway station. It was what Paulie's father would have called an old man's pub, all heavy wood furniture, stained carpets that seemed to suck at your feet as you walked and upholstery that would have looked tired and out of date in the seventies. It was also the preferred watering-hole of Danny 'Ding Dong' Moffatt. A former burglar and safe-cracker, Danny had settled into the role of fixer and middle man for anyone involved in shady dealings across central Scotland. From prostitutes and drugs, to semi-automatic weapons and fake passports, it was well known that a call to Danny would sort it out for you. Hence the nickname – Danny Ding Dong; all you had to do was give him a bell and he would see to your needs. At a cost.

When Fraser had told Paulie about his problems, Danny was the first person Paulie had thought of. With his web of contacts, if someone had come into Stirling looking to take Fraser's head, Danny would know. So, he had headed for Leggatt's, found Danny at his usual table, and received a curt 'Fuck off, Paulie,' when he had asked if anyone had been enquiring about Connor Fraser or Jen MacKenzie.

Unperturbed, Paulie had shrugged, leant back, then grabbed Danny by the neck and hauled him into the toilets. He had no qualms about doing this – the last thing that anyone in Leggatt's wanted was the police showing up at the bar. He had thrown Danny into the Gents, bounced him off a wall, then rabbit-punched him in the face twice, the sound of his nose snapping almost musical as it ricocheted off the tiled walls.

'So, Danny,' he said again, ignoring the ache in his knees as he hunkered down, 'why so rude to me when I asked about Connor Fraser? That name mean something to you? Someone been in asking about him?'

Danny wiped at his streaming nose with his left hand, blood smearing across his face like lurid lipstick. 'Please, Paulie,' he said, the words coming out in a rush, 'ah cannae tell you. It's more than my life's worth.'

'Your life?' Paulie mused. 'Look around you, Danny. How much do you think your life's worth at the moment? And how much worse do you think it's going to get if you don't tell me what I want to know?'

Danny's eyes darted from Paulie's face to his hands, which he was slowly curling into fists. 'You know I'll hurt you, Danny. So talk. Who's been asking about Fraser? And what did they want? Did you tool them up?'

Danny's eyes moved frantically over Paulie's shoulder, as though searching for the cavalry charging to his aid. Then he closed his eyes and sighed, blood bubbling from his ruined mouth as he did so.

'They find out I talked, I'm fucked, okay, Paulie? What I'm about to tell you, you didn't hear from me, okay? And I never want to see you again after this, deal?'

'Aye,' Paulie muttered, a mixture of frustration and weariness suddenly settling over him. 'Just tell me what you know.'

'Okay,' Danny said, his voice flattened by resignation. Slowly, he started speaking. Paulie recognised the names he mentioned, wondered how they related to Connor, and the threat to Jen MacKenzie.

CHAPTER 31

It took Donna just over an hour to drive from Stirling to Elderslie, a small village to the west of Glasgow. She remembered the town from her time at the *Westie*, had written a few stories about it when she was on the crime beat there and local properties had been the focus of drugs raids to seize heroin, cocaine and some controlled prescription drugs. Nothing new for small-town Scotland, she thought. The location changed, but the main story, of drugs, unemployment and poor life chances remained. And, judging by some of the stories Donna had seen on the wires recently, the pandemic had done nothing to improve that tired old script.

She drove on, a stone and bronze monument seeming to glow in the warm sun at the top of a gentle hill on her left. With a tall, thin spire that jutted into the sky from an ornate stone base, Donna was briefly reminded of the Mercat Cross in Lenton Barns. She knew the monument was a memorial to the birthplace of William Wallace, who had fought for Scottish independence in the thirteenth century, and whose victory over the English at Stirling Bridge was immortalised on a much larger scale at the Stirling Wallace Monument. It was a towering, Gothic structure that loomed over the Stirling skyline from Abbey Craig, like some giant dagger stabbed into the hills as a warning to anyone who would dare try another invasion. After her discovery in the *Westie*'s library, Donna couldn't help but wonder if Wallace was the only connection between Stirling and Elderslie that she would find.

She turned off the main road as her satnav ordered, into a narrow residential street lined with privet hedges, neatly maintained wooden fences and rows of houses that looked as if they had been built for durability – or a siege.

Donna pulled up in front of a neat, detached house that was encased in scaffolding as a team of workers painted the harled walls an industrial white and scuttled around the roof, another confirmation that she was in the right place. When she had called the owner of the house, she had been given two instructions; turn right off the road at the Wallace Monument, and look for the house being worked on.

She gathered up her notes, checked her phone one last time. When she had found the story in the *Westie* archives that had led her here, she had called Doug, told him of her discovery. It didn't sit easily with her, sharing a line on a story was almost heresy to any reporter, but if she was to be part of the bigger story Doug was trying to tell, she would play along with him. So, she had called him, told him what she had found, and her plan to visit Elderslie. To her surprise, he had rejected her offer of joining her on the trip, saying only that he 'had another line to follow up'.

Donna shook her head and got out of the car. She knew what she was doing – stalling. The death knock, calling on the family of someone who had just died looking for comment, was an ordeal every trainee journalist went through. Sometimes editors sent junior reporters just to see if they were cut out for the raw, exposed edge of journalism, where you probed the bereaved for a soundbite. Sometimes they sent them out as an act of petty malice. Donna had hated death knocks, but knew they could be valuable, giving those who were mourning a way to articulate their grief, anger and pain.

Which, she wondered, would she find behind the door at the end of the garden path?

The door was answered before the bell had finished ringing, leaving Donna face to face with a tall, almost ethereal woman with a crown of steel-grey hair and blue eyes so pale they were almost translucent.

'Mrs Turnbull?' Donna said. 'I'm Donna Blake, we spoke on the phone earlier on, about Peter.'

Something less than a smile but more than a grimace danced across the woman's face, making her seem both older and younger at the same time.

'Ah, yes, the reporter,' she said. 'Come in, please.'

Donna nodded her thanks, followed the woman into the house and along a long corridor. The smell of fresh paint and tar filled the air, causing Donna to cough involuntarily and Mrs Turnbull to turn to face her.

'Sorry, this work's being going on so long now that I've forgotten it's happening,' she said. 'Come on, we'll sit in the garden. It's a nice day, and we can get a bit of fresh air while we're at it. Would you like some tea?'

'No, thank you, Mrs Turnbull,' Donna replied. 'I don't want to take up much of your time. I just had a few questions about Peter.'

Mrs Turnbull's head tilted to the side as her lips pursed, as though she hadn't heard the name Peter for some time. 'It's fine,' she said. 'All I have is time these days, dear. And, please, call me Caroline.'

Without waiting for a reply, she turned and began walking down the hall again. At the end, she opened a door to reveal a large, airy living room, the back wall of which was dominated by two floor-to-ceiling patio doors. She paused beside an oversized armchair, scooped up what looked to Donna like a large, leather-bound book, then got moving again, the patio doors sighing slightly on their runners as she threw them open and stepped out onto a porch. Donna arrived at the doors just in time to see Caroline descend a surprisingly steep flight of stairs into a garden that looked as if it was being prepared for a 'garden of the year' show with a lush, neatly cut lawn and flowerbeds packed with brightly coloured flowers in rich, dark earth.

She followed Caroline to a table and chairs on an oasis of concrete in the middle of the lawn, nodded her thanks as she took the seat the woman indicated. Caroline watched her get comfortable, then slid into the chair opposite. She was older than Donna had first thought, the sunlight showing her hair to be finer, and a good deal whiter, than the gloom of the hallway had at first suggested. She was slim, almost emaciated, with high, sharp cheekbones and a thin, almost predatory nose. But there was kindness in her eyes, and a quiet patience that Donna found at once comforting and unnerving.

'So, you said you wanted to talk to me about Peter?' Caroline said, her soft, almost lyrical accent hinting at a heritage that had little to do with the West Coast of Scotland.

'Ah, yes, yes, I did,' Donna said. 'You see, I found the article on his death while I was doing some research and, as the last victim of the Harbour Street fire, I wondered if there was anything you could tell me about him or what happened that night.'

'I'm sure there are more knowledgeable people out there to help you with that, dear,' Caroline said, as her fingers traced the spine of the book she held. 'Peter was just a good man in the wrong place at the wrong time, and he paid too high a price for it.'

Donna nodded. The story she had found was a small piece, its importance diminished by time and a news cycle that thrived on fresh headlines and stories. It had referred to Peter Turnbull as the last victim of the Harbour Street fire. Based at the Carrigan Street fire station on the outer edges of Glasgow, he had been just another firefighter called in as the fire intensified and threatened to rage out of control. According to the records Donna had managed to track down, he was a well-regarded career firefighter, heavily involved in community events and charity work. What interested Donna about Firefighter Peter Turnbull was that he wasn't included in the initial count of the seven people who had lost their lives in the Harbour Street fire of 2011.

The reason being that Peter Turnbull had died only last month.

The article reported that Peter Turnbull, fifty-four, had passed away peacefully at St Margaret's Care Home in West Lothian. He had been a resident there since suffering life-changing injuries at the infamous Harbour Street fire in Glasgow in 2011. Turnbull was survived by his elder sister, Caroline, who had worked as an administrator for the Firefighters' Association, the charity for those who had served.

'I'm sorry if this is painful,' Donna said slowly, taking a notepad from her bag. 'As I said on the phone, I'm doing a piece on the fire service, and I wanted to mention some of the brave men and women who gave their lives in the line of duty, just as Peter did, tell their stories.'

Caroline Turnbull gave a strange, empty smile, almost as though she could see the lie in Donna's words. She took a deep breath, her hands tightening on the book she held.

'Well, there's not much to tell, Ms Blake,' she said, her voice firm and even as she spoke over the low hum of work being conducted on her home. 'We're from a long line of firefighters, you see. Our grandfather and father were both in the service.' A forlorn smile haunted her lips for a moment. 'Obviously, female firefighters were frowned upon when I was of the age to sign up, but I found an admin position and later moved into the firefighters' charity. Peter joined up as soon as he left school, did his basic training then was assigned to Carrigan Street. He could have been promoted many times over, always refused. He wanted to be a firefighter, simple as that.'

Donna nodded, scribbled some notes, her eyes straying back to the book Caroline was clasping to her chest. 'So what happened at Harbour Street?' she asked. 'Did they tell you? How was Peter hurt?'

Caroline gave Donna an indulgent smile, as though she was a child who had just asked why water was wet or the sky was blue.

'They told me a little,' she said. 'He and his crew were called in when things were getting bad at Harbour Street. Peter was assigned to search-and-rescue operations, something to do with missing security personnel at the site. Anyway, as he was searching, the roof above him gave way, and he was trapped in the building as it burnt.' She closed her eyes. Shuddered, as though someone had just poured vinegar over an old wound that was not fully healed.

'They got him out eventually,' she said at last, her voice wizened and husked now. 'But the damage had been done. He'd suffered third-degree burns over thirty per cent of his body, with some fourth-degree burns as well. His oxygen failed, so he also took in a lot of smoke, which scorched his lungs and deprived his brain of oxygen for an extended period. They did their best for him, we all did, but he was never the same. We got him into St Margaret's, a wonderful residential place that specialises in treating burns victims. I think,' she gave a weak smile, 'I think he was happy in his way. I visited him as often as I could, but eventually his body just gave up. He contracted pneumonia and God decided to end his suffering and take him home.'

Donna looked up at the mention of God, Father Donnelly's words flashing across her mind. 'God,' she said tentatively, as though stepping on thin ice and gauging how much of her weight it would take. 'Was faith important to Peter?'

'Oh, yes,' Caroline said, defiance flashing into her eyes. 'It is to both of us. I know it's unfashionable, these days, with all this focus on individual expression and deciding who and what you are for yourself, but Peter and I were raised in the Church. And the Church was a great friend to us through his trials. It was Father Donnelly who arranged for Peter to be transferred to St Margaret's, who ensured he received the last rites.' A smile softened her face again. 'Not that he needed them at the end, of course.'

'Why?' Donna asked, suddenly noticing the ornate golden inlay on the spine of the book Caroline held.

Caroline chuckled. 'Because he'd already been given the last rites, Ms Blake,' she said. 'He'd been absolved of his sins when they dragged him out of the Harbour Street fire. It was Father Donnelly who gave him the last rites when they thought he was going to die at the scene. But he lived, thanks to the grace of God, and he was sinless from then on. After all, what type of sin could a man confined to a hospital bed, a man who was brain damaged and barely aware of his surroundings, possibly commit?'

'None,' Donna said, the word feeling heavy and alien in her mouth. 'None at all.'

CHAPTER 32

Connor's experience, both as a police officer and since he had quit the force, told him that a summons to a police station from a senior officer was never a good thing. When the officer in question was DCI Malcolm Ford, and the summons took the form of a gruff, two-sentence command, 'Randolphfield in one hour. Don't be late,' he knew he was in trouble.

How much trouble became clear when he pulled into the car park at the police headquarters and saw a large SUV branded with the Scottish Fire and Rescue logo parked in a visitor's bay.

'Shit,' he said softly, suddenly wishing he had agreed to Simon's suggestion to accompany him.

He made his way into the reception area, was met there by DS Troughton.

'They're waiting for you in the conference room,' Troughton said, by way of a greeting, then turned and walked off, leaving Connor to follow him. They made their way to the third floor, Troughton stopping at a door, knocking, then opening it and gesturing for Connor to enter. He thanked Troughton as he passed him, got a look he guessed was usually reserved for pet-killers and politicians.

'Fraser,' Ford said, from the head of the large conference table that dominated the room, 'take a seat. I believe you already know Assistant Chief Officer Strachan.'

'Of course,' Connor said, settling into a seat opposite the firefighter, who was sitting to Ford's right, the neutrality of his expression only accentuating the fury in his eyes. 'We spoke earlier on today, in Kirkcaldy. I'm guessing that's why I'm here now.'

'Why you're here,' Ford said softly as he leant forward in his chair, 'is to help us try to make sense of the shit sandwich you've served up to both of us.'

Connor ignored Ford's dig as he felt excitement pulse across the back of his neck. 'You found something at the station in Banknock?' he asked. 'The drones used in the church attack did come from there?'

Strachan's cheek twitched, and Connor could have sworn he heard the firefighter's teeth grind together.

'Before I say anything, I want to make a few things clear, okay? First, I don't like you Fraser. You attacked one of my men on the job, which makes you shit in my eyes. But, whatever the hell is going on, you seem to be at the centre of it. And since it affects my service and the police, I need you. But we,' he gestured between himself and Ford with one blunt, callused finger, 'call the shots. Malcolm has agreed not to exclude you from the investigation as a person of interest for the moment. But if you mess us about, or any of what we discuss gets back to your friends in the press, he will end you. Clear?'

Connor glanced at Ford, whose eyes were chips of flint in a face that looked like an expressionist carving of exhaustion. 'That's the deal, Fraser,' he said. 'I know you have family wrapped up in this, but this could fuck up a lot of people, so we need to be in control, agreed?'

'Control?' Connor snapped, then forced himself to take a breath. The truth was, none of them was in control. The person pulling the strings, the person who had paid Connor to protect Father Donnelly, then burnt alive an innocent man to send a message, they were in control. But to find that person, Connor needed Ford and Strachan, so he would play along.

For now.

'Agreed,' he said, his gaze returning to Strachan. 'So, tell me, what did you find? Did the drones come from Banknock station or not?'

Strachan exchanged a glance with Ford, then dragged in front of him a laptop from across the table.

'Yes and no,' he said. 'I ordered a full inventory check at Banknock.

They normally have three drones stationed there as, given the rural location, they have to survey a large area of land, and the thermal-imaging cameras are useful for tracking wildfires or some idiot who went for a walk in the hills in shorts and a T-shirt. The inventory check showed that all drones were present and accounted for, and the service logs show they were maintained as normal at the start of the month.'

'Okay,' Connor said. 'That covers the no. What about the yes?'

Strachan sighed, as though he had just lost an argument with himself. 'I asked the duty officer to check the broadcast logs for the Wi-Fi router and the antenna at the station,' he said, 'and during the times of the attack on the church at Lenton Barns, the Wi-Fi and the radio transmitter showed increased broadcast activity.'

Connor blinked, took a moment to let what Strachan had just told him sink in, looked at Ford, who nodded confirmation – he had come to the same conclusion as well.

'You're telling me the drones didn't come from Banknock, but someone controlled them from there?' Connor said.

Strachan's jaw worked again, the soft sound of his teeth grinding together making Connor wince. 'Yes,' he said. 'That's what it looks like. I checked the logs, and the CCTV footage from the station broadcast centre, and no one was near the transmitters at the time. So . . .'

'So someone hacked the fire station and used it as a transmitter,' Connor said. 'But hold on. Police frequencies are encrypted to prevent false broadcasts. Aren't fire-station broadcasts and frequencies similarly protected?'

Strachan's eyes narrowed, as though Connor has just offered him a mouldy piece of fruit and invited him to take as big a bite as he could. 'Yes,' he said slowly. 'I pulled perimeter CCTV for the station because we found this.'

He turned the laptop in front of him to Connor. On the screen a freeze frame from a CCTV camera showed a narrow, rutted road that was lined on one side with trees. The forefront of the images was taken up by a thick ribbon of what Connor guessed was brickwork – the perimeter wall of the fire station. At the corner of the image sat a battered red car, possibly an old-style Volkswagen Polo. Connor leant forward and checked the timestamp on the image. It matched the time of the attack on the church.

'You're telling me someone parked outside the station, on what, from the look of it, is a quiet country lane, then hacked into the transmitters to control the drones that attacked the church? Who could do that, other than a . . .' He trailed off, as the answer hit him.

'Yes,' Ford said. 'The only person who could pull that off would be a technical genius or . . .'

'A firefighter,' Connor said, thoughts crashing into his mind like a storm-whipped sea slamming into a shore.

'So, Mr Fraser,' Strachan said, 'you need to tell us everything. Now. Why would a firefighter want to kill John Donnelly? And why would they want to make you part of their plan?'

Connor blinked, tried to slow the kaleidoscope of thoughts that was churning through his mind, making it difficult to think. 'I don't know,' he admitted, hating the note of defeat in his voice. 'But you said it yourself, this all seems to centre on Donnelly. I've got my people looking into him, seeing if there's any link between us that might give a clue as to why I've been targeted.'

'You realise you're getting very close to interfering in a live police investigation with stuff like that, don't you?' Ford asked.

Connor held Ford's gaze. 'Anything on the man who was burnt to death in the cab?' he asked. It was a classic policeman's trick – when the interview wasn't going the way you wanted, change the topic of conversation, throw the interviewee off-guard. The tight, sour smile that pulled across Ford's face told Connor that the policeman recognised the tactic for the distraction it was.

'Nothing yet. VIN number confirms it was a commercial taxi, registered to a firm that has one of the big contracts to service the railway station in town. Drummond is running them down, seeing who was on call with that cab, see if we can get a name.'

Connor nodded. It made sense, but he had a nagging sense that they would find nothing important. The taxi had been torched by the killer as a way of illustrating his power over them all. He had threatened to kill a police officer, then snatched a taxi driver and burnt him alive with a police hat on the roof of the cab as a message – and a taunt. *I can do what I want, and make you look like idiots as I do it,* the hat said. The killing was a message, nothing more, a message that, again, put John Donnelly at the centre of whatever was going on.

'And now we've got that out of the way,' Ford said, 'let me remind you, Fraser, this is an official police inquiry. One man is dead, another has been threatened and an attempt was made on his life. You're a material witness, and intimately connected to all of this. I appreciate your help, but you cannot interfere in an active investigation. Christ,' he sighed, as though he had just got to his favourite pub as last orders were called, 'if we ever get our hands on this bastard, I need a prosecutable case, one that's not been derailed by you going cowboy on me.'

Connor felt a surge of irritation, swallowed it. If he was being honest with himself, he knew Ford was right. But, still . . .

'Sir,' he said. 'I was at the centre of this the moment that sick bastard took pictures of my gran and Jen. But whatever's going on, whoever is doing this, I promise I'll find them and you'll be the first people to know when I do.'

Ford's objection died on his lips as Connor's phone chirped in his pocket. He gave the policeman an apologetic nod, fished out his phone, a mixture of curiosity and unease churning in his gut. After the last couple of days, messages could be promises of impending doom or fleeting glimpses of hope. What was this one going to be?

He smiled as he read the contact on the message, almost laughed as he realised he was actually glad to see the name.

'If there's nothing else, sir,' Connor said, rising from his chair, 'I have work to do. I promise I'll keep in touch and won't cross any lines that might cause either of you, ah, embarrassment.'

Ford exchanged a glance with Strachan, then gestured for the door with a grunt. Connor didn't push it – they all knew he'd do anything and everything he could to find whoever was behind this madness. And the justice he would deliver would have little to do with a courtroom.

CHAPTER 33

They arranged to meet at the Albert Halls, a large sandstone and lime-stone concert venue a few minutes from the centre of Stirling. Paulie was lumbering around the car park in front of the halls when Connor arrived, studying the selection of vehicles in front of him with a look of disdain that the sunglasses he was wearing did nothing to disguise.

'Looking for a new ride?' Connor asked as he approached Paulie, flicking his phone to silent as he did so. When dealing with Paulie King, it was better to give him your full attention.

'Fuck off,' Paulie spat. 'Nothing here fit for the scrappy, let alone driving.' He glanced across the car park to the dark foliage that shrouded the hill leading up to the castle. 'Let's take a walk. You can buy me a drink at the Portcullis.'

They headed for the Back Walk, which followed the old city walls up towards Stirling Castle and the Portcullis pub. Shaded from the sun by a line of trees, the walkway was quiet, peaceful, with only a few tourists and dog-walkers to disturb their privacy.

'Your text said you'd found something,' Connor said, as he fell into step with Paulie. 'What was it?'

'I found that you've got a knack for pissing off all the wrong people,' Paulie said, as he wiped a thin line of sweat from his top lip.

'I'll take that as a compliment,' Connor said. 'But this isn't just about me, Paulie, it's—'

'I know,' Paulie snapped. 'Jen's the only reason I'm here. What

– you think I've nothing better to do than take scenic walks with you? I'm here for Jen, nothing else.'

'I appreciate it,' Connor said, the words thick and heavy on his tongue. 'But, please, what did you find?'

Paulie swiped at another bead of sweat, this one trickling from his thick bristle of hair down his temple. 'You ever hear the name Tom McGovern?' he asked.

Connor stopped dead, his mind filling with thoughts of Doug McGregor. 'Tom McGovern, the property developer? Came to my attention in relation to another matter yesterday. Why? What the hell's he got to do with this?'

'Seems some of his, ah, associates, have expressed an interest in you,' Paulie said. 'I spoke to, ah,' he grunted, as though laughing at a private joke, 'ah, an acquaintance of mine. Deals in everything from gossip to guns. If a contract had been taken out on you, Ding Dong would have heard about it.'

Connor felt his chest tighten. 'And?' he asked.

'Nothing official,' Paulie said. 'Though he did mention that some boys who have done work for McGovern in the past had been asking about you, background, family, connections, that sort of thing.'

Family, Connor thought, the pictures of Jen and his gran rearing up before his eyes. He blinked. Pushed them aside. 'You said these guys had done work for McGovern in the past. What type of work?'

Paulie stopped, turned to Connor. 'McGovern came up through the buildings trade in the late eighties and nineties. What type of work do you think? He may be all Mr Success now, but Tom McGovern was as hard as the nails he used to drive into walls. If someone wouldn't sell him a piece of land he wanted to develop or an old building he wanted to renovate, his boys would pay them a visit. And on those visits, they would take some of their tools of the trade to, ah, force their point home. Don't know if they went as far as actually offing someone, but I know his crew were no strangers to breaking bones and threatening loved ones to get what they wanted.'

Connor's thoughts raced, trying to make this new information gel with what he already knew. But it was like trying to put together a puzzle with no idea of what the finished product was meant to look like: there were just too many blanks to fill in. 'When did they ask for this background on me?' he asked.

Paulie shrugged. 'Ding Dong said they approached him about a week ago. Asked for background on you, along with any enemies you might have. Makes sense, I guess, to rattle the local trees and see what falls out about you, but still . . .'

'What?' Connor asked, the vague shape of Paulie's thoughts forming in his mind.

'Well, it's a noisy way to do it,' Paulie said. 'If I was coming for you, or thought you were a threat, I'd do it quietly. Not ask the local talent all about you. Risks getting back to you, doesn't it? Puts you on your guard.'

'Yeah,' Connor agreed, even as a thought tugged at his mind. He pushed it aside. 'What about Jen and my gran? You said they asked about family. Did they—'

Paulie held up a shovel-like hand. 'I dealt with it, okay? Ding Dong's going to put word around that Jen and your gran are off limits. I don't give a shit if someone takes a pop at you, but civilians are not on. I mean, who targets an auld woman and a young lassie for Christ's sake?'

Old Bitch, Young Slut, Connor thought, remembering the names given to the pictures he had been sent with the contract he had been forced to sign.

He sighed, and Paulie seemed to read the frustration in the gesture.

'I dunno what shite you've stepped in, Fraser,' he said, as he adjusted his sunglasses, 'but firebombing a church and threatening your family doesn't seem like McGovern's style to me. I only know him by reputation, but he seems like an old-school bribe-and-intimidate kind of a guy. Whatever's going on, whatever he's asking about you for, I cannae see how it ties in to the church and what happened yesterday. And don't gawp at me like that. I watch the bloody news, and I'd recognise that rocket you drive anywhere. Should have known you'd be at the heart of any chaos in or around Stirling.'

Despite himself, Connor smiled. 'Thanks for this, Paulie,' he said. 'I owe you one.'

Paulie stiffened, as though Connor's gratitude stung him. 'I did this for Jen, not you,' he rumbled, and turned away, looking up the hill. 'Fuck it,' he said. 'Too bloody hot for this. And I've got a reputation to think of – don't want to be seen drinking with the likes of you. You can owe me.'

Connor kept his face neutral, trying not to express the relief he felt as he watched Paulie lumber back down the hill towards the Albert Halls. 'No problem,' he said. 'Got a date with a reporter anyway.'

CHAPTER 34

After declining Connor's offer to accompany him to his meeting with DCI Ford, Simon had decided to head back out to Lenton Barns. He knew the church and Father Donnelly were under police guard, a guard that would have been tightened following the discovery of the burnt-out taxi and its murdered driver but, still, there was something about the place, and the priest, that was pulling at him.

He was just passing the Mercat Cross in the village when his phone pinged on the dashboard.

'Hello?'

'Simon, it's Donna. How you doing?'

Simon broke into a smile. He knew Donna had caused Connor a few problems over the years with the stories she covered and the way she attacked them, but Simon had to admit that he liked her fierce independence, quick wit and the inexhaustible energy she showed when working a big story. He knew, after watching her during long, tense hours, that she hid a lot of her insecurities behind bravado and bluff, got the feeling she was as much a victim of imposter syndrome and self-doubt as he was. But still she powered on. He respected that, almost as much as he admired her camera-ready appearance. Shallow, he knew, but, as his grandfather would always tell him, he was only human.

'Donna, hiya. I'm dodging away. How's you?' he asked as he spotted a space and drew in outside a small, freshly painted butcher's shop.

'Not bad, Simon,' she replied, sounding distracted, as though she was only half listening to his voice. 'Look, I'm trying to get in touch with Connor, but his phone keeps diverting to voicemail. You know where he is?'

'Said he had an appointment this morning,' Simon lied. Rule one, never tell a reporter too much, on or off the record. 'Should be around later on, though. Anything I can help you with in the meantime?'

'Hmm, maybe,' Donna replied. 'I did that digging Connor asked for - you know, into the Harbour Street fire - found something that might be interesting.'

Simon sat up straighter in the driver's seat. 'Go on,' he said.

He listened as Donna told him what she had found out about Peter Turnbull, the firefighter who had survived the Harbour Street blaze, and his connection to Father Donnelly.

'You think it's important?' she said, after she had finished.

'Dunno,' Simon said, staring out of the windscreen. 'But it could be helpful, especially in getting the good Father Donnelly to open up a bit about what the hell is going on.'

'You think he knows more than he's letting on?'

Simon thought back to his first meeting with Donnelly, in his study at the presbytery. The nervous way he toyed with the scar on his chin as he spoke. And what was it he had said? *I cannot think of anyone who would consider me an enemy.*

'Definitely,' Simon said. 'This is good stuff, thanks, Donna. I'll let Connor know, and we'll catch up as soon as—'

'Hold on,' Donna said, her voice suddenly sharp. 'This was a quid pro quo deal, remember? Doug and I look into Harbour Street. Connor gets his guy at Sentinel to look into the logs we need on Cunningham and Gareth Hogan.'

Simon smiled – another trait he admired in Donna: a certain stubborn impatience. 'You called Robbie?' he said.

'Yeah, couple of hours ago now, gave him all the details. Haven't heard anything back from him yet. I don't want to lose this story, Simon, especially with all the other newsworthy events happening around you and Connor at the moment.'

Simon felt the urge to counter Donna's implied threat, squashed it. No point in pissing off a national journalist. 'Let me check in with Robbie, see where we are. I'll give you a call back. Maybe we can grab a coffee, catch up on everything that's happened. Feels like it's been an age.'

A moment of silence on the line, just long enough for Simon to remember Donna sitting at her coffee-table, leaning forward into her laptop, legs crossed, a strand of dark hair falling forward.

'Yeah,' she said. 'But try to hurry it up, will you, Simon? I don't know what Doug's managed to dig up, but I've done my bit and, like I said, I don't want this story going cold.'

'Fair enough, I'll give you a call in a bit,' Simon said, then hung up.

He sat for a moment, considering. Should he keep his word to Donna and call Robbie straight away, or give him more time? As talented an investigator as Robbie Lindsay was, there was only so much he could do, and juggling Donna's request with the deep dive into Father Donnelly was a big ask, even for him. He could wait a while, confront Donnelly with what Donna had just told him. But then what? 'Excuse me, Father, I understand you offered comfort to the family of a wounded firefighter, presided over his funeral mass. Care to comment?' It wasn't the strongest line of questioning in the world. And, besides, with the police on guard at the church, how close was Simon likely to get to Donnelly anyway?

He fidgeted in his seat, clenching and unclenching his grip on the steering-wheel. There was something missing in all of this – he could feel it. Some fact, some connection that would shed light on what was going on, lead him to whoever had been stupid enough to threaten his friend and those he loved.

He took the phone from its dashboard mount, scrolled through his contacts. Hit dial.

'Robbie?' he said, as the call was answered. 'It's Simon McCartney. How's it going?'

'Good question,' Robbie said, his voice muffled, almost as if he was holding the phone in the crook of his neck.

A moment later, the soft clatter of keys confirmed Simon's suspicion. 'You found anything in that background check Connor asked you to run for him?' Simon asked.

'Aye, maybe,' Robbie replied, the rustling of papers replacing the chatter of keys.

'Maybe?' Simon said. 'That's not very encouraging. What did you find, Robbie?'

A rasp of static on the line as the phone was moved. Then Robbie's voice, clearer, stronger than before. 'I'm not sure,' he said. 'Something. But I'm not sure what it means. The most interesting thing was what I found in the files Connor had me look up for those reporters.'

'Oh?' Simon said, quietly impressed that Robbie had managed to conduct both pieces of research so quickly.

The phone was juggled again, Robbie giving a vague harrumph at the other end of the line. 'Look, Simon, I'm right in the middle of this now. I can send you the files I've found, but it might be easier if I sit down with you and Connor and go through this face to face. Can you both get over here to the office?'

Simon thought of this. Sentinel's office on the western outskirts of Edinburgh was about an hour's drive from where he was at that moment, with no idea of when Connor would resurface ... 'Better idea,' he said. 'Can you bundle up a laptop and head over here? We can meet at Connor's place, go over everything there.'

'Uhm, I'm not sure ...' Robbie said, wariness in his voice. Simon understood it. Being asked to visit the boss's home for a personal briefing was not part of the average working day.

'Come on, it'll be fine,' Simon said, another thought occurring to him. 'You get moving. By the time you're here, I'll have tracked down Connor.' And, he thought, have had a chance for a coffee with an attractive reporter as well.

CHAPTER 35

The grace of prayer eluded him. He had, over the years, come to terms with this. Come to understand that, although he could close his eyes and voice the words of prayer, it was a pantomime, a farce. He was little more than a child reciting the alphabet in class, regurgitating what he had learnt with no connection to its deeper meaning. It was a heavy price to pay, but one he understood he must face.

After all, with the magnitude of his sin, was it any wonder God was deaf to his pleas?

But sitting there in a silence that seemed to crowd in on him with echoes of accusation and regret, he wished with all his heart for one moment of grace.

He had known this day was coming; had known it since that night, all those years ago. The night he had made a deal with the Devil. And while that deal had saved lives and ultimately served a greater good, he knew that, one day, he would have to face judgement for his crime. And now that the time had come, now that Death and a final reckoning had stepped from the shadows of his nightmares and become as real as the damage he had inflicted on the church, he felt nothing but relief and serenity. The same serenity, he realised, that a more innocent man would find in prayer.

The only problem was Connor Fraser. He had proven himself to be both resourceful and tenacious, and the way he had thrown himself at the police officer to save him from the exploding drone showed him to be a brave man as well.

Brave, but not innocent. Far from that. In his own way, Fraser was as blighted by sin as he was.

He rose from his knees, abandoning the parody of prayer, suddenly finding the act tawdry and offensive.

No, Connor Fraser would die. His good deeds did nothing to erase the smear of sin on his soul. It was, after all, part of the plan. For the resurrection to succeed, rebirth could only be preceded by death.

And Fraser's death would offer a chance to bring justice and closure. Just as his own death would.

He stepped to his desk, rummaged in a drawer for the small phone he kept there. He held it for a moment, smiled at the irony. It was, in many ways, just like him. A basic device, designed for a single purpose, stripped of all the non-essentials that every phone seemed to be crammed with these days. It was a tool designed to do a single job. It was anonymous, untraceable, expendable.

Just like him.

He dialled the number. Waited for the answer. The answer, he knew, that would bring Death to his door at last.

CHAPTER 36

As much as the call from Simon frustrated Connor, he was forced to admit it came as a relief as well. After his meeting with Paulie, he had found himself torn between talking to Doug McGregor about what else he knew of Tom McGovern, and the growing desire to visit the man at his office, kick his door in and beat the answers from him. So the call from Simon, telling him Robbie had found something in his background checks on Father Donnelly and his research for Donna and Doug, at least gave him a definitive course of action that would keep him out of a prison cell.

Robbie was already at the flat when Connor arrived, looking around nervously, standing like a child who had been summoned to the headmaster's office. Simon wasn't helping his discomfort: he was sitting on the couch opposite Robbie, Tom in his lap, stroking the cat slowly as he stared at Robbie silently, as though he had taken up role-playing Bond villains in his spare time. The mischievous twinkle in Simon's eye when he looked up to greet Connor told him his friend knew exactly the joke he was playing at Robbie's expense.

'Ah, Connor, what about ye?' Simon said, as Robbie glanced up from his laptop and began to stand.

'Not bad,' Connor said. 'Robbie, sit down for God's sake, and stop letting this lump wind you up.' He headed for the kitchen. 'I need a coffee. Either of you want anything?'

'All good,' Simon said.

'Ah, no, I'm fine, thanks,' Robbie said, as he sat down again, dragging the laptop across the coffee-table and closer to him.

'Okay,' Connor said, as he busied himself making coffee. 'Simon tells me you've found something in your background checks. Care to share?'

'Sure,' Robbie said, relief tingeing his voice as small-talk came to an end. 'You asked me to look into the background of Father John Donnelly, full name Johnathan Meighan Donnelly, see if there was some link to you, something that would put you in the crosshairs of whoever is gunning for him.'

'Uh-huh,' Connor grunted, as he sipped his coffee. 'You get anything?'

Robbie glanced up from his laptop, a look of bemused frustration on his face. 'Well, yes and no,' he said. 'There's nothing I can find that directly connects you to him. No record of you meeting him, no events I can see where you might conceivably have crossed paths.'

'Damn,' Connor said, his mind returning to Tom McGovern and a more direct form of communication. 'Another dead end.'

'Well, not necessarily,' Robbie said. 'I said I couldn't find any links between you and the priest directly. But I did find something that may link him to Sentinel, and the other matter you asked me to look into.'

Connor sighed as confusion began to press into his temples, soon to take root and bloom into a headache. 'What do you mean?'

'Well, you also asked me to dig out the reports on the work we did for Paradigm Energy and Gareth Hogan, who needed security after threats were made against his person and his business,' Robbie said.

'Yeah,' Connor replied. 'The background for Donna Blake and Doug McGregor. But how does that connect to Donnelly?'

'Tangentially, at the moment,' Robbie said, turning his laptop to Connor, who made his way around the breakfast bar and towards the coffee-table.

'I looked into the case files on Hogan. Sentinel worked for him for three months. He employed our services after death threats, malicious vandalism and an arson attack at one of his refining sites.' Robbie tapped the laptop's screen. 'This was all related to Paradigm's

151

support for fracking in former mining sites across Scotland, a practice that is thought to be dangerous and hated by environmentalists.'

Connor studied the screen Robbie had called up, the initial assessment report and briefing notes from the first meeting with Paradigm. Sentinel had been asked to provide twenty-four-hour security for Gareth Hogan, to ensure there were no attacks on him. They had also signed a contract to review security at Paradigm's offices in Edinburgh and the site in the Borders that had been petrol-bombed. Connor vaguely remembered the work: it was shortly after he had been recruited to Sentinel, and he was still proving to them and himself that he could make the transition from police officer to private security.

'Right,' he said, scanning the page, trying to see what Robbie was driving at and failing. 'All seems fairly standard so far.'

'Yeah,' Robbie agreed. 'It only gets interesting when we take a look at it in the way Ms Blake asked us to.'

He spun the laptop back to himself, hit a couple of keys, then turned it to Connor.

'Activity logs,' he said, as Connor read the screen. 'Standard operating procedure for us. When we're providing security for a client, we log their movements, note anything that might pose a risk at that location at the time or in the future. It also allows us to establish a pattern of movement, see if we're being too predictable in the case of a kidnapping threat or an attack.'

'Right,' Connor said, skimming the file. It was a long list of addresses, mostly in Edinburgh's New Town. The street names he recognised, but the meaning eluded him.

Robbie smiled, as though he could read the confusion on Connor's face. 'When I got this, I took a look at the addresses, tried to establish a pattern. Over the course of the three months we were engaged by Mr Hogan, he made thirty-one visits to Paradigm's main office, which is located at two twenty-seven Forth Street, just off Leith Walk. As well as his regular trips to and from his hotel and to the Scottish Parliament, he also made seven visits to an address in Melville Crescent.'

'Enlighten me,' Connor said, a memory of Doug McGregor's claims of a conspiracy flitting across his mind at the mention of the Scottish Parliament.

'Melville Crescent is home to the Scotland Office,' Robbie said. 'That makes a certain sense. If Hogan was lobbying politicians to give the go-ahead for his company to start fracking operations in Scotland, he would probably be visiting both the Scottish Parliament and the offices of the UK government in Scotland. But this is where it gets interesting. He also visited . . .' Robbie turned the laptop again, hit some keys, then spun it back to Connor with a small flourish, '. . . this address on seventeen occasions.'

'Seventy-one Lauder Street,' Connor said, looking at the Google image Robbie had called up. It was a grand Georgian townhouse, limestone walls stained by years of soot and pollution that streaked the stone like smeared mascara. 'What's there?'

Robbie smiled. 'Officially, it's called a private members' club – you know, one of those elitist retreats where the great and the good still wear jackets and ties for dinner and the ladies retire to the drawing room as the men take brandy and cigars in the library.'

'I take it you're not a fan, then,' Simon said, reacting to the contempt Connor had heard in Robbie's voice.

'Classist bullshit, old-school ties, funny handshakes and who can do what for whom,' Robbie muttered under his breath, darting a guilty look at Connor.

'It's fine,' Connor said. 'Got no time for that crap myself. You said "officially" it's a members' club. What about unofficially?'

'That took a little more digging,' Robbie said, 'but if you know where to look, you can find some of the historic memberships that have been passed down since the club was formed back in 1790. And when you do that, you find that two of the club's founding members were a George Eustace Cunningham and a Bartholomew Jackson-Laird.'

Connor felt a vague pang of recognition, thought back to what McGregor had said. 'I take it you mean Cunningham is a relative of Kerr Cunningham, the list MSP? But what about this Jackson-Laird?'

'Sir Walter Jackson-Laird,' Simon said. 'Right? Secretary of state for Scotland? And I'm guessing this club is entry by member invitation only, so Mr Hogan would have had to be invited by a current member?'

Robbie nodded, a sneer of disapproval contorting his features. 'Exactly,' he said. 'It's not conclusive, but it looks a lot like Hogan was using this club to have private lobbying chats with the secretary of state for Scotland and his pal, the list MSP for Central Scotland.'

'Okay,' Connor said slowly. It fitted with what McGregor had said. In the wake of the Brexit vote in 2016, when Scotland and Northern Ireland had voted to remain in Europe but Wales and England had voted to leave, the calls for independence had ramped up again. Using a controversial policy like fracking, which the Westminster Government supported but Scotland rejected, would create a polarised political debate – do you support them or us? Add in the jobs and investment that would be lost due to the Scottish Government's refusal to back fracking developments, it would be a powerful weapon that the unionist Westminster Government could use against a nationalist administration in Edinburgh. Especially when physical violence was added to the mix.

'One more thing,' Robbie said, after a pause, as though he was giving Connor and Simon time to process what he was telling them. 'Along with the visits to the locations I've already listed, Hogan also made another couple of trips outside Edinburgh.'

Connor almost felt something click in his mind, felt he knew what was coming next. Reading the screen Robbie flicked to confirmed it. On three occasions, Hogan had left Edinburgh and travelled north-west. On one trip he had visited Falkirk, and the constituency office of Kerr Cunningham. On another, he had visited Banknock, where he had been shown a potential fracking development site on the outskirts of the town. Connor read the address, remembered seeing Donna cover it only the day before. The land was now the site of the Wallace Development, where homes would be constructed by Tom McGovern, the man Paulie had mentioned to him hours before.

But it was the last trip that interested Connor most. Reading the Sentinel day log on the trip, he was suddenly aware of the dull ache in his shoulder where the shard of exploding door had lodged itself.

The log detailed that Hogan had left his Edinburgh hotel and been driven into the Stirling area where, after a brief stop at Banknock, he

154

had travelled on, further into the country. To a small village with a neat high street, a Mercat Cross and a church that had recently been attacked by exploding drones.

For some reason, Gareth Hogan had visited Lenton Barns. And the church of Father John Donnelly.

CHAPTER 37

After leaving instructions with Robbie to contact Donna and McGregor with what he had found in Sentinel's logs, Connor and Simon headed out for Lenton Barns. As Connor drove, Simon filled him in on what Donna had told him about Peter Turnbull.

'So this guy dies, then someone targets Donnelly,' Connor said, after Simon had finished speaking. 'That strike you as a bit of a coincidence?'

'Too much of one,' Simon replied, the cold, almost distracted tone in his voice telling Connor his friend was working through the case one step at a time, analysing facts and testing theories.

'What you thinking?' Connor asked.

Simon twisted slightly in his seat to face Connor. 'What do we know?' he asked. 'That a Catholic priest with close links to the fire service has been targeted by someone who can hack secure frequencies, knows how to modify drones to make them weapons and, given the seventy K they dropped into your account, they're not short of cash. We also know that, whatever is going on, it's somehow linked to that fire at Harbour Street, the one that sent Donnelly scurrying from Glasgow to preach in a forgotten village in Central Scotland. The last victim of that fire dies and, less than a month later, Donnelly gets death threats and you're pulled into this.'

Connor tensed his grip on the steering-wheel. 'See, that's the bit I don't get. Okay, someone has a grudge against Donnelly. Fine. But why rope me into all of this? Why pay seventy grand into Sentinel's account and throw down the gauntlet? And why go as far as killing an innocent man just to send us a message? Doesn't make sense.'

'You sure you can't think of a link between you and Donnelly, or another firefighter?' Simon asked.

Connor remembered Strachan's cold contempt at their last meeting. What was it he had said? *My men intervened to put the fire out, and you grabbed one of them by the throat. I wish it had been me. It wouldn't have gone so easily for you.*

'Well, you heard Strachan,' he said. 'I took down one of his men when they were responding to a fire at an event a few years ago, but I hardly think that's grounds for murder, is it? Unless it's something to do with this guy McGovern, who's had his goons sniffing around, asking about me.'

'A property developer,' Simon said, popping up one finger, 'an MSP,' another finger, 'and a priest,' a final finger. 'Apart from sounding like the set-up for a bad joke, how the hell does this all tie together?'

'No idea,' Connor said, slowing as they hit the outskirts of Lenton Barns. 'But as soon as we've had a chat with the good priest, my next stop is going to be the offices of Tom McGovern.'

'*Your* next stop?' Simon said slowly. 'You mean ours, surely. No way I'm letting you go in there alone, big lad. You're as like to kill the guy if he doesn't give you the answers you want.'

'You blame me?' Connor asked, sour anger curdling his words.

'Not at all,' Simon replied, a smile dancing across his lips, 'but at least if I'm with you I can help hold the fucker down.'

They arrived at the church a few moments later, the police tape fluttering gently in the warm breeze like streamers. Connor parked behind a police car, tensed as he killed the engine, leant forward as something cold began to caress the back of his neck.

'What's up?' Simon asked softly.

'The police officers guarding Donnelly,' Connor said, eyes not leaving the church gate. 'Where are they? Car's there, but where are they?'

Simon shifted forward. 'Inside, maybe? Checking on the priest?' His tone told Connor he didn't believe that any more than Connor did.

'Standard procedure would be a visible police presence at the perimeter, for deterrence and logging anything suspicious,' Connor said. 'I don't like this, Simon. Let's take it slow.'

They got out of the car, the sound of the doors closing suddenly very loud in the peace of the day.

'Same as before?' Simon asked. 'I'll take the back, you take the front?'

Connor nodded. 'You carrying?' he asked.

The smile returned to Simon's face as he pulled the left side of his jacket tight, revealing the bulging outline of a gun. 'Standard issue when I'm with you, pal,' he said.

Connor gave him a tight smile. 'Be careful.'

Simon disappeared to the back of the church. Connor took a deep breath, stepped forward. Lifted the police tape over his head and swung the church gate open.

He was about twenty feet up the path when he heard it. A low, almost plaintive moaning. He looked to his left, felt his chest draw tight even as he pulled his gun from its holster. He approached the figure lying propped up against the church wall slowly, resisting the urge to sprint to them and offer help. Dropped to his haunches as he got to the police officer, who was making low, guttural noises as he tried to breathe through a nose that had obviously been broken. The pallor of his skin accentuated the dark red of his blood, turning it into some gruesome parody of lipstick as it smeared across his lips and down his chin.

Connor checked his pulse, felt cold, clammy skin and an erratic heartbeat beneath his fingers. 'I'll call an ambulance,' Connor said, even as he glanced around again. Nothing, just trees rustling in the gentle breeze and the gravestones holding silent watch. 'What happened to you? Who attacked you?'

'Guh,' the policeman grunted, his eyes fluttering open and showing only whites. He was half conscious, and clearly had one hell of a concussion. Connor briefly wondered if someone had fractured his skull, and when he saw a drop of blood dribbling down the man's cheek from his left ear, he became almost certain of it.

He whirled suddenly, raising his gun as he dropped to one knee.

Saw Simon jogging towards him, gun held low as his head swivelled smoothly from side to side, scanning his surroundings as he moved.

'How bad?' Connor asked, reading his friend's grim expression.

'Not good,' Simon replied in a tight whisper. 'There's another copper inside, wee girl who's had her head bashed in. Got her in the recovery position now. Looks like a tornado ripped through the place, signs of one hell of a fight, blood all the way up one of the walls in Donnelly's study.'

Connor felt something cold and oily uncurl in his stomach, as though a snake was nesting inside him. 'Donnelly?' he said.

Simon shook his head. 'Didn't have time to check the upper floor of the house, wanted to get out to you, make sure everything was okay. But the front door was open, and the church is still boarded up with MDF from when the door was destroyed. I'm not a betting man, Connor, but I'd say someone was here, clocked these two poor bastards and grabbed him.'

Connor bit his lip, holstered his gun and grabbed his phone. 'Call an ambulance,' he said to Simon. 'I'll call Ford while you're doing that, tell him what's happened. We can search the rest of the house and grounds while we're waiting for him to arrive.'

'What the fuck is going on here?' Simon asked.

'I don't know,' Connor said. 'But I swear to you, we're going to find out. Whoever is doing this has been one step ahead the entire time. That ends. Now.'

CHAPTER 38

The ambulance for the two injured police officers was leaving just as Ford and an entourage of forensic specialists and uniformed officers arrived. The paramedics hadn't told Connor or Simon much but, watching them work, Connor could tell they were as worried about the head injuries the officers had sustained as he was. The memory of the man he had found trying to speak as his eyes rolled back in his head and blood dribbled down his cheek played on repeat in Connor's mind, as though a needle had stuck on the record of his memory.

'What the hell happened here?' Ford snapped, making no effort to hide the fury in his voice as he glanced between Simon and Connor. For an instant, he looked like a drunk in a pub who was aching to start a fight but didn't know who to attack.

'It's like I said on the phone, sir.' Connor tried to keep his voice calm. 'We arrived to talk to Father Donnelly after receiving some new information. When we got here, we found your two officers had been assaulted and Father Donnelly was gone. From the look of his study and the blood we found on the wall, he didn't go willingly.'

'From the look of his study.' Ford chewed on the words. 'So you've been in, contaminated an active crime scene? For Christ's sake, Fraser, what did I tell you about interfering in an active police investigation?'

Connor opened his mouth to speak, but it was Simon who got there first.

'We ascertained that two police officers had been injured, sir,' he said, his words slow and deliberate. 'Given the situation, we had a duty to see if anyone else was in the property and required immediate assistance. I apologise for entering the locus, but we had little choice. In any case, Connor and I are well versed in forensic techniques and preserving evidence.'

Ford turned his gaze on Simon for a moment, then to DS Troughton, who flinched slightly at the abruptness of his boss's movement.

'Troughton, find Jim Dexter, he's leading the SOCO teams. Tell him two civilians have been in the property, and to prioritise the main study. Blood-spatter analysis and typing, the usual. Then get officers out to the village. Did anyone see any other vehicles around the church? Anyone suspicious been lurking about? Got it?'

'Yes, sir,' Troughton said, and hurried off. Ford watched him go, then turned back to Connor and Simon.

'Give me one good bloody reason that I don't just arrest you both right now, make my life a lot easier,' he said, weariness edging his voice now.

'Sir, Malcolm, I'm sorry,' Connor said. 'When we got here, we followed procedure as best we could. Made sure your officers were well cared for, then secured the locus. We're just trying to help.'

Ford sighed. Massaged his eyes with his fingers. 'And what,' he said, after a moment, 'did you find that was so important you decided to race here to confront Donnelly without informing me first?'

Connor felt the tension in his chest ease a fraction. If Ford was willing to listen to him, he might be talked down. Might even help. He took a breath, then told Ford about Robbie's discovery.

'We've found evidence that links Father Donnelly to the industrialist Gareth Hogan, a site at Banknock. We were on our way here to ascertain the nature of that link and what they might have discussed,' Connor said, noticing Simon's quizzical look as he left out any mention of Tom McGovern, the property developer who had looked into Connor's background. He shrugged slightly. McGovern was personal. He would deal with that without police interference.

'Hmm,' Ford said. 'Hardly a concrete link to you, is it? Or a reason to kill a cabbie.'

Connor couldn't help himself. 'Cabbie? You got something on the man who was burnt to death?'

Ford's jaw tensed, then eased as he shrugged, as though he had just lost an argument with himself. 'We got the VIN number from the chassis. Traced it to Albion Transport, a taxi firm that works out of Stirling station. They've got one driver and car missing. Russell Dorman, fifty-four, lives out in Denny. No family, but neighbours haven't seen him in a couple of days. Search of his property showed nothing out of the ordinary, no sign he had left on a holiday or anything like that. We've requested medical records, should have the formal identification shortly.'

'Anything interesting in his background that could show he was targeted by the killer?' Simon asked.

Ford shook his head. 'Nothing. Quiet man, from what we can see. No criminal record other than a few parking tickets. Nothing suggestive at his house. Too early to tell yet, but it seems the killer chose him completely at random.'

Connor considered this. Did it make it better or worse that the killer had killed an innocent man he had not known simply to send a message? And what did that message mean? *This blood is on Donnelly's hands, Mr Fraser. How bloody are you willing to get?*

'Anything from CCTV at the station?' Connor asked, forcing himself to focus on the present.

'Being checked at the moment,' Ford said. 'But the station is usually busy, and I'm guessing that whoever is behind all this isn't going to be sloppy enough just to turn around and smile for the camera.'

'Check the car-park videos as well,' Connor said, almost to himself as the thought occurred to him. 'Remember what Strachan found at Banknock? An image of an old red car, maybe a Volkswagen, parked on a road outside the fire station when its broadcast tower was hacked. It might give us another link, something to look for.'

'Us,' Ford said, leaving the warning hanging in the air.

'So, what next?' Simon asked, clapping his hands together as though trying to break the tension that was mounting between the three men.

'Next, you give one of my officers your official statements on this shite. Then you bugger off and let us do our jobs. You get any more information about Donnelly, you let me know first, clear?'

'Clear sir,' Connor said. 'But I think you're missing something.'

Ford straightened, and Connor could see the effort it took not to snap out a reply – or a quick left jab. 'Oh, and what would that be, Fraser?'

'It's not unreasonable to think that whoever torched the cabbie now has Father Donnelly, right?' Connor said. 'That being the case, he is at extreme risk of harm, and we need to find him as soon as possible.'

Ford waved at the array of police officers and SOCOs swarming around them. 'And what do you think all this is for?' he asked.

Connor held up a hand. 'Sir, I know you're making every effort. But we've been behind the ball on this from the start. We've got a ticking clock. The killer threatened to murder Donnelly sometime in the next seven days. That could be any time. But he made me part of the threat, challenged me to protect him.'

'So?' Ford said.

'So call his bluff. I've failed. He's got Donnelly and I've breached the contract he wanted me to sign at the start of all this. He's got a taste for the dramatic, so why don't we play into that, flaunt my failure? See if he gets cocky with success, makes a mistake.'

Simon smiled. 'Nice idea,' he said, with a soft chuckle.

'What are you suggesting?' Ford said, his tone telling Connor he knew, and didn't really want to hear the answer.

'Easy,' Connor said. 'We call the press.'

CHAPTER 39

Strachan sat at his desk, staring unseeing at the pictures strewn in front of him. After his discovery that the drones used in the attack on Father Donnelly's church had been controlled from Banknock fire station, he had pulled all the reports from the crew that had attended the incident. In his day, that would have been restricted to typed-up reports and static images like the ones at his desk, but nowadays, he had access to new tools – camera footage from the appliances that attended the scene and from the cameras that were mounted on the uniforms of firefighters.

The problem was, reviewing the footage, the reports and the images told him nothing. The firefighters had arrived at the church after the attack, been relegated to putting out the smouldering embers of the fire and ensuring what was left of the drones wouldn't blow up. The thought of the drones worried him. Why would someone target Father Donnelly with drones? Why would they hack a fire station to do it and why, most importantly, would that person set light to another human being to deliver a message? Strachan had seen too many burns victims at too many fires to know that anyone capable of inflicting that kind of terror and agony on another human was a person who had no right to be walking free. They were an animal, frenzied, lethal, capable of lashing out at any moment.

But, the question remained, how could he help find this person?

He swept the pictures from the desk with a sudden, angry grunt, felt a pang of shame at his petulance. Got out of his chair and knelt down to collect the pictures, found himself at eye level with his lower desk drawer. He could almost hear the bottle in there, whispering to him, calling him to take one little drink. It would soothe him. Relax him. Help him think.

He grunted, stood up. No. Not now. Not when there was work to be done.

He gathered up the last of the pictures, dumped them on his desk and started studying them again, as though the different perspective would let him see something he had missed before. But, no, there was nothing. Just images of the craters left in the stonework of the church by the impacts and the scorch patterns on the grass where one drone had come crashing down.

He closed his eyes, forced himself to think. In fire investigation, he had been taught to look for the cause of the fire: the initial flashpoint where the blaze had begun. It could be anything, from a faulty fuse to an overheating lamp to a satellite box left on too long without proper ventilation. Fire was patient, but it was also opportunistic. All it needed was a lapse of concentration to snatch at life and erupt into a blaze that would consume everything it touched.

So where was the flashpoint that had started this blaze?

On an impulse, he hit his intercom. A moment later, Watch Manager Ogilvy knocked at his door then entered the room, ducking and turning slightly to squeeze his massive frame through the door. 'Yes sir?' he asked, in that unnervingly gentle voice of his.

'Ah, John,' Strachan said. 'I need you to do something for me, but it's delicate, so caw canny, understood?'

Ogilvy tensed, ready for orders. He had worked for Strachan for almost a year now and Strachan had never encountered a firefighter who took his job so seriously.

'Yes, sir,' he said.

'Good. I need you to pull the logs for the Harbour Street fire in Glasgow. You know the one?'

Ogilvy blinked once, stared at Strachan. 'Yes, sir,' he said. 'Every firefighter remembers that one.'

'Of course,' Strachan said. 'And that's why it's delicate. You see,

165

Chief Officer MacAlister was at that fire, and I'm sure that any interest shown in it, especially at the moment with everything that's going on, will get his attention. And the last thing we want is to have the chief breathing down our necks. So pull the records, but do it quietly, okay?'

Ogilvy nodded his massive head, the overhead lights reflecting off the wide expanse of his forehead. 'Yes, sir,' he said. 'I know a way to access the records quietly. Am I looking for anything in particular?'

Strachan thought back to Father John Donnelly, the stories he had heard about his work on the creation of the national fire service and his part in comforting the firefighters who had attended Harbour Street. Whatever was happening, it was linked to that fire, he was sure of it.

'The cause of the fire,' he said to Ogilvy. 'The flashpoint.'

CHAPTER 40

The heat, helping Connor Fraser and the low-level disgust he felt at someone using Jen and a frail old woman as pieces in some kind of sick game all combined to put Paulie in a foul mood.

Which was why he was so happy when he spotted the car tailing him.

It hadn't been hard to see. After concluding his meeting with Fraser, he had headed back to Corn Exchange Road, where he had left his car. He got in and drove down the hill, turning right at the junction onto Albert Place. He was planning to drive towards the castle and then out of town. Maybe hit the bypass and head up to Perth. But then he had noticed the car in his rear-view mirror. The car that was trying just a little too hard to stay one vehicle behind him, the car that had been parked on the other side of Corn Exchange Road, just close enough to keep him in sight.

From the look of it, it was a BMW. Maybe a 5-series. If it was an injected version, it was more than a match for Paulie's Mercedes, which meant getting away from whoever was following him would be a problem.

If, that was, Paulie was in a mood to run.

He drove on for a few minutes, mapping out a route in his head. Smiled as he came to a decision. When he reached the roundabout that led on to Dumbarton Road, he floored the accelerator, surging in front of a grocery van, the sound of squealing tyres and a blaring horn like a symphony to Paulie's ears. He watched as the BMW darted into oncoming traffic and roared after him, abandoning any pretence that they weren't following him. He drove on, found the small side road he was looking for. It led to a smallholding, which had a butcher's shop on site. But the road itself was about half a mile long, narrow and rutted. Perfect for Paulie's needs.

He found a small layby, pulled the Mercedes in, then jumped out, running to the boot. By the time the BMW screeched to a halt behind him, Paulie was at peace with the world and ready for a day's work.

A man he vaguely recognised emerged from the passenger's side of the BMW, his pale face framed by a mane of hair so dark it had to be dyed. The darkness seemed to magnify the emptiness of his eyes, which glared at Paulie with a malevolence that promised pain was only a wrong word away. On the other side of the car, a younger, almost comically thin man emerged from the driver's door, doing nothing to hide the knife that glinted in his hand.

'Be careful son,' Paulie said, tightening his grip on the crowbar he held. 'You could hurt yourself with that, specially if you're as careless with a knife as you are with a steering-wheel.'

The kid's face flushed with anger, eyes narrowing to glittering slits that reminded Paulie of the rats he had seen crawling over the face of a man he had killed many years ago. The boy moved around the driver's door, raising his knife.

'Alasdair, relax,' the older man at the other side of the car said, his voice calm and lyrical in the way only a Geordie's could be. 'Mr King, we wanted to talk to you. We believe you met with Danny Moffatt recently. Is that correct?'

Paulie glanced again at the boy's knife, wondered when it had last had blood on it. 'Aye,' he said. 'I had a wee word with Ding Dong. So what? Hardly justifies you tailing me now, does it?'

The older man smiled, revealing teeth that were as false as his hair colour. Again, Paulie felt a twinge of recognition. 'See, the problem is, we understand Danny might have been a little . . . indelicate in what he told you. We just wanted to set the record straight.'

Despite himself, Paulie smiled, shook his head. 'Fuck off,' he said, suddenly remembering where he had seen the man in front of him before. 'You tailed me from the Albert Halls. You know I've met with Connor Fraser, so you also know I probably told him what Ding Dong told me. You're Mickey Jamieson, right? Thought I recognised the face, but that fucking perm put me off. You run the crew that does the strong-arm work for Tom McGovern. So if that's the case, you're not here to keep me quiet, you're here to teach me a lesson, or shut me up permanently. Is that what you did to Ding Dong?'

Jamieson's smile grew wider and colder. 'We spoke to Danny, yes. He won't be making the same mistake again. But as for you, Mr King, you spoke to the enemy, betrayed confidences. So, yes, I'm afraid corrective measures have to be taken.'

Jamieson raised a gun, pointed it straight at Paulie. Paulie raised his hands, smiled. 'Come on, don't be fucking—'

He never finished the sentence. In one smooth move, he hurled the crowbar at Jamieson, spun and dropped, the sound of Jamieson's shot screaming into his ears as he grabbed his own gun from his ankle holster, raised it and fired.

Jamieson's head snapped back, a halo of misted blood and brains exploding into the sky as Paulie's shot took out most of the left side of his face. Paulie spun around, saw the kid scrambling past the car, slipping on the scree of the road, charging at Paulie with nothing but death in his eyes. Paulie raised his gun, aimed at the centre of the kid's chest.

'Alasdair, stop,' he said, his words muffled by the echoes of gunshots in his ears. 'It doesn't have to go this way.'

Alasdair lurched to a standstill. His face was twisted with fury, tears streaking his flame-red cheeks. 'Fuck you!' he roared, stabbing at the air in front of him with the knife as though he was plunging it into Paulie's chest. 'You just killed Mr Jamieson. I'm going to fucking gut you for that.'

'No, you're not,' Paulie said. He lowered his gun, took aim then fired a shot at Alasdair's feet. The boy flinched back and Paulie surged forward, grabbing his wrist and twisting until he felt the bone start to creak. Alasdair cried out in impotent fury as he dropped his knife. Paulie punched him once, not hard, just enough to get his attention and convey the message that knives weren't toys, especially when they were pointed at him.

'I'm not going to kill you,' Paulie said slowly, his voice gentle, even friendly. 'But you are going to do me a favour. We're going to load Mr Jamieson into your boot, then you're going to take him back to your boss. Tell him that this is what happens to anyone who tries to fuck with me. Clear?'

Alasdair snarled at Paulie, spat a wad of phlegm into his face. Paulie tightened his grip on Alasdair's wrist, rabbit-punched the youth once.

'Fuckin' quit it,' Paulie said. 'I'm too fuckin' tired to pick up Jamieson's body on my own, so you're going to have to do it. You want to do it with a broken wrist, that's fine by me.'

Paulie watched as the fury bled from Alasdair's eyes, replaced by dejection and acceptance. He pocketed the knife, made sure there was no way Alasdair could put his hands on Jamieson's gun.

Felt nothing as he watched the lad struggle with the corpse of the man he had just killed, the dark dye of his hair now glittering with blood and brain as it oozed from the exit wound at the back of his head. He hadn't meant to kill him, only wound him, send him back to McGovern as a bloodied message. But what was done was done. A gun had been pulled on him and, as his father had taught him years ago, the only answer to violence was violence. The trick was to be the one left standing when the fists or bullets had stopped flying. He held the gun on Alasdair as he started up the BMW, kept clear of the vehicle as it bounced back up the farm track. Stood for a moment in the sudden silence of the day, then fished his phone out of his pocket. Cursed under his breath, then made the call.

He hated Connor Fraser, but he was important to Jen. Which meant he deserved to know about the trouble that was coming his way.

CHAPTER 41

The call from the chief constable came just when Ford expected it to – as soon as Donna's report about Father Donnelly going missing hit the air.

'What the hell is the meaning of this?' Chief Constable Guthrie had snapped, the moment Ford had picked up the phone. 'This makes us look like fucking idiots, especially after what happened at that church the other day! Did you know this was going to be leaked? I swear to God, Ford, if I find out this was your doing, I will personally see you assigned to court duty in Dundee before the end of the bloody week.'

Ford smiled, turned to the muted TV in the corner of the office. Donna Blake stood in front of the church, talking straight into the camera, the tag line 'Priest abducted from drone attack church' scrawled across the bottom of the screen. He knew from a quick check that McGregor's news website, the Crucible, was also carrying the story.

'As I said to the communications team when they called,' Ford said, 'we didn't leak this story to the press. It came from that security agent, Fraser. He visited the property, found Father Donnelly was missing, called us, then called Donna Blake.'

It was a version of the truth Ford could live with. He had agreed with Connor's strategy of going to the press in the hope of goading the killer into some rash action that would lead them to him. But he had conditions: one was that no mention was made of the injured police officers found at the church, and the second was that Ford's name didn't come up. He had little time for Chief Constable Guthrie, was quite happy to see him in an uncomfortable position, but he was also aware of a truism in the police: shit rolled downhill, and he didn't need Guthrie piling shit at his door.

'Sorry, sir?' he said, realising Guthrie had finished his rant and he hadn't heard a word of it.

'I said, this is the last bloody thing we need. I've already had the justice secretary on the phone, squealing about possible sectarian motives for this. How is your investigation progressing? We need results on this, Ford. Now.'

Ford rolled his shoulders, tried to keep his voice level. It was always the same. A crime is committed? Fine, stick it in the spreadsheet and tally up the stats at the end of the year. A crime gets committed in front of a camera or the press gets wind of it and starts asking awkward questions? Waste no resource to show that the full force of the law will see justice done. It was a perverse attitude to policing, one that Ford had no time for. He had made his share of mistakes over the years, was trying to atone for them, but he had always thought criminals should be hunted down without mercy, even when the cameras were off and the stories had run.

'We're doing everything we can, sir. I'm working with Assistant Chief Officer Strachan at the fire service to try to ascertain the origin of the drone attacks. We're pulling CCTV in relation to the cabbie who was abducted and burnt to death, and we've got forensics teams going over the presbytery at the church to look for any clues as to who took the priest, and why.'

Guthrie grumbled something unintelligible under his breath. It could have been anything from approval or a curse. 'Very well,' he said. 'But be careful with Strachan. You know what working with the fire service can get like. And their chief, MacAlister, is a political animal.'

'Oh?' Ford said, before he could stop himself.

'Yes,' Guthrie said, his voice dropping to a conspiratorial whisper, like he was the office gossip who was glad to find a co-worker to share the latest juicy titbit with. 'The service review of the national fire service is just under way at the moment. MacAlister was one of the architects of the national service, so if the review is kind, it'll be the making of him politically. And he's made it clear that he wants to move into elected office when he stands down.'

In his mind, Ford heard Fraser whisper something, a fragment of a conversation he couldn't quite hear. 'Ah, I see,' he said, forcing himself to focus on Guthrie.

'Yes, so he'll do anything to make the fire service look like heroes and us look like idiots. So get your leaks plugged, DCI Ford, and get a result on this mess. Quickly.'

'Understood, sir,' Ford said, ending the call before Guthrie could argue.

He hung up the phone, glanced back to the TV. The news programme had moved on, now showing long queues at a petrol station, intercut with shots of a board showing fuel prices so high they could give you a nose bleed.

'Fuel,' he muttered. He turned to his desk, rooted around for the file he wanted. Found it and skimmed it, a flicker of hope sparking in his chest. He reached for his phone again, called for DS Troughton. The young detective appeared a few moments later.

'Yes, Guv?' he asked.

'Any word on the CCTV footage from Stirling railway station?' he asked.

'Not yet,' Troughton said, his face flushing slightly as he spoke.

'Chase it up,' Ford said. 'Then go online. Get a list of petrol stations in a, say, ten-mile radius of Banknock.'

'Ten miles, sir? Why ten miles?'

Ford shrugged. 'Call it a guess. Whoever flew those drones into that church had to get the petrol they used to make the napalm somewhere. Same for the napalm used to burn out the cab. Makes sense that they wouldn't want to stray too far from wherever they were storing the drones, so it's logical to think can't have been too far from Banknock. So check petrol stations in the area, pull their CCTV. If we can get a match on the car seen outside Banknock fire station and if that car is also on the train station CCTV, we can maybe get a card listing for fuel sales, maybe even a shot of whoever we're looking for.'

Troughton smiled, like a child who had just been shown a magic trick. 'I'll get right on to it,' he said, then left the room.

Ford sat back in his chair, looked up at the ceiling. Felt a faint nagging in his mind again, something about what Guthrie had told him about the chief of the fire service: *he's a political animal.*

Ford picked up his phone again, dialled. 'Gary Strachan, please,' he said, when the phone was answered. 'Tell him it's DCI Malcolm Ford.'

'Gary,' he said, as the call was connected. 'It's Malcolm. Listen, you got time to meet up for a coffee somewhere? I think it's time we compared notes.'

CHAPTER 42

'So, how do you want to handle this?'

Connor bit down on his lower lip, leant forward in his seat, staring up at the offices in front of him. They were in a small business park not far from the centre of Stirling, and a little too close to his flat in King's Park for Connor's liking. Squat, blocky buildings clustered around a central roundabout that acted as an oasis of greenery in the desert of tarmac and stone that surrounded it. A glance at the information board at the entrance to the park showed that it was home to everything from insurance brokers and accountants to software engineers and graphic designers. It was also home to the new headquarters of McGovern Homes.

Connor had taken the call from Paulie shortly after he and Simon had left DCI Ford at Lenton Barns. It had been, like the man who was making it, short, blunt and unsettling.

'Had a wee chat with some of the men we were talking about earlier,' Paulie said, the background noise telling Connor he was near a motorway. 'Wasn't the friendliest of chats. Can't see we'll be doing any business again. But watch yourself. If they were that unfriendly with me, who knows what they'll be like with you.'

'So I take it that was the last time you'll see the people in question?' Connor said, picking up the undertone in Paulie's voice.

'Aye, it's a dead end now,' Paulie replied. 'Just caw canny, Fraser. Jen's been through enough, doesn't need to see you getting hurt as well.'

Connor felt a smart answer form in his mouth, bit it back and ended the call. Paulie was no fool, and the hints he had given Connor about dead ends and not doing business again painted a very, very dark picture. Someone had confronted Paulie because of the questions he had asked on Connor's behalf, and they had paid a heavy price for it.

'Hello?' Simon said from the passenger's seat. 'Earth to Connor. How do you want to play this, big lad? I mean, we don't even know if McGovern is here.'

'Let's find out,' Connor said, getting out of the car and heading for the front door of the building. He was just asking for McGovern at the main reception desk when Simon caught up to him.

'Subtle,' he said. 'Real subtle, big lad.'

Connor shrugged. He was tired of acting defensively, reacting to events rather than being the cause of them. One person was dead. Donnelly was missing. Jen and his gran had been threatened. And McGovern was tied up in it all, somehow.

The thin man behind the reception desk coughed apologetically as he put his phone down. 'Gentlemen,' he said, with a smile, 'Mr McGovern says he'll see you in the main conference room. It's just down this hall, last door on the right.'

Connor turned to Simon, whose face was etched with surprise. 'Sometimes the direct approach works,' he said, before marching down the corridor.

He didn't bother knocking when he got to the door, just opened it and walked in. McGovern was standing behind a chair at the head of a large conference table, the self-satisfied smile on his face making Connor's knuckles itch.

'Ah, Mr Fraser,' he said, 'and this must be your associate, Simon McCartney. Please gentlemen, come in, sit down. I believe we've a few things to talk about.'

Connor felt Simon's presence at his side, knew he would be tensed to follow his lead. Took a moment to breathe, calm the sudden urge to cross the room and grab McGovern by the throat.

'I believe you've had your people asking around about me and my family,' Connor said, his voice the sound of concrete being dragged across gravel. 'And given how unsubtle they've been about it, and their reaction to learning that third parties have heard about their enquiries, I'm guessing you wanted me to know you've been asking, and what the consequences of betraying your confidences are. So, Mr McGovern, you've got my attention. My only question is, what the hell are you playing at, and what's your connection to Father John Donnelly?'

McGovern's smile faded. Then it reappeared, like a faulty light that had just been tapped back into life. 'Father Donnelly? Sorry, never heard the name. As for the rest of what you said, you're quite right, Mr Fraser. I did want you to know I was asking around about you. I admit my men's reaction to Danny Moffatt's indiscretion with Paulie King was a little, ah, extreme, but I understand that Mr King has balanced the scales on that point. Please, sit down, let's talk.'

Connor didn't move. 'You don't want me getting any closer to you, McGovern. Believe me. So tell me. What the fuck are you playing at?'

McGovern's face darkened, like that of an ugly drunk deciding whether he was just going to hit someone with his fists or smash a pint glass over their face. Then he smiled, stepped around the chair and sat down, running his hands over his slicked-back white-blond hair as he got himself comfortable.

'It's simple, Mr Fraser,' he said, as he brought his hands forward and started playing with a large, ornate watch on his right wrist. 'I wanted to know about you, and I wanted to see how you would react to certain people asking about you and your family. Why? Because I want you to do a job for me, Mr Fraser. A very important job that I think would suit your particular, ah, talents.'

Connor took a moment, swallowed. 'Job,' he said quietly. 'What type of job do you think warrants having your thugs look into my past?'

Another fiddle with the watch. 'You've no doubt heard of my development out at Banknock and the, ah, little problem I had with a member of the press the other day?'

Connor nodded slowly, felt something click in his mind, bit back the urge to smile as he thought of Banknock, the development and Gareth Hogan's visit to John Donnelly. Knew McGovern was a liar.

'Well, the simple truth of the matter is, Mr Fraser, that the Middletrees Rise Development won't be the last project I'll be unveiling over the coming months. I've got several developments planned across Scotland, some on quite controversial sites, greenbelt land, areas of natural beauty, you know the type of thing. I expect that I'll be getting some adverse press on these, as well as local protests. I want you and your company to provide security for me and my workers, make sure things go smoothly. Obviously, you'll be facing some uncomfortable questions and press attention, like I did at Banknock the other day. So I wanted to see how you would react to that, and assure you of what would happen to anyone who spoke about you, ah, out of turn.'

Connor glanced at Simon, whose face was set halfway between bemusement and disgust.

'So, let me get this straight,' Connor said, remembering his conversation with Doug McGregor and the allegations he had made. 'You're planning to concrete over swathes of Scotland, no doubt with the help of your MSP pal, Kerr Cunningham. And you want me to, what, scare off the local opposition and intimidate the press while I'm at it?'

McGovern's smile grew wider. 'Well, I wouldn't put it quite as bluntly as that but, yes, in effect, you're right. I've vetted you, Mr Fraser. I know you're a man who can get things done. And, trust me, you'll be well compensated for your time, very well compensated.'

Connor shook his head, fury, disbelief and comprehension crowding into his thoughts, giving him a tension headache.

'Okay,' he said, after a moment. 'You've been clear with me. So let me be clear with you, Mr McGovern, just one more time. I have a couple of questions for you. I advise you to keep your answers short and truthful. Understood?'

McGovern nodded, his fingers stealing over the watch as though it was now a security blanket.

'You asked about my family and friends. Are you telling me that you had nothing to do with photographing my grandmother and my girlfriend or a contract for seventy thousand pounds?'

Confusion turned the deep furrows in McGovern's forehead into dark caverns. 'What? No. No! My people were told to ask around, make sure it got back to you. Nothing else. As for seventy thousand pounds, I have no idea what you're referring to. Just as I have no idea what you meant by your reference to Mr Cunningham.'

'Truthful answers, remember?' Simon said softly, his tone as cold and hard as Connor's gaze.

'All right,' Connor said, the sudden desire to get out of the room and away from McGovern almost overwhelming. 'And you claim you know nothing about the threats made against Father John Donnelly?'

McGovern glanced between Connor and Simon, as though one of them was going to give him a hint about the right answer to the question. 'No. I don't know who that is. Don't know—'

'Truth, remember?' Connor said. 'Don't talk shite, McGovern, it doesn't suit you. I'm guessing you know exactly who Father John Donnelly is. After all, it was at his church that you met Gareth Hogan to broker the deal for the land at Banknock, wasn't it?'

McGovern flinched in his chair as though Connor had strode across the room and slapped him. 'How ... how the hell did you know?' he said.

'Simple.' Connor shrugged. 'Banknock's been at the heart of a few events over the last couple of days. I had my people pull some information, tracing certain others' movements. Your friend Cunningham came up and, like the responsible politician he is, he showed a site in Banknock to Gareth Hogan, the industrialist. See, Hogan wanted to carry out fracking at the site, but the Scottish Government wouldn't go for it. So he looked for someone to unload the land on. And guess what? Three weeks after he inexplicably pays a visit to Lenton Barns and John Donnelly, you buy the land with plans to develop it. Now, I'm not a big one for coincidences, Mr McGovern, so you tell me, am I right, or was Mr Hogan suddenly gripped with a spiritual crisis he needed the good father's help with?'

McGovern seemed to deflate in his chair. 'Yes,' he muttered, petulant as a sulking child, 'you're right. When it became clear that Hogan wasn't going to get the go-ahead to develop the land for fracking, I was contacted, asked for a meeting. I knew Father John was at Lenton Barns, asked if he would be good enough to host a quiet meeting, out of sight of prying eyes. Hogan was toxic in the press with everything that was going on, and I had a reputation to protect. He agreed, for the good of the community and the jobs that a housing development would bring.'

Connor crossed his arms, felt like a dog being ordered to sit and wait for a treat.

'So how do you know Donnelly?' he said. 'And no bullshit. If you piss us around, I swear to you I'll take that watch and ram it down your throat so far your shits will be sponsored by Accurist for the rest of the year.'

McGovern's eyes widened as cold hatred bled into them. He glanced from Simon to Connor, as though trying to size up his chances against either man. Obviously came to the conclusion that the answer was 'none'.

'It's no big secret,' he said, as he began to fiddle with the watch again. 'I met Donnelly in Glasgow. Few years ago now. Yeah, that's right, it wasn't long after that big fire. Harbour Street, wasn't it? Yeah, that's it. The fire at Harbour Street. I met him after that.'

CHAPTER 43

Strachan agreed to meet Ford in Stirling, at a café up close to the castle. The call had come as a welcome excuse to get out of the office – after he'd asked Ogilvy to pull the incident logs for the Harbour Street fire, Strachan was sure Chief MacAlister would have uncomfortable questions for him. And, with the query he had just been informed about from the main press office in Glasgow, the last thing Strachan wanted was to be answering questions.

He arrived before Ford, staked a claim to a table on the street outside the café. It was a warm, pleasant day, light clouds in the sky, tourists milling around, taking in the sights and sounds of the historic heart of Stirling which, with its cobbled streets, solid buildings and almost Gothic engravings and adornments, always reminded Strachan of a scale miniature of Edinburgh's Old Town.

Ford arrived a few moments later, shoulders hunched, head down, as though the bright sun and mildness of the day offended him.

'Sorry I'm late,' he said, taking a seat opposite Strachan. 'Got delayed with a bit of news.'

'No problem,' Strachan said, gesturing to the coffee he had ordered for Ford when he arrived. 'You want that, or does this news you're referring to warrant something stronger?'

Ford smiled. Years ago, they had been drinking pals, hitting the pubs after shifts attending crime scenes that required the attention of both police and fire services. But while Ford had had his wife to go home to and a sense of when to stop, Strachan had had neither. It was Ford he had turned to when he had decided to get sober, Ford who had swapped whisky for Diet Coke when they had met for drinks and a chat.

'I'll take this,' he said, reaching for the coffee. 'Thanks.'

'So, what you got?' Strachan asked, curious.

'Well, it's part of what I wanted to see you about,' Ford said after a long sip of his coffee. 'I was thinking about the drones used in the attack on the church, and what was used to make the bombs that were attached to them.'

'Petrol mixed with Vaseline,' Strachan said. 'Crude but effective. Acts like napalm. The Vaseline thickens the petrol to a sludge, so it sticks to anything that it comes into contact with and burns.' A thought occurred to him then, an unwelcome addition to a picture that had been steadily growing in his mind.

'Okay.' Ford nodded. 'So my question was, where was the petrol used in that coming from? Given the range of the drones, I guessed that whoever was doing this would want to get their petrol somewhere between Banknock, where the drones were controlled from, and the site of the attack at Lenton Barns. So I had my people look at petrol stations between the two places, and check CCTV footage for any sign of the red car we saw outside the fire station at Banknock and the railway station at Stirling.'

'So you found it? It was there?' Strachan asked, leaning forward.

Another smile twitched Ford's lips. 'Yeah, one of the CCTV cameras covering a supermarket car park about five minutes' walk from the station recorded an old VW Polo parking up at about the time of the kidnapping. Predictably, the driver keeps his head down and has a cap on to obscure any look at his features, and we ran the plates we managed to get from the footage, but they're registered to a Porsche 911 that was reported stolen from Dunblane last month. But it's something. And it matches with what kept me from getting here sooner.'

'You found footage of the car at a petrol station as well?' Strachan said, feeling a faint buzz that was nothing to do with the coffee he was drinking.

'Exactly,' Ford said. 'Footage from a Shell garage about halfway between Banknock and Lenton Barns recorded the same VW Polo stopping, the driver filling the car and two drums with petrol. You know the type – folk use them on camping trips and the like.'

'Hardly seems enough to make those bombs and torch that cab,' Strachan said.

'Yeah, we thought of that,' Ford replied. 'So we're going back over the last month, see if he's a creature of habit, if there are any other visits he made to stockpile petrol in the run-up to the attack.'

'Makes sense,' Strachan agreed. 'But hold on, you only found out about this while I was on my way here, so this isn't the main thing you wanted to talk to me about. What's up? Why did you want to meet?'

'Got me,' Ford said, holding up his hands. 'Actually, it was my chief who made me want to talk to you. He called me earlier on, gave me a bollocking for Donna Blake breaking the story about Father Donnelly being kidnapped. But he got really defensive when I started to . . . Gary, what?'

Strachan realised his expression must have changed when Ford mentioned Donna Blake's name. 'That reporter,' he said with a sigh, 'Blake. I got a call a little while ago, from our press office, telling me she'd been on the phone, asking for a statement about a firefighter who was injured at Harbour Street and died about a month ago. I know you've had dealings with her in the past. What are we getting into here?'

Ford leant forward, his gaze growing cold, calculating. 'She's a pain in the arse,' he said, 'but a good reporter. Got a knack for sniffing out trouble and stuff you don't want in the public domain. But what about this firefighter who only died a month ago? I thought Harbour Street was years ago.'

Strachan swallowed the last of his coffee, ran his fingers around the rim of the cup. 'Yeah, it was,' he said. 'Seems Peter Turnbull was badly hurt in the blaze but lived. If you want to call it living. He'd suffered massive burns and brain damage.' He shrugged, feeling that niggling, unpleasant thought coil in the back of his mind again.

'What?' Ford asked.

'I dunno,' Strachan said. 'It's just that, with everything that's going on here, Harbour Street keeps on coming up at the heart of it. Then there's the drones, the hacking of the Banknock tower to control them, the petrol bombs that have been used, it all—'

'It all points to a firefighter, or someone with expertise in your operations and techniques,' Ford said, in a tone that told Strachan he'd had the same thought.

'Yeah,' Strachan replied, not liking the way the word felt in his mouth. 'I've asked my junior to pull the incident logs from Harbour Street, see if there's anything in there.'

'Your Chief MacAlister was there, wasn't he?' Ford said.

Strachan cast his mind back. 'Yeah,' he said. 'He was the station commander for the first appliances responding, took command of the incident. Worked the whole night from what I was told, did a lot to get him the job of chief of the national service.'

Ford shifted forward. 'See, that's what I wanted to talk to you about. When I was talking to my chief about all this, I mentioned I was working with you. He got jumpy, started banging on about your boss's political ambitions and a national review of the fire service.'

'Yeah, happening at the moment,' Strachan said. He'd been involved in compiling the reports for the national review and, from what he could see, it was little more than a way for the government to show that their idea of merging the eight regional fire services across Scotland into one national service had been a brilliant idea. Strachan, like a lot of firefighters, wasn't sure he agreed.

He sighed, aware of Ford's gaze on him. 'Well, Chief MacAlister was one of the main architects of the national service, and his voice carried a lot of weight after Harbour Street. So if this review goes badly, then it's the end for him. But if it goes well and we're shown to be a model of efficiency and good practice ...'

'He finds himself a nice wee seat in Holyrood after his term as chief is over?' Ford guessed, remembering the chief constable's words.

'There are rumours,' Strachan replied, 'that MacAlister wants a seat in politics. Feels he's earned it.'

'Any idea which way he leans?'

'No clue,' Strachan said. 'But he loves the Scottish national fire service, so you decide.'

Ford grunted a laugh. 'Fair enough, you—'

He was cut off by the shrill ring of Strachan's phone. Strachan pulled it from his pocket, felt a stab of ice lance through his veins as he read the number calling.

'Control, this is Lema Four Delta Zero Four,' he said, giving his tally number to the caller from the fire service's main control and deployment centre in Johnstone, just outside Glasgow.

He listened as he was given details of the call he had been assigned to, his mind racing with calculations and mapping out routes to get to his destination as quickly as possible. 'Mark me as assigned and en route,' he said, then killed the call.

'You okay?' Ford asked.

Strachan looked across at his friend, blinked. Again the equation rose in his head, the facts they had been discussing merging to form one conclusion too grotesque to be real.

'That car you were looking for,' he said, as he stood. 'Old-style Volkswagen Polo. Probably early nineties. Front bumper hanging loose at the off side, licence plates conveniently missing?'

Ford nodded, his face growing pale. 'Yeah,' he said warily. 'That sounds a lot like it. Why?'

Strachan held up his phone. 'Just had a call in. It's been spotted at Lenton Barns, near the Mercat Cross. Local crews are on their way, but the caller, well . . .'

'What?' Ford asked.

'The caller said the car was a bomb,' Strachan said. 'And that it would go up like the drones at St Ninian's in,' he glanced at his watch, 'forty minutes' time.'

CHAPTER 44

For Connor, the scene in front of him was an unpleasant reminder of his time in Northern Ireland. Police had set up a cordon around the Mercat Cross in the centre of Lenton Barns, pushing everyone back towards the opposite end of the high street. People milled about uneasily at the cordon, anxious chatter filling the air as a mixture of curiosity and fear rippled through the crowd.

Beyond the cordon, Connor could see an array of ambulances, police cars, fire engines and a large gunmetal grey van striped with what looked like yellow reflective go-faster stripes. He didn't need to make out the lettering on the side to know what it said: Explosive Ordinance Disposal – the Army's specialist bomb disposal team.

The call had come from Donna not long after he and Simon had left the offices of McGovern Properties.

'Just got a tip from a contact in the police,' she said, as he answered the phone, her voice tight with distracted excitement. 'Seems there's something going on at Lenton Barns. A bomb threat's been called in. You know anything about it?'

Connor checked his messages to see if his tormentor from the last few days had been in touch. But nothing, no messages or emails. The sudden silence troubled him. Had going public with Donnelly's kidnapping been a mistake, driven the killer further into the shadows instead of dragging him into the light?

He thanked Donna for the tip, told Simon what had happened.

They drove to Lenton Barns in silence, and Connor knew Simon would be thinking of other bomb calls in Belfast. Despite the Troubles being over, the threat of bombs was still used as a weapon of terror and intimidation in Northern Ireland, and it was bred into every police officer's DNA to be on the lookout for abandoned suitcases and innocuous-looking parcels delivered in the post. Even now, Connor knew Simon would check under his car before driving whenever he was at home.

They arrived, parked and made their way to the front of the cordon, both trying to take in every face at once, searching for someone who was looking the wrong way, or ignoring the churn of people around them. It was common enough with bomb threats – the bomber would make the call, then join the chaotic crowd they had created and watch the results of their work play out in front of them. In his gut, Connor knew whoever had planted this bomb would not be in the crowd. Whatever was going on, he wasn't doing any of this for visceral pleasure. There was cold calculation in everything that had happened, like a grand master moving pieces around a chessboard to get his opponent exactly where he wanted them to be.

The question Connor had was what the end game would be.

He turned to his right, his attention drawn by the sound of a siren and the impatient beeping of a horn. Saw a dark SUV roll towards the barrier, blue lights flashing from beneath the front grille and a mounted LED unit on the interior of the windscreen. Connor saw DCI Malcolm Ford sitting in the passenger seat, his face pale and set, Strachan leaning forward from the back seat, squeezing between Ford and his man mountain assistant, Ogilvy, as he gestured to the police officer at the cordon to let them past.

'What you think?' Simon asked.

Connor felt his phone buzz in his pocket, pulled it out and smiled, showing the screen to Simon. It was a message from Donna, who was positioned at the other side of the high-street cordon with Keith, her cameraman. She had sent Connor a picture of Ford and Strachan arriving, with the text: *Guess I know who to get to comment on this.*

'I think Ford's going to be pissed off with Donna again,' Connor said.

'Couldn't happen to a nicer guy,' Simon replied. He held the moment of levity for a second. Then his voice dropped as his face tightened. 'But what about this? Dramatic enough for yer man but, again, why? Why blow up a car in the middle of the village? He's already got Donnelly, so why do this? It doesn't damage the church, doesn't get to you or anyone you're close to.'

Connor shrugged, as though the action could relieve the itch he felt in the back of his mind. Simon was right: there was something here, something he wasn't seeing, something . . .

'Oh, fuck,' he whispered, the sudden realisation slamming the breath from his lungs as his mind filled with the messages the killer had sent him. He was moving before he knew it, barging through the crowd, sprinting for the cordon.

'Connor, what?' Simon called, as he tried to catch up.

'He's flushing the mark!' Connor shouted back. 'Get on the phone now! Warn them!'

He saw the police officers at the cordon turn as they registered the turmoil in the crowd, people parting like waves as Connor sprinted through them. One officer took a step forward, but Connor had no time to stop. He grabbed the man's outstretched arm, dropped his hip and drove up, putting everything he had into a shoulder check into the police officer's ribs, just behind his protective vest. The officer was thrown off his feet, crashing into his fellow officer, who was charging towards them both to offer help.

Connor barely heard the screams from the crowd behind him, just kept moving, praying he was going to be fast enough or that Simon would get through. He dodged through bemused emergency staff who were clustered around their vehicles, sidestepped a firefighter who seemed to appear out of nowhere, like a cardboard cut-out bad guy on a firing range.

Saw Ford and Strachan in front of him, standing in front of Strachan's SUV, talking to a man in what looked like an exaggerated American football player's uniform.

Pain exploded in his side as he was suddenly driven off balance and tumbled to the ground, the rough surface of the road biting into his palms, elbows and knees. Felt a heavy weight on him, strong arms grabbing for his hands and pushing them back, trying to pin him.

Connor threw back his head, bucked his hips, flung off his attacker. Was aware of other bodies closing in on him, knew he had to get up before it was over. Scrabbled to his feet, warm blood dripping from his hands and scraped knees. Saw the police officer who had rugby-tackled him in front of him, getting to his feet, teeth bared in an almost feral snarl.

'Fraser!' a voice shouted. Connor turned to his left, saw Ford rushing towards him, something between miscomprehension and naked hatred tattooed across his face. 'What the hell are you—'

Connor stepped forward, grabbed the policeman by the collar, dragged him towards him. Turned and started dragging him away. Away from the car.

'Think about it, sir,' he said, noticing the uniformed police officer shifting closer, other officers moving in to surround him. He would have done the same. A man had just assaulted three police officers and breached a cordon at a bomb site and was now trying to kidnap a senior police officer? If he had been on duty, Connor would have taken the man down himself.

But he wasn't. And, finally, Connor knew what the killer was trying to tell him: Things aren't always what they seem.

'What the hell are you talking about, Fraser?' Ford asked, as he thrashed against Connor's grip.

'Think about it, sir,' Connor said again, forcing himself to talk slowly and clearly. 'What did he say in the warning to me after the attack on the church? *Good to see so many faces from the boys in blue. I'll kill one of them as well.* He was watching us, knew who was there. Knew you were there, sir, knew you were involved in the case, knew you'd respond to any subsequent calls. This,' Connor gestured back towards the car, 'is flushing the mark. Using a distraction to get you where he wants you, then. . .' He let his voice trail off, saw Ford put the pieces together in his head.

'Jesus,' Ford whispered, eyes growing wide as they darted around, trying to take everything in at once. 'Then that means—'

And then everything exploded.

CHAPTER 45

It was as if the world had suddenly been put on fast forward.

Connor heard a sharp cry of warning, felt rather than saw frantic, panicked movement around the car. Then, before he could react, there was a deafening roar and Ford was thrown into his arms, as though some vengeful god had reached down from the heavens, snatched the policeman and hurled him with all its might. Connor grabbed Ford, then felt himself shoved off his feet, flying through the air backwards on what felt like a wave of arid air. A memory of his first visit to Las Vegas flashed through his mind, of stepping out of the air-conditioned plane into a heat so dry and intense it felt vengeful. It was like being hit by a wall of that heat.

A strange moment of weightlessness, then he crashed to the ground, Ford's body adding to the force of the impact. He cried out as agony tore across his back like a lightning bolt, his injured shoulder exploding with searing, ice-cold shards of pain. Dark stars exploded across his eyes as the back of his head cracked onto the tarmac, and he felt the sudden urge to vomit. The blackness crowded in on him, eager, warm, inviting, but he bit down on his tongue, used the pain to focus, drive back the oblivion that called to him. Dared to move his head, saw Ford lying on his chest, eyes closed, having given in to the unconsciousness that Connor had beaten back. He fumbled for the policeman's neck, his fingers thick, clumsy, alien, felt a surge of relief when he detected a strong, steady pulse beat.

'Connor! Connor!' A voice was calling to him, far away and muffled, as though he was sitting at the bottom of a swimming-pool and someone was shouting for him. He leant his head back and smiled. Simon: always there when he needed him.

'Jesus Christ, Connor. You okay?' Simon said, as he hauled Ford off Connor's chest and placed him in the recovery position. Around them there was a riot of activity as firefighters sprang into action and ambulance workers helped triage the wounded.

'Aye, I'm just bloody wonderful,' he said, aware he was shouting. Was this, he wondered, how his gran heard the world as her hearing faded? Far away, muffled, unimportant?

He sat up, the dull, copper tang of blood biting at the back of his throat. Hung his head and spat out a thick wad of reddish-pink phlegm. It didn't help. He raised his head slowly, wincing as rusty nails of pain dug into his neck and the back of his skull. Squinted. Could just see what was left of the car that had exploded, nothing more than a mangled, twisted husk of metal.

'How many hurt?' he asked, more to himself than Simon as an idea solidified in his mind.

Simon turned back to the wreckage. 'No idea,' he said. 'But it looked like everyone was fairly far back, and you know those bomb-disposal boys don't leave the house without strapping their G-shocks to their wrists and body armour to their cocks.'

Despite himself, Connor laughed, his chest feeling as if it was filled with churning hot coals. He held the pain close, nurtured it, made it a part of him. A part he would share with the man who had just lured DCI Ford into a trap and detonated a car bomb to try to kill him.

A man, he realised, who had just made his first real mistake.

Connor thought back to another smouldering wreck and the sign in front of it: *This blood is on Donnelly's hands, Mr Fraser. How bloody are you willing to get?*

'As bloody as it takes,' Connor muttered. He hauled himself to his feet, spat out more blood.

'You need to get a paramedic to look you over,' Simon said, as his eyes darted across Connor's face, no doubt inventorying injuries as he went.

Connor shook his head as he saw a paramedic making a beeline for him. 'No time for that. Let's get Ford looked at, then get the hell out of here before the police decide to hold us.'

'Oh, aye,' Simon said cautiously, as though he had heard the intent in Connor's voice. 'And just where will we be going?'

'Back in time, Simon,' Connor said. 'Back in time.'

CHAPTER 46

They used the chaos of the blast to get past the cordon, the officers who were there more interested in keeping bystanders who hadn't fled away from the wreckage than stopping Connor and Simon leaving.

Connor gave Simon the keys to the Audi, tried his best to get comfortable in the passenger seat despite the symphony of pain that was echoing through his body. Closed his eyes for a moment, felt the darkness call to him again. And what would it hurt? Just a few minutes in the numbing silence. After all, he deserved it. He—

'You sure this is a good idea?' Simon asked, forcing Connor back to consciousness.

'Not got many options,' Connor said. 'We've no time to be slowed up answering police questions, and they know where I live and the company offices. We need somewhere off the grid to work. Somewhere with supplies. Think I've got an idea about what's going on, but I'm going to need some help to prove it.'

Simon turned to Connor, gave him a quizzical glance. 'Care to share with the class?'

Connor shifted in his seat, thought again of the twisted wreckage of the car. A car that had been detonated only when Ford was nearby, in an explosion that, from what Connor could tell, was controlled.

He fumbled for his phone in his pocket, winced as he saw the screen was cracked. But it still worked, unlocking as he tapped in his passcode. Battered but still working. Connor knew the feeling.

'This whole thing revolves around the fire service,' he said, as he scrolled through his contacts. 'From the drones that were controlled from a hacked fire-station tower, to the Vaseline-laced petrol used to make napalm, to the car bomb, everything about this indicates that whoever is behind this has knowledge of fire and how the fire service works. So you add that to the car bomb, and how it only went off when Ford arrived on scene, then . . .'

'Then whoever blew the car up was there to see Ford arrive,' Simon said, picking up Connor's train of thought.

'Exactly,' Connor said. 'And with all those firefighters, coppers and ambulance staff milling around, what would be the perfect camouflage?'

'A uniform,' Simon said, his voice a barely audible whisper above the growl of the Audi's engine. 'Christ, you really think a serving fire-fighter is behind all this?'

Connor shrugged, his shoulder instantly telling him it had been a bad idea. 'It fits the facts we have. Even Donnelly is connected to the fire service, through what happened at Harbour Street and the last victim Donna tracked down.'

'Makes sense,' Simon said. 'So what's our next move? I know where we're going, but . . .'

Connor hit dial on his phone, raised it to his ear. 'Harbour Street,' he said. 'Everything ties back to there. Donnelly, the dead firefighter – hell, even the property guy, McGovern.'

'Speaking of whom, do you really believe his story about . . .'

Connor held up a finger, silencing Simon as his call was answered.

'ACO Strachan? It's Connor Fraser. Are you okay, sir? I didn't see you in the scrum after the blast, not sure how close you were.'

'Fraser,' Strachan growled, his voice hoarse, as though he had been shouting. 'I saw your little stunt with Ford. You might just have saved his life. Though your vanishing act won't have made you too many friends in the police.'

'Just did what I had to,' Connor murmured, embarrassed. 'Look, sir, the reason I'm calling is I need your help. I think I can find who-ever the hell is doing all this, but I can't do it without you.'

Strachan barked a laugh down the line. 'Ford really was right about you, wasn't he?'

Connor ignored the dig. 'Look, I need to know about Harbour Street. What happened there. I think this is all tied to it. I know some of it from what my reporter friends have dug up, and I can find a fair chunk online. But I need to know all of it. Is there any way you could get me the incident logs from Harbour Street, let me see the big picture?'

'You've got to be joking,' Strachan snarled. 'You want me to share confidential files with you? For what? To try to pin this on a firefighter?'

'Nice to see you came to the same conclusion I did,' Connor said, sudden weariness seeming to push him down into the passenger seat. 'Look at it this way, sir. Either I find it is a firefighter behind all this, or I prove it isn't. If it is a firefighter, do you really want a killer in one of your uniforms loose on the streets? I want to find this bastard. He's killed one person, grabbed Donnelly, almost killed DCI Ford. Threatened my family. I want to stop him, but I don't have time to go through official channels. If you've talked to Ford about me, you know I can get things done. So, please, help me. Or do you want to see someone else get hurt?'

A moment of silence on the line, then Strachan gave a frustrated sigh. 'Fine,' he said. 'My assistant, Ogilvy, is heading back to pull the logs now. As soon as he gets them, I'll share them with you. But this is confidential, Fraser. You do this off the books, and you tell me anything you find, clear?'

'Totally, sir,' Connor said. 'You have my number. Call me when you have the files.'

He hung up, stared ahead. Something in what he had just said to Strachan nagged at him, like a half-remembered dream. Something about uniforms . . .

He snapped out of his thoughts as Simon pulled up at their destination.

'You sure about this?' Simon asked again.

'No,' Connor said, as he studied the blunt façade of Paulie King's home. 'But let's do it anyway.'

CHAPTER 47

'Jesus Christ,' Paulie snarled, as he opened his front door. 'What the hell did I do to deserve this shite? I did you a favour, had a gun put in my face as a thank-you, and now you're back again looking like an extra from a zombie movie. You're bloody cursed, Fraser. Anyone ever tell you that?'

The pain rolling through Connor's body made it hard to disagree. 'Paulie, I'm sorry,' he said. 'Got to keep my head down for a bit, and I need a favour.'

'And what's in it for me?' Paulie said, leaning against the door frame, obviously enjoying Connor's discomfort.

'Nothing,' Connor said simply. 'But you'd be helping me find who-ever threatened Jen.'

Paulie bared his teeth, sighed. 'They responsible for that blast in Lenton Barns?' he asked.

'Maybe,' Connor said. 'How did you. . .?'

'All over the TV,' Paulie replied. 'That reporter you know, Donna Blake, she's been reporting on it. Nice wee lassie by the look of it.'

Simon stiffed slightly at Connor's side and Paulie smiled, held up his hands. 'Just saying,' he said. 'Look, come on in - you're making the place look untidy standing there.'

Connor and Simon exchanged a glance, then followed Paulie into the house. The smell of bleach hung in the air, and Connor could guess why.

'So what happened with McGovern's thugs? You didn't say much on the phone.'

'And what was I going to say?' Paulie said, gesturing to one of the couches in the living room. 'They followed me, pulled a gun and a knife on me so I blew one of their heads off? I'm not a total fucking arsehole, Fraser, give me that much.'

'Jesus,' Simon said.

'Aye,' Paulie agreed.

'That seem like an overreaction to you?' Connor said. 'We spoke to McGovern. He claims he was asking around as he wanted me to do a job for him. Look after some development sites he's got in the pipeline, make sure things run smoothly, use my press contacts to keep the bad headlines to a minimum. He said he wanted me to see how he worked so I knew he was serious. But sending someone to kill you after you did some digging for me, isn't that a bit . . . extreme?'

Paulie gave Connor a look that could almost have been mistaken for sheepish. 'I don't know if they were sent to kill me,' he said. 'They were tailing me, and when I confronted them, one kid pulled a knife, the other a gun. They might have been putting the shitters up me, or they might have been going to put me down. I didn't give them the chance.'

A moment of silence, the weight of Paulie's words settling in the room.

'Still, it doesn't track. It's an overreaction. Unless McGovern was covering something else up.'

'Like what?' Paulie asked.

'I don't know,' Connor said, more to Simon than to Paulie. 'McGovern did mention that he knew Father Donnelly from his time in Glasgow, something about meeting him because of the Harbour Street fire. You know anything about that?'

'What the fuck am I? Your personal encyclopaedia?' Paulie snapped. 'Christ. But, yeah, as I remember, McGovern was building homes in Glasgow at the time. Only know that as MacKenzie Haulage got the contract to deliver some of the materials to the site, and I had to co-ordinate it. Bastard of a job, with all the safety regulations.'

'What type of homes?' Connor asked.

Paulie gave him a warning look, and Connor felt the temperature in the room drop. 'Community homes, social housing, that type of thing.'

'So how would that lead him to cross paths with a firefighters' pastor?' Connor asked.

'Because McGovern helped with the clear-up at the Harbour Street site after the fire,' Simon said, stepping forward and showing Connor his phone. He had opened a web page, found a news article in the *Western Chronicle* reporting on the aftermath of the Harbour Street fire in the days after the blaze. Scrolling down, Connor found a picture. A crane sat in the centre of a rubble-strewn site, the skeletal remains of the Harbour Street warehouse rising from the ground, like gnarled fingers that had been stripped to the bone. The side of the crane bore a logo, and the name 'McGovern Homes'.

'So he helped with the clean-up,' Connor said, skimming the article below the picture. It stated that McGovern had offered his services with the clean-up, and donated generously to the fund Father Donnelly had set up in the wake of the tragedy to support the work of the Firefighters' Association. 'What happened to the site afterwards?'

Simon took his phone back, fiddled with it for a moment. 'Flats and shops,' he said, showing Connor a street-view image marked 'Harbour Street'. 'Looks like they bulldozed the site and redeveloped.'

Connor suddenly remembered McGovern's words in his office: *I've got several developments planned across Scotland, some on quite controversial sites.* 'Controversial,' he muttered.

'What?' Simon said.

Connor looked up, a thought uncurling in his mind. 'We need those files from Strachan,' he said. 'Now.'

'Does that mean you're going to piss off and leave me in peace?' Paulie rumbled.

Connor smiled. 'Sure, Paulie,' he said. 'But, first, I've got one more favour to ask.'

CHAPTER 48

Strachan sat in a mobile command unit that the police had brought in to Lenton Barns, drinking a cup of coffee that was doing nothing to improve his mood. He almost envied Ford, who had been taken to hospital for assessment after being knocked out by the blast. At least that way he was missing out on all this.

The bomb that had been detonated in the car had been small and lethal, just powerful enough to destroy the vehicle and any real chance at forensic evidence, but not so forceful that it had detonated the car's petrol tank. It was, Strachan was forced to admit, a very professional, expertly handled piece of work.

And that was what troubled him.

He knew that police forensics officers were picking through the car with fire investigation staff, preparing their reports. He also knew that, as it was a car bomb, counterterrorism officers would be involved. All of which had turned up the pressure on Chief Constable Peter Guthrie, and Strachan's boss, Chief Fire Officer Arthur MacAlister. Pressure they had been only too happy to share with their officers, making it clear that a quick result was needed to placate the angry gods that roamed the halls of the Scottish Parliament, set their budgets and decided who got the top jobs. Strachan suspected MacAlister would see it as an opportunity to boost his reputation as the review of the national fire service was under way, which meant that, if there was fault to be assigned, he would have no problem in finding a sacrificial lamb.

And, as the most senior firefighter on the scene, Strachan knew that role would fall to him.

He sighed, got out of his chair, suddenly needing to be away from the confinement of the mobile unit, which was little more than an oversized Transit van that had been fitted with tables, chairs and extra power outlets for laptops.

He hopped out into the street, the wreck of the car sitting opposite, hidden by a white tent SOCOs had erected around it. The street glittered with glass from windows shattered by the force of the explosion, and Strachan was again amazed that no one had been seriously hurt in the blast.

He grunted, pulled out his phone and checked his call logs and emails. Nothing yet from Ogilvy on the files from Harbour Street. He felt a flash of irritation: it wasn't like Ogilvy to be so sloppy. Usually when he asked the young officer for something, it was done almost before he had finished speaking.

He flicked through his phone for Ogilvy's number. Dialled it. Got nothing but a voicemail recording. Gave a sigh of frustration, then dialled his station in Kirkcaldy.

'Ah, Debbie,' he said, as the phone was answered. 'I'm looking for Ogilvy. He's got some files for me and I've not heard from him. Could you put him on, please?'

'Sir?' Debbie said, uncertainty in her voice. 'I'm not sure what you mean. Ogilvy logged himself as off duty and left the station a couple of hours ago. I've not seen him since.'

CHAPTER 49

Connor studied his phone as Simon drove, heading back to the flat. It was a risk, but one Connor thought worth taking. They were in a small, pristine hatchback: Connor's last request to Paulie had been the use of a car and storing the Audi at his place until he knew the police weren't actively looking for him. After a storm of expletives Paulie had reluctantly agreed, and Connor had watched in the rear-view mirror as he circled the Audi as they drove away. Knowing Paulie, he could be considering anything from blowing it up to giving it a full valet.

'What's up?' Simon asked.

Connor grunted. 'Something's been bothering me. Why has he gone quiet?'

'You mean the guy doing all this?' Simon asked.

'Yeah. Think about it. This all started with him sending me images of Jen and Gran and that bullshit contract. Then he taunts me about killing one of the "boys in blue", sends me a pic of the burning taxi. But since he's grabbed Donnelly, nothing. I mean, I thought getting the news of the kidnapping out there would force his hand, make him get in touch and gloat, but no. Then he blows a car up and not a word. Why?'

'Maybe we got lucky and he blew himself up with one of his own petrol bombs,' Simon said, no humour in his voice.

'Better not have,' Connor said. 'I want a word with this bastard before he stops breathing.'

They drove past the flat once, checking for marked police cars or unmarked surveillance. Seeing nothing, Simon U-turned, then powered up the small, gravelled driveway that led around the back of the building to the entrance to Connor's flat. They got out quickly, neither speaking as they scoped out the terrain and checked the door for signs of tampering. Satisfied that the flat had been left undisturbed, they let themselves in.

'I'm going to get changed,' Connor said, the smell of smoke and spent petrol from the blast suddenly very strong in the calm of the flat.

'Aye, crack on,' Simon called. 'I'll get some coffee on the go, see if Tom's around for a snack.'

Connor smiled to himself as he headed for his bedroom. While Simon doted on the cat, Connor could hardly get her to come near him. In a way, it wasn't much different with people: Simon was the outgoing, welcoming one, Connor the introvert who found forming new relationships and friendships difficult. He had long since made peace with his social awkwardness, but he still felt a vague pang of jealousy when he saw how easily Simon related to people.

A shower and a change of clothes later, he walked into the living room, saw Simon behind the breakfast bar, a pot of coffee in front of him, the wall-mounted TV on low.

'I see Donna caught your good side,' Simon said, gesturing to the TV. Showing on loop was footage of the car explosion in Lenton Barns, Connor's back half turned as he tried to drag Ford away from the scene.

'You spoken to her?' Simon asked.

'No,' Connor admitted. 'Been too caught up with everything else that's going on. But I should give her a call, see how she and that other guy, McGregor, got on with the information we gave them.'

'You think he can make his story about Hogan being involved in a government conspiracy stick?' Simon asked.

Connor shrugged. It was one thing to put people in positions of power in the same place at the same time, quite another to prove that they were holding meetings aimed at destabilising a government over its energy policy. Given everything he had seen, Connor couldn't discount the possibility, but proving it would be for Doug and Donna. He had other problems to deal with.

'I'll give her a call later, see how it's going,' he said. 'Mind you, I'm kind of surprised she's not been in touch with us. She saw us in Lenton Barns, got me on camera with Ford. She's usually the first person to . . .'

Connor stopped talking, felt something cold and grotesque skitter through his thoughts as he remembered his conversation with Simon in the car.

'Connor, big lad, what . . .?' Simon said, his face growing pinched and concerned.

'Call Donna, now,' Connor whispered, panic and an ugly certainty clawing at his throat. Why would a killer who loved attention go quiet? What would he do to make a point? And if Connor was right, if he was a firefighter at the scene of the blast, virtually invisible until he made a request or issued an order, what could he do? He closed his eyes, could almost see the scene unfolding. *Just step this way, please, ma'am, for your own safety . . .*

Connor looked up again at the TV, Donna staring into the camera. It wasn't a live feed – he could tell by the smoking wreckage of the car and the position of the fire engines. Felt the panic in his chest curdle into something darker and more poisonous as he saw a firefighter just over Donna's shoulder, watching her present to camera.

'No answer,' Simon said, as he waggled his phone at Connor.

Connor cursed. 'Come on,' he said. 'We can call her news desk while we move, and try McGregor as well, find out if he's seen her.'

'Hold on! You think he's got her?' Simon asked.

'I don't know,' Connor said, hearing the lie in his tone and hating it. 'But it would explain why our friend hasn't been in touch with me. And Donna's been the face of this story from the start – from the attack on the church to Donnelly's kidnapping. And it's no secret she knows us. So, yeah, if I was going to make a point, she'd be a target for me.'

'Shit,' Simon hissed. 'Okay, let's go. You drive, I'll make the calls.'

They were halfway to the car when Connor's phone rang. He froze, glancing up at Simon, whose expression betrayed nothing.

'Hello?'

'Fraser? It's ACO Strachan. We need to talk *now*. How fast can you get back to Lenton Barns?'

CHAPTER 50

Simon confirmed with the Sky newsdesk that Donna had been covering the Lenton Barns car-bomb story, and hadn't returned. There had been no word from her cameraman, Keith, either. A call to Doug McGregor made the bad news worse – he had arranged to meet her in Stirling to go over their story on the conspiracy, but she hadn't shown up.

'Shit,' Connor hissed, as they drove into Lenton Barns, tensing in his seat as the police cars and vehicles clustered around the Mercat Cross came into view.

Simon seemed to read his thoughts. 'Strachan said he'd had a word with the police, straightened things out. You're here at his request. Unlikely he's going to set the boys on you when he's got whatever he wants.'

Connor nodded, but didn't share Simon's optimism. He had seen the hostility in Strachan's eyes when he had brought up Connor's assault on a firefighter during a previous case, knew the man had a deep distrust of him. And while he couldn't blame him for that, he couldn't let it stop him either. If he was right, Donna was in trouble – and it was his fault.

He pulled the car into the kerb near the cordon, sent a text to Strachan. The firefighter appeared a few minutes later, strode towards them as Connor and Simon got out of the car.

'Let's take a walk,' he said, jutting his chin back up the main street.

They walked in silence, then crossed the road and went into a small park where an old slide and swings stood, rusting and forgotten as weeds rose up to choke them.

'What I'm about to tell you is off the record and should not be taken as incriminating to the officer in question. Is that clear?' Strachan said, eyes darting between Connor and Simon.

Connor felt a tingle of excitement. 'Go on,' he said.

Strachan sighed. 'My assistant, the officer I told you about, the one I asked to pull the files on the Harbour Street fire, has gone AWOL.'

Connor thought back, remembered the giant he and Simon had met in Kirkcaldy. 'The watch manager, Ogilvy, you mean him?'

'Yes, that's him. A fine officer. I can't explain it. But I checked with Control as well. He left his beeper at Kirkcaldy station and signed himself off the run – off duty, that is – and hasn't been seen since. And the records department at our HQ confirmed to me that they haven't received any requests in relation to Harbour Street.'

'So you asked him to pull the records and he disappeared?' Simon said. 'Why? What do you know about him?'

'As I said, a good officer. A career firefighter from what I can tell. Joined straight out of school, excelled at basic training. On the fast track to be an area commander and a future assistant chief or even chief.'

'That's not what Simon asked,' Connor said, as pieces of a puzzle he hadn't known he was working on clicked home in his mind. 'He asked what you know about the man. Not the firefighter. Who is this guy?'

Strachan shrugged. 'He's a quiet man, which I suppose is odd given his stature, keeps himself to himself. And, I'll admit, I don't go out of my way to get involved in the personal lives of my men.'

Connor nodded approval. Took a breath, then exhaled. 'Pull his personnel file,' he said. 'We need to know who he is and why he dis-obeyed a direct order, then went AWOL.'

'As I said, this is not to be taken as incriminating,' Strachan replied, warning in his voice now. 'I can't explain it, but he may have any number of reasons for walking off the job. I wanted you to know, just in case . . .'

'Yeah,' Connor said, 'just in case I was wrong.'

'Wrong?' Strachan said. 'What do you mean wrong?'

Connor closed his eyes. Stupid, he thought. Stupid Connor. And slow.

'I thought the car bomb was for Ford,' he said. 'But what if it wasn't? Police aren't the only boys in blue. Think about it. You ask for files relating to Harbour Street, then all of a sudden there's a bomb call in Lenton Barns. Now, how would you stop someone looking into something you didn't want them to?'

'You'd flush the mark and lure them into a trap,' Simon said.

'Exactly,' Connor replied. 'I was right about that. Our killer was flushing the mark to get rid of someone he wanted – no, needed – to get out of the way. I thought that was DCI Ford. But what if it wasn't, sir? What if it was you?'

'You can't possibly think—' Strachan began.

Connor raised his hand. 'A career firefighter, that's what you called him. So he's trained. You also said he was capable. So he would know how to make napalm with Vaseline and petrol, how to hack the radio tower in Banknock to control the drones. Drones that, coincidentally, are the same type used by the fire service. Then you ask for the Harbour Street files and suddenly a bomb goes off in your face. That's all a bit of a coincidence, isn't it?'

'But . . .' Strachan said, his voice distracted, thin as he scrambled for an alternative explanation.

'You said he logged himself off duty at Kirkcaldy,' Connor said. 'How did he do that? In person or via a call? He drove you and Ford here, then you sent him scuttling back to Kirkcaldy. But, in reality, after seeing his little bomb trick fail, he could be anywhere.'

'But why?' Strachan said, after a moment. 'What could possibly motivate him to do that? What the hell happened at Harbour Street?'

'Pull the records,' Connor said. 'Personally, right now. Get them emailed to you and we can look at them together. And pull Ogilvy's personnel records as well. We need to know who he is. Might give us a clue as to where he's gone and . . .' Connor paused, another realisation hitting him '. . . and where our friend Donna is as well.'

CHAPTER 51

Doug sat in his room at the Stirling Highland Hotel, frustration and unease making it impossible to concentrate. Before the call from Simon asking about Donna, he had been working on his story about Gareth Hogan and Kerr Cunningham. The information that Connor Fraser had provided was compelling but circumstantial: he had an MSP and an industrialist involved in the controversial process of fracking in the same place at the same time, and visiting the Scotland Office. Looking back at the headlines from the time, the debate over energy and fracking had been used by all political parties, and there was plenty of rhetoric, especially from Cunningham and the secretary of state for Scotland accusing the Scottish Government of undermining potential new energy resources.

The facts fitted, Doug could feel it. But he needed more. He needed some kind of proof that Hogan was colluding with the UK Government, and that Kerr Cunningham was complicit in that. He had contacts at Holyrood and Westminster who could help, and he was on the point of contacting them, but he also needed Donna to start asking the type of questions that would rattle Cunningham. He wanted the politician off balance, nervous that a camera was about to be stuck in his face and some very uncomfortable questions asked of him.

But now, after the call with Simon, none of that seemed to matter. He didn't know Donna well, but he'd worked with her enough to get a feel for her – an ambitious, driven reporter with a nose for news and the tenacity to get at the truth. Had that tenacity led her into trouble, as it had him so many times before?

He sighed, gave up on any pretence of working on his story. He needed to find Donna - something in Simon McCartney's voice had told him as much. Flicked to his email, and the notes Donna had sent him on her digging into Father John Donnelly. She had found a link to a firefighter who had recently died, Peter Turnbull, the last victim of the blaze at Harbour Street. Was there something in there that would give a clue as to where she might possibly have gone, a line in the story that she'd decided to track down? It wasn't much, but it was all Doug had.

He skimmed over the notes Donna had made of the interview with Turnbull's sister, Caroline. It seemed straightforward: the grieving sister talking about her brother's life in the fire service, their family's firefighting history and their close relationship with Donnelly, who had provided comfort over the years Peter had been in a coma, and presided over his funeral when he had finally died.

He sat back in his chair, considered. What would he do if he was in Donna's position? After reporting on the car bomb in Lenton Barns, she would have gone back to the Turnbulls. Their close association with Donnelly, who had now gone missing, would have guaranteed it. But what . . .?

He read Donna's notes again, concentrating on what Caroline Turnbull had said about the priest. *It was Father Donnelly himself who arranged for Peter to be transferred to St Margaret's, who ensured he received the last rites.*

He flicked over to his search engine, typed in 'St Margaret's long-term care, firefighters' and hit search. Skimmed through the results, felt his stomach lurch as he saw the third entry. Opened the link and read, then started typing again, more quickly this time, breath short with excitement and a cold, ugly realisation.

He called up the files he had hacked from Sentinel, and the pictures that had been sent to Connor. Zoomed in on one, jotting down a name. Then started another search, his gut telling him the answer even before the screen had refreshed.

'Shit,' he muttered, reaching for his phone.

Donna really had been on to something with the Turnbulls. And, if he was right, it might just be enough to get her killed.

CHAPTER 52

The call came as they were driving back to Stirling, the plan being to check at Donna's place for any clues as to what she might have been working on. Connor wasn't looking forward to the task: if Donna's parents were at the flat looking after her son, he would have to think of a way to search the place without alerting them to what was going on. The last thing he wanted to do was alarm them until he had to.

'Connor Fraser,' he said, putting the phone on speaker as he drove.

'Fraser, it's DCI Ford.'

Connor exchanged a glance with Simon, who raised an eyebrow.

'Sir, it's good to hear you. Are you all right?'

Ford sighed, and Connor could hear exhaustion and pain in his voice. 'Banged up and got a headache that makes me think I had a bottle of whisky before I went to bed, but other than that, I'm in one piece. I understand I have you to thank for that. Second time in as many days.'

'Ah, yes, sir. I, ah, I apologise for manhandling your officers, but I needed to get to you as quickly as I could when I realised what was going on.'

'Manhandling,' Ford said, with a grunt of a laughter. 'Way I hear it, you just about took their heads off, put on a show that would put a scrum-half to shame.'

'Yes, sir,' Connor said, not sure what to say. Beside him, Simon grinned, clearly enjoying his discomfort.

'Anyway,' Ford said, his voice growing serious, 'that's not why I'm calling. Have you heard from Donna Blake recently?'

Another glance at Simon, the grin on his face gone now.

'No, sir. We were looking for her. Why?' Connor asked.

'We just had a call. Her van was found in a layby just outside Lenton Barns. Driver was in the back, badly injured, possible fractured skull. Nothing was taken and there was no sign of Blake. So she either wasn't with her cameraman or she was taken.'

Connor sucked air in through his teeth. 'Shit,' he hissed, thinking back to the two injured officers he and Simon had found back at the church. Both concussed, one with a possible fractured skull. A sudden image of Ogilvy ushering them to Strachan's office in Kirkcaldy, ducking and turning sideways as he manoeuvred through doorways, shoulders the size of boulders, hands like shovels.

Hands that could quite easily fracture a skull when they were curled into fists.

He told Ford what they knew about Ogilvy's disappearance, and his theory that the car bomb had been aimed at Strachan.

'Makes sense,' Ford said, after Connor had finished. 'I'll speak to Gary, get officers looking for this man Ogilvy. In the meantime, see what you can find. If you do turn up anything, you let me know, okay?'

'I thought you didn't want me involved in an active police investigation?' Connor asked, before he could stop himself.

'That was before this arsehole blew a car up in my face,' Ford said, before his voice dropped and he added: 'Two people are missing, Fraser. Father Donnelly and now Blake. I've no love for the woman, but I won't see her hurt by this lunatic. So if you can find him, find him. Just let me know if you do.'

'Understood,' Connor said. 'And, ah, sir, about my run-in with the police officers at Lenton Barns . . .'

'I've had a word. No further action will be taken and you're not wanted for questioning. But a word of warning, Fraser. It would be in your best interests not to attract my boys' attention for a wee while, understood?'

'Completely, sir. I'll be in touch.'

He cut the call, focused on the road.

'He's got her,' Simon said, his phone chirping with a text message as he spoke.

'Looks that way,' Connor agreed, feeling an impotent rage churn deep inside him. Where did they start looking for him? Where could Ogilvy take two people against their will and have no one notice? His sheer size would ensure he stuck out in a crowd, so how did he . . .

'Least we've got a place to start,' Simon said, rousing Connor from his thought.

'Oh? How so?'

Simon held up his phone, waggled it. 'Message from Doug McGregor. Seems he's been going through Donna's files, found something that may help. He also has a question for you.'

'Go on,' Connor said.

Simon looked back at his phone, read the message: '*Got something from Donna's notes. Need to see you both. And ask Fraser, his gran's nursing home is in Bannockburn, isn't it?*'

'What the hell?' Connor whispered, unease tickling the back of his neck at the mention of his gran.

'No idea,' Simon said. 'But I think we should go and ask McGregor what he's talking about, don't you?'

CHAPTER 53

'Just what the hell do you think you're playing at, Gary?'

Strachan closed his eyes, let static hiss down the line for a moment. He had been expecting the call ever since he had requested the files relating to the fire at Harbour Street. The fire in which Arthur MacAlister had forged himself a reputation as a skilled, courageous leader, the perfect man to lead Scotland's new national fire service. The man who was now on the other end of the line.

'Sir?' he asked, deciding the less he said, the better.

'We've had two major incidents in less than seventy-two hours, I've got the First Minister breathing down my neck about car bombs and response times and drone attacks, and then I'm told that my senior officer on the ground, the man I'm trusting to run clean-up operations, fire investigation liaison and personnel deployments, is taking time out to delve into ancient history. So again, I ask, what the hell do you think you're playing at.'

Strachan stared at the ceiling. Tell his boss the truth, or keep him in the dark - try to find out what the hell was going on first? If he told him, the poisoned chalice marked 'scapegoat' would pass from him to Ogilvy but, still . . .

'Sorry, sir,' he said, decision made. 'It's what you said about major incidents. Harbour Street was one of our biggest deployments back in the day. I wanted to have a look at the files, see what you did, how you handled it. And . . .' he took a breath - sod it '. . . I know Father

Donnelly was involved with Harbour Street. I wanted to know if that was related to what's happening now somehow.'

'I seriously doubt it,' MacAlister snapped, his tone telling Strachan that his attempt at distraction through ego massaging hadn't worked. 'Harbour Street was years ago, and if you have any operational questions, you call me. Clear?'

'Absolutely, sir,' Strachan said.

'Good. Then get on with the job in hand. Work with the police, get a report on the car bomb as soon as possible. Do you have any preliminary conclusions?'

Strachan had to bite back an urge to laugh. Conclusions? He was getting there, and this call was helping to solidify them in his mind.

'Well, sir, it was a small device. Probably a shaped charge, from the blast pattern and scorching we've seen. Remote detonation, no sign of a timer device in the wreckage.'

'Well, that's encouraging at least,' MacAlister said.

'What?' Strachan said, almost sure he had misheard. 'How do you—'

'Think about it. If this was remote-detonated and not just on a timer, it's less likely to have been a random car bomb, which will calm the First Minister. She's terrified this is the start of some kind of bombing campaign which is either religiously or politically motivated.'

Strachan closed his eyes, forced himself to remain quiet. He found MacAlister's spinning of the facts to suit his purposes not only disgusting but potentially lethal. So it was unlikely to be a terrorist campaign? Fine. That meant they had just one lethal psychopath to deal with instead of an army.

'I'll get the report to you as soon as possible, sir,' he said, hearing the coldness in his voice, not caring.

'See that you do,' MacAlister replied. 'And leave Harbour Street where it belongs. In the past.'

'Sir,' Strachan said. He put down his phone, considered for a moment. So the chief had a flag on the Harbour Street files, ensuring that he was informed every time they were accessed. It was almost understandable, given it was the fire that had made his career, but something about that bothered Strachan.

213

He grunted, stood up and stretched. Eyed the bottom drawer of his desk, heard the bottle of single malt it held whisper to him. Sat down again, swallowed the last of a mug of coffee that had long since gone cold, and returned to the files on Harbour Street.

Twenty minutes later, he stopped. Flicked back through the incident logs for the night, and the tally numbers of which fire-fighters had entered and exited the building and when. Found one, double-checked it. Glanced at the door, expecting it to have been blown open by the sudden chill that seemed to have permeated the room. He sat in silence, processing what he had just found.

And in that silence, the whisky in his bottom drawer didn't whisper to him.

It screamed.

CHAPTER 54

By the time they arrived at Doug McGregor's hotel, Connor's unease at the questions about his gran's care home had curdled into something sharper and more dangerous. He knocked on McGregor's door as if he was back in Belfast and about to issue an arrest warrant at a suspect's house. When Doug opened the door, Connor strode in, sending the reporter staggering back into the room.

'Jesus Christ!' he spat, as he regained his balance. 'Take it easy!'

'You asked Simon about my gran's care home,' Connor said. 'Why?'

Doug straightened, took a breath. If he was intimidated by Connor's looming presence, he was doing a good job of hiding it.

'I'll get to that,' he said, raising a placatory hand. 'Just give me a minute, okay? It's better that we go through this one step at a time, it'll make more sense that way.'

Connor folded his arms, tucked his hands into his armpits, as though he didn't quite trust them not to act of their own accord. 'Make it quick,' he said.

Doug gestured for Connor and Simon to move to the table and chairs that sat beneath one of the large picture windows in the room. 'Take a seat. I'll run you through what I've found.'

He grabbed his laptop as they sat down, Connor finding it impossible to get comfortable.

'So,' he said, placing the laptop on the table between Connor and Simon, 'I went back to Donna's notes and the research we did for you on Harbour Street, and it turns out that she tracked down a firefighter who died only a couple of months ago, years after the fire.'

Simon nodded. 'Peter Turnbull. She told us about him and what happened, said he was badly injured in the fire, but survived, finally died of pneumonia.'

'Yeah,' Doug agreed, eyes starting to sparkle in the same hungry, excited way Connor had seen in Donna when she was on a big story. 'And that also gives us a link to Father Donnelly. That was how Donna found Turnbull. She was searching for stories that featured Harbour Street and the priest, and the story on Turnbull's funeral turned up as Donnelly was the priest who led the funeral.'

'Okay,' Connor said. 'I see the link, but what does this have to do with my gran?'

Doug smiled briefly, his eyes glittering as if someone had switched on his full beams. 'It's what Turnbull's sister, Caroline, said to Donna.' He tapped a finger against the laptop's screen. '"It was Father Donnelly himself who arranged for Peter to be transferred to St Margaret's, who ensured he received the last rites." It got me thinking. How? So I had a little dig into St Margaret's and, on first glance, it's a stand-ard care home. Residential care for the elderly and infirm, a range of activities to keep the residents busy, a physiotherapy centre and, of course, regular services and visits by clergy of all denominations.'

Connor blinked. 'Hold on,' he said. 'Clergy visits? You mean?'

Doug toggled the screen on the laptop, brought up the homepage for the St Margaret's Care Home, then highlighted the text he had found: 'Regular services are held by our pastor and non-executive board member Father John Donnelly, while regular visits by clergy of all denominations are welcomed.'

'My gran's care home. That's why you were asking about the name.'

Doug nodded. 'Yeah. I checked for the name of the home on the picture of your gran that you were sent, but no luck, wasn't clear. Didn't take a lot of work to track it down, though. Montrose House, owned by Carson Residential. So I had a wee look at their website, and guess what I found? The same text: ". . . regular services and visits by clergy of all denominations are welcomed'. Oh, and for the bonus point, want to guess who owns St Margaret's?'

'Carson Residential,' Connor said, his words dull, flat things as his mind raced. 'So Donnelly is on the board of both homes.'

Simon leant forward. 'You think those photos of Connor's gran were taken by someone following Donnelly?' he asked.

Doug shrugged. 'That's supposition,' he said. 'But it's a strong possibility. Think about it. Whoever has targeted Donnelly is following him and the priest leads him to Connor's gran's care home and either he was already planning to take the pictures or he sees an opportunity. Either way, it works. And, yes, I checked, St Margaret's is only a forty-minute drive to the rehab centre where your girlfriend, Jen, is staying, so he could have made it there easily as well.'

Connor felt the urge to grind his teeth in time with the headache pulsing through his skull. 'But why?'

'I can't answer that,' Doug said. 'But I can maybe give you another piece of the puzzle. It was something else Caroline Turnbull said to Donna, about them being a firefighting family. So I had a wee look back into Peter Turnbull, see if firefighting was still the wider family business today. Neither he nor Caroline had any children that I could find, but I did find one thing – a godson.'

Doug leant forward again, pulled up another picture. Simon and Connor exchanged a glance.

'Holy fuck,' Connor whispered.

'I take it that means you know him?' Doug asked.

CHAPTER 55

The fire was a living thing. And it was laughing at him.

It roiled and spat and hissed at him as it feasted on the oxygen and accelerants he had fed it, gaining in intensity and size in front of his eyes. Even from a distance, he could feel the heat tightening his skin. Any closer and he would blister, and the scorching air would force its way into his lungs, burning and consuming, just as it had with Peter, all those years ago.

Was it, he wondered, the fire that scalded his eyes as he read the words in front of him, the blaze that blistered his tongue as he spoke them? He could feel moisture on his cheeks, the path of his tears etched by their sudden coolness on his fire-warmed cheeks. He told himself he had to leave, that the job was done. He had taken no pleasure in the killing, but he knew it was essential. And, besides, she would be at peace now, born anew, away from the pain and betrayal and hypocrisy of a fallen world. He had not thought he would be called to kill, but he had no choice but to do as he was commanded. He was a pawn, an instrument of a higher power, nothing more. His soul did not matter – unlike the one he had just sent to the Lord.

He closed the book he held open in front of him, pressed it together tightly, as though he could squeeze from it the strength to do what was needed. He took in the fire one last time, to run through what had happened. He had acted swiftly and decisively: she would not have suffered, would not now feel the fire as it devoured her, urged on by the petrol and vaseline he had doused her body in before he had released the flame.

He turned, wiped his eyes as he heard the first wail of sirens in the distance. In response, the fire seemed to grow louder, its laughter more spiteful. But it did nothing to drown the scream he heard carried on the smoke-soured wind.

A scream that echoed in his mind and soul. A scream that told him he was damned.

A scream that told him it was time for one final sacrifice.

CHAPTER 56

Doug had suggested some other lines of enquiry he could follow up, so Connor and Simon left him at the hotel and headed back to Lenton Barns to search the presbytery after stopping at Paulie's to retrieve the Audi. What Doug had found had planted a terrible thought in the back of Connor's mind, like the half-remembered terror of a fading nightmare, and he needed to drag it into the light.

They drove along the main street, past the Mercat Cross where the car had been detonated. It looked strangely empty, like a park after an outdoor concert. The car had been removed for further study, and the police and fire engines had long since gone, leaving only the empty, glassless windows staring out at the scene. Some buildings had been taped off as a safety risk, most probably waiting for structural engineers to make sure the blast had not shaken anything loose, but what drew Connor's attention most was the scorched, scarred tarmac where the car had blown up. It would be repaired in time, he knew, but in a small village like this, would the scar of the bombing ever truly heal?

They arrived at the church a moment later, no sign of any police guard now. What was the point? Donnelly was gone, and so had whatever evidence that could be collected from the place. So officers had been redeployed, hopefully, Connor thought, to help in the hunt for John Ogilvy, the godson of Peter Turnbull.

It hadn't taken Doug long to track down the link. He had used the Firefighters' Association's pride in their members' service and traced back the 'brave firefighters whose history of service runs through the generations'. The association had published an obituary mourning the loss of Peter Turnbull, mentioning that 'his legacy was carried by John Ogilvy, his godson'.

They got out of the car, ducked under the police cordon tape and walked up the gravel driveway. Connor slowed, glancing over at the wall where he had found the injured police officer, eyes rolling back in his head, blood oozing from one ear. He wondered, vaguely, how the officer was, and whether he would ever put on the uniform again.

Somehow he doubted it.

'So, how do you figure it?' he said, turning to Simon. 'Ogilvy blames Donnelly for something that happened to his godfather, Turnbull, at Harbour Street. So, when questions start getting asked about that fire, he flips, makes his way here, beats the shite out of two uniforms, makes off with Donnelly, and grabs Donna at some other point?'

Simon took a deep breath. 'Makes a certain sense,' he said. 'And from what we saw of Ogilvy, he's definitely got the size to inflict the type of injuries those coppers had.'

'But why? Why go to all this trouble? You said it yourself, the man is a walking monster. If he wanted to get some kind of revenge on Donnelly, why not just come here and kill him quietly? Why all the shit with the drones and burning that cabbie alive to make a point? And why pay me seventy grand to protect Donnelly from him? Why drag Jen and my gran into it?'

Simon shrugged. 'I don't know,' he said. 'But then there's those photos. Donnelly being a regular at your gran's care home and close to Jen gives Ogilvy the perfect opportunity to follow him and take the photos. It also solidifies the link between you and Donnelly, and gives Ogilvy a way to get at you.'

'Question remains, why me? And why all the cloak and dagger? Why get into this game of cat-and-mouse with me, hire me to protect a man he's determined to kill?'

'No way we can track down where that seventy grand came from?' Simon asked.

'Not really,' Connor said, hating the edge of frustration he heard in his voice. 'According to Robbie, it was bounced through a few dummy corporations in the United States before getting to us. They're notoriously secretive about who really owns what out there, part of the reason being it's a hotspot for money laundering. He said we could maybe get there in time, but it would take a lot of legal legwork and a hell of a lot of money to do it.'

'Say seventy grand's worth?' Simon said, with a humourless smile.

'Aye,' Connor said. 'Come on, let's have a look around inside, see if we can get some answers.'

The door to the presbytery had been sealed with police tape and locked. Neither obstacle presented much problem for Simon, who sliced the tape with a knife he produced from his jacket before picking the lock.

'You know, a police officer really shouldn't be able to do that so easily,' Connor said, as they stepped into the gloom of the hallway.

'Says the ex-copper packing a gun and his own set of picks,' Simon retorted, with a smile.

They followed the hallway back to Donnelly's study, the room they had first spoken to him in. It was filled with the musty, dry smell that book-filled rooms had, the atmosphere somehow charged, as though the house was holding its breath, waiting for its owner to return.

'What we looking for?' Simon asked.

'I'm not sure,' Connor admitted. 'Anything that's out of place. Anything that might indicate either a connection to Ogilvy or a motive for Donnelly to be involved in this himself.'

They split up, Connor taking Donnelly's paper-strewn desk, Simon the shelves of books that lined the walls of the room.

Connor studied the desk, remembering Donnelly barricading himself behind it after the drone attack. He had been shuffling the papers on the desk, his movements jerky, erratic, almost panicked. At the time, Connor had put it down to shock over what had happened, but what if . . .

He sat at the desk, closed his eyes, remembered Donnelly's position. Reached out to his left for a bundle of papers, just as Donnelly had, and began to sift through them. They were mostly notes on upcoming services, spidery handwriting copying out Biblical quotes and the priest's thoughts.

Psalm 71:9: *Do not cast me off in the time of old age; forsake me not when my strength is spent,* Donnelly had written. The verse meant nothing to Connor, but the note below it did: *Every generation has a duty to the one that came before, an obligation to care and honour them.*

Below this was another verse:

1 Timothy 5:8: *But if anyone does not provide for his relatives, and especially for members of his household, he has denied the faith and is worse than an unbeliever.* Again, Donnelly had scrawled a note below this: *We must provide for our households. It is our duty and our obligation to God. Is your house provided for?*

Connor leant back in the seat, chewed his lip. There was something here, something he was almost seeing, something . . .

'Anything?' Simon asked, as he approached the desk.

'Huh, not really,' Connor said, holding up the sheaf of papers. As he did, an old-fashioned Kodak picture fell from the pile, fluttered to the desk and landed face down. Connor reached for it, dragged it across the desk, his hand covering it. 'You find anything?'

'The man likes to read,' Simon said, gesturing back to the bookshelves. 'Some beautiful old editions, Dickens, Shakespeare, that sort of thing. Few local history books as well, couple of framed maps of the parish. It's funny, though, that with all these books, there's not a Bible in sight.'

'Oh?' Connor said, his thoughts turning back to the scrawled notes, the feeling of missing something obvious rising in his mind again. He looked around the room, trying to remember his last visit. Hadn't he seen a Bible then? 'That's—'

He was interrupted by the ringing of his phone, shrill in the silence of the room.

He took his hand from the picture, fished his phone from his pocket as Simon reached for the photograph on the desk.

'DCI Ford,' he said, in lieu of 'Hello'. Felt a weight start to push down on his shoulders, massive and irresistible, as he listened to the policeman's words. 'We're on our way,' he said, then killed the call.

'What?' Simon asked.

'Ford,' Connor replied. 'Just had the call. A fire was reported in

Elderslie about an hour ago. Confirmation just came in that it was at the home of Caroline Turnbull, the sister of Peter Turnbull. Ford's got officers on the scene, but firefighters have reported that a body has been found in what's left of the house.'

'Jesus,' Simon whispered, his face growing pale.

'Yeah,' Connor replied. 'Not sure what good we can do, but I said to Ford we'd meet him there.'

He started to rise from the chair, but Simon stopped him.

'Got a better idea,' he said. 'There's not much we can do, so why don't we go and ask about this instead?'

He raised the picture that had fallen from the papers to eye level, flipped it over to Connor. Three men stood, smiling into the camera. On the left of the picture stood Father Donnelly, an awkward smile on his lips. He was dwarfed by the massive, looming form of John Ogilvy, who was standing stiffly in the middle, his face impassive. The other man in the picture had one hand held up to shield his eyes from the glare of the sun. On his raised wrist, a large watch glinted like a jewel, flaring back at the camera.

'Jesus,' Connor whispered. 'Tom McGovern. But what . . .'

'Maybe this will help,' Simon said, flipping the photo around to show Connor another quote, scrawled there in the same hand as the other notes he had read: *The sins of the father are to be laid upon the children.*

Connor looked between the two men in the picture, searching for similarities. Was there something around the eyes, the nose? The lips? The broad shoulders? The jaw?

'Call Robbie,' he said. 'Get him to pull Ogilvy's birth certificate. Now.'

CHAPTER 57

The drive to McGovern Homes gave Connor just enough time to put the pieces of the puzzle together. McGovern's questions about his past and his family, his men's extreme lethal reaction when Paulie had started asking questions. It made sense now. And yet there was still something he was missing, some last piece of the puzzle that he could feel but not understand.

Not yet.

He didn't bother stopping at Reception, ignored the startled cry 'Stop, please, sir, stop!' from the skinny guy behind the desk. Marched down the corridor, found the conference room and walked straight in, McGovern rising, surprise and anger twisting his face as he moved.

'Mr Fraser,' he said, as he re-established a veneer of composure. 'I wasn't expecting to see you again so soon.'

'I bet you weren't,' Connor said, aware that Simon had followed him into the room and had taken up a sentry position at the door. 'After all, you gave me just enough to keep me away from your boy, keep my focus on you, didn't you?'

The colour seemed to drain from McGovern's face and pool around the collar of his shirt, which suddenly looked about two sizes too small for him. 'I'm not sure I know what you . . .'

'Oh, quit it,' Connor said. 'See, we pulled John Ogilvy's birth certificate. Mother, Jane Louise Ogilvy, father, surprise, surprise, one

Thomas Eugene McGovern. Didn't take much to trace his mum back, find that Peter Turnbull was her cousin, the man she asked to be her son's godfather. Was that to counteract the fact that his real father was a nasty little piece of shite or that you dumped them both when you'd had your fun?'

'Choose your words carefully, Mr Fraser,' McGovern hissed, hate sparking in his eyes. 'I never married Jane, but that didn't mean I didn't love her. She was ill after John was born – they call it post-natal depression, these days, but we didn't really have a proper diagnosis for it then. She wanted John to know her family, so we made Peter her godfather, Caroline his godmother. Good people, they did John proud, especially when ...' He trailed off, his eyes darting away from Connor, as though looking at him was forcing him to remember something too painful to bear. He didn't need to say anything, Connor had seen the death certificate Robbie had found showing that Jane Ogilvy had taken her own life.

'Good people, both now dead,' Connor said, his voice flat.

McGovern's head darted up. 'What do you mean?' he asked.

'Haven't you heard?' Connor said, studying McGovern. If he was lying, he was doing a good job of it. 'I had a call from the police a little while ago. Seems Caroline Turnbull's house caught fire earlier on today. They've found a body inside.'

McGovern collapsed into his chair, splayed his hands onto the table in front of him as though it was a life-raft. 'My God,' he whispered. 'Oh, my dear God.'

Connor took a step forward. 'Was it John, Mr McGovern? It was him that was asking about me, wasn't it? Not you. See, I couldn't understand why your thugs would be asking about me, why they would react the way they did and try to silence Paulie when he asked about them sniffing around. But if you were doing it for John, a favour from father to son, it would explain why you tried to sell me that line of shit about offering me a job. Take the heat off John and get me focusing on you. That's what happened, isn't it?'

McGovern blinked, his eyes shimmering with tears. He looked from Connor to Simon, then leant back in his seat, gazing at the ceiling as though the answers were there.

'John came to me, asked me to get some of my, ah, associates, to look into you. Your past, your friends, family, that sort of thing. I didn't understand, but couldn't see the harm, so I arranged it for him. But then I heard about what had happened at the church, and Paulie King was pushing for answers so . . .'

'So you got your men to try to take Paulie out, and sold me a line so I wouldn't look into John Ogilvy. And now Caroline Turnbull is dead, just like Peter. So my question, Mr McGovern, is this. Is your son capable of torching a house that his godmother was in?'

McGovern dragged his hands across his eyes then down his cheeks. 'I saw her last week,' he said, his voice a low, empty whisper. 'She was using Peter's money to get the roof on the house done, and I put a crew in place to do the work at cost. Least I could do. And now . . .'

'Back up,' Simon said, stepping away from the door and towards McGovern. '"Peter's money". What do you mean?'

McGovern looked up, a small confused child in a man's body. 'What? The life insurance, of course. It paid out when Peter died. Around seventy-five thousand, I think. I know, Caroline could have afforded to get the roof done with anyone, but I wanted to help. Why does that matter?'

'Mr McGovern,' Connor said, 'how often have you done business in America? And do you have any bank accounts based there?'

CHAPTER 58

The smell of whisky hit Ford as soon as Gary Strachan walked into his office. The firefighter looked around the room, face pale, eyes red. He swayed slightly as he shut the door behind him, then walked to a seat opposite Ford at his desk, dropping his briefcase clumsily as he fell into the chair. Ford studied his friend for a minute, had a sudden, nightmarish flash of Strachan behind the wheel of his car as he made the trip to see him.

'Gary, Jesus, you okay?' Ford said.

'Oh, yeah, I'm absolutely wonderful,' Strachan said, he voice low and husky, stained with whatever whisky he had been drinking.

'Tell me you didn't drive like that,' Ford said.

Strachan's face twitched into a smile. 'Doesn't matter,' he said. 'Got a wee present for you.' He reached down, produced a thick sheaf of papers, tossed them onto the desk. 'There you go, the reports from the Harbour Street fire.' He gave a choked, wet laugh. 'No fucking wonder the chief didn't want me looking at them.'

Ford reached for them, pulled them towards him. Reading them was like listening to a favourite song in the wrong key. He recognised some of the formatting and markers of a police report, but the vocabulary was alien to him.

'Care to translate for me?' he asked.

Strachan shifted forward in the seat, his eyes focusing. 'Not sure I understand it completely myself,' he said. 'But I can give you the basics. At every fire, we have something called a tally system. These are call-sign numbers assigned to breathing apparatus. They're used to log which firefighters are actively on a scene so we can track who is where, how long they've been in the fire, how much air they've got left in their tanks, that kind of thing.'

'Okay,' Ford said, thinking of the similar log system police officers used in major deployments. 'So?'

'So I had a look at the deployments, all fairly standard. The three firefighters who were killed in the fire are all logged as entering the first floor of the building looking for civilians. Peter Turnbull is also logged as entering on the fourth floor, which subsequently collapsed, leaving him trapped on the third floor before he was later found.'

'Okay, but what does that have to do with—'

Strachan held up a hand that wasn't quite steady, blinked as though he was trying to clear his vision. Maybe he was.

'When I was looking at the tally numbers, one didn't make sense.' He leant forward, tapped a string of numbers and letters he had highlighted. 'Golf four Zulu seven four,' he said.

'Huh?' Ford said, looking at the page. 'What does that mean?'

'Nothing,' Strachan said, his eyes growing dark. 'It's a dead tally, retired from service in tribute to an off-duty firefighter called John Evans who died saving a boy from drowning in Loch Fyne thirty years ago. It was his tally number.' He waved away Ford's questioning glance. 'I had to do lectures on fire history at the fire service museum, I know a few things. And,' he added, embarrassment washing over his face, 'studying the service's history kept me off the bottle, for a while.'

'Okay, so it's a mistake, then,' Ford said.

'Aye, maybe,' Strachan said. 'But look at this. That tally was logged as active on the site of the blaze, then wasn't logged back out of the fire until three hours later, just at the time that the three firefighters who died on the scene, George Logan, Derek MacRae and Michael Lawson, were dragged out.'

'So?' Ford said, feeling like he was trying to understand the incoherent ramblings of a relapsed alcoholic.

'So that's not possible,' Strachan said. 'A firefighter's BA, the breathing apparatus, holds enough air for an hour at most. So how does he stay in the fire for three full hours without logging off the site to replenish his BA? And why is he using a dead man's tally?'

'I don't know,' Ford said, the first glimmerings of an idea forming in his mind. He felt something putrid turn in his guts as he thought of the drones, the burnt-out cab, the car bomb, the images mounting in his mind, like a stack of cards, one horror played on top of another. He felt a dull thirst, which he knew would only be quenched by the same bottle Strachan had been drinking from. 'So you're saying a dead man was stalking the fire for three hours, only emerging after injured or dead firefighters were pulled from the blaze?'

'Aye, and I think he was scavenging. I had a look at the reports. The firefighters who died all had severely depleted BAs – their oxygen levels were way down. Explained at the time as them breathing more rapidly as they panicked, but . . .'

'But it could have been whoever this was, using their oxygen so he could stay in the fire longer? Is that even possible?'

Strachan nodded, and Ford could see hard sobriety return to his friend's gaze. 'Aye. Not easily, especially in an active fire, but there are ways to do it if you swap the lines from the tanks to the masks, take what you need, then swap them back.'

'But who would do that? And why?' Ford asked. 'And why would whoever this was log themselves into a fire anyway? Why not just sneak into the building another way?'

'Because they're trained,' Strachan said, voice flat and matter-of-fact. 'They knew how to hack Banknock's tower to control the drones. They knew how to rig the car bomb. If it's the same person, they would know at Harbour Street that the safest way in or out of the blaze was the one established by crews going in. Why risk sneaking in through a window or a back door and walking straight into an unsafe area when the firefighters on the scene have done all the hard work for you? Look at how this guy has been working. He's a professional. He doesn't take risks he doesn't have to.'

A picture Ford didn't want to see was forming in his mind. Was it possible? Had a killer been stalking Harbour Street all those years ago, picking off firefighters as they worked? Why? And, more importantly, why were they back now, targeting Father Donnelly, who had been at the fire that night, comforting the men?

'Hold on,' he said. 'You found this, saw the irregularities about the log-in and log-out times and the drained air tanks. Wouldn't someone else have seen that too? Who signed off these logs?'

Strachan gave a smile that told Ford he was wondering where he was going to get his next drink.

'Who else?' he said, after a moment. 'Our esteemed chief fire officer, Arthur MacAlister.'

CHAPTER 59

'So, where the hell has he gone?'

Connor looked around the Spartan flat, his mind a bubbling cauldron of impotent fury and an uneasy guilt that throbbed through him like toothache. After their conversation with McGovern and the revelations of John Ogilvy's links to Peter and Caroline Turnbull, it was a simple matter to get Robbie at Sentinel to track down the missing firefighter's address. Home for John Ogilvy was a flat in a nondescript new-build development on the outskirts of Airth, not far from Falkirk. The location made sense, with its proximity to Kincardine Bridge: Ogilvy could easily get to Kirkcaldy for his work, while also remaining within striking distance of Lenton Barns and Father Donnelly.

Connor was about to answer Simon's question when his phone buzzed. He answered, listening closely. 'Thanks, Robbie,' he said, then ended the call.

'What?' Simon asked.

'Some more information on Ogilvy, the stuff we asked Robbie to look into after our chat with McGovern. It seems Ogilvy had power of attorney over Peter Turnbull's estate, was a co-signatory with Caroline Turnbull. When Peter died, the seventy-five-thousand-pound insurance policy on his life was paid into an account to which both Ogilvy and Caroline Turnbull were signatories.'

'Lemme guess,' Simon said. 'Not long after that, seventy grand or so was paid to an American-based bank, the same one that just happened to dump seventy grand in Sentinel's account the day this all started.'

Connor nodded, a thought forming in his mind. 'Christ. You think that's why he killed Caroline Turnbull? She was asking about the missing money and he wanted to keep her quiet?'

'Makes sense,' Simon said. 'We need to find this guy. What's next? There's fuck-all here for us.'

'One more sweep, then we'll get out?' Connor said.

'Aye,' Simon said, weary resignation in his voice. They had approached the flat cautiously, wary of booby-traps or even finding Ogilvy himself. But after picking the lock, they had found nothing except a neat, almost monastic living space, with minimal decoration and nothing that gave away the personality or motivations of the man who owned it. There were a few books sitting in half-empty bookshelves in the living room, a kitchen that looked as if it had never been used since it had been installed, a neatly made bed and a drawer half full of clothes in the bedroom. A dress uniform hung in the wardrobe, still wrapped in the plastic bag in which it had been collected from the dry-cleaner. The whole place had such a feeling of absence and loss that it almost made Connor feel sorry for Ogilvy, and the apparent emptiness of his life.

Almost.

He moved closer to the bookshelf, inspecting what was there. A range of crime and horror novels mostly, the spines of which looked as though they had never been cracked.

'Who the hell is this guy?' Connor asked.

'Huh?' Simon said.

'Look at this place,' Connor said. 'No family pictures, no personal effects, save for the fire-service citations and awards hung in the hallway. Some clothes and a few books, but nothing that tells us about the man. Who is he? Does he like sports, music? Got a girlfriend? A boyfriend? What?'

Simon shrugged. 'I know what you mean,' he said. 'This could almost be a show home. It's like an impression of what someone who's never had a real home thinks a home should be. It's almost as if . . .'

Connor nodded, picking up Simon's thought. 'Almost as if he doesn't really live here. But if he has another place, and this is just for show, then where the hell is it? Robbie couldn't find any other properties listed in Ogilvy's name, and he's only got one mortgage for this place. So where else could he be?'

'What about McGovern?' Simon asked. 'Handy that Daddy Dearest is in the property game. Could he have set Ogilvy up somewhere else?'

'Maybe, but I doubt it,' Connor said, thinking back to their conversation with McGovern. As he told it, Ogilvy had never forgiven him for what had happened to his mother, and his father's inability to tame the demons that ultimately drove her to take her own life. They had little contact, which was why McGovern had been so eager to go along with Ogilvy's request to look into Connor. He saw it as a bridge, a way to form a connection with his son.

A connection that had come at a deadly cost.

'So what do we know?' Simon asked. Connor turned to his friend, the feeling he had missed something rising in his mind. Something about the books . . .

'We know it's likely that Ogilvy had the skills, knowledge and, thanks to Peter Turnbull's death, the money to orchestrate the attack on the church and the car bombing in Lenton Barns. We know he's targeted me, and that he's connected to the Harbour Street fire, thanks to Peter Turnbull. We know from what Strachan said that he's a dedicated firefighter who keeps himself to himself. Other than that . . .'

'Okay,' Simon said, holding up a hand. 'So he wants revenge on Donnelly for something, presumably linked to Peter Turnbull. But what? From everything we know, Donnelly was nothing but helpful to the Turnbulls. And why grab Donna as well? As an extra hostage, to get at you, what?'

Connor felt the guilt sting like bile in his throat at the mention of Donna's name. This was the second time she had been put in danger because of her association with him and his work. Her son, Andrew, had already lost his father, thanks to a case Connor had been working on. Was he now doomed to lose his mother as well? Connor had long known he was damaged in some way, cursed with an anger that could flare like a Roman candle and burn out of control at any moment. It had cost him relationships in the past, and denied him many close friendships. But was he also cursed? Cursed to blight the lives of those around him, those who he cared for? Simon had suffered a broken jaw and a serious beating for knowing Connor, while Jen had almost died after being run over by a car. And then there was his gran, sitting in her care home, the past overwhelming her present more and more every day as she lost her sense of self and the walls of her identity eroded a little more. Was he the cause?

The revelation hit him like a tidal wave, almost dropping him to his knees. How could he not have seen it sooner? The answer was simple. He had been too busy reacting to the situation, to the threats to Jen and his gran, to see what had been right in front of him all the time. What was it the blackmailer had said when he had called Connor after the pictures of Jen and his gran had been sent to him? *You can call me a fan, I suppose, Mr Fraser. You see, I've read about you, and I'm very impressed by your work.*

Then Gary Strachan's words when they had met in his office in Kirkcaldy. *I know you hit one of my men at Alloa House a few years ago. I wish you'd taken a swing at me. I wouldn't have gone so easy on you.*

'Connor, what?' Simon asked.

'Justice,' Connor replied, the picture forming in his mind now, like a blurry photograph coming into focus. 'That's why Ogilvy is using me. He must have read the incident reports about me hitting a fire-fighter a few years ago. He said he was a fan of my work. What if the work he's talking about was me knocking out a firefighter?'

'Okay,' Simon said slowly. 'I can almost see that. But why would a firefighter side with a guy who's beaten the hell out of one of his colleagues? And what about the seventy K? This guy can make a car bomb or aim a drone at you, why bother paying you seventy K for the pleasure of your company?'

'I don't know,' Connor said, feeling the frustration prickle across his back and settle in the wound on his shoulder. 'Why keep this place like this? Why . . .'

He trailed off as his eye caught the sparse collection of books again. Books that looked as though they had never been read or loved . . . 'Simon, when we were back at the church, you said there was something odd about the books in Donnelly's study, right?'

'Yeah,' Simon agreed. 'Stuffed with local maps, historical books and the like, but no Bible. Why?'

Connor smiled. Nodded to himself as another piece of the puzzle fell into place.

'Why would a priest not have a Bible in his study?' Connor asked.

Simon shrugged. I don't know. Maybe he was working somewhere else, took it with him. Maybe . . .'

Connor saw the thought dawn on him. 'Exactly,' he said. 'Just like this place. The church is a front. Donnelly wasn't working there when Ogilvy took him. He was somewhere else. Somewhere away from the police who were guarding him.'

'But in that case why were they attacked?' Simon asked. 'Why beat the shit out of two coppers when you don't even have to face them? Why go to the church just to attack two coppers? Why leave the blood on the study wall?'

'Distraction,' Connor said. 'Get us looking at this the wrong way. Come on, we need to speak to McGregor. Now.'

CHAPTER 60

Doug greeted them eagerly, hurrying them into his hotel room and sitting them down at the table below the window. Connor noticed that the space looked a lot messier than it had on their previous visit. Papers and printouts were scattered on the bed. A notepad lay on the floor beside Doug's chair, face down and abandoned. Post-its crowded the wall above the laptop, Doug's spidery notes scrawled across them.

He also noticed that the bottle of whiskey he had seen on his previous visit had been opened, a large glass filled beside it.

'So,' Doug said, his eyes flitting from Connor to Simon restlessly, 'what did you find out from your visit to McGovern?'

Connor told him about the links between McGovern and the Turnbulls, how McGovern had been asking about Connor's past on Ogilvy's behalf, and their discovery of Ogilvy's soulless flat in Airth. As he spoke, Doug nodded, quick, birdlike motions that made Connor think less about the whisky on the desk and more about cocaine. But Doug's eyes were sharp and clear, the skin around his nostrils clean and unblemished by white powder. Whatever he was on, it was, as far as Connor could tell, natural.

'Okay,' Doug said, as Connor finished talking. 'That all kind of confirms what I've found.'

'Which is what, other than a thirst?' Simon asked.

Doug blinked, momentarily confused, then broke into a sheepish smile. 'Oh, you mean the Jameson,' he said, eyes sliding towards the glass. 'I've not had any, I promise. It's a ritual I've got, a test you might say. I, ah . . .' he paused to clear his throat, colour rising in his cheeks '. . . I used to have a bit of a problem. I keep the whiskey as a reminder of that, only open it when I make a breakthrough in a story. See, I want the drink, but I want the story more, so it focuses me.'

Connor shook his head, unable to follow Doug's logic. He was no stranger to addictive behaviour, knew his gym habits bordered on the obsessional, but McGregor's method of self-torture seemed cruel, almost sadistic, as though he felt he deserved to be punished for some past sin.

'So, what have you got, then?' Connor asked, focusing on the present problem.

'Well, after I found out about John Ogilvy being a godson to the Turnbulls, I thought it was reasonable to assume he was the one who had been following Father Donnelly. So I took a look back, tried to find some links between the two, see if I could find a motive to what Ogilvy is doing.'

'And?' Simon said, a jagged edge of impatience in his tone.

'Well, I found it,' Doug said, gesturing to the drifts of papers in front of him. 'I looked back at Donnelly and what happened after the Harbour Street fire. Both he and the firefighter who was in charge at the fire, now Chief Officer Arthur MacAlister, appeared in front of the Scottish Parliament's justice committee to give evidence about merging the eight fire services around Scotland into one national service. Both men spoke eloquently about it, used Harbour Street as a reason why frontline firefighters needed to be retained in the merger, why community fire stations were the key to keeping people safe. Hell, Donnelly even went further. . .' he reached over to the bed and grabbed a highlighted printout '. . . claiming, and I quote, "Firefighters are a family, and that family is grieving. The Bible states that *If anyone does not provide for his relatives, and especially for members of his household, he has denied the faith.*" Basically, Donnelly was saying that the wrath of God would fall on the heads of anyone who used the merger to cut firefighters.'

Connor nodded, thinking back to Donnelly's study and the notes he had found. Notes which included that verse, and the note Donnelly had added: *We must provide for our households. It is our duty and our obligation to God. Is your house provided for?*

'Right,' he said. 'But how does that connect to Ogilvy?'

Doug gave Connor a smile: the child in the classroom who had answered a tough question first. He sifted through his notes again, found the page he was looking for, handed it to Connor. 'That's the minutes for the meeting when Donnelly quoted the Bible to MSPs,' he said. 'Have a look at the list of attendees at the meeting.'

Connor scanned down the list. Spotted the name four down.

'Ogilvy,' he said. 'John Ogilvy.'

Doug nodded. 'Yup. I went through another four meetings of the justice committee on the merger and, surprise surprise, he was at all of them. The minutes of one meeting explain why he was there. MacAlister, the fire chief, refers to his assistant, Watch Manager Ogilvy, giving him notes. From what I can tell, he was effectively the administrative gofer for MacAlister while he and Donnelly were at the committee meetings.'

'So they knew each other,' Connor said, thoughts starting to race across his mind. 'Worked together.'

'And then some,' Doug replied, gesturing to more papers. 'The fire service had a lot of internal meetings about the merger, mostly held in Perth for some reason, probably because it was seen as neutral territory for the firefighters from Glasgow and Edinburgh. They spoke about everything, from the new logo for the unified service, to deployment numbers, chaplaincy and spiritual support for firefighters of all faiths.'

Simon exchanged a glance with Connor. 'Hold on. Chaplaincy, you mean . . .'

'Yup,' Doug replied. 'At least seven meetings on providing for the spiritual needs of firefighters in the national service, looking at what happened at Harbour Street as an exemplar of why faith leaders were needed on the ground. And, yeah, before you ask, both Father Donnelly and Watch Manager Ogilvy were on those working groups.'

'So they worked together,' Simon said, more to himself than Connor or Doug. 'And it sounds like they had a common goal. So if that's the case, why the hell would Ogilvy turn on Donnelly and suddenly want him dead all these years later?'

'That's where I fall down,' Doug admitted. 'I can put them together, establish the link between them. What I can't do is explain why Ogilvy suddenly went Biblical on Donnelly.'

'Went Biblical,' Connor repeated, his voice a low whisper.

Simon straightened, alerted by the change in Connor's tone. 'What?'

'The church, the missing Bible. The battered police officers,' Connor said. 'Jesus, I'm a fucking idiot.' He looked between Simon and Doug. 'Doug, thank you, you've been a huge help,' he said, as he headed for the door.

'Don't thank me, give me a quote and first crack at the story when it's done,' Doug said, before his smile faded and his voice grew serious. 'And find Donna, will you? Didn't work with her long, but I'd hate to break this story without her.'

'I promise,' Connor said. 'Swear to God.'

CHAPTER 61

Simon sat at the steering-wheel, grim-faced, as Connor spoke to DCI Ford on the car's hands-free system. He had called him to give him an update on what he and Doug McGregor had found. Ford was terse, distracted, his tone telling Connor he was engaging in a conversation he wished he didn't have to have.

'That fits with what ACO Strachan found in the Harbour Street incident reports,' Ford said.'Seems there was an unidentified person on the scene the night of the fire, maybe even attacking firefighters who were in the building at the time.'

Connor ground his teeth, an ugly picture forming in his mind. 'Hell of a risk for Chief Officer MacAlister to go in front of MSPs and talk about Harbour Street when he knew something was wrong with the incident reports,' he said.

'Yes and no,' Ford replied. 'He was the only one who would know something was wrong, if indeed he did know. The tally number for the dead firefighter was fairly unknown. Strachan only recognised it because of his work with the Firefighters' Association. And the depleted oxygen supplies on the dead firefighters were easily explainable.'

'So you think MacAlister didn't know anything was wrong that night?'

'I'm saying it's not impossible,' Ford said, with a sigh.

Connor knew why. His next step would have to be to speak to

MacAlister about that night. And a detective chief inspector talking to the head of the fire service, no matter how casual or off the record that conversation was, would attract attention. The kind of attention that was normally focused on running a country.

'You going to be okay, sir?' Connor asked.

'I'll have to be,' Ford said. 'This is all tied to Donnelly, Ogilvy and Harbour Street. If MacAlister missed the odd tally numbers at the fire, then so be it. It's a mistake, but one he can downplay, being chief, especially with this government service review coming. But if there's something more to it, if he's covering for someone . . .'

'Understood,' Connor said. 'I'll keep you appraised.'

'Do that,' Ford said. 'And, Fraser, just remember, I'm breaking almost every rule of a major investigation by letting you freelance on this. I'm doing it as I want results. I need this lunatic off the streets, before he hurts anyone else.' A pause, Ford sucking in his breath as if he had just realised what he'd said. 'I take it you've not heard anything else from Donna Blake?'

'No,' Connor said, his voice a whisper as he forced down the tide of icy panic he felt at the mention of her name. 'Nothing, sir.'

A moment of silence, both Connor and Ford unsure of what to say next. Then Ford broke the stalemate with a terse 'Good luck,' and ended the call.

'So,' Simon said, 'care to tell me why we're going to the presbytery again? Thought we'd found everything we could there. Aren't we just wasting time?'

'Where else can we go?' Connor asked. 'You said it yourself. Ogilvy is one hell of a big guy. He attracts attention. If he grabbed Donna and Donnelly, I doubt he could take them far without some sighting being reported. And we know that he had to be close by to detonate the car bomb aimed at Strachan. So the best bet is to try the presbytery, see if we missed a clue to where he could have taken Donnelly. Somewhere he wouldn't attract too much attention being out in public. Isolated. Private. And there's a lot of countryside around the village, so maybe . . .'

Simon shrugged, the unasked question forming between them seeming to give the air in the car a physical weight.

'She's not dead,' Connor said softly. 'Think about it. When he torched that taxi driver, he boasted about it. The car bomb, the drones weren't subtle attacks. He's trying to make a point. Just killing Donna and dumping her does nothing for him. No, he needs her for something, even if it's just to draw me out. So she's alive, she must be.'

'I fucking hope so,' Simon hissed.

They arrived at the presbytery a few minutes later, parked. Approaching the front door, Connor saw nothing to warn him that the house had been visited since he and Simon had been there hours before. They made their way into Donnelly's study without debating it, both deciding that it was the heart of the house.

'So, what we looking for that we missed before?' Simon asked.

'Not sure,' Connor replied, his mind returning to the missing Bible. 'But think of this as ground zero. If I'm right, Ogilvy couldn't have gone far, so he'd have to find a bolthole nearby that would be easily accessible. Or he's using wherever else it was that Donnelly was working from. Maybe there's a clue to that in here.'

Simon nodded, drifted towards the bookshelves. Connor stared down at Donnelly's desk, and the raft of papers on it. Saw nothing new. In frustration, he pulled out his phone, opened the search engine and entered the name of the church, St Ninian's. He was rewarded with the usual tourist information on the village, as well as some pictures of the church and the surrounding grounds. He scrolled down, found a listing on a website called Scotland's Hidden Histories. Clicked on the link, which led to a picture of the church and a headline: *Death and Rebirth in Central Scotland, the Tale of Lenton Barns.*

He flicked down, reading the article.

The roots of the Catholic Church in Lenton Barns can be traced back to the thirteenth century, when priests ministered to farmers, and a small church was established on the site of the current church. Though records from the time are scarce, the original church was burnt down in 1530, around the time of the Reformation. The current church was established by Lord Gordon Lassiter, a landowner, in the late 1880s, as part of his desire to restore the religious heritage of the village. However,

243

the persecution of Catholics has left its mark on the village as, around the time of the Reformation, many Catholics observed their faith secretly, with an altar to the Virgin Mary that could be dismantled and hidden from the state deep in the woods that border the southern edge of the village. A stone chapel was built on the site, under the guise of a byre. This was abandoned some years later when persecution of Catholics diminished.

Connor scrolled down further, felt his breath catch in his throat as he looked at the image on his screen. A small bunker-like construction, its stone walls glistening as though it had recently rained. A second photograph showed the interior of the structure: surprisingly spacious, with three rows of pews and, at the front, an altar with a statue of the Virgin Mary atop it. Sitting in front of the statue was a large, ornately decorated Bible. He scrolled through the site, trying to find a more exact location to the altar, frustrated that he could not.

He called Simon, showed him what he had found. 'A bolthole?' he asked.

'Maybe,' Simon said. He retreated to the bookshelves and returned with what looked like a folded poster. 'I found this earlier, didn't think much about it,' he said, unfolding the document and spreading it on Donnelly's desk. 'It's a map of the village. Look,' he pointed down at the map, 'here's the church. And look here. To the south of the church, just as that site says, there's this. I thought it marked a grave or something, but what if . . .'

Connor looked down to the small red cross that Simon was pointing at. Thought back to what Ford had told them about where Donna Blake's van had been found. Just outside the village, almost on a direct line of sight to the point marked on the map.

'What do you think?' Connor said. 'That Ogilvy found out about this place, or forced Donnelly to tell him about it? Is using it as a hidey-hole?'

Simon twisted his neck, studied the picture. 'Or Donnelly hid there when he knew Ogilvy was after him,' he said. 'Either way, it's a place to start looking. Want to pay it a visit, see if anyone's home?'

'Love to,' Connor replied.

CHAPTER 62

The confused, almost incredulous tone with which Ford's request to speak to Chief Fire Officer Arthur MacAlister was met was little more than he had expected. As with the police, senior officers in the fire service were not normally bothered by mere mortals making requests on their time. Especially mere mortals with awkward questions to ask. The woman who answered his call to Scottish Fire and Rescue headquarters in Cambuslang had told Ford, 'Chief Officer MacAlister's diary is entirely too full to entertain a visit any time within the next month.'

'That's not a problem,' Ford replied, wondering how long it would take for news of this call to get back to his own boss. 'Just tell the chief I'll take it up with your press office, get what I need from there. Should be easy enough. Harbour Street was a big fire back in the day.'

He had hung up before she could answer, waited. It had been a calculated risk, and he wondered what MacAlister would do – call his boss and get him to tell Ford to back off, or bite the bullet and talk to him directly. He got his answer a moment later when his phone rang.

'Chief Fire Officer MacAlister for you, DCI Ford,' the caller told him, her voice even colder and harder now.

'Thanks,' he said, even as the line clicked and the call was transferred.

'DCI Ford, how can I help you?' MacAlister boomed down the line. His voice was hard, unyielding, and Ford wondered what the man had done to prepare himself for this. Anything from a strong cup of coffee to slaying a junior officer, he guessed.

'Thanks for your time, sir. I wanted to ask you one or two questions about the fire at Harbour Street a few years ago. I think it might have some bearing on a case we're working on at the moment in relation to Father John Donnelly.'

'And where would you get such an idea?' MacAlister replied. 'Actually, don't bother telling me, I already know. I assume you've been speaking to ACO Strachan and he's been spouting some nonsense to you. Rest assured, I intend to clear that matter up with ACO Strachan in person and in full, very quickly.'

You'll have to wait until he sobers up, Ford thought. 'Sir, I'm sorry for taking up your time. But there are a few discrepancies in the Harbour Street reports that I need to clear up. It'll only take a couple of minutes, unless, of course, you'd prefer I speak to another of your officers.'

A sharp intake of breath at the other end of the line told Ford that MacAlister understood the implied threat, and wasn't too happy about it.

'Go ahead,' he said, after a moment, 'but be brief, DCI Ford. My time is extremely short.'

'Quite so, sir. Three officers died in the Harbour Street fire, correct? George Logan, Derek MacRae and Michael Lawson. Peter Turnbull was badly injured at Harbour Street, but only died recently. Is that right?'

'Indeed,' MacAlister said. 'But I'm not sure how that relates to—'

Ford cut him off, not wanting to give him the chance to settle into the dominant position he normally inhabited during meetings. 'Reading the reports, I see that the air tanks on Logan, MacRae and Lawson were all seriously depleted, more so than should be commonly expected in a fire of that nature. Yet you signed off the reports without any further investigation. Why was that, sir?'

'There was no need,' MacAlister said, sounding as though he was reading from a prepared statement. 'The examination of the BAs after the men were rescued was routine. The three of them were obviously in an extremely distressed state – being in a burning building does that to you, DCI Ford. They were obviously breathing heavily, taking in larger amounts of oxygen than normal.'

'Possibly, sir,' Ford said, ignoring MacAlister's dig about being in a fire. 'But if that's the case, why was Peter Turnbull's oxygen level significantly higher than that of the other three victims? After all, he was the last man to enter the blaze and the first to be pulled out, badly injured but still alive. How do you account for his breathing apparatus being better supplied than his colleagues'? Surely he would have been breathing just as heavily as they were. More so presumably, as the report into his death states that he was trapped underneath the remnants of a collapsed ceiling before being rescued. There's also reference to a neck wound around the windpipe, caused, according to the reports, by his fall from the floor above. Surely a man with a neck injury would struggle to breathe as deeply as you say the other firefighters did.'

'I can't say,' MacAlister said, after a pause. 'This was years ago, DCI Ford, ancient history. I can't be expected to remember—'

'You remembered details from the night well enough when you gave evidence to the Scottish Parliament, though, sir. Speaking of which, at those hearings, you were assisted by one John Ogilvy, a fire-fighter who is now a person of interest in my enquiries. Tell me, Chief MacAlister, how well did you know Mr Ogilvy?'

'Ogilvy?' MacAlister said, confusion in his tone, as though Ford had taken a corner too quickly for him to follow. 'What do you mean? He was attached to my office at the time, to assist with the paperwork for our evidence submissions to the Scottish Parliament about merg-ing the eight fire services into one national service. He was extremely efficient, perhaps a little too zealous for my liking but—'

'Zealous? How?' Ford asked.

'He took it all personally,' MacAlister said. 'Always going on about how the fire service was doing God's work by protecting the innocent and the weak, and that the politicians had no right to be propos-ing cuts as part of the merger. But he spent a lot of time with Father Donnelly, so I suppose that sort of outlook was to be expected. And it helped in the committee hearings. The rhetoric and the deaths at Harbour Street helped to make a powerful case for us.'

Ford swallowed down a shiver of revulsion. In his way, MacAlister was no different from his own chief constable. A man willing to spin any tragedy to his advantage, use it to make his—

He snapped forward in his chair, the thought squeezing the air from his lungs, robbing him of the power of speech. He closed his eyes, forced himself to think everything through logically, one step at a time. The dead man's tally at the scene, Father Donnelly giving the last rites to Peter Turnbull not once, but twice. Peter Turnbull, godfather of John Ogilvy, the man he now suspected of bombing the church in Lenton Barns, kidnapping Father Donnelly and burning another man alive. The idea blossomed in his mind, obscene in its elegance and beauty. What was it Fraser had said? *Hell of a risk for Chief Officer MacAlister to go in front of MSPs and talk about Harbour Street when he knew something was wrong with the incident reports.*

But what if that was the point all along? What if that was why Ogilvy was now hell-bent on revenge? What if—

'DCI Ford, if you have no other questions, I really do have work to be getting on with,' MacAlister said, his voice regaining its earlier cool hostility.

'Sorry, sir,' Ford said, leaning forward and massaging his forehead with his fingers, as though trying to dig out the sudden headache that had exploded there. 'Just one more question. And, please, think very, very carefully before you answer this. When you prepared for the committee hearings, who drafted your evidence? You or John Ogilvy? And was Father Donnelly involved in any of that work?'

'Well, I . . . I . . .' a clearing of the throat rattled down the line '. . . as I recall, Ogilvy did the bulk of the work, possibly with Father Donnelly. Then I would get the draft and give it my approval before it was submitted to the committee.'

Ford almost smiled. 'You got a junior officer to do your work for you, right?' he said. It was a tale as old as time, common in the police as well as the fire service. It was summed up by that old motto in the force – 'Shit rolls downhill.' If there was long, tedious work to be done, like compiling stats on staff deployments or preparing statements for official reports, the senior ranks delegated it to the juniors. It was standard practice, a way to ease your workload.

And in this case it might have been fatal.

'Tell me, sir,' Ford said, even as his mobile began chittering on his desk, the caller ID telling him the chief constable was calling, 'when was the last time you were at church? And when you were there, did you go to Confession?'

CHAPTER 63

They were walking up a dirt track into the forests that surrounded the southern edge of Lenton Barns when Connor took the call from Ford. In short, terse sentences, the policeman told Connor what he had learnt about the fire at Harbour Street, the dead men, the mystery firefighter and the depleted air tanks. Connor nodded as Ford spoke, adding the information to what he already knew. And as he walked, the thought of the missing Bible grew more vivid in his mind.

He thanked Ford, ended the call, then sent a quick request to Doug McGregor.

'What was all that about?' Simon asked softly, as though someone was eavesdropping from some hidden vantage point in the trees. Who knew? Connor thought. Maybe they were.

'Details,' Connor muttered, jarred from his thoughts. Simon shrugged, and Connor knew that his friend wasn't really interested – at that moment, all that mattered to Simon was getting to the shrine in the woods, and seeing if Donna was there.

They walked on, the light growing dimmer as the canopy of trees above them thickened. Beneath their feet, bark and fallen leaves rustled softly, like static being discharged from the ground with every step. In the quiet, the sound seemed deafening.

A few moments later, they came to a gentle curve in the path and, in the sloping crook of a hill, saw the small, stone-walled chapel Connor had found in the history of the church and the village. It was angled away from the path, as though turning its shoulder to it and the rest of the world. The stone walls looked ancient, with an almost greenish tinge from the lichen and moss that had taken root in the pointing and cracked mortar over decades. But the whole building seemed robust, substantial, and Connor noted that the tiling on the roof was neat and clean, the slates new and as yet untarnished by the forest around them.

'Well, someone's been taking care of the place,' Simon said, as they hunkered down.

'Yeah, and look there,' Connor said, pointing to the left side of the building, where a motorbike lay propped against a stack of freshly cut logs. 'Whoever's here has transport as well.'

Simon twisted slightly, and Connor watched as a gun suddenly appeared in his hands. He checked it smoothly and effectively, the clacking of the chamber gentle as he muffled it with his hands. 'I say we circle round, check out the perimeter,' he said. 'You take left, up beside that hill. I'll hook round right, meet you at the gable end.'

Connor nodded, pulling his own gun, the weight of it at once disconcerting and comforting. 'You wouldn't be sending me left because it's less exposed, would you?' he said.

'Not bloody likely,' Simon said, with a smile. 'I'm being lazy. Ground that way is less even, and you'll have further to travel. Me, I prefer the straighter route.'

Connor returned Simon's smile. 'Be careful,' he said. 'You've seen Ogilvy. The guy's shadow could crush us both. And if he's got Donnelly in there with Donna and he feels cornered . . .'

'Copy that,' Simon said, as he moved off, somehow making no noise.

Keeping low, Connor got moving, his gaze flitting between the building and the path in front of him. As Simon said, it was uneven as the ground slowly rose into a hill, with the trunks of trees and fallen branches littering the path. There were no windows on the side of the building Connor was following, which meant Simon was at greater risk of exposure. Connor cursed under his breath, wishing he had taken the frontal route.

After a few minutes of carefully picking his way through the fallen tree branches, Connor came to the end of the building. He smiled as he saw what was sitting there, at the end of another rutted path that presumably led out of the forest.

Simon came into view a few seconds later, gun raised.

'What the hell?' he said, as he saw the red Volkswagen Connor was looking at. 'I thought this car was blown up in the village. So what is this?'

'The last piece of the puzzle,' Connor said, annoyed it had taken him so long to put it all together. 'What did you see?'

'Not a lot,' Simon said. 'No windows on the front side. One door, wooden, but the hinges and bolts on it look brand new.'

Connor had been expecting this. 'So we've only really got one option,' he said. 'No other ways in or out of the structure, so we go in head on.'

Simon nodded. 'Still time to call Ford in,' he said, 'get some of his armed boys here to handle this.'

Connor raised his gun slightly. 'And where would the fun in that be?'

Connor checked the car to make sure there were no unpleasant surprises in it. Then he and Simon crept around to the front of the building. They took up positions at either side of the door, and Connor inspected the lock and the hinges bolting it to the stone arch of the entrance. He felt his heart sink as he saw everything was as Simon described – brand new and solidly built.

'Shit,' he whispered.

Simon dropped his head, shook it. Connor wasn't sure, but he was fairly certain that his friend was laughing softly. 'What's so funny?' he asked.

'Not funny, ironic.' Simon said. 'We saw what happened to a church door when a drone hit it. Nice of Ogilvy to give us the idea. Come on, let's get our own drone ready.'

Connor followed as Simon retraced his steps, returning to the motorbike they had seen propped against the stacked logs.

'What are you thinking?' Connor asked, not sure he wanted to know the answer.

Simon tucked his gun away, straddled the bike. Leant forward and prised a wire from the centre of the handlebars, then followed the wire down around the petrol tank. He smiled, reached into his pocket and produced a paperclip. 'You never spent enough time in Belfast, big lad,' he said. 'Easiest thing in the world to grab a bike when you needed a ride.' He disconnected a wire coupling, then straightened the paperclip and jammed the two ends into the wire connecter.

'Good to go,' he said, rocking the bike off its stand and rolling it gently back to the front of the building.

Connor followed, watched as Simon lined the bike up with the door before unlooping his belt from his jeans. Then, to Connor's amazement, he clicked the ignition switch and the bike growled into life. He wrapped his belt around the right handlebar then secured the other end to the bike's frame. The bike screamed as the belt twisted the throttle open and jammed it.

'Knock, knock, motherfucker,' Simon said, as he released the clutch and threw the bike forward. It dug in and spurted towards the wooden door, which shattered like kindling. Connor watched as the bike disappeared into the darkness, heard a dull crash as it hit something in the building.

'Go, go, go!' Simon shouted, then sprinted forward, pulling his gun as he moved. Connor raced after him, swallowing the sudden insane desire to laugh as adrenalin and terror burnt through his veins.

They got to the door, stepped into the darkness, both men flattening themselves against the wall at either side. It was a long, wide room, almost like a church in miniature. At the head, beyond a row of pews packed with what looked like plastic containers, Connor could see a small plinth with a statue of the Virgin Mary looking down on the motorbike, which lay like a wounded animal, engine screaming, at the bottom of it. Connor exchanged a glance with Simon who nodded and they stepped forward cautiously. Connor felt an icy flush as he got closer to the pews, saw that the containers lying there were jerry-cans. As he stepped further into the gloom, the smell of petrol burnt his nose and stabbed for his eyes. He got to the bike, killed the ignition, then looked at Simon.

'No one home,' he said.

'On the contrary, Mr Fraser,' a voice said, as a figure emerged from the shadows just behind the altar. 'This is the Lord's house, and he is always at home, as am I.'

Connor felt a moment of vertigo-like confusion as Donna emerged from the shadows, her eyes wide and glinting with terror. Then he saw the knife at her throat, followed the arm holding it back. Cursed himself at being so slow to put it all together.

'Father Donnelly,' he said, in a voice as cold as the stone that surrounded them.

CHAPTER 64

'Donnelly?' Simon said. 'What about Ogilvy? I thought he was the one behind all this.'

Connor smiled, not taking his eyes from Donnelly. Madness danced and glittered in the priest's, magnified by the thick, heavy glasses he wore. But it was the calmness that worried Connor more. The relaxed, almost dreamy smile on the man's face, as if everything was right with the world and exactly where it was meant to be.

'Oh, Ogilvy's part of it, a big part, if I'm right, but Father Donnelly is pulling the strings, aren't you, Father? Or are you going to tell me now that you weren't the one who took those pictures of Jen and my gran, sent me that bullshit contract and dropped seventy grand into my business account?'

Donnelly's smile lost its dreamy look, turned hard and sharp, like the blade he held to Donna's neck. 'Quite right, Mr Fraser. After all, I must protect myself, and the work I do in the name of the Lord.'

Connor sneered. 'The Lord's work? That includes killing firefighters and innocent old women, does it?'

'I did not kill them!' Donnelly roared, his voice loud in the charged silence of the church. 'They were sacrificial lambs, anointed by God and sanctified by me to play their part in the glorious rebirth and resurrection of our family.'

'Your family?' Connor said, thinking back to the notes he had seen on Donnelly's desk, and the Biblical verses he had written down. And as he did, another thought occurred to him, the reason Donnelly had targeted him as his protector and, ultimately, his final victim.

'Why, yes, my family, of course,' Donnelly said, as though talking to a child. 'They needed to be protected. The brave men who died were sacrifices to the cause. Their courage will not be forgotten.'

'It was you, wasn't it?' Connor said, thinking back to what Ford had told him about the fire at Harbour Street. 'You snuck in, made sure the firefighters who died were put in harm's way or attacked them yourself. Then you snuck out to give them the last rites, make sure they got to Heaven. You sick bastard. But Turnbull surprised you, didn't he? When you saw that the ceiling collapse hadn't finished him off you slashed his neck to make sure the job was done. But you didn't count on him surviving, did you? Or Ogilvy finding out what you had done.'

'It was God's will,' Donnelly replied. As he spoke, he tightened his grip around Donna's waist, brought the knife further up her throat. She squealed, eyes pleading with Connor for help.

'You really went into a burning building to make sure firefighters died?' Simon whispered, his voice robbed of any strength by disbelief. 'But why, for fuck's sake? They saw you as a hero, their saviour. Why kill them?'

'You heard the man,' Connor said, eyes flitting between the knife and Donna's pleading gaze. He had to keep Donnelly talking. 'You were doing God's work, weren't you, Father? They were talking about merging the fire services, cutting stations and men. And you couldn't have that. So when a big fire broke out, you made sure that firefighters were killed in it, that you had a tragic story of heroic sacrifice and honouring the work of heroes to fight off those who would wield the axe and use the merger to cut costs, staff and stations.'

'Jesus,' Simon whispered.

'Quite right,' Donnelly said. 'God sacrificed his own Son to save us, how could I be expected to do any less? I needed to make them understand, to tell the story. And it worked.'

'And all it cost was six lives,' Connor said. 'What is it the Bible says about "Thou shalt not kill", Father? Seems to me you've kind of screwed yourself on getting into Heaven.'

Donnelly gave Connor a smile that was almost sympathetic. 'I never thought I was going to Heaven, Mr Fraser. I know my fate is to go to a darker place. But I accept that happily, as I have served a greater good and my legacy will endure well beyond my death.'

'Legacy,' Simon hissed, his voice jagged with contempt. 'You've killed six people. And what about Ogilvy? Did you kill him as well?'

'Enough!' Donnelly roared, Donna flinching in his arms. 'I have work to complete to ensure my legacy.' He started forward, forcing Connor to back up as the blade flashed closer to Donna's neck. 'We will leave here, now. You will stay exactly where you are and—'

A low, almost animalistic moaning cut Donnelly off, rumbling from the darkness behind the altar as though all the lost souls that had sought comfort and shelter in the building had been awoken by the commotion and were demanding to be heard. Donnelly's head snapped backwards, towards the sound and Connor surged forward, grabbing the hand holding the knife and wrenching it from Donna's throat.

'Run!' he shouted as he grabbed Donna's arm and wrenched her from Donnelly's grasp. The priest bared his teeth, spun and punched Connor in the ribs before pivoting his weight onto the knife, trying to drive it down into Connor's chest.

From what seemed like miles away, Connor heard Simon cry: 'Can't get a shot. Get clear, Connor!'

And then there was that sound again, a low, guttural moan that seemed to vibrate through the stones of the building. It galvanised Connor and he tightened his grip on Donnelly's knife hand, felt the fingers bear down on the handle. He twisted his hand abruptly, flipping Donnelly's grip and forcing his shoulder down as the priest straightened his arm and bent to ease the pressure on his wrist. Connor slashed a knee forward, felt the bone in Donnelly's elbow explode as he connected. The snap echoed through the church like a gunshot, Donnelly's howl of pain joining the low moaning from the shadows, like some hellish chorus. Connor lifted the priest by his ruined arm, dragging him almost off his feet as though he was a child's toy. He spun him, looked into the man's eyes, saw nothing but hatred and madness glaring back at him across a void he knew he would never understand.

He jabbed Donnelly in the face with his free hand, the man's nose and glasses shattering on the impact. Then he pushed him back, felt his ribs snap as he drove a stamping kick into his chest. Donnelly collapsed to the floor and rolled into a ball, as though trying to hold the agony he was experiencing close to him.

Connor stepped over him, felt the urge to stamp down, grind the man who had threatened those he loved into a paste on the stone.

'Connor,' Simon said, his voice a warning as he approached, one arm around Donna. 'Enough. That gobshite's not worth it. Leave him.'

Connor blinked once, took a breath, forced back the searing rage that flared through him, demanding only blood and pain. He looked down at Donna, felt his fury reignite as he saw a rivulet of blood roll down her neck. 'You okay?' he asked, the words seeming hollow and inadequate.

Donna grunted, something between a laugh and a cry. 'I've had better days. Last thing I remember is that bastard,' she jutted her jaw to Donnelly, 'knocking on the van door then launching himself at Keith.' Her eyes grew wide, panicked. 'Oh, God, Keith. How is he?'

'He's okay,' Connor said, laying a hand on Donna's shoulder.

'Donnelly grabbed you?' Simon said, before shifting his gaze to Connor. 'Big lad, would you mind telling me just what the fuck is going on?'

Connor smiled. 'In a minute,' he said. 'First, let's see what's making that God-awful noise.'

CHAPTER 65

They found him behind the altar, in a small anteroom, which also held a table, a laptop and various other electrical components. Unlike the main area of the church, this room was well lit, with battery-powered spotlights attached to the walls and trained on the desk. Connor could also see a small petrol-powered generator tucked into the corner of the room.

He gestured for Simon and Donna to stay back, stepped into the room and, with a grunt, turned over the figure who was lying on the floor, moaning. John Ogilvy's face was a mask of blood and bruises framed around a strip of tape that had been stuck across his mouth.

The skin around his eyes was crimson, dried tears crusted around his cheeks, and the whites of his eyes were scarlet. His massive hands had been folded across his chest and bound with clip ties that Connor could see were biting into his wrists. Connor grabbed his knife from his pocket, cut the wrist ties and pulled the tape from Ogilvy's mouth.

'Thanks,' he coughed, in a voice too small and gentle for his size as he sat up slowly.

'Take it easy,' Connor said, putting a hand on the giant's shoulder. 'Looks like you took a hell of a knock. Donnelly, I presume?'

'Yeah,' Ogilvy said, massaging his wrists. 'He told me he had your reporter friend, called me here. Jumped me when . . .' His voice trailed off, eyes suddenly wide and wild with an almost feral panic. 'Donnelly? Where is he? Did he . . .'

259

'Don't worry, he's dealt with,' Connor said. 'Passed out by the altar. We'll get to him in a minute. But let me guess, he clocked you with that oversized Bible of his?'

Ogilvy nodded slowly. 'Might have been. I knew it was a trap, but didn't know what else I could do. He had your friend, and this is between us. No one else needed to get hurt. So I came here, thinking I could get the jump on him, but he sprayed something in my eyes then hit me with what felt like a brick.'

Connor nodded. 'Yeah, he did the same to the two police officers who were guarding him at the church,' he said, annoyed at how wrong he had been about most of this case.

'Wait, you mean Laughing Boy here is innocent in all of this?' Simon asked. 'You're saying that Donnelly wasn't grabbed but he beat the shit out of two cops then fled here? But why did he attack his own church with drones? Christ, he could have been killed himself.'

Connor turned, smiled at Simon. He understood his friend's confusion, had shared it until that last call from Ford and the message from McGregor telling him that a check of the official reports from the Scottish Parliament and Donnelly's comments confirmed that the four dead firefighters, Turnbull, Logan, MacRae and Lawson, had all attended Donnelly's former church in Glasgow.

'Donnelly didn't attack the church with the drones. That was you, wasn't it, John? After you found out what he did at Harbour Street.'

Something hardened in Ogilvy's crimson eyes, uglier and angrier than the wounds to his face. 'When Uncle Peter died, I had to know why,' he said, the softness of his voice somehow emphasising the sorrow in his words. 'So I went back, into the incident logs. I mean, I knew most of the story from my work with Donnelly and MacAlister on the merger hearings, but I wanted to know more. And that was when I found the dead man's tally and the discrepancies in the BA levels. I called Donnelly, asked him about it and . . .' he choked back a sob, a desperate pleading in his eyes '. . . he admitted it. No attempt to lie to me or deflect blame. Jesus, the twisted bastard thought I would understand. He had preached for years about the value of sacrifice, about what was expected of him. So when he saw Peter in the fire at Harbour Street, he said it all made sense. He said Peter had played his part in God's plan and had lived sin free since the fire, that he had given him the last rites at the time and he was going to Heaven with a clear conscience and an open heart.'

'So you didn't know what Donnelly had done when you helped him with the statements on the joint service at the Scottish Parliament?' Simon asked.

'No!' Ogilvy cried. 'Of course not. I thought we were doing the Lord's work, using the sacrifice and pain of the men who died at Harbour Street to protect the fire service and see it reborn as something new and good. Something that would protect people. But it was all a lie! All based on sin, not virtue!'

'Yeah,' Connor said. 'And that's why you tried to kill Donnelly with the drones, isn't it? You knew illegal drones were an issue. What better way to get people talking about it and taking action than using them to kill a priest? Win-win for you. You keep the secret of Harbour Street, that the fire service we have now is built on the work of a killer, and give your boss, MacAlister, an issue to fight on into the service review.'

'I'm sorry you got hurt in the attack,' Ogilvy said. 'I found out Donnelly was looking into you. He kept talking about your gran and girlfriend, when I called him, and a "sinful protector". So I asked McGovern to find out about you. Were you a threat or a possible ally? He must have taken the seventy grand from Aunt Caroline and used that to hire you.'

'Yeah,' Connor agreed. It made sense now, all of it. What was it Caroline Turnbull had said? *Father Donnelly has always been so helpful. It was him who got Peter into St Margaret's.* Was that altruism, or a way to keep an eye on Turnbull, make sure he kept his secrets, took them with him to the grave? And would he have used the power he had over Turnbull to force him, under the shroud of confession, to tell him of any confidences he had betrayed, that he had told his godson of what he had done in God's name? Connor thought of the serpent in Eden, whispering into Eve's ear. Could see Donnelly doing the same. Inveigling himself into Caroline Turnbull's life, offering support and counsel. Persuading her, oh so gently, to transfer the seventy thousand pounds from Peter Turnbull's life assurance to the

US. Shuddered as he thought of Donnelly walking the halls of his gran's care home, asking after her, talking to her, then wandering the grounds, taking pictures that would ultimately be sent to Connor to blackmail him into protecting Donnelly. And, of course, a fee would have to be paid. After all, it was written in the Bible. *To the one who works, his wages are not counted as a gift but as his due.* In Donnelly's twisted mind, he was only acting honourably, paying Connor for his services.

'Hold on,' Simon said. 'You're telling me that he only orchestrated the drone attack? Not the car bomb or the killing of the cabbie? So why?'

'Think about it,' Connor said. 'We were right about Donnelly flushing the mark, just wrong about who the mark was. After Ogilvy attacked the church, Donnelly had to take him out of the equation. So he grabbed a car similar to the one Ogilvy drives – no doubt he'd been told all about the car by good old Aunt Caroline – then booby-trapped it in the village. He knew Ogilvy would get the message, would have to visit the scene himself. And he drove Strachan and Ford to the site. Just me causing a commotion by grabbing Ford, thinking he was the target, who got in his way.'

'The cabbie,' Simon said, after a moment, understanding dropping his voice to a whisper. 'Jesus Christ, the cabbie. He told us he did it. "This blood is on Donnelly's hands." But the police helmet?'

'A threat,' Connor said, his guess hardening into certainty in his mind now. 'After the attack on the church, Donnelly grabs the cabbie and uses him to send a message. *Come after me and this will happen to a policeman or a firefighter.* Ogilvy here was on the scene that night, would have got the message. And, as he said, he didn't want innocents to get in the middle of a private little war.'

'Fucking hell,' Simon muttered, 'and to think—'

A harsh scraping sound from behind them cut Simon off. He whipped his head round, gun rising as he did.

'Simon, check on Donnelly, get him and Donna out of here,' Connor said.

Simon nodded. Donna looked like she was going to object, then seemed to think better of it.

'So what happens now?' Ogilvy asked.

Connor stood and offered him a hand. 'We get out of here, call the police. You'll have to answer for the attack on the church, of course, but we'll see what happens with—'

'No police,' Ogilvy whispered.

'What?' Connor said, unease tickling the back of his throat as Ogilvy rose from the floor, as if it had suddenly given birth to an avenging demon.

'No police,' he repeated. 'I can't let what he did at Harbour Street come out. It would destroy the service, especially now, with the review at Parliament coming up.'

Connor forced himself to keep his voice calm, even as he closed his grip on his gun.

'That's not your call,' he said. 'We've got to bring the police in. No one will believe that anyone in the fire service supported what Donnelly did. Please, Ogilvy, let's end this the right—'

Ogilvy moved almost too quickly for Connor to register what was happening. He surged forward, grabbing Connor's wrist as he brought his gun arm up. Excruciating agony scorched up his arm as Ogilvy twisted Connor's wrist and squeezed it with his massive hand. Connor held on as long as he could, but the gun fell from his grasp and clattered to the floor.

'I can't let you tell everyone what he did,' Ogilvy whispered, his voice still singsong and soft, like a child at play.

Connor felt his knees begin to buckle with the pain. Forced himself to think. Relaxed his arm and stepped into Ogilvy's chest, almost as if he were inviting the man to dance. He dropped to his knees then sprang up with all the force he could draw from his legs, smashing the top of his head into Ogilvy's massive jaw, the shock reverberating through Connor's head, blurring his vision and momentarily deafening him.

Ogilvy staggered back, and Connor felt hot blood splash on his face as the bigger man coughed and spat, clawing for breath. But still he had Connor's wrist in his iron grasp, yanking him back towards him.

'I didn't want this,' he said, lips pulling back from blood-smeared teeth. Connor said nothing but went with Ogilvy's yank, adding his momentum to it, pivoting at the hip as he brought the elbow of his free hand up and smashed it into the giant's temple.

He felt the pressure on his wrist ease, twisted his hand away, breaking Ogilvy's grip. Dipped, then twisted up with a left hook to Ogilvy's ribcage. It was like hitting a brick wall, but Ogilvy grunted again, staggered back, banging into the table behind him.

Not daring to give the giant a moment to recover, Connor lashed out with a sweeping leg to Ogilvy's ankle, throwing him off his feet. He leapt onto the man's chest as he fell, dug his elbow and forearm into the massive exposed neck.

'Quit it!' he shouted, his hearing still muffled. 'I understand what you did, but you have to—'

'No!' Ogilvy roared, blood flecking Connor's face again. 'You can't do this. I won't let you!'

He threw his hips up, almost throwing Connor off him. Connor held on, bore down on the arm across Ogilvy's neck.

'Sorry,' he whispered, as he pressed harder, Ogilvy's eyes bulging, his skin flushing an ugly purple. Connor swung with his free hand, aiming rabbit-punches at Ogilvy's cheek. Felt a bone splinter with one blow, saw something flicker, then dull in the man's eyes as they rolled back in his head. Felt a moment of nausea as he remembered the stunned policeman he had found at the church, the same dazed eyes, blood oozing from one ear.

He waited for a moment, then eased off his choke hold gradually. Ogilvy lay underneath him, chest rising and falling, blood oozing from his mouth.

Connor rocked back, let the world into his consciousness. And as he did, a thought occurred to him.

With all the commotion, why had Donna and Simon not come to help?

CHAPTER 66

Connor retrieved his gun, made his way back to the main church. Saw Simon standing in the middle of the row of pews, gun out and trained on Donnelly, who was sitting propped up against a pew, a jerry-can abandoned further up the aisle. Connor didn't need the sudden onslaught of petrol fumes to know what had happened – the priest had regained consciousness, dragged himself to the pews and emptied a can of petrol over himself. Connor felt a flash of panic as he saw the lighter in Donnelly's hand, held up as though it was a talisman that could ward Simon off.

Donna was nowhere to be seen.

'Got her out of here, sent her for help,' Simon said, as though he had read Connor's thoughts. 'Just trying to convince Father Donnelly here not to send us up like a bad Eleventh Night bonfire.'

Connor glanced over Donnelly's shoulder, to the pews cluttered with cans behind him. If they were even half full, the explosion would raze the building to the ground.

He took a step forward, eyes not leaving Donnelly.

'You don't want to do this,' he said slowly. 'You conned Caroline Turnbull out of seventy grand, took pictures of my gran and my girl-friend to persuade me to protect you from Ogilvy when he found out what you'd done. You wanted to live then. I can't see how that's changed. So put down the lighter, let's get out of here together.'

Donnelly smiled as though he was watching a tranquil sunrise.

'My work is ended,' he said at last. 'My life is not mine any longer. And my death will secure my legacy, ensure firefighters for years to come can protect the innocent. They must, you see. They must.'

'Why?' Connor asked, playing for time, trying to think of something, anything he could do to stop Donnelly. Not just for him and. Simon, but for Ogilvy too. He had beaten the man, true, left him unconscious, but he was still responsible for his life.

'Why?' Donnelly said, his voice an incredulous sneer. 'Why, to make sure no one else suffers the mark, as I have.' As he spoke, he gestured lazily to the scar that ran from his lip, down and around his jaw.

'What happened?' Connor asked, his mouth suddenly dry.

Donnelly's brow furrowed, as though he was peering into the gloom in front of him at something only he could see. 'We were only children,' he said, more to himself than to Connor. 'Back in Glasgow, a tenement flat in the Gorbals. Our parents had left us for the evening. Father was a factory worker, on the night shift, and Mother worked ... Well, Mother worked nights as well. We needed the money – we had nothing but each other. So it was just Anne and me that night. Sweet Anne. She was cold, so cold. So she put on the fire, you know, the old ones that connect to the bottles of gas. But she was young and innocent. And the fire, she didn't understand it was a living thing. She let it get free. And it ate its way through the flat, burning, searing ...' His voice trailed off as he touched the scar again, traced it almost lovingly with his finger, then reached down, ripping at his shirt. Connor winced at what he saw, heard Simon give a choking cough.

It was as if someone had taken a flesh-coloured candle and dripped it over his chest. The skin swooped and twisted in strange, almost abstract whorls where the flesh had bubbled and melted, distorted by fire. His right shoulder was a dark, almost purplish knot of flesh, a graft that had failed or an injury from that night, Connor couldn't tell.

'The firefighters found us, of course,' Donnelly said, his voice an echo of the past. 'They were heroes. Angels emerging from the flames to rescue us. I don't remember how I got the scar – something about the gas bottle, I think. But by the time they got to us, the damage was done and Anne was ... was ...'

He closed his eyes for a moment, and Connor saw his shoulders shudder. Despite himself, he felt a sudden wave of pity for the broken, deranged man in front of him who had obviously sought shelter in God and found only damnation and madness.

'I'm sorry for your loss,' he said. 'But surely Anne wouldn't want this. Wouldn't want you to—'

'This is not about what Anne would want, it's about me!' Donnelly snarled, eyes glinting, face contorting as he spat the words. 'And you, Fraser, are not one to lecture me about family, given what you did to your grandmother.'

Connor nodded, remembering the note he had seen in Donnelly's study. The note that had made him a fitting target in the priest's eyes. '*Do not cast me off in the time of old age; forsake me not when my strength is spent*,' he said, feeling fury prickle at his eyes, tears that were nothing to do with the petrol fumes that soured the air. 'Is that really what you think I did? Dumped my gran in a care home and left her to rot? Abandoned her? She gets the best of care they can provide. I make sure she—'

'And what of Jennifer?' Donnelly snapped. 'You did the same with her. The moment she was broken, you discarded her, shipped her off to Glasgow. Made her someone else's problem. You are a sinner, Fraser. A defiler. Men like you deserve nothing but violent ends and, by God, that is what I'll give you.'

Connor was moving before he realised it as Donnelly closed his eyes and pulled the lighter closer to him.

A sudden blur of movement beside him, the sensation of some massive force shoving him from behind into Simon. He grabbed his friend, staggered forward, then pirouetted around Simon to see Ogilvy launching himself at Donnelly, his bloodied face a grotesque etching of mindless hate.

'Bastard! Everything I did was a lie. A lie! For you! Not for God, not for the service. You!'

Connor grabbed Simon, dragged him towards the ruined door of the church. Nothing else mattered except getting Simon to safety, no matter how hard he struggled and fought against him, possessed by the urge to get to the men who had threatened his friend.

He got Simon to the door, pushed him through it. Simon landed roughly, rolled, sat up.

'Stay there,' Connor yelled. 'I'm going to—'

The explosion was deafening, as if the church itself was screaming in agony. Connor felt himself lifted off his feet, hurled back by an unrelenting wall of boiling force. He felt his skin tighten, smelt burning hair as the heat rolled over him. What breath he had left was punched from his lungs by the unforgiving forest floor, fallen branches and twigs skewering him. He was aware of a strange, cooling numbness on his chest, then Simon was on him, roughly flipping him over, turning his chest into the cool earth.

'I've got you, big lad,' he heard Simon say, his words muffled and distorted by the ringing in Connor's ears. Felt Simon grab his shoulders and roll him back, was gripped by an almost obscene urge to laugh when he looked down at his chest and saw smoke rising from his jacket where the fire had leapt from the church and tried to devour him as well. What was it Donnelly had said? That fire was a living thing? Connor could almost believe it.

The laughter died in his throat when he looked up at the church. The old stone walls had held, mostly, reflecting the force of the blast back on itself. Smoke gouted from the ruined door, almost as if the church was a living thing exhaling a cigarette.

He looked at Simon, no need to ask the question, unable to form words as the numbness faded from his chest and cold, scalding agony dug into it with a thousand tiny needles.

Simon shook his head, eyes not leaving Connor's. 'No way they survived that,' he said, after a moment. 'Donnelly was doused in petrol or whatever the hell he was using, and Ogilvy forced him back into the jerry-cans he was stockpiling. The big man's bulk probably smothered some of the blast, but still . . .'

A sudden wave of nausea hit Connor and he lay back, looking up at the canopy of trees overhead. Felt hot tears prickle at his eyes, let them come. Thought of his gran in the care home, Jen in rehab. Was Donnelly right? Had he abandoned them, given up when they became too difficult to deal with? Failed them in the same way he had failed to save Ogilvy?

He sat up, forcing back the churning of his guts. Grabbed onto the pain in his chest, focused on it. He refused to be judged by a killer who turned faith into a weapon to justify his twisted goals. Connor had no great belief in a higher power, but he knew that, if it did exist, it wasn't to be found here, or in the actions of Father John Donnelly. Maybe Donnelly was right, maybe he was a man who would face a violent end. If so, Connor could live with that. At least he would face that end standing. At least it would be on his terms.

'You gonna be okay, Connor?' Simon asked, eyes strobing to the smouldering ruin of Connor's jacket.

Connor shrugged off his jacket. Saw his T-shirt was as tattered as the jacket. It didn't look pretty, and it felt worse, but Simon had acted quickly, smothered the flames before they could really take hold. 'I'll live,' he said. 'Donna?'

'Should be halfway back to the village by now. Gave her my phone, told her to call for help as soon as she got to a place with signal.'

Connor got to his feet, the world growing overly bright and lurching in front of his eyes as he did so. 'Come on,' he said, knowing what needed to be done, despite how he felt about it. 'We need to confirm they're both dead. Then you can hotwire that car, like you hotwired the bike. Get us the fuck out of here. Don't know about you, but I'm done walking for the day.'

CHAPTER 67

Three days later

Strachan sat at his desk, unable to decide if the grainy headache behind his eyes and the oily roiling he felt in his stomach was due to the previous night's whisky, the files that sat in front of him or the phone call he had just taken.

After reading the police statement taken from Connor Fraser that Ford had given to him 'off the record, of course', it hadn't taken long to track down the missing pieces of the puzzle. It was all there, just waiting to be found, if anyone had taken the time to look.

A search through the records showed a fire in a tenement flat in Glasgow, just as Donnelly had described. Firefighters who attended found an established blaze, and rescued one child, John Donnelly, twelve. A female, his sister, Anne Donnelly, was found dead at the scene, thought to have been killed instantly when the gas bottle that was the cause of the blaze had exploded.

Donnelly disappeared off the radar for a while, until he became the parish priest covering Spaven Street, and the fire station sited there. Over time, he became the pastor for the station, and then for the whole of what had been Strathclyde Fire and Rescue Service. He had organised fundraisers for the service, set up prayer groups for men who were still wary of declaring their faith and openly worshipping in a city that was riven by sectarianism. And, Strachan found,

Donnelly had also trained as a 'retained firefighter': an on-call firefighter, who could be summoned to duty when needed but otherwise retained their day-to-day job. Donnelly received all the training a regular firefighter would have had at the time – including instruction in the use of breathing apparatus. He was also given his own safety equipment, with everything he would need to enter a burning building.

A building just like the warehouse on Harbour Street.

Strachan had gone back to the files on that night, found what, deep down, he knew he would and wished he would not. The cause of the blaze at the warehouse was attributed to a defective bottle of LPG gas that was stored on the site, attached to a small flamethrower used for melting the asphalt that was being applied to the roof of the building. It was found that the bottle had leaked over time, filling the storeroom where it was held with gas that ignited when a cleaner stepped into the room and flicked on the light. Strachan didn't need to compare the report from the Gorbals fire to know that the gas bottle that caused the Harbour Street fire would be the same as the one that had exploded in John Donnelly's home.

He sat back, felt the sudden urge for a drink, fought it with the knowledge of what would come next. The reports that Donna Blake, the journalist Donnelly had kidnapped to blackmail John Ogilvy, had produced had been bad enough, but with the Scottish Government's service review looming, the story, and the scrutiny, from press and politicians alike would only intensify. And what, Strachan wondered, would that scrutiny reveal about his boss, Chief Fire Officer Arthur MacAlister, the man who had built his career on his action at Harbour Street, action that now looked at best sloppy and at worst complicit. Four men had died because of the Harbour Street fire and Donnelly's actions in the blaze, all to protect a fire service that this story could ultimately destroy.

If, that was, Strachan allowed it to.

No. He would not. Could not. He wasn't the political animal that MacAlister was, but he was a firefighter, and he knew that an inferno could sometimes be stopped by a cutting a firebreak, letting the fire feast on what it had already consumed and not move any further.

A call from the justice secretary's office told Strachan that MacAlister had already been consumed by the blaze, and that his career was to be the firebreak. Strachan had never wanted the chief's job, only ever to be a good firefighter. But now being a good firefighter meant stepping in and leading a service that was reeling from a scandal that could haunt it for decades.

But to do that, he would have to be sober.

He reached into his bottom drawer, brought out the bottle that was alarmingly empty. Swilled the last of the liquid around the bottom, considering. Then, decision made, he popped the cork, the sound sweet and soothing.

It wasn't a drink, he told himself. It was a toast.

A toast to his future.

CHAPTER 68

Donna sat across from Simon in Connor's flat, a glass of white wine and a bottle sitting on the coffee-table between them. On her lap, Tom was curled, purring contentedly as she stroked the cat's luxuriant fur.

'You should be honoured,' Simon said, gesturing to the cat with his own glass of wine. 'She's normally very selective about whom she lets pet her.'

'Like my mum always says, "Dogs have owners, cats have staff,"' Donna replied, with an absent half-smile.

'How is your mum, anyway?' Simon asked. 'Must have been hell to pay when you got back home after everything that happened.'

Donna grunted at Simon's understatement. Her mother had never liked Donna's choice of profession, the long hours and the numerous calls from her daughter to help look after her grandson, Andrew, while Donna worked. But to have her daughter kidnapped as part of that work, to have her life threatened? It had hardened Irene Blake's contempt for journalism into a blunt hatred that was only softened by the tears of relief she shed when she had hugged Donna as she stepped through the door of the flat.

'Aye, you could say that,' Donna agreed.

'More importantly,' Simon said, standing and offering Donna her wine glass, 'how are you doing?'

Donna looked up at him, at the gentle concern in his eyes, and considered. She wasn't sure if it was concussion or her mind trying to

273

process what had happened, but the events of the last couple of days would only come to her in snatches. When Donnelly had barged into the Sky News van and attacked Keith, she had attempted to fight back, fuelled by terror and fury. But he had been strong, almost manically so, and then there had been blackness. She had awoken somewhere cold and damp, the air filled with the harsh tang of petrol, a giant trussed up next to her, his face bloodied and broken. Then a growling scream that seemed to echo through the old stone that entombed her, a rending crash that sounded like the end of the world. The scalding cold of a knife blade at her throat, Connor grabbing her, then . . .

She blinked, picked up her wine. Drank. 'Honestly, Simon, I don't know,' she said. 'I mean, between this and the story McGregor is working on with me, I've not really had time to take it all in, just felt like I've been riding the whirlwind, if that makes sense.'

Simon nodded. 'Aye, I know that too well,' he said. 'Used to happen all the time in Belfast, one case blurring into another. It was all we could do to keep our heads above water. But, trust me, Donna, holding things in doesn't help. So if you want to talk, or I can help with anything, just shout, okay?'

'Okay,' she said, a heavy silence falling between them, Donna wondering what type of help Simon really meant. She was a single mother with a demanding career and a knack for getting into trouble. The last significant man in her life, Andrew's father, had died partly because of a story she was working on. She had thought finding someone to share her life with was a distant dream, but then there was Simon with his easy humour and his genuine concern for her. Was she imagining the spark she felt between them, the feeling that there was something to be explored and developed? Or was she seeing something that didn't exist, an illusion given substance by the extreme situations they had confronted together and the common cause they had made?

She was stirred from her thoughts by the ringing of the front-door bell. She looked up at Simon, who exchanged a puzzled glance with her.

'You expecting someone?' he asked, his voice low as he stared at the living-room door.

'Who knows I'm here?' she replied. Andrew was spending the night with her mum and dad, a situation her mum had insisted on, despite her complaints about how often she looked after Andrew, and anyone on the news desk who needed her for a story would just call.

'Hmm,' Simon grunted. He put his glass down, reached under the settee, then stood up. Donna felt her breath catch in her throat as she saw the gun he held. It was almost comically small in Simon's hand, yet it demanded her attention, as though it was emitting some irresistible force that drew her eyes towards it.

'Stay here,' he said, moving with silent grace towards the door. 'If you hear me shout, get into the bathroom, lock the door and do not come out for anyone or anything but me, clear?'

'Clear,' Donna whispered, her lips numb.

Simon nodded, moved to the door. Opened it silently, then disappeared through it. Donna got to her feet, took a step towards the door. Heard muffled voices, then the sound of the front door opening and closing. A dull banging echoed into the living room from the hallway, and Donna felt the urge to run judder through her legs in electric bolts.

The door opened slowly and she shrank back, eyes darting around the room for a weapon or a place to hide. Then Simon stepped through, Doug McGregor draped over his shoulder, like a discarded puppet, his clothes ripped and smeared with mud and blood.

'Oh, Jesus, Doug,' she whispered, as she rushed towards him.

Doug brought his head up, revealing a face that was a riot of bruises and blood crusted around his nose and lips. He tried to smile, exposing ragged stumps where his two front teeth had been.

'Hiya, Donna,' he whispered, his voice hoarse, as though he was a smoker who had just finished his fifth packet of the day. 'Know that story we were working on? I think it's a wee bit bigger than we thought.' He gave a laugh, clutched his side.

'What the hell happened to you?' Simon asked.

'I'll get to it,' Doug whispered. 'But, first, two things.'

'What?' Simon asked.

'Get me a drink,' Doug said. 'Then call Connor, will you? Somehow, I think we'll need him on this one.'

CHAPTER 69

Jen punched Connor, pain arcing through him from the burn to his chest. He had been lucky: the wound was merely superficial thanks to Simon's quick thinking.

Unfortunately, Father Donnelly and John Ogilvy hadn't been so lucky. Simon and Connor had found their bodies in the church, Donnelly little more than a blackened, twisted husk with just enough human characteristics remaining to make Connor's stomach turn. Ogilvy was lying slumped against the far wall of the church, thrown clear by the blast from the jerry-cans. His skin was blackened around his face, the bruises Connor had inflicted standing out in obscene contrast across his neck. His massive head drooped down, as though he was looking at his chest, and the catastrophic damage that had been done to it. When Connor lifted Ogilvy's head to check for a pulse, he felt the grinding of bones that told him Ogilvy had broken his neck, his empty eyes glaring back like accusing marbles, glassy and cold.

Jen punched him again, and Connor hissed out a sharp breath.

'I said, Connor,' she said, pointing to the TV in the corner of the room, 'you should have told me about this.'

Connor looked up, saw Donna on the screen, standing in front of a large warehouse-style building that was branded with the Scottish Fire and Rescue Service logo. The picture then cut to the church in Lenton Barns, followed by footage of Chief Fire Officer Arthur MacAlister at the press conference after the drone attack. After Donna had called for help, she had brushed aside concerns for her condition and got herself in front of a camera as quickly as she could. Over the course of the next twenty-four hours, she had, with Connor's help, uncovered the rest of the story: Donnelly being the killer of Harbour Street, Ogilvy's discovery of the truth, Donnelly's plan to hire Connor to protect him from Ogilvy's wrath. Connor had dug into that, thought he'd found an explanation for the contract Donnelly had insisted he signed in scripture, and a verse stating that 'If a man vows a vow to the Lord, or swears an oath to bind himself by a pledge, he shall not break his word.' In Donnelly's mind, Connor thought, it had made sense to have Connor pledge himself to the task of saving him. Just like it had made sense to Ogilvy to move back in with Caroline Turnbull, to protect her from Donnelly. They had found his personal belongings in the fire-gutted house. It explained why the flat in Airth had been so barren, empty: he had taken the bulk of his belongings to the Turnbulls', set up camp there in the hope of protecting the only family he had left. It hadn't been enough.

Connor reached for the remote, muted the TV. Looked down at Jen. They were lying on her bed in the rehab facility, Jen resting her head on Connor's chest, looking up at him with a mixture of concern, anger and confusion.

'I'm sorry,' he said, swallowing another hiss of pain, 'I was just trying to . . . well, I don't know . . . protect you. You've already been through so much because of me. I didn't want you to—'

'Stop that,' Jen said, her gaze hardening to match her tone. 'This,' she indicated her legs, 'was not your fault. Neither was what happened with this nutcase Donnelly or the other firefighter who died.'

'Ogilvy,' Connor said quietly, the dead man's accusing eyes flashing across his mind as he spoke his name. He knew those eyes would haunt his dreams.

'Yeah, him. Look, Connor, I told you when I was first hurt that I didn't want you to stay with me because you felt sorry for me. The same goes for some outdated idea you have about being my personal White Knight. I don't need a protector, okay? I can take care of myself. All I need is you. And for you to be honest with me.'

'Okay,' Connor said, brushing a strand of blonde hair away from her forehead and behind her ear, hearing the lie in his voice and hating it. He loved her, but he could not bring himself to be honest with her. About what he had seen, about how he had failed to save John Ogilvy's life. About how her life, and his gran's, had been reduced to nothing more than a bargaining chip in the delusional scheme of a man who had long since sailed off the edge of the world into a parallel reality where murder was part of a grander plan and the ends justified the means.

He had spoken to his gran the day after Donnelly had blown himself and Ogilvy to hell in the church in the woods. She had confirmed that she had met Donnelly on several occasions, had even taken tea with him in the day room of the home a couple of times.

'I was glad of the company, son,' she said, oblivious to the dagger the words stabbed into Connor's heart. 'And he was a lovely man. Happy to talk, interested. Wanted to hear all about you and your work. And Jennifer, of course.' And then she gave Connor a smile that was so warm and filled with pride that it made him wish Donnelly hadn't died so quickly, that he had survived and been forced to endure the same non-life to which he had condemned Peter Turnbull, a life of constant pain and suffering, borne only with the fervent belief that his suffering held some kind of deeper meaning.

He realised Jen was talking, gave a smile that he hoped was apologetic but felt false and empty on his face.

'Sorry, what?'

She tutted at him, lifted her head, pulled back her hand to punch his chest playfully again, then paused. Reached forward gently. 'How bad is it?' she asked.

'I'll survive,' Connor said. It was, after all, his credo. No matter what, survive.

'So, when are you getting me out of here?' she asked. 'The doctors say I can continue treatment as an outpatient after the next clinical review.'

Connor gave another smile, this one feeling genuine, whole. 'As soon as they say,' he replied. 'Can't come soon enough, to be honest. It'll give me an excuse to kick Simon out. Between you and me, he's not all that tidy, and the place smells of fish, thanks to all the tuna he feeds Tom in the kitchen.'

Jen pushed herself up on an elbow, her eyes suddenly very wide, her face serious. 'Connor Fraser,' she said, her voice low and even. 'Did you just ask me to move in with you?'

Connor blinked. The thought hadn't even consciously occurred to him. He had always assumed that Jen would move in with him as soon as she was released from hospital. But what was it she had said? *I don't need a protector. I can take care of myself.* He loved her, but was that why he wanted her to live with him? Or was it to keep her close, protect her from the insanity he had seen in the world? The insanity, he realised with a cold stab of guilt, he often seemed to attract.

'Absolutely,' he said, after a moment, reaching up and touching her cheek. 'After all, someone's got to pair my socks for me.'

She punched him again, harder this time. And as the pain rolled through his chest, stirred by the burn and the laughter that blended with Jen's, he grabbed for it, held on to it tight. A reminder of his failure to save John Ogilvy, a vow never to fail to save another person.

No matter what, he thought. *Survive.*

ACKNOWLEDGEMENTS

My dad died before I finished this book, and he spent his last month in hospital being cared for around the clock. It's become an easy slogan to call those who work in the NHS heroes, but I've seen first-hand that that is exactly who they are. My deepest thanks and gratitude to Tess, Janna, Sara, Claire, Laura C, Laura S, Jen, Valerie, Emma, Leigh, Theresa, Louise, Rosalie, Lauren, Lucy, Kirsty, Amy, Tracy, Helen, Sheela, Megan, Kirsty B, Kirsty C, Joanna, Debbie, Lee, Alfred, Fernanda, Kelly, Hayley, Joanna, Jodie, Amber, Madison, Nicole, Gillian, Millie, Rundolf, Emile, Vicky and everyone else on Ward 207 at Edinburgh Royal Infirmary who made sure my dad passed with dignity.

Thanks also to those who got me through the nightmare. To Ed James, Derek Farrell, David Gray, Douglas Skelton, Mark Leggatt, Vic Watson, Helen Fields, Joe Farquharson, Stephen Galbraith and, of course, MLYP, your kindness and love kept the lights on in a time of utter darkness and made sure I stayed standing and was able to do what needed to be done. I'll never forget that – and my dad would kill me if I didn't promise that the first round is on me the next time we meet.